And then it happened

Linda Green

Quercus

First published in Great Britain in 2011 by Headline Review,
an imprint of Headline Publishing Group

This edition published in 2018 by

Quercus Editions Ltd
Carmelite House
50 Victoria Embankment
London EC4Y 0DZ

An Hachette UK company

A CIP catalogue record for this book is available
from the British Library

PB ISBN 978 1 78648 706 3
EBOOK ISBN 978 1 78648 705 6

10 9 8 7 6 5 4 3 2 1

Printed and bound in Great Britain by Clays Ltd, Elcograf S.p.A

For Jean Dennis
and in memory of John Dennis

Prologue

I was eleven years old the first time I saw him but I still knew straight away. It was something about the darkness of his eyes and the way his face scrunched up when he smiled. I didn't tell him, of course. That wasn't how it worked, I understood that even then. I had to wait for him to realise. Two years it took. Though it felt more like an eternity to me. Still, it was worth the wait. I knew it then and I know it now. Nineteen years, ten months and twenty-one days later.

PART ONE

One

MEL

Saturday, 27 March 2010

According to Wikipedia, it was Aesop who came up with that line about familiarity breeding contempt. Which kind of vindicates my belief that Greek philosophers are, on the whole, rather overrated. I have known Adam for two-thirds of my life now. Admittedly, that's only a dot backwards on the great history timeline of things towards Aesop's era in 600 BC. But the fact remains that for me it is a struggle to remember life BA (as I tend to think of the years before I met Adam). There is a blurry childhood involving a one-eyed teddy bear, under-the-knee socks and grazed knees, blackberry-picking along the canal bank, a less than perfect ponytail and sticking my tongue out at my older brother Martin, who was always the apple of Mum's eye. And then there is the day I started high school and met Adam. That is when life as I know it really began.

We have barely gone a few weeks without seeing each other since that point. Yet far from make me look at him with a mixture of irritation and loathing, that familiarity has bred something deeper, stronger and altogether more wonderful than I ever thought possible. Don't get me wrong, Adam is not perfect. He's a man, for goodness sake. And this is a marriage not a fairy tale. There are, inevitably, a few things about him that cause me to roll my eyes and make the odd sigh or tut every now and again; he snores (though only when lying on his left side), appears to have a pathological fear of baths (I should point out in his defence that he does shower), refuses to go anywhere near a tapas restaurant (something to do with not being able to get one big plate of what you want to eat and having to go home and make cheese on toast afterwards because you're still hungry) and is prone to going off on a bit of a rant if anyone expresses even the merest hint of admiration for either Margaret Thatcher or Tony Blair (perhaps the most excusable of his foibles).

But that is as bad as it gets. A handful of silly little things that bug me. Nothing even approaching the foothills of contempt. Instead, I have all the lovely things that familiarity brings: knowing that he understands when to back off and give me space and when to throw his arms around me and give me a hug; the fact that we can be comfortably silent together because sometimes we just know and we don't need to say; the reassurance that if I have a headache he knows the exact spot on my shoulder where the knot causing it is and how to massage it away. And the fact that I know, as he sits opposite me at a rather swanky restaurant in Sowerby Bridge, top button of his shirt undone, brushing back the bit of dark brown hair which has always got in his eyes for as long as I have known him, exactly how he will respond to what I am about to say.

'Just in case you were thinking of planning anything, I

don't really want a big fuss. You know, about the anniversary thing. I think we should keep it low key.'

On 6 May we will have been married ten years and, as we got married exactly ten years after Adam asked me out, it will also mark twenty years of us being together. That makes me feel happy and incredibly fortunate. It does not, however, make me want to throw a party.

A hint of a smile creeps on to Adam's face, confirming that this whole conversation we are about to have is already fully scripted. We both know our lines and each other's lines. But we are going to run through it all anyway so we can test how well we have learnt them.

'Oh, why's that, then?' he says. I was right. Word perfect, in fact. He knows exactly why, of course, but he is not going to let me get away without offering some kind of explanation.

I take a sip of my Rioja (I prefer white, but it is his birthday today so it is my turn to compromise. We are experienced enough parents to know you do not drink a bottle of wine each when your four-year-old daughter will be jumping on your bed at 6 a.m. the next morning.)

'Well, it's not like ten years is a big anniversary, is it?' I say.

'So you mean the tin can I've got you will be fine?'

I grin and pull a face at him. I know he hasn't got me a tin can. He is good at presents. Always has been. Partly because he knows me so well and partly because he likes getting surprises so he has to work really hard to think of something I won't have thought of.

'Maybe for our silver wedding we can have a big do but

there's no need this year, is there? I know it's a bit different for us because of the twenty-year thing but people don't really celebrate the anniversary of when they started going out together, do they? At least not in public. And anyway, twenty years together makes us seem really old and my family will forget that we're not and will buy us com-memorative plates and stuff like that and you can't really give them to Oxfam, not if they've got a personal inscription, which they will. Mum would expect to see theirs hung up somewhere and she'll be offended if you put it in the toilet, you know she doesn't get your sense of humour. Besides which, I have bad memories of having to go to my aunt and uncle's silver wedding anniversary party under duress and being forced to do the birdie dance while my friends were enjoying *Ghostbusters* at the cinema, so really, I guess what I'm trying to say is, if you were thinking of planning some big do, I just don't want to go there.'

Adam is smiling some more.

'Oh, piss off, you,' I say.

'What? I haven't said anything.'

'No but you've sat there grinning at me while I've said all that stuff which you knew already.'

'I didn't know I was going to have to wait until our silver wedding to get a party. Jeez, you know how to keep a guy keen, don't you?'

'Don't count on the party then,' I say, picking up one of the tortilla chips which I can vaguely recall appearing at some point during my little spiel. 'I'm not promising we'll have one then, only that I'll consider it. Although obviously not in a depressing church hall somewhere with the Virgin

Mary looking down on us or some dingy community centre which smells of wee and still has sand from the toddler group on the floor. And wherever it is, please, please, do not hire some naff DJ who says things like "now, one for the laydeez out there", we'll just use the compilation tapes we did for our wedding.'

'Right,' says Adam, still smiling. 'I'll be sure to remember all of that. Although I should point out that as the iPod has been invented since our wedding, compilation tapes are now obsolete.'

'See, you're already making me feel old. Imagine what we'll feel like by our silver anniversary when Maya finds out that our wedding photos are on negatives, not a hard drive.'

'So you're already worrying about what she'll think when she's nineteen?'

'Not worrying, just saying.'

'Are you actually going to eat that at any point?' asks Adam, nodding towards the tortilla chip which is still poised between my thumb and forefinger.

'Possibly, but only when I'm sure that you're clear about what I've said.'

'Fear not, I have been left in no doubt about what you've said, although I'm also well aware that it has nothing to do with the real reason you don't want a party.'

I watch Adam expertly use two tortilla chips to shovel a pile of guacamole on to a third before devouring the whole ensemble and selecting two new tortilla chip shovels. He even manages to look sexy as he does it; if I did it I'd probably manage to spill the whole thing down my top. I don't know what age other people grow out of spilling everything but for some reason I haven't got there yet.

'So come on then, please enlighten me,' I say, deciding I might as well ask for the theory as he is clearly going to tell me anyway.

'It's obvious, isn't it? You think that if we pull so much as one celebratory party popper, he, or she, I know you're unsure about the gender of whoever it is that decides these things, will decide that we've had far too long an innings and will send down a plague on our house and seven years' bad luck to all who live in it.'

I finally eat the tortilla chip in my hand in order to give me time to think of a suitably robust denial. I eat three more while I think a little longer.

'You make me sound like some kind of crackpot,' I say, having failed to think of anything which Adam won't see through.

'You are. A loveable one, though,' says Adam, reaching over to squeeze my hand.

'I simply don't think we should tempt fate by making a big song and dance about it, that's all. You know what happens to those Oscar winners who use their speech to publicly pledge their undying love to their husbands. The next week they have to release a statement that it's all over because he's run off with some party hostess.'

'I guess you've got a point, the waitress tonight is kind of cute.'

I smile at him and shake my head. He can get away with it because I don't have an ounce of insecurity about our relationship. Not because I think I'm such a great catch that he'd never leave me but simply because we are Mel and Adam. If we were available in the supermarket you would not be able to buy us singly, only in a pack of two. We are probably at the top of all our friends' 'Least Likely To Split Up' list (I'm presuming everyone else has one of those too, even if they don't actually write it down). So it's not that I fear Adam running off with anyone. It's that somewhere along the line I figure I am owed a huge great dollop of something bad. Adam says it himself, I have lived a charmed life; the first boy I fell in love with fell in love with me and we have stayed in love ever since, I have never even had my heart broken. How many people can say that? We have a gorgeous, happy, healthy daughter who, apart from being obsessed with dinosaurs, seems reasonably well adjusted, we live in our dream home, a converted schoolhouse in Cragg Vale, a couple of miles from here, with views across possibly the most beautiful valley in West Yorkshire, I have a great job lecturing in child development at Bradford University, my parents are still together and although I wouldn't go as far as to say they are blissfully happy, they seem content enough to stick it out. All four of my grandparents are still alive, living in sheltered housing, in reasonably good health and in full possession of their marbles, none of my close family or friends have ever died, had cancer or been stricken with an incurable disease. Indeed, Adam jokes that the worst thing that ever happened to me was when my pet hamster died. It's not true, of course, but then he doesn't know about the worst thing. Only one other person does. And as Adam doesn't know I can see why he would think that. Why most people would think that. Because what is undeniably true is that my life appears to be borderline perfect. But because of what I did I obviously don't deserve that. Hence my conclusion that it is only a matter of time before someone will shout on a loudhailer, 'Come in, Mel Taylor, your time is up,' and something the equivalent of being shat on by the world's biggest seagull will occur.

'I just think we should leave well alone and have a quiet celebration for the two of us rather than publicly rub our happiness in other people's faces.'

'For someone with a psychology degree,' says Adam, 'you really are completely round the bend.'

My enchiladas arrive. And Adam's jambalaya. We don't do that couple thing of sampling each other's food in restaurants. Mainly because it is skin-crawlingly gross but also because we hardly ever fancy what the other one is having.

'Well, if that's what you want,' continues Adam with a shrug as he picks up his fork. 'As long as you don't complain when we spend our anniversary at home watching some crappy programme about a B-list celebrity who wants to fly his kite in the most inaccessible places in the world and have TV licence payers foot the bill for it.'

'You sound like my mother. Anyway, I shan't complain. I'll simply turn it off and put some music on to dance to.'

'Not your flamenco stuff again.' I go to a class once a week with my friend Louise. It is an opportunity to don a swirly long skirt and stomp around in clompy shoes like you are a little kid dressing up in your mother's clothes and consequently it is very good for the soul.

'No, I was thinking of something a bit slower.'

'Hey,' says Adam, 'something for the laydeez.'

'Enough,' I say, laughing as I shake my head. 'You really are old enough now to know better.'

It is gone eleven by the time we get home. We shut the car doors as quietly as possible. Instinctively, I pull my coat across me, though it is unusually mild for March, especially a Yorkshire March, and hurry up the steps to the big wooden front door like a teenager trying to dash back to beat a curfew.

'At what age roughly do you think you'll stop worrying about what your mother will say?' whispers Adam.

'Probably around about the same time you stop taking the piss out of me.'

'It's hardly like we're still at school and rolling in at two in the morning, is it?'

'No, but I said we'd be back by eleven and you know full well that if you give her even the slightest reason to go off on one, she will do. Besides, she looked like she had a bee in her bonnet when they arrived and in case it's anything to do with us I don't want to make it any worse.'

I jiggle the key in the lock and open the door. I love the entrance to our house: a huge dependable door behind which is a wood-panelled hallway with a flight of stone steps rising steeply in one corner (utterly impractical for a toddler and the cause of more 'shit, I've left the stairgate open' moments than I care to remember). I knew it was right for us the second I first stepped inside. I should have said to the estate agent at the end of the tour, 'Actually, you had me at "this is the hallway".'

All is quiet inside. We go through to the lounge where my father is sitting in the armchair doing that one eye open, one eye closed thing he is so good at, and my mother, who is dressed in a jumper with a cardigan over her shoulders and a scarf twirled around her neck in a not very subtle way of suggesting that our house is too cold, is leafing through a copy of *People's Friend* (she brings them with her when babysitting, they are not our choice of coffee-table material). She looks up at me with a 'so what time do you call this?' expression. I am about to launch into a long-winded denial when I remember that I am thirty-three years old.

'Hi, sorry we're late,' I say. 'They took forever with the desserts. How's Maya been?'

'Took ages to go off as usual but we've not heard owt from her since,' says Dad, opening the other eye and smiling. He should be used for sofa adverts, his face screams 'comfy' at you. He also has an Alistair Darling thing going on; his hair and most of his beard are white but his eyebrows remain resolutely dark. When they finally succumb and go white he will make the most amazing Father Christmas. I have already told the local toyshop that I know a Santa-in-waiting.

'So what made-up story did she get you to do?' I ask.

'Something about a T-rex getting his foot stuck on a train track and having to be rescued by a giant purple butterfly.'

I nod. While to outsiders it would sound like a bad LSD trip, it all makes perfect sense to me; Maya's favourite things are dinosaurs, butterflies and the colour purple, and my father, who is retired but runs a model railway museum in Halifax, always manages to get some sort of train reference into his made-up stories.

'So, what did you have for dessert?' asks Mum, as if oblivious to the fact that the conversation has moved on from there.

'I had bitter chocolate torte,' says Adam, 'and Mel went for the blueberry cheesecake.' Mum raises her eyebrows and nods slowly, managing to suggest that she is either disappointed in our choices or the dessert menu itself.

'Well, I'm glad I brought me magazines,' she says. 'Nowt worth watching on TV as usual. Certainly nowt to take me mind off bad news.'

Dad looks up with a start from his armchair and gives Mum a look.

'Well, I've got to tell them sometime, haven't I?' she says.

'Tell us what?' I ask, my stomach tightening.

'I didn't want to mention it earlier because I didn't want to spoil your evening.'

'Just tell us, please,' I say.

'Bill's left Sylvia for some woman at work. A cleaner, not even one of secretaries.'

The knot in my stomach releases. Sylvia is Mum's friend from the surgery. The two of them do for GPs' receptionists what Sweeny Todd did for barbers. I see her occasionally at Mum's house and bump into her every now and then at the Co-op. She is a terrible gossip and impossible to get away from once she's started. I feel sorry for her, of course, as I would feel sorry for any woman who is left by their husband. But the very idea that imparting this news earlier would have spoilt Adam's birthday demonstrates how much Mum has lost the plot. I glance up at Adam who is clearly trying to resist the temptation to comment on the notion that Bill's actions would somehow have been more honourable had he run off with a woman of greater social standing.

'Oh dear. That's a shame,' I say. 'Must have been a terrible shock for her. It's not long since their silver wedding, is it?' Sylvia and Bill were late starters, both living at home in the same road until their aged parents died and they realised it was lonely being on their own.

'Three months,' snorts Mum. 'Then he tips twenty-five years of marriage down drain just like that. I can't understand how anyone could do that to Sylvia, can you?'

'No, dear,' says Dad, obviously deciding it is politic to agree with her although I suspect he can understand exactly why Bill did it. And that somewhere he has a sheet of paper on which is a tally of the years he and Mum have been married. A tally which is heading towards fifty. Mum sighs and starts gathering her copies of *People's Friend* together.

'You know worst thing about it?' she says. 'All that effort Sylvia put into that lovely trifle she made for silver wedding party. Such a waste.'

'I suppose,' says Adam as we lie in bed together later, his arm around me as I nestle into the comfortable place my body seems to have worn away in his over the years, 'I now need to add "trifle" to your list of silver wedding party no-nos.'

I let the laugh I suppressed at the time finally escape.

Adam is laughing so much his chest is shaking.

'The thing is,' I say, 'we haven't heard Bill's side in this. Maybe he doesn't like trifle. Maybe he told Sylvia so the day they met and she never took any notice, kept on making it, determined to force her trifle-making talents on him. And then to spite him by making one for their silver wedding party, well, you can see how that could have been the final straw.'

Adam grins down at me, his hand stroking my arm. 'I bet his new woman doesn't do trifle,' he says. 'I bet she whizzes up Angel Delight for him. Chocolate, butterscotch, any flavour he wants. Come to think of it, I haven't had Angel Delight since I was a kid. How come you never make it for me?'

I look up at him, smiling. 'Tell you what. I'll get some in especially for our anniversary.'

'Oh, Mel,' he says, starting to kiss my shoulders. 'You sure know how to turn a man on. Go on, talk Angel Delight flavours to me . . .'

'You either shut up now,' I say, digging him in the ribs, 'or I turn out the light.'

'OK,' he says. 'I'll just lie here quietly and fantasise about you being covered in it.'

I try to kiss him to stop him talking but I can't do it for laughing.

'Right,' I say, rolling over on top of him. 'If you won't shut up I'll have to make you.' Adam raises his eyebrows. A few minutes later he is suitably distracted and finally rendered speechless. That's the other great thing about familiarity. The control panel is the same as it's always been.

So you don't have to waste time getting to grips with the instruction manual.

I lie there in the darkness much later, my body still pressed against Adam as he sleeps. Feeling his chest rise and fall, listening to his breath, unable to move even an inch away from him, lest I might somehow break the spell.

'Happy Birthday,' I whisper, giving him a final kiss goodnight. And trying not to worry about what else, apart from trifle, could destroy a marriage so easily.

Two

ADAM

I pull off the narrow, undulating road and park in the lay-by as usual. Far behind me in the distance lies Manchester, where I work. Cragg Vale is just the other side of the hills. But I am not going home right now. I am stopping off on the top of the world. I see this same view every week. A palette of green, brown, grey, white and blue, framed by my windscreen. But still it has the ability to shake the day out of me when I notice how the light is subtly different, catching some rocky outcrop I have never noticed before. Some places are so beautiful they can still do that to you, however many times you visit. This is one of them.

I take the printed invitation from the envelope in my holdall and read it again while I wait. As surprise anniversary parties go, I think it's going to be a good one. The venue, of course, is the key. Scaitcliffe Hall is where we got married, a country house hotel on the edge of Todmorden and as far removed from a damp community centre smelling of wee as you could wish to imagine. It was all organised months ago. Even then, the weekend after our anniversary was already booked for a wedding so it had to be the Saturday before. The buffet menu has been finalised, a Commitments tribute band booked (if I tell Mel she'll probably worry that they'll split up before the gig – life imitating art and all that). By the time Mel came out with the 'not wanting a big fuss' line, there was no going back. Not that it would have made any difference if she'd told me before I'd booked everything. I have always known she wouldn't like the idea, always known the old stuff about tempting fate would come tumbling out. She's been the same for as long as I can remember. It was her who got cold feet about the wedding. Not about whether I was 'the one' (Mel is not prone to changing her mind or doubting the strength of her feelings) but about whether getting married would somehow spoil things and we would end up cursing the day we put on a big, public show of our love. The fact that nothing of the sort has happened, that we are, if anything, happier now than we have ever been, does not appear to have shaken her belief in the theory. I would never tell Mel this but sometimes it's a bit like living in one of those weather house barometer things. The sun is shining down on us, I come out, dressed appropriately in shades, T-shirt and shorts, and Mel is cowering in the other doorway, resolutely holding her umbrella up – just in case.

It's the only thing I wish I could change about her – and that's saying something when you consider how long we've been together. I long for her to be able to chill out and enjoy our life together without always looking skywards for the big black cloud that must be heading our way. It's weird really because I'm the one who should be paranoid. When you work as a journalist for ten years, dealing with a succession of murders, tragic accidents and life-threatening diseases, it tends to warp your view of life. I have interviewed enough people who have said 'I never thought it would happen to me' to know that 'it' can happen to absolutely anyone at any time. But apart from having a thing about not travelling on the end carriages of trains (I've done two inquests into train crashes and in both cases the only people who died were sitting at the front and back of the train), I don't spend my life in fear of 'it' happening. If anything, seeing things happen to other people has made me more determined to go out there and live life to the full, to appreciate what I've got and bloody well enjoy it.

That's why I want an anniversary party. Ten years of marriage is worth celebrating. So is twenty years of being together. A hell of a lot of people never make that. And it's not like we've clawed our way there, crossing off the years as we go, staying together for the sake of the kids and barely able to have a civil conversation. I love her. I absolutely do. I've had the best twenty years imaginable and I can't wait for the next twenty. And the twenty after that. And I actually do want to shout it from the rooftops, to say, 'Hey, look at me and my gorgeous wife and daughter, what a lucky bastard I am' (though not while Maya is in earshot, obviously). There, that's it; my audition for a Richard Curtis romantic comedy over with. I shall revert to stereotype now by being a pig-headed Yorkshire git with an inability to express my emotions. Or perhaps audition for a part in *Iron Man 3*.

Steve swings into the lay-by in his 4×4 and parks next to me. We are well aware that the whole thing looks a bit dodgy and have long been expecting someone to tip off the police about the strange behaviour of the two guys who meet up at the highest point of the road across the moor at 6 p.m. every Thursday from April to the end of September (we have to switch to Sunday mornings for the darker months). The disappointingly boring truth is that there are no brown envelopes exchanged, no illicit acts taking place; it's simply the best place for us to meet up for our run.

I put the invitation back in the envelope, open the door and get out.

'How's tricks?' says Steve, as he steps out of the car resplendent in his white polo shirt and shorts. He is the only man I know who would dare to go fell-running looking like he's dressed for tennis. And a sad tosser for not only turning up spotless but bothering to iron his running kit too. His whole appearance screams 'Ha, I haven't got children' at you.

'Good, thanks,' I say, handing him the envelope.

'What's this?'

'The usual procedure is to open it and see.'

Steve rolls his eyes and does as instructed. I watch him reading, a slight frown forming across his brow.

'Does Mel know about this?'

'No, hence the mention of it being a surprise anniversary party and request that no one blabs to her.'

'It's a nice idea, mate. Or rather it would be if she didn't hate surprises.'

I suspected he was going to be like this. If Steve is ever on *Mastermind* his specialist subject will be 'knowing best'.

'She hates the idea of surprises. Not the actual surprise itself.'

'Right, so she's totally up for a big bash, is she?'

'No, but people don't always know what's good for them, do they?'

'Well, I hope for your sake you know what you're doing.'

I manage to resist the temptation to knee Steve in the groin. For a best mate he can be a real pain in the arse sometimes. Of course he gets away with it because we've been best mates since the age of eleven. We have far too much dirt on each other to ever contemplate falling out. But the thing that really riles me is when he pretends to know Mel better than me. He's the only person apart from her family who has known Mel longer than me. He went to the same primary school as her. And, boy, does he like to remind me of the fact.

'She's my wife, Steve. I think I've got her sussed by now.'

Steve shrugs, opens the car door and tosses the invite on to the front seat.

'So are you coming then?' I ask.

'Yeah,' he says, locking the door and putting the keys in his belt pouch. 'Let's get going so we're not finishing in the dark.'

'No, I mean to the party,' I say, breaking into a jog beside him. 'Are you and Louise going to come?' There is a moment of hesitation. Maybe he is searching for a get-out clause.

'Yeah, of course. Unless you need Louise for babysitting duties?' For someone who is not child-friendly, the hopeful note in his voice is decidedly unexpected.

'No, don't be daft. Mel wouldn't want her to miss the fun. Anyway, there's no way on earth I'll be able to keep

Maya away once she knows there's a party going on.'

'You're going to tell her?'

'No choice. I'm buying a new party dress for her and I'll need to make sure it fits. And as Maya's interrogation skills are second only to her mother's, I guess she'll get it out of me at that point. I won't tell her until the day before, though. There's a very slim chance she can keep a secret for twenty-four hours.'

'So what are you going to say to Mel?'

'I don't know, I'll think of something.'

'We could invite you out for a meal, if you like. Throw her off the scent a bit.'

'Yeah, that would be great. Thanks, mate.' He still thinks I'm mad, I know that. But I also know I can always count on his support.

We both run on in silence. I love it up here. Bleak, windswept, rugged. Away from it all. It's like playing God for a while, looking down on the rest of the world below. Feeling a little bit smug that you're in a better place than any of them. I love picking my way along the dirt tracks, across the rocks, through the mud. Mel says I must have been a goat in a previous life. But that's probably because she still has to hold my hand for the stepping stones across the river near our home. As far as I'm concerned this is the only way to run. I've never been able to understand those people who go jogging alongside dual carriageways. You may as well just go on a treadmill at the gym and have someone pump exhaust fumes at you and shine headlights in your eyes.

'So what are you doing for your anniversary?' I ask Steve.

He and Louise married almost two years after us. They met through us. Louise was Mel's best friend at uni. She's lovely, Louise. Far too good for Steve really.

'I expect I'll get a Chinese on the way home from work. Maybe even rent a DVD, something girly that she'll like.'

'You old romantic, you. You sure know how to push the boat out.'

'Well, eight years is not such a big deal, is it? I'll give her some flowers too.'

'What, from the petrol station?'

'They're a damn sight cheaper.'

'And that's what you want to say, is it? I love you to the value of three pounds ninety-nine?'

Steve puts a spurt on, pulls in front of me and makes a not particularly friendly gesture at me behind his back.

'I imagine it's your charm Louise fell for,' I call after him.

'Yep, that and my devilishly good looks and formidable intellect.' Steve works in IT. Sometimes it shows.

The gap between us opens up a little. It doesn't bother me. Steve has a long stride on him whereas I'm built for stamina, not speed. I'll still get back to the lay-by before him. I always do. He never says anything but I know it bothers him. Just an occasional glint of resentment in his eyes.

I look up at the sky unfolding its dusk colours. Hear the sound of my breath blown back to me by the wind. Feel the mud splattering up my legs. This is running. This is being alive.

One of the best things about working at a museum is that

the whole place takes a while to come round in the mornings – a bit like myself. When I worked on the news desk at the *Yorkshire Post* in Leeds I was often slapped around the face with something big the moment I walked through the door. It was like being in a car that goes from 0–60mph in one second flat. Great when you're young and get off on that sort of stuff but there comes a time when you want a smoother, more comfortable ride. I guess that's when you know you need to get out. That and the fact that you can no longer be bothered to rewrite less than perfect copy by trainee reporters because you simply want to get home to see your daughter before she reluctantly succumbs to sleep.

So a year ago I did just that. I got out. Applied for a job as Communications Manager at Manchester Natural History Museum. Selling out, the other hacks called it. Crossing over to 'the other side'. And sure, I miss the banter and the thrill of a breaking story. But I haven't regretted the decision once since. Especially not when I arrive in the morning and walk through the eerily quiet exhibition halls, always noticing something new, a little detail I've somehow missed before. I swear things move around in the night. Maybe it's a bit like *Night at the Museum*. The minute we all decamp, the exhibits wake up and have adventures of their own. Then in the morning, as they hear the first of us come in, they hastily resume their positions. Only sometimes not in exactly the right place. Maybe we could do a stakeout one night. Maya would love that. Waiting for the dinosaurs to come alive.

I love how different it is without the people. A sleeping

world waiting to be discovered by probing eyes, keen ears and inquisitive hands (we're very interactive, none of that locked glass cases and stuffy formality here). In an hour's time this hall will be heaving. The Easter holidays are always busy, especially when it's chucking it down outside like it is today. Come to think of it, Manchester ought to be the museum capital of the world, guaranteed museum weather all year round. Legoland has just opened its new Discovery Centre a few miles down the road. All indoors, of course. We're not too bothered about the competition, though. There are plenty of bored, wet children to go round.

'Morning, all,' I say as I sit down at my desk in the communications department. Department is, perhaps, a rather grand word for what it is. A small but airy room, tucked away at the back of the building. 'All' is also somewhat of an exaggeration. I am addressing Chris, the senior press officer, and Hannah, a trainee press officer, who are the only people in my charge.

'Hi,' says Hannah breezily as she looks up and smiles. She is fresh out of university and oozes confidence in a way I can't remember doing when I was her age.

'Morning,' grunts Chris, pulling open a drawer and taking a couple of Jacob's cream crackers from the packet he keeps there. Mercifully, the Wensleydale cheese which used to accompany it went home after I had a 'quiet word' with him about the smell. But if he has any hope in hell of pulling Hannah (which, frankly, I don't think he does) he needs to ditch the whole Wallace and Gromit thing. Men who wear tank tops and nibble dry crackers in a hamster-like fashion do not usually appeal to members of the opposite sex. Well, only ones like Wendolene. And Hannah is most definitely no Wendolene.

'I've had a play-around with the kids' page on the website like you suggested,' says Hannah, leaning back on her chair. 'Do you want to take a look?'

'Sure,' I say, strolling round to her side of the desk and positioning myself carefully so as to leave as much distance as possible between us while still being able to read the words on the screen. I am walking a tightrope between not wanting to give her, or anyone else, the wrong idea but at the same time not appearing rude or aloof. I have, of course, noticed Hannah. Every male in the building has noticed Hannah. Willowy young women with swishy ash-blond hair and a penchant for red stilettos are few and far between in this place. More than a few of the guys have privately suggested that was why I took her on in the first place. I have, of course, explained that as she was head and shoulders above the other candidates, I didn't have any choice in the matter. They have winked at me and tapped their nose. As if saying, 'Hey, you don't have to pretend with me.' But whereas the rest of them either drool silently or make clumsy attempts to chat her up, I'm her boss. Her married boss. Her very happily married boss, actually. It's not as if I even want anything to happen between us. Simply that I'm aware she's an attractive young woman who sits next to me in our very small department and I still haven't quite worked out how to handle that. Even if I did think it would be OK to flirt with her (which I don't), I wouldn't be able to do it because in some weird evolutionary development, my 'flirting with women other than my wife' device appears to have withered, died and fallen off due to underuse. All I have is a chat-up line, devised while trying to idle some time away in a particularly boring management meeting. This is it. 'So, Hannah, have you got any sisters?' It's OK, I didn't actually say it out loud, only in my head. While it may amuse me in quieter moments during the day, I am well aware that she is probably too young to get the Woody Allen reference. In which case I would come across as some sad old git who deserves a slap. At last year's staff Christmas party (before Hannah joined us), Chris was overheard saying, 'So, Julie, what's it like working on the front desk?' to one of our receptionists. In all likelihood, my line would come across as no better than that. So I keep it to myself and do the platonically friendly older boss who maintains a dignified distance thing instead.

'That's great, Hannah,' I say, taking a look at what she's put together on screen. She's arranged the kids' feedback comments as speech bubbles coming out of the dinosaurs. 'Far better than I could have done. Brilliant, thanks.' She smiles and nods at me before quickly looking down again. I feel a bit like a teacher whose attractive star pupil is slightly embarrassed by my praise. I can hear Chris seething in the corner. He can't even seethe silently. I can see the thought bubbles coming out of his head. Read the exact words on them. None of which would be appropriate as content for the children's web page.

'Is it today your wife's bringing your kid in?' Chris asks, looking up at me as I return to my seat. He has no interest in Maya and Mel's visit whatsoever. It is simply marginally more subtle than saying, 'I'd like to remind both you and Hannah that you're married with a child.' All pretty pathetic, really. It's not as if I try to hide my marital status, I have a photo of Mel and Maya on my screensaver, for Christ's sake. And unlike some men who work here, my wedding ring has been on permanent display since Hannah's arrival.

'Yeah, they'll be in at lunchtime,' I reply, throwing Chris a suitable look in exchange for his fake interest.

'Your daughter's so lucky,' says Hannah. 'I would have loved to have had a dad who worked in a place like this when I was her age.'

Chris is looking rather smug now that my status as a married father has been reiterated several times.

'What does your father do, Hannah?' he asks. I shake my head. Clearly his chat-up lines are no better when he's stone cold sober.

'He's dead, actually,' she replies. I watch Chris die a painful, lingering death himself. I can't help thinking he would have been better off using my line about her sisters. Even if she has never heard of Woody Allen.

'Daddy, can we go and see the dinosaurs first?' Maya hollers as she breaks away from Mel and comes charging towards me across the foyer. If I'd ever hoped my daughter would be a demure, softly spoken, shy little thing, I'd have been disappointed. Fortunately, what I wanted is what I got. A loud, excitable, unguided missile who positively fizzes with the joy and wonder of being four years old and having the whole world to discover. Maya explodes into my arms, instantly unleashing a wave of love, pride and the desire to metamorphose into a fire-breathing dragon in order to protect her from all the bad stuff out here.

'Hello, sweetheart,' I say, lifting her up into my arms to give her a proper cuddle. I am promptly covered in a mass of wild light-brown hair with streaks of gold running through it. When I brush it she sometimes tells me to be careful not to brush the gold out. I don't dare tell her that it will all disappear one day and she will have dark hair like mine and Mel's. She will no doubt still look gorgeous. But I know I will always see her with her hair like this.

Mel arrives at our side. Her hair is tied back, apart from those two long bits at the side which frame her face. It is good Maya is here. Sometimes, without her, I would lose track of where we are in our lives and think I was looking at the fifteen-year-old Mel again. And feeling suitably chuffed that I got to go out with the prettiest girl in our year.

I lean across and kiss Mel.

'I take it she's a tad excited,' I say, nodding at Maya.

Mel smiles. 'Next time I think we'll come with you in the morning. Then I won't have five thousand "Is it time for the dinosaurs yet?" before ten thirty.'

'Dinosaurs? Oh, we haven't got any dinosaurs here.'

'Yes you have,' squeals Maya, screwing up her nose and grinning at me. 'Can we go and see Monty first?' Monty is our Tyrannosaurus rex. We ran a competition for the kids to come up with a name for him. We fixed it, actually, because the first name we drew out of the hat was Barney. And whilst I'm usually in favour of playing things by the rules, I have a violent desire to retch every time I hear Barney the purple dinosaur sing the 'I Love You, You Love Me' song in that dreadful American accent. So I put the postcard straight back in the sack and picked another. There, the truth is out. Bit of luck it wasn't a *Blue Peter* competition, otherwise I'd be out of a job now and there would be stories in the *Daily Mail* about anti-American leanings at the BBC.

'Come on then,' I say to Maya as she wriggles in my arms. 'Let's go and see Monty.'

It is only as I put Maya down and we begin walking hand in hand down the corridor towards the prehistoric hall that I notice Hannah coming towards us. She has her trench coat on and her handbag with her. I guess she is going to lunch. She smiles when she sees us and then quickly looks down at her feet. For a second I am not sure whether to say anything then realise it would be ridiculously rude just to walk straight past her.

'Hannah, this is my wife Mel. Mel, Hannah, our new press officer.'

'Pleased to meet you,' says Hannah, holding out her hand.

'And you,' says Mel. 'You have my complete sympathies for having to put up with Adam all day.'

'Oh, he's been a real help.'

'Well, I'm glad to hear it.' Everybody smiles slightly awkwardly. Maya is staring at Hannah's shoes.

'Look, she's got Dorothy shoes on. They're very red and pointy, aren't they?' she says to me. I smile and shake my head.

'And this is our daughter, Maya. Who as you may have noticed is not backwards in coming forwards.'

'Pleased to meet you, Maya,' says Hannah, bending down to shake her hand. 'They are a bit like Dorothy's shoes, aren't they? I don't think they have magic powers though. They just rub my heels, to be honest.'

'You should put some plasters on,' says Maya. 'That's what Mummy does with her new shoes.'

'Thanks for the tip,' smiles Hannah, waving to Maya as she goes.

'Come on,' says Maya, giving my hand a tug. 'Monty will be wondering where I am.'

'She seems nice,' says Mel, as we are dragged along the corridor by Maya.

'She is. Unfortunately for her Chris thinks so too.'

'No way,' says Mel, shaking her head. 'The phrase "out of his league" springs to mind.'

When we arrive in the exhibition hall there is already a crowd of children gazing up in awe at Monty. I lift Maya on to my shoulders and, as requested, start pointing out all the different parts of the skeleton, even though she has heard it all dozens of times before.

'Why have you only got one Monty?' asks Maya after a while.

'I guess he didn't have any brothers or sisters,' I reply.

'Just like me, then. Is he lonely?'

I look up. Her face is serious for once.

'No, love. He's not lonely. Just very, very special.'

I wait until Mel and I are lying in bed later before saying anything. I try to think of a subtle way of raising the issue, although I know it doesn't really matter how the conversation starts because I'm pretty sure about how it will end. I stroke Mel's hair. It has the same fine, flyaway texture as Maya's. Without the gold bits, of course.

'Did you hear what Maya said earlier, about Monty being lonely?'

'It doesn't mean to say she is.'

'So why did she say it?'

Mel shrugs. 'Maybe she just meant because he's the only T-rex. She could have meant anything.'

'I try to imagine what it'd look like, sometimes. If we had another baby, I mean. Whether it would be a mini Maya or look completely different.'

Mel doesn't answer. Her face is turned away from me. I stroke her hair some more.

'All I want to make sure is that we don't regret it some day. Not having another baby, I mean.'

I can almost feel Mel's skin prickle. She pulls away from me slightly. When she finally speaks there is an unfamiliar snappish tone to her voice.

'Have you forgotten about the sleepless nights? The colic, the teething? The strain of me taking a couple of years off work?'

'You chose to do that. You said you wanted to.'

'I know I did. And I don't regret it for a moment. But it doesn't mean to say I'd want to do it again.'

'I'll ask if I can have a sabbatical. We'll do a year off each.'

Mel gazes up at the ceiling and shakes her head. 'You'd go stir crazy here all the time.'

'We'd go out and about like you and Maya did.'

'I can't quite see you at the parent and toddler yoga class.'

'Swimming then, I'd take them swimming. And just for walks and stuff.'

Mel turns to look at me. It's like someone has turned down the brightness control on her face.

'I'm sorry, love. The answer's still the same. I just want to enjoy Maya.'

'She'll be at school by then.'

'Even more reason not to go back to the land of sleep deprivation and cracked nipples. And I haven't even mentioned the birth.'

I go to say something and stop myself. Nothing they said in the NCT classes had prepared me for watching the person I love most in the world go through the excruciating pain of childbirth and not being able to do anything to help. Sure, I tried to be supportive and say the right things and not complain about the fact that her fingernails had actually drawn blood in my palms. But really, what good was I? All I kept thinking was, I did this to her. I persuaded her to try for a baby and then got her pregnant before the ink on the agreement was dry (metaphorically speaking at least, we didn't actually put it in writing). And although the second Maya had been born we were both in floods of tears, mine were actually for Mel, were sheer relief that she'd been put out of her pain, that I didn't have to watch her suffer any more.

'I'm sorry,' I say, pulling her to me. 'I know you had a really rough time. It's just when I see Maya—'

'You can't help thinking how lucky we are to have her,' says Mel, finishing my sentence, though not in the way I'd planned. That is what this is all about, of course, Mel's hang-up about nothing this good lasting forever. I'm not going to push her on it, though. This one has to be her decision. If I ever do get to see her in labour again, I need to know that she isn't going through it just to please me.

We lie there for a while, neither of us saying anything, before Mel finally pipes up.

'Maybe we can get her a pet instead.'

I start laughing.

'What?' she says.

'I like the way you got from a new baby to a goldfish in one swift leap.'

'Not a goldfish,' says Mel. 'Maya's seen *Finding Nemo* too many times. She'd probably try to free it by pinging it into the sink.'

'Well, what do you suggest?'

'Maybe a rat. They're supposed to be really good pets.'

I burst out laughing again.

'What's wrong with that?'

'Nothing,' I say. 'I'm just imagining her trying to dress it up as Angelina Ballerina.'

'OK, so it would be a cross-dressing rat.'

'Fine, one condition, mind.' Mel sighs and raises her eyebrows expectantly. 'Don't ever let me catch you playing her that Michael Jackson song. You know, "Ben", the one about the rat.'

'OK, deal. Can I go to sleep now?'

I nod and kiss her before turning out the light. Trying to erase the picture I have in my head of Maya playing with the new baby we're not going to have. It's hard, though. Especially when all I get instead is the sound of Michael Jackson singing 'Ben'.

Three

MEL

'I hope I've done the right thing, inviting them round on their anniversary.'

'You always do the right thing,' says Adam, squeezing my shoulder as he walks past. His hands are still wet from washing up. I now have a large wet handprint on my top.

'Unlike you.' I grin.

'I'm a man, I'm genetically programmed to screw up at least once a day.'

'It's a bit embarrassing though, isn't?'

'What, being a man?'

'No. Having to invite Steve and Louise round for an anniversary meal because he wasn't planning to take her anywhere.'

'We didn't have to invite them. You chose to.'

'Only because you told me that he was being a tight git and planning to get a takeout.'

'So if this all goes horribly wrong, it's going to go down as my fault, is it?'

I smile at Adam. There are times when he knows me too well. I suppose you could say I am meddling. I am not a meddler by nature. I wasn't one of those girls who were forever trying to fix up people at school, or the sort of woman who tried to get my single friends to go out with my boyfriend's single friends. Although weirdly, that is kind of how Steve and Louise got together. Not through me purposefully trying to fix them up but simply because they kept getting thrown together at our social gatherings. To be honest, I didn't think it would work. Sure, there was an obvious physical attraction – they're both good-looking people. But I always thought Steve was a bit intense for Louise, too prone to take the piss out of people, not nearly as gentle as her. She fell for him big time, though. It was Steve who dragged his feet over marriage; Louise would have said yes within a year of them getting together, she told me that once.

It is lovely, having a ready-made foursome. So much nicer than having to put up with each other's friends' spouses who we don't really know or get on with. And it means I can do this, invite them over without it seeming like an obvious attempt to hide the fact that Steve hadn't planned to take her out for their anniversary. At least I hope it's not obvious.

Maya charges into the kitchen dressed in her dinosaur pyjamas and a purple tiara. She is a walking contradiction. Or rather a running one.

'Slow down, missy,' I say, managing to grab her just before she careers headlong into the Rayburn. 'What have I told you about running in here?'

'Don't. Run outside like Daddy does.' She sidles up to Adam and hugs his legs. As much as I hate all those stereo-types, if someone came along and stamped 'Daddy's girl' on her forehead, I couldn't disagree. I watch as Adam bends down and blows a raspberry on her cheek. It is moments like these, moments when the sheer enormity of their love for each other threatens to overwhelm me, that I start to crumble. Start to wonder if I am being despicably selfish by not agreeing to try for another baby. I know how much Adam wants it, though he is good enough to hide the true extent of it from me. And I know that Maya would make a fantastic big sister and that in lots of ways it would be good for her to have to think about someone else's needs. But at the same time I still remember how difficult the pregnancy was last time. How it brought all the pain to the surface. Pain I still couldn't share with Adam. Pain I have had to work so hard at burying deep inside me again ever since. Besides which, I can't get past the idea that it is wrong to wish for anything more than I already have. That somehow it would be pushing my luck just a little too far.

'When is Loo-eeze going to get here?' Maya pronounces her name like it is some kind of over-the-counter diarrhoea remedy. Fortunately Louise finds it amusing.

'Any minute,' I say. 'But remember, it's bedtime as soon as you've said hello to them, OK?'

Maya nods although I know she will deny any knowledge of this conversation when the time comes. The one thing she hates more than anything else in the entire world is the idea that she may be missing out on something.

Adam checks the moussaka. We both enjoy cooking but have learnt through experience that we don't work well together in the kitchen. He treats recipes as a starting point whereas I never stray from them. So we have come to a working arrangement; he does the main course, I am in charge of the starter and dessert. That way, we are out of each other's hair and if his experimental cuisine bites the dust (as has been known on a couple of occasions) our guests will at least have two reliable courses to fall back on. To be fair, his experimenting mostly leads to dishes people rave about to the extent that my creations are merely the bookends to his meal. I don't mind, though. If you take the risk, you deserve the credit when it works. And Adam does at least hold his hand up when it all goes pear-shaped.

A loud knock at the door sends Maya into the higher stratosphere of excitement. Louise is almost knocked off her feet as Maya rushes up to her.

'Happy annibirthday and Mummy says I can have a pet rat.'

'Thank you, sweetie,' says Louise, bending to give her a hug. 'A rat, eh? Aren't you the lucky one?'

'It'll take up a bit less space than a dinosaur,' I explain.

'Mummy, you can't get dinosaurs now. They were only in the old days.'

'Like when I was a lad,' says Adam.

Maya frowns. 'Even you're not that old, Daddy. They were before cavemen.'

'Oh, we had cavemen when I was a kid,' says Adam. 'Where do you think Steve lived when I met him?'

Maya shoots Steve an inquisitive look. She has seen a couple of clips of *The Flintstones* and I suppose if Fred was put on a diet and stretched he might bear a passing resemblance to Steve.

'Your daddy's winding you up, love.' Steve grins. 'It's actually your grandad who was a caveman.'

'Hey, he's got a point,' says Adam. 'Remember that time I called for Mel and Tom answered the door and said, "Shintin".'

Three of us laugh, Louise and Maya look puzzled.

'Sorry,' says Adam to Louise. 'I keep forgetting you still need a translator sometimes. "She isn't in", they'd probably have said in your neck of the woods.'

'Oh, in Warwickshire they'd phone first to check,' says Steve. 'No one just pops round.' Steve and Adam laugh again. Louise doesn't appear particularly amused.

'They were only joking about the cavemen,' I say, seeing Maya still looking perplexed, 'and a rat will make a lot better pet than a dinosaur ever would.' Maya's face brightens.

'I'll let you stroke it if you like,' she says to Louise.

'I'd love to,' says Louise. 'Though maybe you'd better keep it in its cage for a bit until it gets used to me.'

'Nice get-out,' I whisper as I take Louise's coat. She is looking stunning in a soft pink jersey dress and a purple shrug. But then Louise is one of those people who, being tall, slim and a C-cup, looks good in absolutely anything. As someone who has to loiter with intent around the petite section in Next, I can only imagine what that feels like.

'Come on then, Maya, time for bed,' I say.

'Ohhhh.'

'I'll tell you a good bedtime story if you're quick,' says Adam.

'One about a rat, a dinosaur and a butterfly?'

'The very one I had in mind.'

Maya does her goodnights as if she may never see Louise

and Steve again, before disappearing upstairs with Adam.

'Anyway, happy anniversary, you two.' I kiss Louise and Steve in turn. The mixture of perfume and aftershave is momentarily overwhelming. It's odd to be reminded how well-groomed people are when they don't have children.

'And thank you for this,' says Louise, waving her arm around the kitchen. 'By far the best restaurant in the Calder Valley.'

'We don't know what Adam's cooking yet,' chips in Steve. He smiles at me as he says it. I resist the temptation to point out that if he wasn't such a cheapskate we wouldn't have had to do it. Steve and Louise sit down on opposite sides of the oak table while I get the halloumi sizzling. I love having a big dining kitchen like this. It is absolutely the heart of the house. All warm and busy and sociable. Whenever we go to my parents' place I am reminded how rude it seems to abandon your guests in a soulless dining room smelling of potpourri while you go off to savour the warmth and altogether more enticing smells in the kitchen.

Adam returns five minutes later, just as I am dishing up. Maya can still be heard chattering away to herself on the baby monitor.

'Come on,' says Adam. 'No one thought she was actually going to go straight to sleep, did they?'

'It's a shame they don't come with an off button,' says Steve. Louise throws him a look. It is only then I realise they haven't said anything to each other while I've been cooking.

'So, do you two want us to make ourselves scarce and

leave you to a romantic anniversary meal?' asks Adam. There is an awkward silence, broken finally by Steve.

'I don't think that will be necessary. We are married, you know.' I glance at Louise who appears to be trying very hard to smile.

'What Steve means is,' she says, 'it's lovely to share our celebration with you.'

'And don't forget Basil and Sybil,' says Adam. The first thing he said when Steve and Louise's wedding invite arrived was that 17 April was the Fawltys' anniversary. I did try to persuade him not to put it in his best man's speech but he couldn't resist the laugh he knew it would get.

'How could we, with you reminding us every bloody year?' says Steve. 'Anyway,' he continues. 'We'd like to return the favour for your anniversary. Take you out for a meal, I mean. Not subject you to our cooking.'

'Thank you,' I say, looking across at Adam who is nodding enthusiastically. 'I told Adam I didn't want a big fuss. A meal just for the four of us would be lovely.'

'We were going to suggest the Saturday before, May the first, I think it is,' says Louise. 'If that's OK with you?'

'Should be fine, I'll check out Mum and Dad for babysitting but they don't usually have anything on.'

'And it gets me out of having to organise anything.' Adam grins.

'Not out of getting a present, mind,' I add. Louise looks down at the table. I sense Adam is about to crack a joke about Steve's cheap flowers.

'Anyway,' I say, raising my wine glass. 'To many more happy anniversaries to come.' Four glasses chink together.

Although I notice Steve and Louise's don't actually touch.

'So, who saw the leadership debate then?' asks Adam. 'And have either of you two succumbed to Clegg mania?' For once I think he is on safe ground with politics. Much safer than anniversaries, at any rate.

I have to wait until after the meal is finished before I get a chance to engineer some time alone with Louise. Adam is telling Steve one of his many Twitter anecdotes (he follows lots of journalists and political commentators, it's a wonder he gets any work done. Still, I think it helps with the withdrawal symptoms. Despite what he says, I know it was a big deal for him, giving up the world of newspapers.)

'Why don't you get Steve to show you?' I say. 'You know, all that stuff you were talking about, how to send tweets from your phone and getting different apps and that.'

'You mean I've got permission to be an honorary geek for a while?' says Adam.

'Yeah, as long as you do the washing up later.' Adam looks at Steve. They hesitate for only a millisecond before disappearing upstairs like a couple of schoolboys desperate to play with their Scalextric. Louise stands up and carries her coffee cup over to the sink.

'Not so fast,' I say, taking the cup from her and sitting her back down at the table. 'I want to know what's up with you two.'

The face which has been doing its best to hold itself together all evening finally crumples. A couple of tears squeeze themselves free from her eyes, trickling down her face as if doing a dot-to-dot on her freckles.

'Hey, it's all right,' I say, bending down to give her a hug. 'Me and Adam have rows, you know, usually over stupid stuff, mind.'

'I wish it was just a row. He won't even argue with me. Just kills me with these silences.'

'What do you mean?'

'He didn't say a word on the way here. He stuck Coldplay in the CD player and that was it. When I asked him what was wrong he shrugged and said nothing. It's worse than dealing with the kids at nursery.'

'What did he get you?' I ask. 'For your anniversary.'

'Flowers,' she says. 'From the petrol station on the corner. Although he did at least take the price label off this year.'

'What did you get him?'

'Tickets for Peter Kay in Manchester.'

I have to stop myself crying now. Louise doesn't even much like Peter Kay.

'So how long has this been going on?'

Louise looks up at the ceiling and sighs. 'A long time.'

'Days, a week, a month?'

'Longer than that,' says Louise.

I sit down next to her, wipe a strand of soggy blond hair from her face.

'Why didn't you say anything?'

'It's not the sort of thing you can just drop into a conversation, is it? "By the way, my marriage is in a really bad way."'

'I know but—'

'You don't know, Mel. You and Adam are still in love. You can tell a mile off. You do that whole lighting up when

45

the other one walks in the room thing. All Steve seems to do when I walk in the room is clam up.'

'But you still love him?'

'Of course I do. I want children with him but that's never going to happen, is it? And I know he was straight about that from the beginning but you always think they'll change their minds, don't you? Soften as the years go by, when they see their mates becoming dads.' I decide not to tell her about Adam wanting to try for another baby. It makes me feel really mean. And Louise is in such a state she'd probably offer to be a surrogate mum.

'Sorry,' I say. 'Maybe Maya's scared him off parenthood.'

'Don't be daft, she's gorgeous. Steve's simply immune to the delights of children. I tell him the cute things the kids at nursery say and it never even raises a smile.'

'Is that what you think's eating him? Knowing you want a child?'

She looks at me and shrugs. 'I don't know. It's not like I go on about it or anything. I guess it's kind of the elephant in the room that neither of us mentions.'

'But you still, you know. You're not in separate beds or anything.'

Louise shakes her head. 'Don't get me wrong, I've got no complaints about the physical side but emotionally he's not there for me. He ought to take up smoking, at least then he'd have a genuine reason for not speaking after sex.'

'Oh, Louise.' I give her hand a squeeze. I don't know what to say. It's not like she's complaining about her boyfriend, I can't suggest dumping him. He's her husband. And Adam's best friend, come to that.

'Do you want me to get Adam to talk to him, try to find out what the problem is?'

'No. Steve'd go mad if he knew I'd said anything. Anyway, they'll be down soon. I need to go and do my face, I don't want him to see I've been crying.'

Louise gets to her feet, picks up her handbag and heads towards the downstairs toilet. Adam has just put a photo of the three of us having a family hug up in there. I wish we didn't look quite so happy.

'Well, that went well, didn't it?' I say as I shut the door later.

'At least my moussaka provided a welcome distraction.' Adam puts his arms around me and kisses me. 'Have they had a domestic or something?'

'It's a bit more serious than that.'

'What do you mean?'

'I'm not supposed to tell you this.'

'But you're going to anyway. Don't worry, unlike you, I'll be the soul of discretion.'

'I'm not gossiping. I'm worried about them.' Adam frowns and leads me over to the table where our second coffees are going cold. I tell him what Louise said. When I am finished he leans back in his chair.

'Jeez, I had no idea it was that bad. I thought it was some spat over his crappy flowers.'

'It just shows you, doesn't it? How it can happen to anyone.'

'Hang on a minute. They're not divorced yet, you know.'

'They soon could be.'

'No, it'll blow over. Steve can be a moody sod sometimes.'

It's probably some kind of mid-life crisis. He just needs a kick up the arse.'

'I promised you wouldn't say anything.'

'I'm not going to tell him what Louise said. I don't need to. It was pretty damn obvious that something was up.'

'I don't know. Maybe we should keep out of it.'

Adam smiles and shakes his head. 'How can we? We're supposed to be their best friends.'

'I don't want to make things any worse.'

'I'll deal with Steve. You just be there for Louise.'

I nod and take a sip of my lukewarm coffee. It is only then I remember.

'Shit.'

'What?'

'Well, they're Maya's guardians, aren't they? What would happen to her if they split up?'

'Nothing would happen to her. She'd still be here with us.'

'No, I mean, if anything then happened to us.'

Adam rolls his eyes. The guardian discussion had lasted almost as long as my pregnancy. Not being religious, we hadn't wanted to go through the whole christening thing but we had wanted to appoint legal guardians. Actually, that's not strictly true. I had wanted to appoint legal guardians, Adam had nearly pissed himself laughing when I'd suggested the idea and said I was the only woman he knew who would insist on making a will before decorating the nursery. Once he'd calmed down and agreed to my request, the discussion had moved on to who those guardians should be. It's only when you come to draw up a list of people who are: a) alive (Adam's father ruled out and Princess Di, who was an outsider on the longlist); b) fit (as in capable, not good-looking); c) solvent and responsible (most of Adam's friends ruled out); d) resident in this country (my brother and sister-in-law ruled out due to living in Belgium and Adam's mother ruled out for being in Australia had she not already been ruled out for leaving Adam's father for another man and not even bothering to send a wreath for his funeral); e) young enough to be able to get 'down with the kids' when the baby was in its teens (which ruled out my parents); f) not raving fascists (Adam insisted on that one); and g) not disciples of the Gina Ford contented little baby method (yes, that one was my call), that you realise how hard it is to find someone suitable to leave your child with if you die. We ended up with a shortlist of two couples: Louise and Steve (although there was a question mark over Steve's distinct lack of child friendliness) and Susan Sarandon and Tim Robbins (*Thelma and Louise* and *The Shawshank Redemption* being in our top three films, they'd both spoken out against the Iraq war and I'd read an interview with Sarandon where she explained how they each spend six months working and six months on childcare duties, which had all seemed perfect requisites for the job at the time). When I'd asked Louise if she and Steve would be willing to consider being Maya's guardians, she'd burst into tears because she thought I was going to say I'd got cancer or something. But when I'd calmed her down and explained, she'd said yes straight away and Steve had grudgingly agreed after Adam had pointed out he was extremely unlikely ever to be called upon and it was a damn sight better than having to go through the godfather bit in church and fork out for a christening present.

I look across at Adam. He has that smile on his face.

'What? It's a fair point.'

'Mel, they're going through a rocky patch. We can hardly ask them to stick together for the sake of our child.'

'No, I'm not saying that. I'm just saying it's awful. Even people you think are really happy . . .' My voice trails off as it starts to break. Adam puts his arm around me and pulls my head into his.

'You're a daft bugger, sometimes, Mel Taylor. But it's one of the reasons I love you so much.'

I look up and give him a watery smile.

'I think that bloody list we drew up for guardians is cursed,' I say. 'First Susan Sarandon and Tim Robbins split up and now this.'

'I would still have loved to have seen the letter you were going to write to them.' Adam smiles. 'The one which would have started, *Dear Ms Sarandon and Mr Robbins, you don't know us but we'd like to ask if you'd mind looking after our future child should anything ever happen to us.*'

'I still think they'd have agreed to do it.'

'Well, I guess we'll never know.'

I bury myself against Adam's shoulder. 'It is scary though, isn't it? What can happen to people.'

'Yeah, but it's other people, not us. We're fine. Way better than fine. And we're going to stay that way, OK?'

I nod my head and wipe my eyes with my sleeve.

'Now come on, let's get to bed. A certain young lady I

know is going to be jumping up and down on top of us in about five hours' time.'

I let Adam take my hand and lead me upstairs. Wondering if Louise and Steve are asleep yet. Or still lying awake in the same bed. Backs turned against each other. The silence weighing heavy in the air.

Four

ADAM

'Come on then, who is she?'

'What are you on about?' says Steve. We are running along a narrow ridge, high up on the crag. There are no hiding places here. There isn't room to get past me. If he drops back I will simply turn around and run after him the other way. That's why I waited until we got here. To make sure I had him where I wanted him.

'The other woman,' I say.

'What other woman?'

'Well, quite clearly Louise isn't getting your full attention. So I'm wondering who is.' Steve gives me the very same look he once gave me when I accused him of stealing my Panini World Cup sticker album in 1990.

'What's Louise been saying?'

'You know full well that Mel doesn't tell me anything Louise says about you.'

'Well, who else has put this idea in your head?'

'I was there at the meal, remember? It was possibly the most painfully embarrassing experience of my life.'

'Your moussaka wasn't that bad.'

'You know what I mean.'

'Things aren't great between us at the moment.'

'Because of the other woman?'

Steve actually stops running for a second. I run straight into the back of him.

'There is no other woman, OK?' The anger and heat in his voice feels like a blowtorch. I'm half inclined to touch my cheek to make sure I still have some skin there.

'OK, OK,' I say. 'I believe you. Keep running.' Steve starts up again, slowly at first, as if testing the ground.

'So if there's not someone else, what's the problem between you?'

'Jesus, what is this? I came out for a run, not marriage guidance counselling.'

'Louise looked pretty miserable. I consider her a friend. And for some inexplicable reason I consider you a friend too, I don't like seeing the two of you unhappy.'

'Who said I was unhappy?'

'Well, you're not exactly full of the joys of spring, are you?'

'It's just a bit of a rocky patch. Honeymoon period's over and I'm contemplating spending the rest of my life with her.'

'Bloody hell, you make it sound like you've washed up with some old minger. Louise is gorgeous. She's also one of the nicest people I know.'

'Yeah, well. That's easy for you to say.'

'What's that supposed to mean?'

'Nothing.'

'So why did you say it?'

'Because not everyone can be as loved up as you and Mel, OK? The rest of us live in the real world.'

I run on in silence for a bit, unsure of how to answer

that. It's the degree of resentment which surprises me. I thought you were supposed to be happy for your friends' good fortune. Clearly Steve's got a problem that he's not telling me about.

'Are you getting enough?'

'What sort of question is that?' Steve calls back over his shoulder.

'The sort you ask when you're trying to work out why your best mate's being such an arse.'

'Thank you for your concern, Dr Raj, but there's not a problem in that department,' says Steve. 'If you must know, she wants a baby. I don't. And the thought of that needling away for the next ten years does not fill me with glee.'

'Have you talked to her about it?'

'There's no point. Neither of us is going to change our minds.'

I snort a laugh.

'What's so funny?'

'I want another baby but Mel doesn't.'

Steve slows to a jog and looks round at me. 'Sorry, I didn't realise. Why doesn't she want another one?'

'She thinks we should be happy with what we've got. Says it's because she had such a tough time with Maya's birth. It's not, though. It's this whole bloody not wanting to tempt fate thing.'

'What do you mean?'

'Because, as you pointed out, we're so loved up, she thinks nothing this good can last forever.'

'Oh. Right,' says Steve. 'Not much you can do about that, I guess.'

'No. Bloody ridiculous, isn't it? Both of us wanting the opposite thing. I don't suppose you'd be interested in a wife swap?' I wait for the sound of Steve's laughter. It doesn't come.

'It was meant as a joke,' I call out as Steve accelerates away from me.

'I know,' he replies. 'I'm afraid my sense of humour has deserted me.'

'Are you sure I look OK?' asks Mel, straightening her jacket as I pull the front door shut behind us.

'You look great. And it's not a job interview, remember.'

'So why does it feel like one?'

I throw Mel a reassuring glance, knowing she gets far more worked up about things like this than she should do, having somehow managed to convince herself that the new parents meeting has been arranged to assess whether she is of the required calibre of mother of the new intake.

'Are you going to get a job at my new school, Mummy?' asks Maya, who is skipping along in between us. She doesn't have a 'walk' programme installed. Skip, run or dawdle are the only settings.

'No, sweetheart. Daddy was only joking,' explains Mel. 'I work at the university, don't I? Mrs Hinchcliffe is going to be your new teacher and that's why we're going to see her now.'

Maya nods and carries on skipping. I give her hand a squeeze, knowing full well that Mel will be doing the same to her other hand. Not that Maya needs it. She is positively fizzing with excitement at the prospect of going to big school. Nothing daunts her. Never has, possibly never will. You always hope that your offspring will get the best bits of both of you and in Maya's case she has, having inherited her mother's looks and determination and my laidback genes and sense of adventure. I wonder if Mel has somehow concluded that any future child of ours will therefore get the worst bits of each of us. I guess it must happen to some couples. There's probably been an article about it in the *Guardian's* women's page.

We reach the bottom of the steep steps to Vale Road Primary School. It's a small Victorian village school with less than eighty pupils. The stone building is cut into the hillside and while that means it doesn't have enough flat land for a school field, they do take the children out for walks in the countryside. Imagine that; walks, adventure, learning about nature firsthand. I bet that isn't in the national curriculum.

Maya eagerly climbs the steps. I hope it will always be like this, that she'll be one of those kids who enjoys school, not one of those for whom the novelty wears off after the first week and it's a daily battle to deliver them to the school gates without a screaming match and tearful exit. At least if that does happen, Mel will know what to do about it. Being an expert on child development has its benefits. It has its downsides too, of course. Which is probably why Mel is so anxious about Maya starting school. That's the trouble with knowledge. Sometimes you can have too much of it.

We walk into the small hall, which is decorated with the usual mixture of children's painting and artwork. The cynical former hack in me wonders if there is a Third World sweatshop somewhere exploiting child labour by pumping this stuff out and exporting it to schools where the children are too busy being groomed for their SATs to be able to do art. Maybe the heads buy it in cheap to impress parents. What is it about pictures of owls made out of egg boxes and feathers which instils a feeling that your child is being well cared for? Our fridge is already covered with Maya's weird and wonderful creations from nursery; I can see the time when Mel will suggest buying a second fridge to accommodate all the new stuff from school. Having already discreetly dismantled and recycled a huge junk model of a palace made out of toilet-roll holders and washing-up liquid bottles because Mel couldn't face doing it, I know I am going to be the one charged with creeping around the house disposing of this stuff in the dead of night. I also have reason to suspect that nursery staff are posted at the household waste centre to reclaim their materials and distribute them straight back to your child the next day.

The head, Mr Groves, who struck us as a bit of a maverick when we looked around the school, and Maya's teacher Mrs Hinchcliffe are there to welcome us. I wish I'd changed out of my work suit now. Mr Groves is dressed casually in chinos and an open-necked shirt. Obviously he's not one for formality.

'Nice to see you again, Mr and Mrs Taylor,' he says. Admittedly the new intake is only ten strong but I'm still impressed that he's managed to remember who we are. 'And how are you, Maya?' he adds, bending down. 'Looking forward to September?'

'Can I start now?' asks Maya.

'You're keen, aren't you?' Mr Groves laughs. 'You'll have to wait a bit longer, I'm afraid, but perhaps Mrs Hinchcliffe can take you down to your class so you can have another look around.'

Mrs Hinchcliffe must be in her fifties but looks impossibly glamorous for a schoolteacher: high heels, sleek glossy hair, dangly earrings and a very stylish scarf. She squats down to Maya's level and takes her hand.

'Come and help me, Maya. I need some ideas for what to turn our topic corner into next.'

'Dinosaurs,' says Maya without hesitation. 'You need a great big dinosaur. My daddy can get you one if you like.' I smile at Mrs Hinchcliffe before she disappears down the corridor with Maya.

'She's going to be fine,' I say to Mel as we lie in bed later. 'You saw what she was like, she can hardly contain herself.'

'I know,' says Mel. 'And I really like Mrs Hinchcliffe. It's just getting my head around it. It doesn't seem five minutes since she was learning to walk.'

'And before you know it she'll be snogging boys behind the bike shed at high school like you did.'

'Oi,' says Mel, hitting me with the spare pillow. 'I only snogged one of them.'

'Yeah and look where that got you.'

'It's funny, though, isn't it?' says Mel. 'I met Steve when I was Maya's age. She could be friends for life with one of those kids we saw earlier.'

'You called Steve a bastard last night, when I told you what he said about Louise.'

'Yeah, well, I think he is being a bastard to her but he's still a friend, isn't he? Just one I'm glad I'm not married to.'

'They'll sort themselves out, you'll see. By the time Maya starts school, it will all have blown over.'

'And you think he was being honest about there not being anyone else? About it just being the baby thing?'

'Yeah. I think he was. Anyway, I'm not spending another night talking about their marriage.' I roll across and kiss Mel on the lips. She smiles at me, though I can tell her mind is still elsewhere.

'And whatever it is you're worrying about Maya, don't. It's six years until she goes on the outdoor adventure residential. And I assure you I'll find something to take your mind off it when she does.'

Mel smiles again, a bigger smile this time. And kisses me back.

Five

MEL

'Are you sure you don't mind taking her?' I ask as I fly around the kitchen, attempting to eat toast and drink tea while brushing my hair and looking for my umbrella at the same time.

'Of course not. It's one of the perks of being the boss, you get to go in late and nobody bawls you out. Anyway, I can easily make an hour up next week.'

'Thank you,' I say, kissing Adam on the top of the head, 'you're a complete star.'

'I'm hoping I'll be rewarded for that in heaven,' he says.

'Or maybe by me later, if you're lucky.'

Adam grins up at me and raises an eyebrow. 'You're perky this morning.'

'I have a good feeling about today.'

'You think something's going to come out of this meeting with Margaret?'

'She doesn't usually ask to see staff before lectures. And she knows I want to increase my hours in September.'

'I'll keep my fingers crossed for you. Let me know how you get on. Now quit fussing and go.'

'I still can't find my brolly.'

'The forecast's dry.'

'Just in case,' I call over my shoulder as I walk out into the hall where I am greeted with the sight of Maya jumping off the bottom step with my red umbrella held aloft.

'What are you doing?'

'Trying to fly like Mary Poppins.'

I shake my head but can't help smiling at the same time. 'Well, I'm afraid I've got to fly now and I need that brolly. Tell you what, how about we try sliding up the banisters when I get home later?'

Maya nods and hands me the umbrella. 'Are you taking me to nursery?'

'No, it's Daddy's turn today.' Maya grins. I have learnt not to feel hurt by this. I give her a big hug and kiss. 'Have fun. Mummy loves you lots.'

Maya hurtles into the kitchen. I glance up at the clock and gasp.

'Bye, love. Got to dash,' I call out to Adam as I grab my coat and briefcase.

'Hope it goes well,' shouts Adam from the kitchen.

The last thing I hear before I pull the door shut behind me is Maya asking if she can have chocolate ice cream instead of yogurt for breakfast.

I hurry up the steps of the main campus at Bradford University. I love this place. It's like the backdrop to a sizeable chunk of the film of my adult life. I did my degree here, as did Adam; it wasn't that our relationship couldn't have survived going to different universities, simply that Bradford offered us both the courses we wanted and therefore there was no reason to be apart. I did have to move to Leeds to do my MA in Childhood Studies, but by that stage Adam and I were living together anyway (he commuted to Sheffield for his journalism course), so it was no big deal. I never really took to Leeds. It's so sprawling and it's very hard to work out where the centre is. I used to get lost all the time. There's a lot to be said for familiarity. Which is probably why I ended up coming back here to do my teaching in higher education qualifications. Bradford is my kind of city; big enough to be interesting and diverse but small enough to navigate across it without the need for a map.

So when the opportunity came up to stay on and actually teach here, well, it just felt like it was meant to be. I still get a kick out of seeing my name on the departmental staff list. I'm Melanie Summerskill here, of course. Just as I was when I arrived as a rather green eighteen year old. I like that. The feeling that I've grown up here. So much so that I can't imagine ever wanting to work anywhere else. And I know how few people can say that – and therefore how lucky that makes me.

I button up the jacket of my trouser suit and hurry across the car park towards the social sciences and humanities buildings. Margaret Carmichael is the head of the department. She is scarily efficient and businesslike but despite this I like her. Firm but fair, I suppose you could say. She is also one of the most intelligent and well-read people I know, which can be rather daunting. She caught me reading a copy of *Take a Break* magazine once; it wasn't mine, someone had left it in the canteen, but even so I suspected I had been filed as an intellectual lightweight in her mind.

I knock on her door and enter when I hear the familiar, gravelly voice say, 'Come.' Her voice softens when she sees me.

'Aahh, Melanie. Thanks for coming. Do take a seat.'

I perch on the black vinyl chair on the other side of her well-ordered desk and try my hardest not to look like a child waiting to find out what she's getting for Christmas.

'Now, there's bad news and good news. Which would you like first?'

My stomach lurches – maybe Santa hasn't got what I was hoping for after all.

'Don't worry,' says Margaret, who has obviously seen my previously composed expression slide off my face and fall crashing to the floor. 'I'm hoping the good news considerably outweighs the bad.'

'Bad first, then,' I say, bracing myself.

'Well, I'm afraid we've taken the decision to suspend applications for the part-time Working with Children and Young People foundation degree. It won't be running next semester.'

I nod, aware that I have just effectively been told I am out of a job.

'But the good news,' continues Margaret briskly, 'is that we are going to run a full-time Early Years BA honours degree and I'd like you to teach on it.'

My previously composed expression picks itself up off the floor, returns to my face momentarily before turning into an inane grin.

'I take it that's a yes,' says Margaret.

'I'd be delighted. That's fantastic news. Thank you.'

'Now we'll discuss your hours in more detail later but I know you were keen to increase them from September anyway. Is that still the case?'

'Yes, definitely. With Maya starting school I'd be happy to do five days, though I'm afraid they couldn't be full days.'

'I'm sure we can accommodate that. It's a big step, starting school, for children and their parents. I understand that you'll want to be around for her.'

I nod and smile, unable to speak for a second. I glance down to check I am not swinging my legs. I used to do it as a girl when I was excited and being on the short side it can still happen. Adam takes the piss about it but I think other people would still do it too if their feet didn't always touch the ground. I glance up again. Margaret is looking at me expectantly. I realise the conversation has finished and she is waiting for me to leave. I scramble to my feet.

'Thanks ever so much,' I say as I grab my trench coat and briefcase.

'You see, the bad news wasn't so bad after all, was it?'

I smile and leave the room, shutting the door quietly behind me. The first thing I do is get my mobile out and text Adam. His reply reads, 'Woo-hooo, well done you! Can I retire now? X' followed by, 'And don't worry, Maya didn't have choc ice cream for b' fast!'

I am on a high all morning. Adam always says I come home buzzing after teaching; like it turns on some switch inside me that nothing else can reach. But today I am feeling so alive, so enthused with everything that my students probably think I have taken something. I imagine them gossiping after lectures, starting all sorts of rumours about what I've been dabbling in.

I am still smiling when I meet Nadine in the canteen at lunchtime.

'Jesus, cat that got the cream and all that,' she says, looking up as I sit down next to her with my ciabatta and coffee.

'Well, cat that got increased hours teaching on a full-time honours course, at any rate.' I grin.

'Yay, congratulations, you. That's fantastic.' Nadine leaps up, dashes across to my side of the table and gives me the most enormous hug. She teaches youth studies. Which is maybe why she says 'Yay' a lot.

'Thank you. It feels like I'm finally starting to get my career up and running again.'

'So no blubbing on Maya's first day at school, then.' Nadine smiles as she says it. She has three school-age children. She knows the score.

'I have no doubt I shall bawl my eyes out but at least I'll be at work every day, which will take my mind off missing her.'

'And you'll have more money, although it won't feel like it because it will all go on keeping her in school uniform and shoes. And you'll have no time to yourself because every evening will be spent baking for school fundraising events or making costumes for dress-up days, and weekends will be entirely taken up with children's parties and dance and gymnastics classes.'

'Thank you for taking the gloss off.'

'No problem, you know you can count on me to bring you back down to earth.' She grins.

'Well, I shall have to make the most of the next four months, then.'

'Starting with your big anniversary next week. I still can't believe you and Adam have been together twice as long as me and Paul.'

'Don't, you're making me feel old.'

'You're not old. You just never played the field like the rest of us.'

'That's what happens if you get lucky first time, I guess.'

'You must at least have kissed another boy.'

I hesitate for a second. I know it is utterly ridiculous but I have still never told anyone about Steve. About him kissing me at the Christmas disco in the last year of primary school. I had no idea he was going to do it. And I hadn't even met Adam then, so it's not as if I did anything wrong – I was eleven, for Christ's sake. But it's the fact that Steve's now Adam's best friend and married to my best friend that makes it rather embarrassing. Adam and Louise would probably laugh themselves silly if I told them. But as Steve obviously never has and it's more than twenty years since it happened, I think it would simply be weird to mention it to them now. It'll be OK with Nadine though. Nadine isn't married to him.

'A lad snogged me under the mistletoe at the school Christmas disco when I was eleven but that was all. I met Adam nine months later.'

Nadine puts down her coffee and leans across towards me.

'Yeah, but you must have fancied other boys.'

'Nope. I've had a twenty-two-year crush on Adam, that's it.'

'But when you were at uni, before you were married, you're not telling me you didn't notice the other lads.'

'Yeah, there were a couple of good-looking ones. But I was happy with what I had.'

'Some people,' says Nadine, lowering her voice, 'still like to go for a test drive even when they've got no intention of buying.'

I smile and shake my head.

'Some people,' I whisper back, 'but not those who have already got the top of the range model.'

'Jesus, you really are a saint.'

'I just know when I'm on to a good thing and I've never wanted to do anything which would risk losing it.'

'Well,' says Nadine, 'all I can say is that if they should ever bring back *Mr and Mrs*, I shall back you two to win it. There can't be anything you don't know about each other.'

I smile at her and take another mouthful of ciabatta. Not wanting to confess that there is one thing. Although admittedly not the sort of thing that Derek Batey would ask about on a quiz show.

I'm in the corridor, on my way back to my classroom when my mobile rings. I always keep it turned on because of Maya. I answer it straight away.

'Hello.'

'Is that Mrs Taylor?' says the unfamiliar voice at the other end. And I know just from the way they say it that it's bad news.

Six

ADAM

Maya is giving me that look. The one which says you can't say no to me, not when I'm this cute and angelic. The first few times it worked without fail but I have wised up to it now. Besides, I know I can turn down her request without risking a full-scale tantrum because I have an ace up my sleeve which will trump even chocolate ice cream.

'We don't have ice cream for breakfast, young lady,' I say, tickling her under the arm. 'But as soon as you've eaten up your yummy raspberry yogurt, I've got a surprise present for you.'

Maya squeals, practically jumps up on to her chair and starts shovelling down the yogurt. I am well aware what the parenting books which Mel subscribes to say about the issue of bribing children to eat their food and normally I wouldn't go there. But it's the day before the surprise party and if I have any hope of getting Maya to keep quiet I need to have her on side.

'Finished,' says Maya, holding up the empty pot as proof. I love the way kids do that. They should open a restaurant called Clean Plates, where you have to hold up yours to catch the waiter's eye. It would be so much more fun than all those stuffy table manners.

'Great,' I say, wiping Maya's face with a flannel as I crouch down next to her. 'Now, can you keep a secret?'

Maya nods enthusiastically although I know this not to be the case.

'Good, because the present I've got for you is something to wear at a surprise party we're going to have tomorrow.'

'Are we going to play pass the parcel?'

'No, sweetheart, because it's not a children's party, it's a tenth anniversary party for Mummy and Daddy. Only Mummy doesn't know about it because I want it to be a surprise, OK?'

'OK,' says Maya. She is cutting to the bit where she gets the present. I'm still not sure she understands the importance of keeping it secret but I will have to give it to her now, otherwise we'll be late for nursery.

'Wait here,' I say before dashing to the study, taking the dress, which is wrapped in purple tissue paper and tied with a silver bow (the lady in Monsoon was very good at making me feel grateful for the free gift-wrapping service when they had just charged me a small fortune for a tiny piece of material with a few sequins on) from the drawer of my desk and carrying it back through to the kitchen where Maya appears to be in danger of spontaneously combusting.

'Here you are,' I say, smiling as I hand it to her. Maya tears open the tissue paper, gasps as she catches sight of the purple and silver sequinned dress inside, holds it up and starts to dance around the room.

'Do you like it then?' I ask, smiling.

'It's my best dress ever,' says Maya, throwing her arms

around my legs. 'Thank you, Daddy.' I feel churlish now for baulking at the price when I first looked at the tag. She is such a grateful child. She only ever asks for one thing from Father Christmas. And she was very understanding last year about the pony not being a real one.

'Good, let's go upstairs to try it on, make sure it fits.'

We hurry up to her bedroom. I whip her butterfly pyjamas off and pull the dress over her head. It is a true Cinderella moment. I almost gasp myself. She is four years old and already I'm scared stiff about how beautiful she is. I dread to think what I'll be like by the time she's thirteen. I am starting to empathise with fairytale kings who lock their daughters in castle towers. I know it's wrong but I can kind of see where they're coming from.

Maya twirls around in her dress.

'Can I wear it to nursery?'

'Sorry, sweetheart. We need to keep it nice for tomorrow.'

Maya's face crumples. I should have realised she'd ask that. I have to think of something quick to avoid the onslaught of tears.

'We can't have Mummy picking you up from nursery in it, can we? That would spoil the surprise.' The dam wall holds. I need to follow up fast to make sure. 'How about I put you to bed tonight and you try it on again then? You won't be able to sleep in it, though. We can't have Cinderella turning up to the ball in a crumpled dress, can we?'

Maya grins and lets me remove the dress without any fuss. I point to the clothes on her bed which Mel laid out for her earlier.

'Now, you get ready for nursery while I pop and hide

your dress somewhere Mummy won't find it. You can change into it when I drop you at Grandma's tomorrow evening and then it'll be a surprise for Mummy to see you in it when we arrive at the party.'

'Is it at a palace?' asks Maya.

'Not quite, but it is a lovely big hotel. The one where Mummy and Daddy got married.'

'Will Mummy be wearing her wedding dress?'

'No, sweetheart. She'll still look beautiful, mind. I've got her a new dress too.'

'Has hers got sparklies on like mine?'

I shake my head. I hadn't realised how early this not wanting anyone else to wear the same as you business starts for women.

'No, love. And it's a different colour too.' Maya nods, satisfied. I disappear into our bedroom and hang her dress inside the same suit bag as Mel's in my wardrobe. I so hope Mel will love it. The dress and the party.

We drive up to the Ark, past the hedge monster which keeps the children entertained (and safely within the grounds). Mel and I started out with the intention of walking to nursery, it only takes twenty minutes or so from our house. But the combination of the chaos which is our home in the mornings and Maya's dawdling means we invariably join the ranks of the other hassled, multi-tasking working parents on the nursery run.

Maya could have gone to the crèche at Bradford University, it would have been cheaper for a start. But when we came to see this place, the beautiful outside play area overlooking the valley, well, we were sold and so was Maya.

I help her down from the car, she holds my hand until we are through the gate then skips off up the path. I place my right forefinger on the entry pad and the door to the main building buzzes open. I still think it's a bit much for a nursery in a wooded valley in rural Calderdale but it reassures Mel that they take such things seriously.

I follow Maya through to the nursery, where the early arrivals are already playing. What reassures me is the way she is always so keen to come here, we've never had any clinginess or tears from her when we drop her off.

'I've got a new dress and my Mummy and Daddy are having a surprise party,' blurts out Maya to everyone within earshot, namely a dozen children and three members of staff. Becky, Maya's key worker, turns and smiles at me.

'So much for the surprise then,' she says.

'The new party dress was a rather crude attempt to buy her silence. Not money well spent, obviously.'

'I'm sure she loves the dress.'

'Oh, she does. But I'd be very grateful if you could remind her not to mention it when Mel comes to pick her up later.'

'Of course,' says Becky. 'I'll tell her it's a game of fairy secrets.' I wonder if I should ask how that game works for future reference but a glance at the clock reminds me it's time to go.

'Have fun then, Maya,' I call out. 'Daddy's going now.'

'OK,' calls Maya. She runs over to give me a hug, a dinosaur in one hand and a Bob the Builder drill in the other. I decide not to ask what game she's playing.

'See you later, sweetheart,' I say, bending to give her a kiss. A second later she is gone again. The sound of drilling comes from within the Wendy house. I make my excuses and leave.

I listen to 5 Live on the drive to work. I shouldn't do, of course, because the phone-in with Nicky Campbell is the one thing guaranteed to get my blood pressure rising in the mornings. Having been a journalist for ten years you would think the ability of the great British public to talk complete rubbish at times is not something which should surprise me. There's always one, though. One person who manages to take my breath away with their sheer stupidity. This morning it is Graham from Doncaster. A fellow Yorkshireman but sadly misguided nonetheless. Graham says he is not going to vote for Gordon Brown because he called that woman a bigot. When Nicky asks who he is going to vote for instead, he says the BNP. As if that is a perfectly reasonable course of action to take. I am none too enamoured with Brown myself, but Graham's argument is a bit like saying that because Father Christmas was overheard criticising one of the elves, you are going to sack him and give the job to Satan. I consider stopping the car and calling in to make that very point when Mel's voice of reason floods over me from afar. I switch over to Absolute Radio and am relieved to hear the Kaiser Chief's 'I Predict a Riot'. There won't be a riot when Labour lose (as they surely will now), of course, because this is Britain. And Britain simply tuts and sportingly gives someone else a chance to mess everything up. And never questions the fact that the other lot are only in opposition because they screwed up last time. I pull up at the traffic lights. There is a copy of the *Daily Express* on the passenger seat of the car next to me. Brown is so obviously dead in the water that they are turning their attentions to Nick Clegg now. Jesus, it's enough to make a guy wear a yellow tie in public. I hear Mel telling me to calm down. See her face sporting that serene, gentle expression she wears when I go off on one. And I smile at how she can catch me doing that even when she is not in the car.

Chris gives me a 'and what time do you call this?' look as I walk past him. He has never got over the fact that he didn't get my job. He applied for it and by all accounts thought he had it in the bag and the interviews were merely a formality. Apparently after he was told his application had been unsuccessful he stormed out of the building uttering something about not being appreciated and the interview panel being impressed by spin rather than substance. Which coming from a PR man was a bit rich but there you go. He has never said directly that he thinks he could do the job better than me, of course. But it is implied in virtually everything he says and does and the permanent look of distaste and disappointment he wears on his face.

'Thanks for holding the fort, guys. How's things?'

'Wet,' says Chris.

'What do you mean?'

'Plumbing problems in the loos on the second floor,

there was a massive water leak overnight. The Bug's Life hall has been closed for safety reasons.'

'Shit. Is there much damage?'

Chris shrugs. 'Don't know. Haven't asked.'

'They're assessing it at the moment,' says Hannah, somewhat more helpfully. 'Roger's been in meetings all morning.' Roger is the museum's director. He belongs in academia and is hopeless at dealing with anything practical. This does not bode well for the rest of the day and especially my hope of getting away at a decent time tonight so I can pop into the hotel on the way home and make sure everything's in hand for the party.

I sit down at my desk and read the yellow Post-it note written in Chris's spidery handwriting.

'Adrian Bashforth's coming in at twelve noon instead of two today?' I ask.

'Yeah, that was the message,' replies Chris.

'Did they say why?'

'Not really.'

I nod, deciding it's not worth trying to extract any further information from Chris. The words 'blood' and 'stone' spring to mind.

'Who is he?' asks Hannah.

'Oh, some big cheese from Orange. They're being lined up as a sponsor for the Dinosaurs in 3D exhibition in the summer. Roger wants me to give him the guided tour and sound him out about possible web links and text stuff we could do.'

'Sounds good,' says Hannah. For a second I wonder whether to delegate the tour to her. I could really do without it today and I know she's far more comfortable with the whole corporate schmoozing thing than I am. But I stop myself from asking her just in time. It's not fair of me to dump my crap on her just because she's very willing and able.

'Yeah, it's a shame about the timing with the second floor out of action but I'll have to find a way around it.'

'You'll just have to linger a bit longer with Monty in the prehistoric hall,' says Hannah.

'You're right. If I get stuck I can always tell him one of Maya's dinosaur stories.'

'Is she excited about the party tomorrow?' she asks. I still feel bad about not inviting Hannah. It was awkward because I didn't want to invite Chris but at the same time I didn't want Hannah to feel that I was singling her out for any special treatment. I realise now that young, attractive women are probably telling the truth when they complain they never get invited anywhere. Older women simply wouldn't want them there and older men don't want to look like prize lechers by asking them. There's no going back now, though. Last-minute invites look the worst of all.

'You could say that. I told her this morning and she went that far off the scale she could probably power the National Grid at the moment.'

'And your wife still doesn't know?'

'No. Although she probably will do by the time I get home tonight.'

'That'll be good then. Seeing as she doesn't like surprises,' says Chris. Hannah looks at me questioningly.

'You know what it's like,' I say. 'When women say they

don't want a big fuss, they don't always mean it, do they?'

Hannah nods and smiles. It is a rather forced smile. Oh shit. Maybe I'm not right about that at all.

'So, welcome to the Manchester Natural History Museum,' I say in the most enthusiastic voice I can muster. I am shaking Adrian Bashforth's hand. He is one of those people who holds on far too long. 'Have you been here before?' I ask.

'No. I've not long moved up from London. And I haven't got kids.'

'Oh, it's not just for kids,' I say. 'We do a lot of After Dark events for corporate clients. The main halls are available for Christmas parties too.'

'Great. Top hole. Shall we get going then?' Adrian Bashforth doesn't want to be here. That much is clear. He has come over from Orange's Leeds office but is clearly in the north under protest. I imagine him sympathising with all those London BBC types who have been grumbling about relocating to Salford. I am reminded of that Victoria Wood sketch. The one where the continuity announcer says, 'We'd like to apologise to viewers in the north. It must be terrible for you.'

'We'll go up to the first floor then,' I say. 'The prehistoric hall is where everyone wants to start. I'll show you what we've got there now and then I can fill you in on our plans for the 3D exhibition.'

I lead the way up the stairs. I could have taken the lift but I don't want to risk the doors opening on to the chaos of the second floor by mistake.

I push open the double doors. Monty is standing proudly at the far end of the hall, towering over everything else. I glance at Adrian to see if the wow factor has registered on his face. Nothing.

'Now this is Monty, our star attraction,' I say, guiding a clearly underwhelmed Adrian briskly down the hall. I realise that I shouldn't have told him his name. It's made me sound too *Blue Peter*y.

'An amateur palaeontologist discovered the skeleton in an outcrop near Buffalo in South Dakota.'

I glance across at Adrian. Still not impressed. There are only a handful of other people in the hall. Friday lunchtime is quiet for us. But I guess that doesn't look very impressive either.

'Come and take a closer look,' I say, stepping over the rope barrier until I am standing directly under Monty's skull. I'm aware I am flogging a dead dinosaur here. However I have to keep going because it's the best we've got and if we've got any hope of getting an all-singing, all-dancing 3D dinosaur, this guy needs to be on board.

'He's, er, big, isn't he?' says Adrian, who hasn't moved an inch. I resist the temptation to point out that of course he's big, he's a fucking dinosaur. The sound of drilling and hammering can now be heard coming from the floor above.

'That's our Bob the Builder exhibition upstairs,' I joke. Adrian isn't laughing. And clearly still isn't impressed. Maybe it's only my daughter who is. I wish Maya was here now, wish I could capture some of her enthusiasm in a bottle and empty it all over Adrian.

I hear a creak and a tearing sound from above. I look up, half expecting to see a plumber's leg sticking through the ceiling. That would just about finish this off. The chain which supports Monty's skull appears to be shaking. There is another creak, longer and louder this time. Followed by a tremendous clank as the ceiling attachment comes away. My brain is telling my feet to move. I trip as I forget to step over the rope barrier and fall backwards. I look up to see Monty's head falling towards me. Crashing. Plummeting. Down. There is a shout. A scream. And sheer, excruciating pain. My pain. As Monty's head connects with mine. And then nothing.

Seven

MEL

'Yes, speaking,' I say into my mobile in a voice which does not sound like my own.

'Hello, Mrs Taylor. It's Roger Simpson at the museum. It's about Adam.' I shut my eyes. I'd thought it was Maya. I thought the call was going to be about something happening to Maya. 'I'm afraid there's been an accident,' he says.

The roller coaster plummets downwards, taking my stomach with it. I am screaming inside but still composed on the surface. I am not sure if he is pausing for effect or because he has watched too many episodes of *Casualty* and thinks you can't give bad news any other way. I want to shout at him to tell me; just bloody tell me what has happened. But I wait while the roller coaster starts its crawl back up to the summit, not knowing whether the next drop will be bigger than the one before.

'The chain supporting the skeleton of the Tyrannosaurus rex came away from the ceiling,' he continues. 'Adam was underneath it.' A noise comes out of my mouth. I am aware that it sounds like laughter. Nervous laughter, of course. Because it is ridiculous and because I am scared of what he's going to say next.

'Is he dead?'

'No. No he's not dead but he has been seriously injured. He was knocked unconscious. He's been taken to A&E at Manchester St Cross.'

I nod, which is crazy as he can't see me but I cannot find any words for now. Students are walking past me in the corridor. I am aware that tears are streaming down my face although I can't understand why because I am not crying. Not crying at all.

'I am so sorry,' says Roger. 'We will, of course, be having a full investigation into this matter. My next call will be to the Health and Safety Executive.' I nod again. 'If there's anything we can do to help. Anything at all.'

Put the dinosaur back up. That's all I can think of. Put the dinosaur back up. Fix it so this can't happen. Rewind the tape. The emotion is bubbling to the surface. I can't listen to this any longer.

'Bye,' I say and end the call. My hand is shaking so much I can barely get the phone back in my bag. I know I have to move but I don't know how. Something inside me takes over. Turns me around and starts walking my legs back down the corridor. I am swimming against the tide of students returning to their lessons. I am vaguely aware that some of them are staring at me. I find myself standing outside Margaret's office for the second time that day. Hear myself knocking on the door and entering again.

'Sorry to disturb you,' I say. 'My husband's been in an accident. He's unconscious. I need to go straight to the hospital. Someone will have to cover for me. I'm very sorry.' I am crying now. Proper gulping breaths of air and tears. Margaret sits me down. She takes my car keys out of my hand and puts them back in my bag. I wasn't even aware I was holding them.

'Where's your car?'

'Mytholmroyd train station.'

'I'll order a cab,' she says. 'The train will take too long and you're in no fit state to drive when you get there anyway. Which hospital is he in?'

'Manchester St Cross,' I hear myself say. Margaret makes the call. She pours me a glass of water from the carafe on her desk and hands it to me.

'Would you like someone to go with you?' she says. I think of Nadine. Her lesson will have started by now. I don't want to put anyone out.

'No, no, I'm fine, thanks. Deep breaths and all that.' I think I manage a smile but I cannot be sure. Margaret passes me a tissue. I dab at my cheeks before scrunching it up in my hand.

'Is there anyone we need to phone? Is your daughter in the crèche?'

'No. She's at nursery near home. I'll phone my mum and dad to get her. I don't want to worry her now. Adam will probably have come round by the time I get there.'

Margaret nods. I put the water down. I haven't drunk any.

'We'll go down to the main entrance,' she says. 'The cab will be here soon.'

I stand up. Crank the automatic pilot on again. We make swift progress along the corridor. My legs surprisingly capable of functioning on their own. We only wait in the foyer for a minute or two before the cab pulls up outside. I am aware of the door opening, of Margaret helping me inside. She says something to the driver. Comes back and pats my hand.

'Please do let me know if I can do anything to help. Anything at all.'

I nod and thank her, although I'm not sure she hears me before she shuts the door. The driver pulls away. He is small and wiry and has greasy hair. He is not wearing his seat belt. They piss me off. People who think they are immune from having an accident. They're not. Nobody is. Nobody at all.

The driver makes no attempt at conversation. I am relieved. Radio 2 fills the silence. I realise I will never be able to listen to Jeremy Vine again without remembering this moment. It is as if someone has picked me up and is driving me away from my normal life, from the cosy, safe existence I have known. And in a short while they will drop me off and I will have to step from the cab into unknown territory. The world of my nightmares, except they are no longer my nightmares, they are real. I look down. I still have the scrunched-up tissue in my hand. I put it in my bag, get my mobile out and dial my parents' number. It rings for a long time. I hang on, waiting for the answering machine to kick in. Until I remember they are the only people left in the country who don't have one. Which is probably just as well as I have no idea what message I would leave anyway. I realise that it's Friday afternoon. Mum will be at the surgery. I could ring her there. She will probably answer. But I don't want to. She will talk to me like I am one of the patients. And the whole waiting room will hear her end of the conversation. I do not want that. I don't think Adam would want that. I call my father instead. He will be at the model railway museum. It will be much quieter there.

'Hello?' Dad sounds surprised that someone has phoned. He obviously doesn't get many calls.

'Dad, it's Mel. I need you to do me a favour.' I am aware my voice is in danger of breaking. I pause for a second, trying to hold it together. 'Can you get Maya for me later, please? I've got to go to the hospital in Manchester. Adam's had an accident.'

There is a momentary silence on the other end of the line. I feel mean, telling him in such a matter-of-fact fashion but for some reason that is the only way I seem to be able to deal with it.

'Oh dear. What sort of accident?' he says. I stop myself from saying a dinosaur one. I realise it would sound ridiculous. Facetious even.

'Something very heavy fell on him. He's unconscious. I don't know much more than that. I'm on my way to the hospital now.'

'Do you want me to ring your mother?' Clearly Dad has no idea how to deal with this.

'No, there's no need. If you can just pick Maya up at five-ish, take her back to our place and get her overnight bits and pieces. Her ready-bed, pyjamas, toothbrush, Iggle Piggle water bottle. She'll show you where it all is.'

'Yes. Yes, of course.'

'Please don't worry her. Tell her Daddy's had a bump on the head and Mummy needs to look after him in hospital.

Make it sound like a big adventure staying at your place. Let her have ice cream for tea. Anything, really, to keep her happy and stop her worrying. If she gets upset please phone me and I'll talk to her.'

'OK, love. You'll call us later, will you?' I can tell from his voice that he is struggling to hold it together too. I picture him standing there, the old-fashioned receiver pushed to his ear, his shoulders sagging further under the unaccustomed weight of bad news.

'Yes. Yes I will.'

'Bye, love.'

I put the phone back in my bag. I catch the cab driver's eye in the rear-view mirror. He doesn't say anything. Just turns off Radio 2.

When we pull up outside the accident and emergency department, I rummage in my bag for some cash.

'It's OK,' the driver says. 'It's on the university account. I hope your husband's all right.' I nod and thank him before scrambling out of the car. He pulls away, leaving me standing there in front of the modern glass and steel entrance. I bite my bottom lip as I hurry through the main doors. I have no idea what I am going to be faced with. All I know is that I need to see Adam. I am desperate to touch him, to hold him. To tell him I am here.

There is a long queue at the reception desk at A&E. A woman with floral patterned kitchen roll held over a cut finger, a boy with his arm in a makeshift sling whose mum has a 'been here before' expression on her face. No one here is in danger of dropping dead. I decide I have the right to be very un-British and push in.

'Excuse me,' I shout out to the receptionist as I squeeze my way through to the front. 'I'm looking for my husband, Adam Taylor. He was brought in earlier. He's unconscious.' The other people in the queue stop tutting at me and move to the side. The receptionist scrolls down the screen on her computer, picks up the phone and makes a call.

'Mrs Taylor's in reception,' she says, before turning to me and saying, 'Someone will be along for you shortly.' I nod and thank her. Which is daft. She's acting like this is some bloody GP's waiting room. Only I'm not here for a cervical smear. I'm waiting to see my husband who for all I know is lying half-dead on a trolley a few yards away. I turn back to the receptionist.

'No, really. I need to see him now,' I say, my voice quivering. I sense I am about to get a 'you'll wait your turn like everyone else' sermon when a side door opens and a nurse pops her head around. I am oddly reassured by the fact that she is considerably older than me.

'Mrs Taylor?' she says. I nod. 'Dr Perryman will see you right away.'

That's bad. I know that's bad. Doctors are ridiculously busy, they cannot just drop everything to see relatives. I realise that Adam could be dead. He might have died here.

'Is he still alive?' I ask. 'I need to know.'

The nurse turns and smiles gently. 'He's alive, he's still unconscious. Dr Perryman will explain everything.' I am shown into a small side room off the corridor. A silver-haired doctor is sitting there, clipboard in hand, serious expression on his face.

'I need to see him,' I blurt out, tears streaming down my face as whatever semblance of composure I had disappears. 'I need to see my husband now. Please.'

Dr Perryman hesitates for a second then nods. A sign that he is human after all. 'OK,' he says. 'We'll talk afterwards. But you do need to prepare yourself for the fact that your husband has suffered a serious head injury. He's still unconscious. He's had an endotracheal tube fitted and is on a ventilator. He's been sedated and we've also used a drug to induce paralysis.'

I stare at him. I realise my gasp was audible.

'It's standard procedure. We need to ensure there are no sudden movements which could damage his spine.'

I nod through the tears. Dr Perryman stands up and leads me out of the room and along the corridor. We stop outside a door which says 'Resuscitation Room'. He turns to me, I nod to indicate I am ready and follow him in.

There is a man lying on the trolley. His eyes are shut. His face is deathly pale. Patches of purple and red are starting to jostle for position on his forehead. A thick tube leads from one of the array of machines surrounding him into his mouth. The man is my husband. The man is Adam.

It is only as she checks one of the monitors that I am aware there is a nurse in the room.

'Can he hear me?' I ask her.

'We don't know,' she replies. 'We suggest that relatives speak as if the patient can hear.'

I step forward to the bed. I am too scared of hurting him to kiss his face. So I take his hand instead. It is limp and heavy in mine. I squeeze it but he doesn't squeeze back. I sink to my knees, bury my wet, hot cheeks against the palm of his hand.

'I'm here now,' I say. 'I came as soon as I could. It's OK. You're going to be fine.'

Dr Perryman opens the door again after a minute or two. I get to my feet and go quietly without being asked. I have seen him. I have let him know I am here. I need some answers now. I follow the doctor back into the side room. He shuts the door and pulls out a chair for me. I sit down heavily.

'I know this must have come as a huge shock for you,' he says. 'Your husband has suffered a severe blow to the front of his head. We understand from staff at the museum that he was unconscious from the moment of impact.'

'He will regain consciousness though, won't he?' I ask.

Dr Perryman fiddles with the pen on his desk. 'It's too early for us to say. We've done an initial assessment, something called the Glasgow Coma Scale. We have detected some involuntary muscle straightening and extending and there have been a few incomprehensible sounds but no eye opening and no response to pain.'

'What does that mean?'

'He scored five on the test, the minimum he could have scored was three. That would indicate there has been serious injury to the brain but we won't know any more until we do a CT scan.'

'When's that likely to be?'

'We'll be taking him down within the next few minutes. The scan uses X-rays and a computer to create images of the inside of his head. The radiologist should be able to give us some more detailed information after that.'

I nod. I still can't believe this is actually happening. I'm half expecting Adam to come striding through the door at any moment, apologising for a practical joke that went way too far. No one comes though. The door remains resolutely shut.

'What might the scan find?' I ask.

Dr Perryman hesitates for a second. 'Essentially what we're looking for is the extent of brain swelling. It's an extremely delicate organ with the consistency of firm blancmange. Any sudden jolt causes it to slide around, compressing and expanding as it goes.'

I have an image in my head now of Adam's brain being the sort of disaster area I remember from my O-level cookery exam.

'And what if his brain is badly swollen?'

'We would need to operate, remove a piece of the skull to give the swelling a place to go. We'll also be looking for internal bleeding and any indicators of haematomas or a haemorrhage.'

'What about brain damage?'

'We can't predict possible brain damage from trauma at such an early stage.'

'But it is a possibility?'

'Yes. I'm afraid it is.'

I nod again. I'm not imagining blancmange any more. I'm imagining Adam; alive, vibrant, running across the moors like there's no tomorrow, Adam, ending up lying there for the rest of his life like some bloody vegetable. I am aware from the fact that Dr Perryman is offering me a box of tissues that I must be crying again.

'Like I said, that's the worst-case scenario, there are altogether more manageable ones.'

I go to ask what they might be but stop myself because I am not sure I want to hear them. In my best-case scenario there is no internal bleeding or swelling or lasting brain damage. Adam comes round shortly afterwards, we all have a good laugh about it and Adam dines out on the story of how he was floored by a dinosaur for years to come. Somehow, I don't think Dr Perryman's best-case scenario is going to be anything like that at all.

I sit and watch Adam being lifted on to the sliding bed in the scanning room. There is something disconcertingly morgue-like about it. I am aware that in a moment the bed will slide away and Adam's body will disappear from view. I have a sudden sense of him being taken away from me. Of wanting to smash down the glass panel and claw him back. Tell them he is mine. That they have no right. No right at all. Someone presses a button. The bed starts sliding. I press the stop button on my side of the glass panel but nothing happens. Nothing happens at all. Because there is no stop button. I am pressing glass. Flat, fucking glass. I have no power. I cannot change anything. There are loud whirring noises as Adam disappears inside the machine. He will hate this. Adam does not like confined spaces. Does not take well to being enclosed. What if he is aware of this happening? If he's screaming inside but nothing is coming out because of the drugs. I have to help him. Have to stop them.

I bash the glass panel with my fist. A second later I am lying in a crumpled heap on the floor, sobbing uncontrollably. A nurse comes and picks me up. Puts her arm around my shoulders and leads me away. I am taken to a tiny side room. Four walls, a couple of chairs. Not much more than a cell. I am given a glass of water. Why does everyone think water will help? My husband is unconscious. He could be brain-damaged and all anyone can do is give me a glass of water and pat me on the hand. I want to wake up now. I have seen the future, been shown the error of my ways. A Scrooge-like conversion has taken place. I will be happy. I will enjoy every second of life. Will not spoil things by worrying about something which may never happen. But of course it has happened. I am being punished. This isn't a nightmare any more. This is my life.

I sit in Dr Perryman's room later, trying to work out from his facial expression how bad the news is going to be. We're talking degrees of bad. There is clearly no chance the news is going to be good.

'I'm afraid the scan has shown considerable swelling in Adam's brain,' says Dr Perryman. 'We're going to need to operate. The impact was on the front of his head so there is particularly severe swelling to the frontal lobes. At some point when the swelling subsides, we will need to do further scans, including an MRI, to try to get a more accurate picture of the situation. But that will all happen after surgery.'

I nod. It is sounding very much like a worst-case scenario to me.

'Is there any good news?' I ask.

'There has been some internal bleeding but there's no sign of significant haematomas or a haemorrhage, although they can develop at a later stage.'

'I see,' I say, even though I don't.

'I know this is a very worrying time, Mrs Taylor. But you can be assured your husband will receive the highest possible standard of care during and after his surgery.'

'And have you any idea how long he might remain in a coma?' I ask. There. I have said it. The C word. Because that is the situation. My husband is in a coma.

'We simply don't know. Every case is different. But it is fair to say the longer he remains unconscious, the more serious the prognosis will be. He'll be going straight to the intensive care unit after surgery. The next twenty-four hours will be critical. That's as much as we can say at this stage.'

I go with Adam as they wheel him down to the theatre. I've only ever been to hospital myself once, when I had Maya. Neither she nor Adam have ever been admitted, not even as outpatients. And yet here I am, thrust in at the deep end without even the benefit of a late-night dash to A&E to have got me acclimatised.

They stop at the doors, a nurse comes out and asks me if I'd like to kiss my husband before they take him in. I know why. It's in case I never see him alive again. I sit down in a small room across the corridor wondering just how much of a comfort that kiss would be if it is indeed the last one.

It's a long wait. The longest of my life. I don't do anything, just sit staring at the wall. My mind empty apart from the single wish that Adam should pull through. When a man who I presume is the surgeon finally comes into the room, I know it is all right simply by the way he opens the door. It is quick and noisy. If it was bad news I'm sure it would be quiet and slow.

'Your husband's out of theatre. We did have to remove a sizeable piece of skull but everything went smoothly and he's now in the recovery room.'

'Thank you,' I say. Those words have never sounded so insufficient.

I think I prepare myself before I go in to see him. But in truth I don't think you can prepare yourself for seeing your husband lying in a coma after major brain surgery. It is not something we are naturally equipped to deal with.

His head is swathed in bandages. They do at least cover most of the bruising but can't conceal the fact that his hair has been shaved. Adam always used to say that if he started to go bald he'd have a comb-over because he reckoned he'd look ridiculous with a shaved head. Although right now, that is the least of his worries.

I can see some dried blood on the bandages. And notice, even through the bandages, that his forehead is flatter, almost sunken. I want to ask someone what they have done with the bit of skull they removed. Have they kept it? Does it get put back later on? Or do I get to take it home as a rather macabre souvenir?

I take Adam's hand. Stroke the nail on his thumb. I stroke it for a long time before I am able to say anything.

'I know you're in there,' I whisper eventually. 'Please come back to me. Please come back soon.'

Eight

I hear Mel's words, rolling in through the fog between us. I am not dead. The relief floods through me. The papers would have had a field day if I'd died: 'T-rex kills museum man', 'First dinosaur victim for 65 million years'. I'd have probably got in the *Guinness Book of Records* as the only human ever to have been killed by a dinosaur. And I'd have won one of those Darwin Awards, which are given out (posthumously, of course) to people who improve the gene pool by accidentally removing themselves from it in a really stupid way. I remember looking at the website once and chuckling at the guy who died while testing whether his new jacket was stab proof.

It wouldn't be so bad if this had happened while I was carrying out some kind of heroic act; pushing a group of schoolchildren out of the way to save them or something. But no, I'm here because I tripped over a barrier rope six inches off the ground and didn't get myself out of the way of a falling dinosaur skull in time. I believe the word the Irish use is eejit. That's what I am. And a prize one at that.

I can imagine the smirk on Chris's face when I go back to work. I'll never live it down. And as for Monty. I thought he was my friend. Of all the low-down, two-faced, double-crossing dinosaur skeletons. If he felt the need to perform a head butt he should have picked on someone his own size.

Mel is still talking to me. Her words intermittent like a poor signal on a radio station. I have a weird understanding now of how Prince Eric in *The Little Mermaid* feels when he awakens and remembers hearing a beautiful voice but no one is there. I'll have to tell Maya when I come round. Maybe I can claim that is what this is all about. An elaborate attempt at method acting for my role as Prince Eric in Maya's plays. And then I remember. The party. Maya will be in bits about it. Not getting the chance to wear her new dress. And Mel will have no idea what she's going on about. I suppose the in-laws will have to tell her. That her husband was planning this fantastic tenth anniversary party for her but has gone and blown it by getting into a fight with a dinosaur. I don't suppose I'll come round in time. And even if I do they'll want to keep me in for observation. Fuck. Of all the stupid ways to spoil a party . . .

I drift off somewhere for a while. Somewhere where I can't hear Mel's voice. I feel like I am in some kind of flotation tank, not that I have ever been in one but Mel tried it at a spa once and told me all about it. I am barely aware of my body at all. My head is strangely numb. They've probably given me something. Drugged me up to the eyeballs. When it wears off the pain will return. But how will I tell them? I know already I cannot speak. I tried the first time Mel came in. My brain sends the words but they fizzle out somewhere before they get to my mouth. It's the same with trying to move. It seems my limbs have gone AWOL. I think of that poor guy in *The Diving Bell and the Butterfly*. Bauby his name was. The book blew me away. And the film. I remember Mel digging her nails into my hand at that bit where they sewed his eye up. Locked-in Syndrome, that's what he had. How can I be sure that's not what's happened to me? He was a journalist too. Maybe we're somehow more prone to it. Our brains just go on spouting words when other people's shut down. I know one thing, mind. I'm never going to have the patience to blink my way through dictating a paragraph, let alone an entire book.

The lack of sensation is the most disconcerting thing. I knew I wasn't dead when it happened because of the pain. But later the pain disappeared, to be replaced by this overwhelming sense of numbness. That was when I thought I was dead. That I had slipped through to the other side. I was waiting to see the bright light and go down the coloured tunnel that all those people who claim to have had near death experiences talk about. When the buzzing and clanking started I thought that was all part of it. It wasn't, though. They were doing something to me. Probably scanning my brain. They must have been surprised to find I had one after getting myself into this mess. They did find it, though. I think they went inside my head afterwards. All I could think of was that *Spitting Image* sketch about Reagan; the one in which the President's brain was missing.

And now? How do I feel now? I don't know. I can't see my body, I can't feel it. It's as if the fuse has gone in my head. That if only someone would put a new one in, all the lights would come on again. Normal service would be resumed. I wish I'd paid more attention in physics at school now. Maybe I could rewire my own brain.

'It's daft, isn't it? I thought we'd be celebrating my new job tonight. And here we are instead.' It is Mel's voice. She has come back. Or maybe she has never been away and I have simply come back to her. Her job. I'd forgotten about that. My brilliant, scarily clever wife teaching an honours degree. She'll love it so much. I've never seen her teach. Weird, isn't it? You spend two-thirds of your life with someone and yet never get to see what they spend their working days doing. I can imagine what she's like, though. She's still buzzing with it all when she comes home. I have this image of her fizzing around the classroom like an Alka-Seltzer tablet dropped in a glass. She is good at explaining things. And patient too, patient beyond words with Maya. When I remember how she was with the whole potty-training thing. She never once lost her temper, even when we had to stop at every service station on our way to Sheffield that time. She's like that with her about every-thing. Always reassuring, encouraging, praising. And look how it's paid off. Look what Maya's like. It's as if she's wearing this invisible cloak of confidence. Nothing fazes her. And so much of that is down to Mel.

I feel bad now. So bad for letting her down. I wanted this party for her. It was my big gesture, my way of saying thank you for everything. And I know she would have been thrown by it all at first and probably would have called me a few names in private but she would have loved it. She really would. Maybe they'll do it without me. I wouldn't mind. Well, not much. And at least it would give

Maya the chance to wear the dress. Jeez, she'll be gutted about the dress. She doesn't even know where to find it. This whole thing is getting stupid now. I've had enough. Very funny joke, God, but I'd like my life back now please.

'Maya's going to come in the morning,' says Mel. 'She's desperate to see you. I spoke to her on the phone at Mum and Dad's and she was chuntering on about some surprise the two of you are cooking up for me. I told her what happened to you. I wanted to be honest with her about it. You know what the first thing she asked was? Whether Monty the bloody T-rex was all right.'

I cannot tell from Mel's voice whether she is laughing or crying. Maybe a bit of both, like me.

Nine

MEL

I wake up in the chair next to Adam's bed with a cricked neck. Which bothers me for a second until I look over at Adam and remember I have nothing to complain about. Nothing at all.

The nurses did tell me to go home. And part of me was desperate to see Maya, to make sure she was OK – well, as OK as you can be when you've been told your daddy's having a big sleep in hospital and won't be coming home for a while. But I couldn't leave Adam. I had this vision of him coming round in the night and not knowing where the hell he was or what had happened. I needed to be here. The only night we've spent apart since we moved in together was when I had Maya. Adam always jokes that I'm trying to outdo Paul and Linda McCartney. I'm not though. I simply don't want to be without him.

'Morning, love,' I say to Adam, leaning over to kiss his cheek. I am secretly hoping that this is the point where everything goes a bit Disney on me. The prince awakens from his long slumber. The princess declares her undying love for him and they all live happily ever after. Actually, nothing happens. The prince sleeps on. The princess sighs heavily and tries not to cry. I am quite sure

Maya wouldn't like that one. Wouldn't like it at all.

The nurse comes in. The same one who was here when we arrived at the ICU. Jacinta her name is. She smiles at me. One of those sympathetic smiles that nurses do so well.

'So, how are we this morning, Adam? It's a beautiful day outside. Rise and shine, Mr Lazybones. You need to get your butt out of bed.' I smile at her. I like the fact that she chatters away to Adam like this. He'll like her. I'm sure he will. Much better than the nurse on the night shift. She didn't utter a word to him. It was as if he wasn't here.

'You need to get yourself some sleep, young lady,' she says, turning to me. 'I'll look after your man here.'

'I can't,' I say. 'My daughter's coming in soon. She's desperate to see her daddy.'

'Did you hear that?' she says, turning back to Adam. 'I didn't know you were a daddy cool. Now you really have gotta get your butt out of bed.' She shakes her head and busies herself checking all the machines and monitors and scribbling on the clipboard.

'How is he?' I ask.

'The same,' she says.

The same as what? Not the same as he was when he woke up yesterday morning, that's for sure. But what if he's the same as this tomorrow, and the next day and the day after that? How soon will this become normal? How long until I get my Adam back?

I sit and hold his hand. Talk to him about happy days past. It feels like being old long before our time. That all we've got left to cling on to are the memories. And the chances of any happy new ones being made are fading by the hour.

'You've got visitors today,' I tell him. 'Mum and Dad are bringing Maya in soon. And Steve and Louise are coming at lunchtime.' It was all I could do to stop Louise coming last night when I phoned her. The sense of disbelief on the other end of the phone was palpable. 'Oh Mel,' she kept saying. Over and over again. People aren't used to getting phone calls telling them that someone close to them is in a coma. And there's nothing they can say after you've told them. Apart from 'Oh Mel'. And to offer to come and visit. I didn't want anyone to come last night though. I just wanted to be alone with Adam for a while. To try to get my head around what has happened before I have to face anyone.

I look at my watch. It's a quarter to ten.

'I'm going to go and meet them. I'll be back in a bit, OK?'

It's hard to stop saying things which would normally solicit a reply. Maybe that's what I'm trying to do. Trick Adam into saying 'sure' or 'that's fine' as if this is simply a game of non-communication he's playing and if I say the right thing rather than ask a direct question I might just catch him out. Adam says nothing. He is clearly too good at this game.

I go to the end of the corridor to wait for Maya. I want to see her before she sees Adam. I need to prepare her, although how the hell I can do that I have no idea. I spend my working week teaching other people about children; how to educate them, how to help them through difficult issues, deal with illness, violence in the family home. But when it comes to your own child, it is another matter entirely. I know too much. Know how these things can undermine previously well-adjusted children, can fuel all sorts of insecurities. I know I have to be strong for Maya. To make her believe there is a way through this. That everything can be OK again. But how can I do that when I'm not sure I believe it myself?

The double doors open and she is here, exploding into my arms in a ball of tears, hair and hurt. Any idea I had of holding it together for her sake evaporates in an instant. My tears mix with hers, love like antiseptic trying to soothe the pain away. She attaches herself to me like a limpet and I in turn hold on to her, ensuring she has at least one secure thing to cling to.

'I want to see Daddy,' she sobs into my ear.

'I know, sweetheart. I'm going to take you to see him now. I just need to talk to you first. Explain what he's going to be like.' She pulls back a fraction, allowing me to breathe and look up. I am aware of my parents hovering above us, a living sculpture entitled 'Not knowing what to say or do'.

'Has he got a big bump on his head?' asks Maya.

'Sort of. He had a big operation and he's got bandages around his head. They had to shave his hair off for the operation but it will grow back. He's also got a big tube in his mouth because he can't breathe on his own.'

'If you can't breathe you die.' Clearly Adam's biology lessons have been rather too successful.

'It's OK, the doctors have got a machine that does Daddy's breathing for him.'

'Why can't he do it himself?'

'His brain is all swollen inside his head and it's not

working properly. The bit that sends the messages to other parts of his body has stopped working.'

'Does it need oiling?'

I smile. Maya loves watching Adam tinkering with his bike.

'Kind of, sweetheart. It needs time to get better.'

'What if he doesn't get better? Is he going to die?' Jeez. I think she's been having interviewing technique lessons from Adam. I swallow the lump in my throat and pull her back tight to me.

'The doctors don't think he's going to die, love. But he is very poorly. His eyes are shut and he can't move or talk to you. He can hear you though.'

'Have they oiled his ears then?'

'The doctors say we all need to keep talking to Daddy. To let him know we're here.' Maya nods, the torrent of questions momentarily subsides. I stand up. Dad kisses me gently on the cheek. Even his glasses have a worried expression. Mum takes hold of my hands and pats them. Clearly they are finding words hard.

'Did you have a nice time at Grandma and Grandad's?' I ask Maya.

'Yes. We had ice cream. But Grandad wouldn't do me a story about Monty.' I look across at Dad who shrugs apologetically. He'd probably been worried about nightmares.

'Never mind. Let's help Daddy to get better first. Maybe then we can do some more Monty stories.'

'Is Monty going to get better too?'

'I expect so, love. Daddy's friends at the museum are probably putting him back together.'

'Can I go and see?'

'Let's see Daddy first, eh?'

I take her hand firmly in mine and start walking back down the corridor. I turn to my parents as we reach the door to Adam's room.

'Can you give us five minutes alone first?'

Dad nods. Mum does her Sunday best smile. I open the door and lead Maya into the room. There is a moment's hesitation when she clings tightly to my hand before she pulls free of it and hurtles towards the bed.

'Daddy,' she cries, throwing her arms over his legs and pressing her head against his knees. I stupidly hadn't warned her to be gentle, to be careful of his head, not to knock or touch any of the equipment. But it turns out she didn't need me to. She appears to have this inbuilt knowledge of how to be when your daddy is in a coma.

'Monty did a naughty thing, Daddy. Hurting you like that,' she says. 'I'm going to tell him off when I see him. I think he was only playing. I don't think he meant it.'

I blink the tears away so I can see this properly. My daughter and my husband, the two people I love most in the world, still managing to take my breath away with the scale of their love, even when one of them is in a coma.

'You've got lots of tubes and things, haven't you, Daddy? I hope the doctors make you better soon. I think you need a bit more oil.' She has hold of his hand now. She is twiddling his fingers as if she's trying to tune a radio in. She walks further up the bed towards his head, leans over towards his ear and whispers something. She waits a few seconds and whispers again.

'What are you telling Daddy?' I ask.

'I can't tell you, it's a secret.'

'Oh, is this the one you mentioned on the phone?'

'Yes. I can't tell you, though. I promised Daddy.' She looks at Adam and back to me, her face crumples. 'I don't know where my dress is,' she says, her voice cracking.

'What dress, sweetheart?' I ask, kneeling down next to her and putting my arm around her.

'The one Daddy bought me for the party.' She claps her hand over her mouth as soon as she says it, then starts to cry. Big, gulping sobs.

'What party?' I ask, smoothing her hair.

'I can't tell you. Daddy said it was a surprise.'

Something was going on. Something I didn't know about.

'Who else knows about it, sweetie?'

'Grandma and Grandad but they said we wouldn't be having a party now. They're wrong though, aren't they? Daddy will wake up in time for it, won't he?'

'When is it, love?'

'Tonight. Daddy said I was allowed to stay up late. Until midnight like Cinderella if I'm really good.'

I open the door. Mum and Dad are standing right outside. It is clear from the expressions on their faces that they have heard every word.

'Come in,' I say. They do as they're asked and shut the door behind them. I see them look at Adam and look down at the ground, the way people do when they see a disabled person in the street.

'What's this about a party?' I ask.

105

'We didn't want to bother you with it last night,' says Dad.

'Bother me with what?'

Mum sighs. I knew she'd be the first to crack. 'Adam had organised a big anniversary party for you. It were supposed to be tonight.'

'How big? Where? Who else is supposed to be coming?' I am aware I am rivalling Maya in the bombarding someone with questions department.

'At Scaitcliffe Hall,' says Mum. 'He'd invited about eighty people I think. Family and friends. There were going to be food and a band and everything.'

I nod, unsure what to make of this new information. Part of me wants to hug Adam for doing all this for me. Another part wants to bash him around the head with a pillow for not listening when I said I didn't want a big fuss. Because now look what's happened. I glance over at Adam. A tear manages to escape from the pool which has welled up in my eyes. Maya rushes over to me.

'Don't worry, Mummy. We can still have the party. Daddy won't mind.'

I look up at the ceiling and screw up my face. It is all too much. I can't cope with this. Not on top of everything else.

'We phoned hotel last night to cancel it, love,' says Dad.

Maya bursts into a fresh round of tears. I wrap my arms tighter around her.

'They are at least going to give your deposit back,' adds Mum. 'Because of circumstances, like.'

'We rang round the family,' says Dad, 'to let them know.

But we didn't have numbers for your friends.'

I nod and look down at Maya whose face is broken in two.

'I'm sorry, love. But we can't have the party without Daddy.'

'You want us to have it, don't you, Daddy?' Maya rushes over to Adam. The pause while she waits for the answer which doesn't come tears me apart. It also jolts me into realising that if Adam can hear us, this is not going to help him. In fact, it's going to be excruciating. Jacinta enters the room, providing a welcome distraction.

'Hey, Adam, is this your beautiful girl?' she says. Maya turns to look at Adam expectantly as if Jacinta may have some secret way of communicating with him. 'Well, you're one very lucky man,' Jacinta continues. 'A beautiful wife and a beautiful daughter. You make sure you wake up for them soon.'

'Me and Daddy were having a surprise party for Mummy,' says Maya. 'But we can't have it now because Daddy's poorly so I can't wear my new dress.'

'And I bet you look pretty as a picture in it,' says Jacinta. 'And when your Daddy's better, I reckon you'll have a party then to celebrate when you can wear your dress.' Jacinta looks at me and winks. I smile appreciatively. Maya appears mollified. Adam sleeps on.

I am on my own when Louise and Steve arrive. Mum and Dad have taken Maya home, she's had to cope with quite enough for one day. Louise knocks on the door. I see her face at the window, solemn and drawn. It feels like someone has died. That people are coming to pay their respects now as the body lies in state.

I stand up, Louise rushes straight over and throws her arms around me. We stand like that for a long time. It feels good to have someone my own size to hold on to. Neither of us says anything. We don't need to. When I finally look up, I see Steve standing awkwardly at the end of Adam's bed. His dark eyes appear to be set back even further than usual, his tall, lean frame seems to be struggling to remain upright. I let go of Louise and walk over to him. Steve is not normally one for hugs and kisses. But this is not a normal situation. I wrap my arms around him. He doesn't seem to know where to put his hands at first. His body is shaking. Finally I feel his fingers pressing lightly on my back.

'It's OK,' I whisper, stroking his back. 'He's going to be fine.' I feel his stubble brush against my forehead. It's the only thing that tells me he is a grown man. Otherwise, it feels for all the world as if I am holding a boy in my arms. That same boy who was always at Adam's side as we were growing up together. Whose friendship has never wavered. I look up at him and he nods. It is an uncertain nod, though. Like Louise's uncertain half-smile. And what nobody says is the thing that all of us are thinking. What if he doesn't get better? What if he isn't going to be fine at all?

I walk over to Adam's bed. Touch his hand lightly.

'Louise and Steve are here,' I say.

Steve appears startled at the sudden realisation that he is supposed to converse with Adam. It is Louise who speaks first.

'I hope your head doesn't hurt too much. At least they've come a long way since vinegar and brown paper.' Louise glances across at me, uncertain. I nod to let her know she's doing fine.

'Don't worry about Mel,' she continues. 'We're going to look after her. You just concentrate on getting better.'

Louise steps back from the bed. The room is silent for a moment. I see Steve swallow hard.

'If I ever see the dinosaur that did this to you, I'll be sure to give him a good hiding.' For a second I think I see Adam's chest shaking, am sure he is about to burst out in laughter. It's just wishful thinking though. I smile at Steve instead. On Adam's behalf.

'And now you're here,' I say. 'One of you can own up about whose idea the party was.'

'Oh, you know about it,' says Louise.

'Maya told me. Mum and Dad have cancelled it.'

'It was nothing to do with me,' says Steve, holding his hands up. 'It was all Adam's own work. I did try to tell him, mind. I said you don't like surprises.'

Louise gives him a look. 'Adam was really excited about it,' she says quickly, turning back to me. 'He'd been planning it for months. I've no idea how he managed to keep the whole thing a secret from you.'

'Nor have I. I need to know who was coming, though. So I can ring round everyone. I'd hate to think of them having a wasted journey.'

'Don't be daft. We'll do that,' says Louise. 'We've already started actually. Steve rang a few people from the running club last night. And everyone we could think of from uni.

We're just not sure exactly who else he invited. I guess he must have a list somewhere.'

'I expect it's on his BlackBerry,' I say. 'Because he'd know I wouldn't look on there.'

'Where is it?' asks Steve.

'It's probably in that carrier bag,' I say, pointing to his bedside cabinet. 'The hospital gave me all the stuff that was on him when it happened. I haven't even looked at it yet, to be honest.'

'Why don't I take it and text everyone in his address book? I'll do the same on your mobile as well if you like.'

'Would you? Thanks. That would be great.'

'Do you know his passwords for Facebook and Twitter?'

'MayaGrace,' I think. 'Like everything else.'

'Well, I could post something on them as well. Just in case we've missed anyone. Where's his laptop?'

'Probably in the boot of his car.'

'Where's his car?'

'At Littleborough station. Hopefully his keys are in the bag. Oh God, I haven't thought of anything, have I? There's so much I need to do.' I slump down on to the chair again. Louise gives Steve a 'back off' look and crouches down next to me.

'You've had a huge shock, Mel. Of course you haven't thought of anything. You've been here with Adam, where you should be. Anyway, you don't need to think about all that stuff. We'll take care of it. It's the least we can do and it'll stop us feeling so bloody helpless. Now, when did you last eat?'

I stare blankly at Louise. I had a Toffee Crisp I found in

my handbag for breakfast and I have a vague recollection of Jacinta bringing me a cheese ploughman's sandwich at some point yesterday but I can't be sure.

'Right,' says Louise. 'I'm taking you to the café. Steve will sit with Adam. What about sleeping? You can't stay here again tonight.'

'I want to go home to Maya, she needs some sort of normality. But I can't bear the thought of leaving Adam on his own. Just in case he, you know . . .'

'I'll stay with him,' says Steve. 'I'll get all the practical stuff done this afternoon, go and get his car and do the texts. Then I'll come back to relieve you for the night shift.'

'Thanks,' I say. 'That would be a huge help. I expect Adam will be glad of your company as well. You can talk guy stuff with him. He's probably fed up with me wittering on by now.'

'Come on,' says Louise. 'Lunch.'

'The nurse will probably be here in a minute,' I tell Steve. 'She's called Jacinta, she's really nice. Any problems you just press that buzzer.' I point to the panel next to Adam's bed. Steve nods.

'You go,' he says. 'We'll be fine.'

It is only as I enter the hospital café that I am rudely reminded that the world is carrying on outside Adam's room. People are eating and drinking, chatting, dashing outside for a quick fag. I wonder why they are all here. Who they're visiting, what state they're in, how long they've been coming here. I feel like shouting, 'Shut up, will you. My husband's in a coma.' I don't though. I sit down quietly at a corner table while Louise gets lunch.

111

'Sorry,' she says, coming back five minutes later with a bowl of tomato soup and a tuna salad sandwich, 'there wasn't much of a choice.' I opt for the soup. I catch a glimpse of my reflection in the spoon. I have on yesterday's make-up and yesterday's clothes. I no doubt smell of yesterday as well. I am reminded of W.H. Auden's poem 'Stop All The Clocks'. How I bawled my eyes out at John Hannah's rendition of it in *Four Weddings and a Funeral*. Adam gave my hand a squeeze at the time. I'd give anything for him to do that now.

I put my spoon down and stare into my soup as the tear clouds gather again.

'Hey,' says Louise, leaning over to rub my shoulder. 'It's all right.'

'It's not though, is it? This wasn't in the plot, you know. This wasn't supposed to happen. I was supposed to be going to my tenth wedding anniversary party tonight.'

'The nurse was right. We'll have a big celebration when Adam's better.'

I shrug. It's lovely that people are saying 'when' instead of 'if' but it doesn't change the situation. 'If' is what we're dealing with.

'You know the really stupid thing?' I say. 'I can't help thinking this is his fault. That it was tempting fate to plan a big do like this. That's why I didn't want a fuss.'

'That's crazy. No one could have predicted what happened.'

'I know. And then I hate myself for blaming him. And I blame myself instead for being so bloody happy yesterday. I got offered increased hours teaching an honours degree.'

'That's fantastic, Mel.'

'It's not now. I couldn't care less, to tell you the truth. All I want is my Adam back.'

Louise drops me off at Mytholmroyd station later. My car is at least still there. It looks slightly forlorn, though. As if it was beginning to wonder if I was ever coming back. I drive the short distance home on automatic pilot. It is only when I see Adam's car parked outside where Steve has left it that it hits me. It has lost its driver. And I have no idea if he will ever be coming back.

I hesitate before putting the key in the door. Summoning up the requisite cheery face and positive attitude Maya needs right now. But bracing myself for the fact the house will seem horribly empty without Adam.

The first thing I see when I go inside are a couple of his jackets hung up in the hall. A second later I hear 'Mummy's home' and Maya comes hurtling out of the kitchen, still propelled by hurt and fury. I scoop her up in my arms and let her squeeze me so hard I am half expecting to find a pool of water on the floor when I look down.

'When's Daddy coming home?' she asks.

'As soon as he's better, darling.'

'When's that going to be?'

'We don't know, love.'

'I wanted to go to your party.' Maya's tears spill over again as Dad appears in the kitchen doorway behind her.

'She's been trying to find her party dress,' he says. 'She's not sure where Adam put it. Says he were going to hide it somewhere. We can't find it in her wardrobe.'

'Come on,' I say to Maya. 'Let's go upstairs. We'll look for it together.' I slip my shoes off and follow Maya who is heading up the stairs on all fours. I am well aware that regression is common in childhood trauma. A wave of panic starts to rise in me until I remember she did this just last week. Maybe she can simply go faster this way. I realise it's going to be like this from now on, though. Me constantly looking for signs of the hurt inside.

'We'll start in our room,' I call after her. I go straight to Adam's chest of drawers and begin riffling through them. Trying not to think about the feel of his clothes in my hands. When the last one has been checked without success, I throw open the doors of his wardrobe and the scent of Adam hits me square in the face. A couple of these shirts are undoubtedly members of his worn once collection. Those he resorts to if there's not a freshly laundered and ironed one there. They're not smelly but they smell of him and it is enough to make me bite down hard on my lip. It is a glimpse of something sparkling through the plastic window of one of his suit covers which catches my eye. Adam is not one for sequinned shirts. I take it down from the rail and unzip it and pull out the tiny hanger inside.

'That's it,' screams Maya in delight. 'That's my dress. It's beautiful, isn't it, Mummy?'

I nod, unable to speak as she twirls around the room clutching it to her.

'Have you found yours too?' asks Maya.

'My what?'

'Your dress. Daddy said he'd got one for you as well. It's not the same colour as mine.'

I turn back to the wardrobe. Reach inside the suit bag and take the other hanger from inside. A midnight-blue bias cut dress in wafer thin silk is hanging from it. I have shoes and a handbag in exactly the same shade. I am always saying I bought the accessories before finding the dress to go with them.

'It's lovely, isn't it, Mummy? Not as nice as mine because it hasn't got sparklies but you'll still look pretty in it.' I smile through my tears as I hold the dress to me. 'Let's put them on,' says Maya. 'We can surprise Grandma and Grandad.' I'd love to say yes to please her but I fear I may break down entirely if I do.

'You put yours on, sweetheart. I think I'll keep mine for when Daddy comes home.'

Ten

'All things bright and beautiful, all creatures great and small.'

What the fuck? I must have died during the night. The angels are welcoming me to heaven. Although you'd think that angels would be able to sing in tune.

'All things wise and wonderful, the Lord God made them all.'

Oh God, it's hell, isn't it? And these are some sort of anti-angels who welcome the fallen. Jeez, I wish I'd paid my poll tax now. I had no idea their records went back that far.

'Each little flower that opens, each little bird that sings.'

Hang on a minute. I recognise this voice. Family gatherings, weddings and funerals. It's Joan. It's my mother-in-law. This is worse than hell. It's a living hell. She's decided to sing to me. She's trying to wake me from the coma. Jeez, I thought they could have done better than that. Was Susan Boyle busy or something? Come to think of it, Katy Perry would have been nice. Or Cheryl Cole even, I'm not going to be snobby about it.

'The purple-headed mountain, the river running by.'

I'd forgotten there were more verses. At least three, I think. The trouble is I have no idea if she'll stop at one hymn. She's not a spiritual woman really. I think she only goes to church for the social side. She's a *Songs of Praise* devotee, of course. The passing of the late, great Harry Secombe was akin to the death of the Messiah for her. Although the fact that Aled Jones then got the gig was something of a second coming. I let the words drift over me, willing them to drift faster.

'The Lord God made them all.' Is she pausing for effect or is there more to come? No, no. I think it's finished. Hallelujah. See, she's got me at it now.

'Morning, Adam. I thought that would be a nice way for you to start the day. It won't be every day, of course. There are other people on rota. But Tuesday and Thursday mornings I shall be with you.'

There's a rota? Whose idea was that? Rotas are for chores – washing up, putting the bins out – not for coma-sitting, surely? Can I get a pass out of here for Tuesday and Thursday mornings? Maybe I could spontaneously combust and set off a fire alarm. Shit, I wish I could talk. And move. Wish I could do something biblical and pick up my bed and walk. How long has it been now? I don't know exactly. All the stupid things people talk to you about and nobody tells you what day it is. Maybe they think it would sound patronising if they did. Or simply think I wouldn't want to know, that it would make it worse to be aware of how many days are slipping away while I lie here. Days I will never get back again. I thought it would last a few hours. Maybe a day or two. But it's been longer than that, I know that much. I am not using a calendar, I am using a noise cycle system. I can recognise the difference between night and day because of the different voices of the hospital staff and because of the lack of visitors during the wee small hours. What I have difficulty doing is keeping count as the days and nights pass. A simple tally system would be enough. But as I'm incapable of even making a notch on my bedpost, all I can do is try to visualise it in my head. And unfortunately my head seems to be pretty rubbish at remembering how many there were the day before.

'Mrs Westwood came into surgery yesterday. Her haemorrhoids are playing her up again. Terrible trouble she's had with them.'

Oh no. I can see where this is going. Religious singing followed by a medical update on the good people of Mytholmroyd. I wouldn't want to know about Mrs Westwood's haemorrhoids if I wasn't in a coma, so what on earth makes her think I'd be interested because I am. Unless, of course, she's trying to bore me into submission. Almost as if those in comas are actually being a bit lazy and if their lives are made dull and mundane enough they will be forced to open their eyes and speak. It doesn't work like that, though. I've lain here and hauled at my eyelids, sent messages until I've ached with trying but it's as if there's some kind of Bermuda Triangle that the messages fall into before they ever reach their destination.

I find myself unreasonably jealous of Jean-Dominique Bauby, *The Diving Bell and the Butterfly* guy. At least he had one eye he could blink. He also, as I recall from the film, had a bevy of beautiful women in attendance (unless of course that was simply the film director wanting to make the whole thing more aesthetically pleasing). I have my mother-in-law singing hymns to me and discussing people's embarrassing medical complaints. When I come out of this coma, and I will come out of it, I will have her up for contravening patient confidentiality. That would be fun. I let out a snort of laughter. Except of course it doesn't come out at all. Gets trapped somewhere along with everything else I have tried to say. I wonder if when I do finally manage to speak, it will be like a dam wall bursting and all those trapped words will escape in a torrent.

'Anne Robinson were wearing another new pair of glasses on *The Weakest Link* last night. I don't know where she gets money from. Well, I do, of course. The stupid BBC that pays it to her. To think that she used to present *Points of View*. Supposedly sticking up for licence payer. I wish I'd never written all those letters to her now. Not that she ever read any of them out.'

Stop writing them then. I won't mind. In fact, I'll dance a celebration conga through Mytholmroyd.

'I took Sylvia out last night, you know. Still at a loss to know what to do now that Bill's gone, she is. It shouldn't happen, should it? Not to women of our age. At least give us dignity of being a grieving widow if we're going to be left on our own.

'We went to the Indian at Luddendenfoot. Half-Moon I think it's called. I had omelette and she had scampi and chips. Lovely they were too. Of course it's a bit smelly, all those curries everyone else is having, but we put up with that because of service. So polite and attentive the waiters are. Nothing is too much trouble for them.'

I wonder for a moment if this is how I'll go. By choking on my own laughter. I feel myself drifting away. Perhaps I am losing the will to live. Or maybe just going to whatever place it is I go to when my head appears to 'tune out' for a bit.

I am on a train journey. I can hear the steam whooshing past, the pistons pumping. I am trying unsuccessfully to place it in my memory. It is clearly not the Santa Special on the Keighley and Worth Valley Railway as the sounds are not accompanied by the screams of hundreds of over-excited children. And I can't remember any other steam train journeys I have undertaken. Not since childhood anyway. Maybe it isn't from my memory. Maybe I am imagining this. Taking myself off to some place I would like to go. Although that doesn't make sense either as I'm not particularly keen on steam engines. I mean they're OK but I'd rather be running on the moors. I'm not sure why I've chosen to be chugging along the tracks.

I hear a click. The sounds stop. 'Hang on a sec, Adam. I'm just turning tape over.' It's Tom's voice. Joan must have given up on me and let him take over. I should have guessed, of course. My father-in-law is a complete train buff. Why else would anyone run a model railway museum in Halifax that struggles to survive on the meagre entrance fees? I suspect it actually makes a loss. That Tom simply doesn't mention that to Joan, goes on propping it up with his pension from the council. I can't say I blame him. I think I'd need somewhere to escape to if I'd been married to Joan for God knows how many years. I have a soft spot for Tom. I feel the words 'long-suffering' were invented to be a prefix to his name. He has an air of hopelessness about him. That to resist is ultimately futile. He is a brilliant grandad to Maya, though. She appears to ignite a childlike enthusiasm in him which would otherwise go untapped. Mel's brother lives in Belgium with his wife and sons so although Maya isn't Tom's only grandchild, she's the only one he has any real involvement with. It's one of my biggest regrets that my own father didn't live to see Maya – he died when I was nineteen, six years after Mum had left him. Perhaps she saw it coming. Thought she'd trade him in for a younger model before his engine conked out. Maybe that had always been the plan. She never even came over for his funeral. Said she was too busy to take the time off work. Which was actually worse than if she'd said she couldn't afford the air fare from Australia. It was a clear case of 'won't' not 'can't'. She didn't send a wreath either. So much for twenty years of marriage.

'While you're listening to train sounds, I thought I'd read to you from *Inside Track*, magazine of the Model Railway Enthusiasts' Society.'

Shit. No. It sounds like one of the guest publications on *Have I Got News For You*. Paul Merton would be cracking jokes about two-inch gauges already. And I've got no choice but to listen to it. They're not getting this. They're supposed to be trying to get me out of a coma, not induce one.

'It appears collectors are having difficulty getting hold of the Bachmann No.41241 model in maroon. These are a limited edition model and unfortunately we have no further information about possible supplies. On a brighter note, the Calderdale Model Railway Society has commissioned Dapol to produce a 00-gauge flat-topped tar wagon, limited to 191 models.'

I tune out and switch off. Tuesdays and Thursdays are going to be exceedingly long days.

When I tune back into my room again, some time later, Joan and Tom have gone. I am enveloped by silence. Not the silence within my head. This is a different sort of silence. A lonely one. Immediately I feel mean for wishing them gone. I know they were trying their best. It's not their fault that their best is lousy. To be fair, it was so bad it was actually funny. Besides, it's good of them to give Mel a break. And I guess that's what this whole rota business is about. She's been here every day, I know that. I have heard her voice between every long night-time silence. I can't imagine how she's managing it. What with Maya to look after and work. Doh. She isn't working, is she? Because I'm in a coma. I wouldn't be working if she was in a coma. They must have given her special leave. They're very good like that at the uni. I feel guilty now. All these people who I'm putting out because I was stupid enough to get into an argument with a dinosaur.

I jump as the door opens (well, in my head I jump, I am presuming my body stays exactly where it is). I listen to the footsteps entering my room. It is not Mel as she would have spoken by now. Not one of the nurses, as they sound much more purposeful. No, these are hesitant footsteps. A woman's. A woman who clearly hasn't been before.

'Hello, Adam.' I know the voice instantly. It is Hannah.

'I spoke to your wife on the phone. She said it was OK

to come. I hope you don't mind. I wanted to drop these off.'
There is a pause as she puts something down on the floor.

'Sorry,' she continues. 'I'm being really dense. It's your
briefcase and things from your desk. I wasn't sure if there
were any valuables. Anyway, I wanted to return them to
you. I've put them by your bedside cabinet.' The pause is
longer this time. She is struggling. She's very young to be
dealing with this.

'I'm so sorry about what happened, Adam. We're all just,
well, in shock really. Even Chris.' I have a sudden pang for
the museum. The sights, the smells, the sounds. The general
tittle-tattle. It's weird, the things you miss when they're
taken away.

'Anyway, there's a big investigation going on. They think
the flood caused more damage underneath the floors than
they'd realised. And the workmen seem to have cut through
a cable which was connected to Monty's ceiling fitting. I
probably shouldn't be telling you this. Not that it bothers
me. You're the one person who has a right to know.'

Another pause. I hear her footsteps go round to the
opposite side of the bed. She is looking at me. I wish I
could see her face. Wish I could tell her it is OK. Whatever
it is she is thinking.

'You've always been so good to me, Adam. I do
appreciate it. I want you to know that. And I've learned so
much from you already. I just want you back. We all do.'

I follow her footsteps back round to the side of the room
she came in. I picture her wringing her hands, fiddling
with her nails, being totally at a loss for words.

'Anyway, I can't stop, I'm afraid. I've just popped down

in my lunch hour. Chris is in charge and, well, you know what he's like.'

The footsteps are heading away from me. They stop abruptly.

'I know you probably think I'm just a silly young girl but I want you to know you mean a lot to me. I remember that time I saw you in the foyer with your wife and daughter. You looked such a perfect family. And now . . .' Her voice chokes. I swallow hard. At least I think I do.

'I just hope you can all be that happy again. One day. Not too far away.'

The footsteps retreat further. I whisper, 'Thank you.' I know she can't hear me but I want to say it anyway. The door shuts behind her. I am left alone with my thoughts.

'Happy annibirthday, Daddy,' Maya bounds into the room. It's my anniversary. I didn't know. Which is different to forgetting. Although I have to say that being in a coma is probably the best excuse for forgetting a guy can come up with.

Maya obviously hasn't come on her own. Mel is with her. I can sense her in the room. But clearly she isn't able to speak at the moment. She takes my hand instead. I can't feel her fingers, only her softness.

'Happy anniversary, darling,' she whispers eventually.

'Mummy loved her dress so much she cried,' announces Maya. 'But she isn't going to wear it in case she spills something down it before you see it. I wore my dress and I spilt my blackcurrant down it. Mummy washed it and it's dry now. It just needs ironing.'

I wouldn't know whether to laugh or cry first, if I was able to do either. I so want to hug her, to pull her to me and never let her go. What use am I to her like this? I was the party pooper and now I can't even iron her dress. Mel is brilliant at a million and one things but she's crap at ironing.

'I made you and Mummy this at nursery.'

'Daddy can't see it, sweetie. You have to tell him what it is.'

'It's a card. I've done hearts on it. Dylan wouldn't give me the red crayon so I had to use green instead. And I've done lots of kisses in it.'

'There,' says Mel. 'We've put it on your bedside cabinet.'

'You've got lots more annibirthday cards at home,' says Maya. 'Mummy hasn't opened them yet. She's going to wait until you get home.'

I hadn't thought of the cards. I wouldn't do. I'm not really a card kind of guy. I did get Mel one. It's in the bottom drawer of my wardrobe. I wonder if she's looked for it. Found it even.

'Mummy's brought you her one.'

'You open it, love. Daddy won't mind. You need to tell him what's on it.'

'There's two hearts. Big red ones. Read him what it says, Mummy.'

'To my husband . . .' There is a pause. A long one. I want to finish the sentence for Mel. Put her out of her misery. 'On our tenth wedding anniversary,' she finishes. I hear a zip. I know exactly what Mel is getting out of her handbag. This is doing my fucking head in now. I want to punch something, though the truth is I couldn't punch my way out of a paper bag right now. What sort of husband am I? A lame duck one. That's what.

Mel whispers something. Maya's voice goes up an octave.

'And guess what? We're not just getting one rat, we're getting two. Mummy read that they like to have company. Mummy's going to buy me them as soon as she finds two brothers or two sisters. She says I can't bring them in to show you in case it scares the nurses but when you come home, I'll show you them then. They won't bite or anything, I'm going to train them.'

Poor kid. She must be finding it hard. Really hard. I know we promised we'd get her one but we wouldn't have got around to it for ages. I guess getting the two of them is kind of like a daddy substitute. Something to take her mind off the fact that I'm not around. This is what it's come to. I'm being replaced by a couple of rats.

Maya witters on, seeming utterly unperturbed by the fact that I don't say anything in response. Mel hardly gets a word in edgeways. Though I suspect that's a welcome relief for her today.

'We're going to go now,' says Maya, eventually. 'Mummy's going to put the radio on for you. She took me to vote with her after nursery. You have to do a cross in pencil because felt tips are too messy.'

Of course. It's the general election. I didn't realise that either. I can't vote. I can't fucking vote. Or can I? Maybe there are special rules for people in comas. Maybe I can vote by proxy. Maybe Mel's already done it for me. Why don't I know if you can do that? Call myself a bloody journalist.

'Bye, Daddy. Love you lots.'

'Love you,' says Mel, squeezing my hand again. She is just about holding it together. For Maya's sake, I know that. When Maya's not around, I don't think she's doing very well at all.

They leave. The darkness gets darker still. Peter Allen is on 5 Live. I have an awful feeling the country is about to turn blue.

Eleven

MEL

I am sitting in a consulting room waiting for answers. Adam has been in a coma for nine days now. Weirdly, it is starting to feel normal. When I say normal, I mean I am struggling to remember the last day we had together before this happened. To all intents and purposes, the intensive care unit is now our home. As friendly as the staff are, I'd rather that wasn't the case.

'Now, Mrs Taylor,' says Dr Brooke, who is Adam's consultant in the ICU. 'The latest CT scan shows there is no fresh bleeding in the brain, nor is there any midline shift, which as I explained before is good news. The MRI found no evidence of haemorrhaged blood although both scans showed there is still considerable swelling. I'm afraid it did also show some lesions and this, together with the swelling, does point to a severe brain injury.'

'What does that mean?'

'It means you need to prepare for the fact that this is a long-term coma.'

What does he mean, prepare? What am I supposed to do, get some extra ready-meals in, cancel the summer holiday?

'You don't think he's going to come out of it, do you?'

Dr Brooke looks down. He is younger than Dr

Perryman and not so adept at telling it to you straight.

'I'm simply saying that this looks like it could be a long haul. It's still early days and if Adam opens his eyes within the next twenty-one days, the prognosis will improve, although as I mentioned before, not all patients who open their eyes do regain consciousness.'

What he is trying to tell me is to get used to the idea that my husband will not be coming back to me. I know the score. I've been researching on the internet. There was a time, not so long ago, when you could easily remain in blissful ignorance. It's much harder now. Google 'comas' and you get more information than you can get through in a lifetime, although I'm giving it a good try. Staying up every night to plough through the articles. Some of the medical jargon has washed over me. But there are certain statistics which stick in my head. Only fifteen per cent of people who remain unconscious for six hours or more will have returned to work after five years. That's six hours. I dread to think what the figure is for six days.

Here's another one: in patients with a Glasgow Coma Scale of 5 after twenty-four hours, more than half will die or remain in a vegetative state. I read them then file them in my head in the folder marked 'not helpful'. It is the other websites I save to my favourites. The ones full of hope. An American one called 'Waiting'. It has lots of posts from people who are going through what I am. Many of them citing stories of loved ones who have defied the odds, proved the doctors wrong. There are newspaper articles too. A man called Terry from Arkansas who came round after nineteen years. His mother never gave up on him.

Like I will never give up on Adam. And there's the book, of course. Adam's copy of *The Diving Bell and the Butterfly* which is now even more dog-eared than it was. I found it painful to re-read at first but then I realised that every word is full of hope. Bauby was written off for dead by the doctors. But we know he wasn't dead. We know he thought and felt and hurt just like us. We know he was in there. Alive, if not kicking.

'How do you know he hasn't got Locked-in Syndrome?' I ask.

Dr Brooke raises his eyebrows, shuffles some bits of paper on his desk.

'If it's the book you're referring to, that really was an extremely rare case, Mrs Taylor. And when it does happen it tends to be when people have suffered strokes.'

He can't deny it, see. He doesn't know. None of them do. They haven't done proper tests or anything. They are as much in the dark about this as I am.

'What if he doesn't open his eyes within the next twenty-one days?'

'Let's cross that bridge if and when we come to it, shall we?' Dr Brooke says. What he is trying to tell me in his rather awkward, avoiding the subject way, is that if that happens, I have lost Adam. And I will not get him back. 'In the meantime we're going to set up a PEG feeding system for your husband. It's essentially a tube which goes directly into his stomach. It will remove the need for his nasal feeds and is the most effective long-term feeding method.'

I stare at him. They are going to put a hole in Adam's stomach, a hole that shouldn't be there. He could wake up tomorrow, what the hell would he make of having a stomach tube then? Clearly that doesn't bother the doctors because they don't think it's going to happen. It bothers me though.

I stumble out into the corridor. The world has gone blurry. I cannot face going straight back into Adam's room. I would have to try to be cheery. And I do not feel at all cheery right now. Besides, Adam is very good at knowing when I am not strictly telling the truth. And even though he can't see me, I think he would know just by the tone of my voice.

I set off down the corridor. I have no real idea where I am going. The person I walk into has her arms out ready to catch me. It is only when she speaks that I realise it is Louise.

'Hey, it's OK. I've got you.'

'What are you doing here?'

'It's my slot on the rota. I came straight from work to relieve you.'

I nod. The rota was Louise's idea. I've never been more grateful for it. I dissolve into a blubbing mess. Louise puts her arm around me and guides me down the corridor to the café. She finds a quiet corner and sits me down. She makes no attempt to get me a glass of water or pat my hand. She's the kind of friend I need.

'I take it you've seen Dr Brooke?'

'Yeah. He says I need to prepare for the fact that Adam could be in a long-term coma.'

'They're just talking worst-case scenario. It doesn't mean he won't come out of it, Mel.'

'No but it means they don't think he will. They're going to put a stomach tube in now to feed him. They wouldn't do that if they thought he was going to wake up tomorrow.'

'Listen, Adam's got you and Maya to get back to. He's going to be fighting like hell.'

'I know he is. But it feels like everyone's given up on him already.'

'Well, I haven't. And I know for a fact Maya hasn't either.'

I look down. 'I don't even know if I'm doing the right thing there. Maybe I'm storing up trouble for later. This is so hard for her. I'm worried she's not going to be able to cope with all this.'

'Come on, you, of all people, know how resilient kids are. Maya's a tough little cookie.'

'Only on the outside. She's all gooey in the middle. Especially where Adam's concerned.'

'She'll be fine. She's got a brilliant mum to help her through. Now, I'm going to get you some chocolate.' I dab at my eyes with a crumpled tissue I find in my handbag while Louise goes up to the counter. I have a whole stack of tissues in there. It's like they're on some kind of rota too. Rising to the surface when they've dried out from last time.

'You know what I haven't heard you say yet?' says Louise, arriving back at the table with a stash of chocolate.

'What?'

'Why me? That it's not fair. You have a right to say that, you know.'

'No I don't.'

'Why not?'

I have to stop myself from blurting out the truth. Now is not the time. So I tell her the obvious thing instead.

'I had it good for so long, didn't I? While everyone else was having problems and heartbreaks and crises. Now it's my turn.'

'You've got to stop thinking like that. You weren't owed this. No one deserves to have their husband lying in a coma.'

'What's the good of saying "it's not fair"? It won't change anything, will it?'

'No but it might make you feel better. Get some of the anger out of you.'

'But I don't feel angry.'

'Well, I'm angry that it's happened and Adam's not my husband. Which reminds me, have you heard anything more from the museum?'

'Only that it's in the hands of the Health and Safety Executive.'

'You need to get a lawyer, Mel. If this is going to be a long-term thing, you have a right to some compensation. I know the uni have been great, but they're not going to allow you to be on special leave forever.'

I chew on my Toffee Crisp while I mull it over.

'I know you're right. It's exactly what Adam would say—' I stop short. I was going to say if he was still here. I look down at the table. A large tear falls on my Toffee Crisp. Louise offers me a fresh pack of tissues.

'It's OK, thanks,' I say, reaching into my handbag and taking out one from earlier. 'I'll re-use one of these.'

★

'Hello, sweetheart,' I say as I hover in the doorway of the pre-school room at the Ark. Maya looks up from literally trying to hammer a square peg into a round hole. She appears surprised to see me, which is understandable. It's the first time I've picked her up since the accident and I'm relishing this dose of normality. Louise suggested I do it. She was right, of course. I would have been no use to Adam this afternoon. And it feels good to be here for Maya.

'Mummy, come and see what I made,' says Maya, dropping her hammer, grabbing me by the hand and pulling me towards the kitchen area. There on the counter sits a delightfully sticky mound of white icing decorated with what looks like an entire packet of hundreds and thousands and a liberal helping of Smarties. It's just possible that somewhere deep beneath lies a small fairy cake.

'Wow, that's fantastic, love. Did you do that all by yourself?'

'Yes. I wanted more sprinklies on it but Becky wouldn't let me. She said the sprinkly fairy had run out.'

'Well, you've done a great job. Let's see if I can borrow a container to take it home.' I look at Becky. 'Has she been all right?' I ask quietly.

'Fine, honestly. We're keeping a special eye on her.'

I nod and go through to the kitchen where one of the staff gives me a small plastic pot. I drop the cake into it and Maya peers at it as if it is an exhibit in a museum.

'I'm going to save it for Daddy,' says Maya.

I was doing so well until this point. I look up at the ceiling so Maya doesn't see me biting my lip.

'That's really kind of you, sweetheart, but why don't you

share this one with me, then we'll make a big one for Daddy one day when he's better.'

Maya appears satisfied with my response. Far more satisfied than I am. It feels wrong to build her hopes up by saying things like that. But the alternative of telling her the truth seems far too cruel.

Maya whoops with delight when she sees her scooter which I've parked outside. I'd needed the walk down and knew she'd love to ride back. I take her hand and we cross the road together before I fix her helmet on. She jumps on the scooter and whizzes off up the path ahead of me, her long hair streaming backwards in the breeze.

'Not too fast, love,' I call after her, although I know it is futile. She is headstrong. And she's four years old. She has the world at her feet. One day I am going to have to let her go and I know that's going to be the hardest thing for me to do. I wondered out loud once why all pavements couldn't be replaced with that springy material they use in children's playgrounds. Adam roared with laughter. Mainly because he knew I was being serious. Yes, I understand that children must face risks, that assessing them is how they learn. That is all very well in theory. Until it is your child flying along the pavement on a scooter, your child going river-walking on a school trip, your child heading out into the big wide world on their own.

Maya has always been so precious. Every child is. But I have a heightened sense of it now. Because of what has happened to Adam. I walk on briskly, trying to banish such thoughts from my head. It should be possible. The valley is positively bursting with spring. It's as if the local children have been out putting scrunched-up pieces of green tissue paper on the trees overnight. The smell of May, of freshness, of new beginnings, is all around. And yet all I feel is resentment. How dare it be so in-my-face beautiful when Adam is not here to see it.

We get back to the house and Maya dismounts from the scooter, pink in the face, hair matted.

'Will Daddy mend the gate when he gets home?' she asks as I take off her helmet. I look down. The wood's been rotten for a long time but it has finally come off its hinges. I have no idea how long it's been like that.

'It's OK, love. I'll do it as soon as I get a minute.'

'But you haven't got tools.'

'I'll use Daddy's.'

'Do you know where they are?'

I realise I don't. Well, not exactly. And the last time I looked, the shed wasn't the sort of place you could find something if you didn't know exactly where it was. I feel like some ridiculous 1950s housewife who is incapable of doing any practical jobs.

'Come on. We'll have a look now,' I say.

On my way to the shed I notice that the young vegetable plants we put out a couple of weeks ago have been eaten by slugs. Maya ate fresh peas from their pods in our garden last year. I suspect we'll be relying on Captain Bird's Eye this summer.

I rummage around in the shed, trying to pretend I know what I'm doing. I find some screws but no screwdriver. A hammer but no nails.

'You can borrow my tool kit if you like,' says Maya.

'Thanks, love. I might just need it. Come on, let's go in now. I'll have a proper look tomorrow.' As I open the front door, the back of the letter box falls off.

'Everything's dropping to bits,' says Maya. I do my best to muster a smile.

It's eight thirty by the time I finally get Maya to bed. We used to read her one bedtime story each. I read her three tonight. My way of trying to make up for it, I guess.

I go into the lounge to sit down and am immediately greeted by a stack of ironing on the sofa. I'm also aware that Maya only has one pair of clean knickers left. The house hasn't been cleaned for a fortnight now. I know it's pathetic. Single mums have to cope on their own all the time. But there again, none of them are going back and forth to hospital every day to visit their husband who is in a coma.

I go through to the kitchen where dirty pots and pans are piled up on the counter. I sit down at the kitchen table and open up my laptop. I've been inundated with messages since the accident, people who Steve texted or emailed on my behalf, offering their commiserations, if that's the right word, and wanting news of Adam's progress. There hasn't been any, of course, which is the reason I've used to justify the fact that I haven't replied to most of them. Only Nadine from college because she's been texting every few days and I felt so bad about not getting back to her.

I scroll down the emails until I see one from Australia. Adam's mother has got back to me. I wouldn't normally dream of emailing someone to tell them their son is in a coma but I had no choice. Annabel has never given us her phone number. We only got the email address from the public relations website she runs with her husband Graeme. I haven't spoken to her since I was a teenager. Neither has Adam. He still bristles at the mention of her name. But as much as I hate her for hurting Adam so much, she is still his mother. I figured she had the right to know.

I click on the email and start reading. The phrase that sticks out is 'obviously if the business wasn't such a drain on my time'. That and 'do pass on my best regards'. Regards? She's his fucking mother. He's lying unconscious in hospital and she's too busy with work to come. I slam the laptop lid down before my tears drip on to it. Adam always used to say me and Maya were all the family he needed. I wish that wasn't the case right now, though. I wish I had someone else to lean on. Someone who shared our love for him.

I hear a soft tap at the door. I've no idea who it is and I don't want to answer but I have this stupid thing in my head that if Adam died they might not phone me. They may send the police round. I have to answer. Just in case.

I turn the latch and open the door a fraction, half expecting to find two uniformed officers on the doorstep. I don't though. I find Steve.

Tears of relief stream down my face. Steve slips quietly inside and shuts the door behind him.

'I'm sorry. I should have texted first. Did I scare you?'

I nod. 'I thought you were—' I stop as my voice catches again. Steve wraps his arms around me. He seems much more certain this time.

'Hey, it's OK. Adam's still the same. I've just come from the hospital. I wanted to make sure you were all right. Louise said you'd had a tough day.'

'Thanks,' I say when he eventually lets go. 'Sorry, you've got a soggy shoulder now.'

'It doesn't matter. At least you had one when you needed it. I'll go straight home if it's not a good time.'

'No. Don't be silly. Come on through.'

The state of the kitchen hits me as I walk back in. The sort of thing you see on BBC2 documentaries about students in shared digs.

'I'm sorry about this,' I say, waving my hand around. 'I know it's a complete state. I simply haven't had the time.'

'Don't apologise. It doesn't matter, does it?' I know from Louise that Steve is fastidiously tidy. I imagine him going home and telling her I've let it all slip. I fill the kettle and flick it on. I can at least manage to provide coffee.

'Everything's getting on top of me. I was dealing with it by waking up in the morning and thinking maybe this will be the day Adam comes round, but now the doctors are talking about a long-term thing, I, well, I don't know how I'm going to cope with it all.' I look away, determined not to let Steve see me blinking back the tears again. The kettle boils, I pour the coffees. Steve has his black, no sugar. Which is a bit of luck as I realise I haven't got any milk in. I hand Steve his mug. He hesitates for a second. I have given him Adam's 'World's Best Dad' mug, without thinking. He takes it without comment.

'Let me help you,' he says.

'You and Louise have done enough already.'

'I can take some stuff off you. Louise is right, you need to get a lawyer. I can sort that. Find you someone good.'

'Would you? That would be a huge help. It feels awful to be even thinking about money at a time like this.'

'Well, you need to. You've got Maya to think of. I'll also come round this weekend and fix your gate. And I'll get you a cleaner.'

'Don't be daft. You don't need to do that. I'll get on top of it.'

'And when are you going to do that?'

I shrug.

'Exactly. Me and Louise have got one and she's worth her weight in gold. The last thing you need when you get home from hospital is to have to face this lot.' He's right, of course. It would be a godsend. I had no idea Steve would be this good in a crisis. Maybe I don't know him as well as I thought I did.

'Thank you,' I say. 'You're a complete star.' It is Steve's turn to shrug.

'Adam's my best mate. I owe it to him to look after you. I know he'd do the same if it had been me.' He walks across to the sink with his coffee mug. I sense again that he is finding this hard himself. Maybe I didn't realise how hard.

'You miss him, don't you?'

'Yeah. I do. I went for a run on Thursday. It was so bloody quiet without him giving me a hard time.'

'You wouldn't be saying that if he was here. Imagine the stick he'd be giving you about the election. Your friend Cameron desperately scrabbling around for some more mates.'

'And Brown clinging on for dear life,' adds Steve. 'It's hardly dignified, is it? Maybe Adam planned this on purpose. If Labour manage to hang on, he'll come round straight away.'

I smile. The first proper smile in a long time.

'That's better,' says Steve.

'I can't promise it'll last.'

'I know. But it's a start.'

We sit and talk for a while. About who Nick Clegg will end up in bed with, work, Maya, anything apart from Adam really. And just for a little bit, I feel almost human again.

'Anyway,' says Steve, setting down his empty mug. 'I'd better let you get to bed.'

I follow him through to the hall. He almost falls over the broken letter box. 'I'll fix that for you at the weekend as well.'

'Thank you. For everything, I mean.'

'It's the least I can do in the circumstances.' He bends to give me a peck on the cheek. 'You take care now. And remember nothing's too much trouble, OK?'

I nod and watch him stroll to his car, jingling the keys in his hand.

Twelve

I have clearly lost the plot now. What else could explain the fact that I am hearing David Cameron and Nick Clegg giving a joint press conference from the Downing Street garden? I had a bad bump on the head and now I think Nick Clegg is Deputy Prime Minister. I'll be imagining Boris Johnson and Ken Livingstone dancing the sugar plum fairy next. A journalist is asking Cameron how he feels about having once called Clegg a joke. They're mucking about now like a comedy double act. Laurel and Hardy are running the country. Or is it Cannon and Ball? Never in my wildest nightmares . . .

Oh God. It's over. They've gone back to Peter Allen in the studio. This is 5 Live. I'm not imagining things at all. This is really happening. Just as well I'm in a bloody coma. Best place for me to be right now. Unless, of course, Cameron chooses to visit this hospital. I used to carry a spoof donor card around with me in the eighties, cut out of *Private Eye* magazine. It read, 'In the event of me being seriously injured I wish it to be known that I do not want to be visited by Margaret Thatcher under any circumstances whatsoever.' I could do with one of those now. Something along the lines of, 'In the event of me being in a coma, I do not wish to be visited by David Cameron or Nick Clegg in order to boost the pro-NHS credentials of a coalition government.'

I'll kill Steve for this when I come round. All that guff about Cameron being the rightful successor to Tony Blair. I bet the Calder Valley's gone Tory. The blue flag will be flying over Hebden Bridge. How weird is that?

The analysis on 5 Live rumbles on in the background. I'm grateful to Mel for bringing the radio in. It does at least keep what's left of my brain active. But there are times I'd rather have one of Maya's Jo Jingles CDs on a loop, 'My Bicycle Has a Bell' over and over again until what's left of my brain is pickled. That way I wouldn't have to think about my predicament. Wouldn't have to worry about how Mel is coping. Wonder if I'll ever be able to see Maya again. Utter even one bloody word. Move a muscle. Any muscle. I'm not fussy. And this from the eternal optimist. The guy who could always be relied upon to see a silver lining. I'm trying. I'm trying so hard. But with every day that passes, every rendition of 'All Things Bright and Beautiful' I am subjected to by Joan, it gets a little bit harder. There doesn't appear to be anything I can do to help, that's the difficult thing. Sometimes the more I try to speak, to move so much as a finger, the further away I seem to drift. The blackness is getting to me now as well. I long to see colours. Deep, rich, vibrant colours. Even when I imagine what things look like in my head, it is starting to be in monochrome. It's like I've forgotten what scarlet and emerald green look like.

I crave sensation, any kind of sensation. Good or bad. It is the numbness, the nothingness, the stillness which drives me crazy. When I picture myself now, I just see this huge head. A bit like the Wizard of Oz, projected on to a screen. My limbs are a dim and distant memory. And if I don't find them or my voice again soon, I fear they may all simply wither and die. That is if they are not dead already. I have a feeding tube in my stomach now. I know because the doctor told me they were about to do it and Mel had warned me the night before. The stupid thing is I can't feel it. If you have a hole in your stomach you should bloody know about it. I have never felt less alive than I do now. I am dead wood. The rot has well and truly set in. And only the uppermost branches show any signs of life.

'Hey, beautiful day outside. Too beautiful to be stuck in here listening to yak, yak, yak on the radio.' I like Jacinta. I like it that she gives me a hard time. The rest of them are always so bloody nice. I love the fact that her voice is different to most of the others too. The lilting Jamaican accent with just a hint of Mancunian thrown in for good measure. I have a picture of her in my head. A big, soft, no-nonsense woman with red lipstick, pearly white teeth and a smile so big it can hardly fit through the door. I'm looking forward to seeing her in the flesh. The day I open my eyes.

'At least it's not a Tuesday or Thursday today. Man, I've heard that woman sing. I reckon she trying to scare the shit out of you. When you come round, you be sure to tell her to go get some singing lessons, OK?'

I laugh so much inside that I think I wet myself. Not that I can do such a thing. Jacinta has told me that I have something called a convene attached to my penis. I think it leads to some kind of bag which she has to change regularly. It is times such as these that I am actually relieved I can't see. It is bad enough feeling like a helpless vegetable. Seeing myself as one might just tip me over the edge.

The door opens. Footsteps. Steve's. It's a game I play, a variation on Name That Tune, called Name That Visitor. I can sometimes name them in three footsteps. Occasionally I even get it by the way they open the door. Louise is the quietest, Tom the loudest. I think that comes from slamming a lot of train carriage doors in his time. Steve is somewhere in the middle. A firm closing of the door and certain footsteps. I wish he'd try to catch me out sometimes by coming with Louise but they haven't been together for ages. Not since that first time. I guess that's because they have separate slots on the rota.

'Hello, mate. It's Steve.' They don't realise, of course. That I have worked out who it is long before the greeting. That's the whole point of the game, to guess before they say anything. It's funny how they all introduce themselves by name as well, as if the voice wouldn't be enough. Apart from Mel and Maya, that is. They know I do not need to be told.

Another round of political analysis of the potential pitfalls of a coalition government is beginning on 5 Live.

'I guess you've heard enough about that,' says Steve, turning the radio off. 'But honestly, it won't be as bad as you think. I reckon they'll make a decent job of it.'

Bollocks. That's what I'd say if I could speak. I can't, though, so I simply lie there and take it without a whimper.

Steve's got better at this. Talking to a guy in a coma. He found it really hard at first. Was so awkward, so hesitant. He's getting the hang of it now, though. Just talking. Not asking questions.

'I've brought something in for you,' says Steve. 'Something I should have given back to you long ago.' I hear a thwack as something lands on my bedside cabinet to my right. 'It's your Panini World Cup sticker album 1990. It didn't go missing at all. I kind of took it without asking.'

Bastard. He's supposed to be my best mate. And all this time I've been blaming Neil Wentworth for taking it. Neil Wentworth is innocent. I shall look him up on Facebook when I get out of here and publicly apologise.

'I was kind of mad at you about something, at the time. Thought I'd get you back and when you went off the deep end I didn't have the balls to own up. And then I just forgot about it. It's been in a box of school stuff all these years. All the stickers are there, I checked.'

Well, I'll be checking myself at the first opportunity I have. I was the only kid in school with the complete set. It ruined the World Cup for me. Well, that and England going out on penalties in the semi-final.

'Anyway, I'm sorry, OK.'

You mean you feel better now you've confessed and you're glad I didn't have the chance to call you a thieving little toerag. Jeez, I may as well advertise myself as a confessional. Just pop in, tell me anything you need to get off your chest and I won't even raise so much as an eyebrow.

'As a pathetic attempt to try to make up for it, I've got a solicitor sorted for you. They've taken all the details and are putting together a claim for compensation. They reckon it'll take years to come through but at least we've set the ball rolling.'

God. Compensation. I hadn't even thought about that. He's right, though. I don't know how long the uni will let Mel be on leave for. I presume she's on full pay. I don't know, though. I've no idea how it works. Is the museum still paying me? I'm assuming they are but I don't suppose they'll go on indefinitely. I don't know what it says in my contract. It's not something you do, check the small print to see how long they'll go on paying you for if you're in a coma.

'I've done a few odd jobs around the house and garden for Mel too. Just trying to make myself useful and take a bit of pressure off her.'

That's good of him. I mean, really, it is. The only trouble is Mel will realise he's a damn sight better at all that DIY stuff than I am. Life's too short to get a spirit level out to check if a shelf is straight. That was always my philosophy. Turned out I was right as well.

'She's doing fine. Coping at home, I mean. You don't have to worry about all that stuff. I check in on her when I can. Usually on the way back from seeing you. I guess it's not until something like this happens that you realise what people are made of. She's made of bloody strong stuff, Mel. You wouldn't think it to look at her, would you? She still looks fifteen to me sometimes. I have to remind myself we're not all at school together any more. Me playing gooseberry as usual.'

Was he a gooseberry? I don't remember it that way.

Although I guess I was too wrapped up in Mel to think about it. I remember him hanging out with us. Maybe he did come to the cinema with us a couple of times. And I suppose I must have snogged Mel in front of him once or twice. Perhaps he did feel a bit awkward. I never really thought about it at the time.

'I'll look after her for you. Make sure she's OK. Whatever happens in the future I don't want you to worry about her. I can't begin to imagine what you're going through, lying there like that. I feel so utterly helpless. I've had bloody Rolf Harris lyrics going round in my head. "Two Little Boys" for fuck's sake. And all I keep thinking is, I wish you *had* been injured in some battle. That I could simply gallop in and haul you to safety. Not that I'd ever have the balls to do it but you know what I mean. So I figure that as I can't help you, the least I can do is look after Mel for you. Help out with the practical stuff around the house. Just be there if she needs someone to talk to.'

I'm glad my eyes are still shut. Otherwise he could see the tears gathering. Probably give me a right ribbing about it. Not that he can talk. Turns out that behind the veneer of a cocky piss-taker there's a big softy trying to get out. I'm glad about that. Glad Mel's got someone to take care of her. Someone I know won't let her down.

Thirteen

MEL

It is like stepping back in time, going to Dad's model railway museum. It's a few roads away from the main shopping area in Halifax. In a rundown-looking building which no one else wants to rent. The sign above it is faded and the 'm' of museum is hanging at a precarious angle. In the window is a dusty-looking model railway set with a couple of tunnels and a bridge. But on the outside of the window is a button. A button which no child in Halifax is capable of walking past without pressing. It sets the train in the window going. Simple but incredibly effective. If I didn't know better I'd say Dad was a marketing genius. Kids drag their parents away from the shops just so that they can press it. Unfortunately for Dad, the vast majority of them then get dragged straight back to the shops. But every now and again there's a child persuasive enough to be allowed inside. Added to which are the fathers and grandfathers who are only too willing to escape the shops in favour of an hour or so of nostalgia. And so it is that it survives. And Dad manages to justify spending his afternoons playing with train sets.

'Mummy,' shouts Maya as soon as I walk in. She loves it here, of course. Which is just as well as she's been spending rather a lot of time here lately. I've had no choice. It's not fair to keep dragging her over to Manchester every day to see Adam. I take her every other day but that's quite enough. She loves seeing him but it's hard for her. It takes its toll. It's important she has time away from it. Time to do normal things that other children do. Time when she can stop being the little girl whose dad is in a coma for a bit and simply have fun.

'Hello, sweetheart,' I say, bending to give her a big hug. 'Have you had a great time?'

'Yes. Grandad's shown me how to change the points and he's let me eat a whole packet of Maltesers and a tube of Smarties.'

I walk over to Dad who looks suitably abashed.

'You should know by now you can't get away with it,' I whisper as I kiss him on the cheek.

'Well, it's not going to do her any harm, is it?'

I resist the temptation to point out that both me and Maya's dentist would disagree with that.

'Anyhow,' he continues, 'I figured she deserved a treat.' This is Dad's code for saying 'because her father's in a coma'. I still don't think he's actually said the C word. The whole thing puts him way outside his comfort zone. 'And so do you,' he says, pressing a bar of Dairy Milk into my hand. It's kind of him, I know, but I can't help wanting to scream at him, 'Dad, I am thirty-three years old and my husband is in a coma. You can no longer cheer me up with something from the sweet shop.' I don't, though. I smile at him instead. Because he doesn't have the words or emotional capacity to comfort me any other way.

'Thank you,' I say, putting the bar in my pocket. 'I'll save it for later.'

'How was Adam?'

I resist the temptation to say, 'How do you think? The same as he was yesterday and the day before that.'

'Oh, you know,' I say instead. Dad nods, looks down at the floor and scratches his beard. I know he has a great time with Maya while I'm at the hospital. I hear all the tales of what they've been up to here from her. But as soon as I arrive to pick her up, it's like a dose of reality blows in the door with me. He can no longer hide in a make-believe world where everything is fine. And that clearly makes him feel uncomfortable.

'Anyway, missy,' I say. 'Time for us to go now.'

'Ohhh,' comes the predictable reply.

'You'll see Grandad again on Saturday.'

'Yippee.' I love the way Maya can do that. Go from dejection to joy within a few seconds. Yo-yo emotions, I call them. She runs over and gives Dad's legs an enormous hug. He bends down and allows her to tickle his beard. It's a little ritual they have. She won't kiss him because of it so she tickles instead.

'Thanks, Dad,' I say.

'No problem. I'm always happy to have her. You know that.'

I nod and we leave, Maya running round to press the train set button on the outside one more time before we go.

Maya chatters excitedly all the way home. Stuff and nonsense mostly but it comforts me, the knowledge that she can still be like other children despite all of this. Although I worry about the long-term damage, now that this is apparently turning into a long-term thing.

I have a surprise waiting for her at home. I finally found her a couple of rats. I was going to take her to the pet shop so she could choose them herself but then I realised that there was no way we would get out with just two rats, she would have wanted a whole menagerie. Which is why I decided to go through the local vet instead. Just as well as it turned out. He put me in touch with a breeder, said the rats would probably live longer if they came from someone reputable. And the last thing Maya needs right now is a dying rat. Anyway, the rats are in the kitchen. Hence the fact that I've had that UB40 song in my head for the last hour.

'Now,' I say, turning around to Maya as I pull up outside our house. 'There's a surprise waiting for you inside.'

'Is Daddy home?' shrieks Maya. My heart sinks. I thought she'd grasped the situation now. Understood that Adam will not be coming home any time soon. And then she says something like that and I realise she doesn't grasp it at all. Still thinks Tinkerbell will come along and sprinkle some magic to make it all better again. She is a child. A child that doesn't understand how or why her daddy has been taken away. And I am simply papering over the cracks. I could give her all the pets in the world but it wouldn't matter. All she wants is her daddy back.

'No, love,' I say, scrambling over to the back seat to get to her. Put my arms around her. Give her all the comfort and support I can. 'I'm sorry but I can't magic Daddy back home like that. He's going to be in hospital for a long time, sweetheart.'

'Will he be home when I'm five?'

I smile. Nine months must seem like an eternity to Maya.

'Let's hope so, sweetie. Let's hope so.'

Maya sits sombrely for a moment, then remembers that a surprise is still waiting for her.

'So what is it?'

'Aahh, well, you'll have to come in and see, won't you? But there's one thing I will tell you. They're very small and easily scared so do be quiet.'

Maya gasps as the penny drops.

'Rats,' she screams. 'You've got my rats.'

I smile as I unclip her seat belt and she catapults out.

'Wait for Mummy. And remember what I said. We need to be quiet.'

I hold her firmly by the hand as we tiptoe into the kitchen.

'Where are they?' whispers Maya, peering into the cage.

'Coming out of that tube,' I say, pointing.

Maya gasps again. 'They're the best pets ever,' she says as she catches sight of the sleek white body and long tail of the biggest rat and the smaller black one which follows it. I sigh. Relieved I picked good ones.

'What are you going to call them?'

Maya thinks for a second. 'Roddy and Rita,' she says. 'Like in the film *Flushed Away*.'

I smile, relieved she didn't say Adam and Eve.

'They're both boy rats but it doesn't matter,' I say.

'No,' she says. 'It doesn't. The black one can pretend to be a girl.'

I remember what Adam said about her dressing them up. And I wish like hell he was here to see it.

We spend a long time watching Roddy and Rita. I tell her we're going to give them a chance to get used to us for a day or so before we get them out of the cage and handle them. We look through the 'How to Look After Your Rat' booklet I got. I am about to get up to start tackling the pile of dishes in the sink when there is a knock on the door.

'Who's that?' asks Maya.

'I don't know. I'll go and find out.'

Maya comes with me. She is nothing if not nosy. I open the door. A woman about the same age as me is standing there. She has short brown hair, tired eyes and a ready smile. She is dressed in a checked uniform with a white apron and is holding a large bag. Outside on the road is a car with 'A Spare Pair of Hands' emblazoned on it.

'Hello, Mrs Taylor,' she says. 'I'm Denise. I understand you need a cleaner.'

This is my Nanny McPhee moment. I have to stop myself checking her face for warts.

'Er, yes. I suppose we do.'

Maya tugs my skirt and hisses into my ear. 'Has she been sent by the government? Like in *Nanny McPhee and the Big Bang*.'

I glance at Denise who is politely pretending she didn't hear.

'Steve Dawson sent me. I did leave a message on your answer machine and your mobile. But he said not to worry that I hadn't heard back and come anyway.'

'Oh. Right. Yes, of course,' I say, moving to the side to let her in as I vaguely recall seeing the answering machine flashing.

'Is she going to live with us?' asks Maya.

'No, love,' I laugh. 'She's just going to clean.'

'Oh good. Can you make it all go sparkly?' asks Maya, looking up at Denise.

'I'll do my best, sweet pea.'

'This is my daughter Maya, by the way,' I say.

'Well, you're as sharp as a pin and pretty with it,' says Denise, smiling at her.

'My daddy's having a big sleep in hospital but I've got a couple of pet rats,' announces Maya, by way of introduction.

Denise looks at me uncertainly.

'They're in a cage,' I say, realising that it's the rats she's not sure about, Steve will probably have explained about Adam. 'But if they bother you I can cover them up.'

'As long as they're not getting under me feet or making a mess, we'll get on fine,' she says.

'Right, well. Let me show you where all the cleaning things are.'

'It's OK. I've got all my own stuff in the car. I clean, do ironing, washing up. Just tell me where you want me to get started.'

I smile at Denise. Almost overcome with emotion. She is going to sort our house out. A large weight slithers from my shoulders. Not as big as the ones that remain, but a weight nonetheless.

★

It's only as I pull up outside Steve and Louise's house the next day and notice that his car is not in the drive that I realise it's a Thursday. Steve will have gone for his run. Sometimes I forget that the rest of the world is carrying on as normal. It is only my world in which everything has stopped.

I want to say thank you to him in person for sending Denise. There is something about having a clean house which has engendered a sense of hope in me. Maybe I can get through this. Maybe the doctors are wrong. Adam will get better. Life can return to normal.

Louise answers the door. She has a small green handprint on her top. Clearly it's the teachers who actually need the painting aprons at her nursery.

'Hi,' I say, wiping my feet on the mat and stepping inside. 'Sorry to call round unannounced. I wanted to say thank you. About the cleaner. Only I've just realised Steve will be on his run.' I stop gabbling and look at Louise who has remained silent. It is only then I notice her eyes are rimmed with red. That the familiar smile is not in its permanent position on her face. 'What's the matter?' I ask, the clenching feeling in my stomach which I know so well reasserting itself.

'Steve's not on his run. Well, he might be actually. What I mean is, he's not coming back here afterwards.'

'Why not?'

'He left me yesterday. Said he wanted a trial separation. He's rented a flat. Rishworth, I think he said. I wasn't really listening by that point.'

I stare at her open-mouthed. I had no idea it would

come to this. I thought it was just some sort of rocky patch. That they would sort something out.

'Oh, Louise, you poor thing,' I say, hugging her. Her body is shaking but there are no tears. I guess she is all cried out. 'Why didn't you call me yesterday?'

'You don't need this. It's not as if you haven't got enough on your plate, is it?'

'God, I feel so awful,' I say. 'I haven't even asked you how things have been going, have I? I've been so wrapped up in my own troubles.'

'Of course you have. And rightly so. You've got far more important things to worry about.'

'Your marriage is important too. Come on, we're going to sit down now and talk about this. Mum and Dad are looking after Maya. It's my turn to put the kettle on.'

Louise follows me through to the kitchen. It is one of those modern affairs, shiny enough to see your face in and not an uncoordinated item out of place. Louise sits down at the kitchen table. I notice there is only one place mat out and a pot plant has been moved to the spot where Steve's used to be. I put our teas down and wait for her to start talking.

'I just don't understand,' she says, shaking her head. 'It's not like we'd had a row, or a big fall-out or anything. Things weren't brilliant, as you know, but I had no idea this was on the cards.'

'Didn't he give you any kind of reason?'

'Not really. He said it was time he was honest with me and he wasn't sure if we have a future together. Thought it was best he moved out while he figured out what to do.

Said something about seeing how things were in four months' time.'

'Bloody hell. There's not, you don't think . . .' Louise shakes her head so I don't need to say it.

'He said not. Said it was about him. That I hadn't done anything wrong and he didn't want to hurt me any more than he already had.'

'Well, what is it then? People don't just go off like that for no good reason, surely?'

Louise shrugs. 'I think it's to do with Adam.'

'What do you mean?'

'He's taken it really badly.'

'I know.'

'No. Even worse than he's let on to you. He's been moody, irrational, snappish. Talking about how life's too short not to be doing what you want to be doing. I guess it's been like a wake-up call to get his life in order.'

'But his life involves you.'

Louise shrugs again. 'I don't think he loves me, Mel. I'm not sure he ever has.'

'Don't be ridiculous,' I say, reaching out my hand to squeeze hers. 'Of course he loves you. You're gorgeous. You're beautiful and fun and absolutely the nicest person I know. Why wouldn't he love you?'

'I want to believe that he did, still does even. But he's such a closed book it's impossible to tell. I kept thinking I could get him to change, open up a bit and let me in. And then he goes and does this and I wonder if I really know him at all.'

I sigh. I don't get it either. 'Maybe it's some kind of mid-life crisis.'

'He's only thirty-three.'

'Some people have them early. Maybe like you say, the whole thing with Adam has brought it on. I can't believe this is it, Louise. I can't believe he won't come back. A few days on his own to sort his head out and he'll realise what a prat he's been.'

'I wish I could be so sure.'

'Do you want me to go and see him? Try to talk to him.'

Louise shakes her head. 'Thanks but I don't think that's a good idea. He's such a private person. This is something we've got to sort out between ourselves. I only wish I knew what it was we were sorting out.' We sit silently for a few moments.

'I wish Adam was here,' I say.

'He is still here.'

'You know what I mean. Wish he could go and knock some sense into Steve. Not literally, but you know what they were like. They never took any shit from each other, did they?'

'Do you know what I keep thinking of?' says Louise. 'That meal we had at your place. A month ago we were a foursome and look at us now. It may as well have been a different lifetime.'

'I know. Imagine if someone had told us then. Had fast-forwarded the tape for us to watch. We wouldn't have believed it, would we? Wouldn't have believed that life could possibly go so horribly wrong in such a short space of time.'

'So what do we do about it?'

'You sit tight. Steve'll be back. I don't think he knows

what he wants right now. I think the whole thing with Adam has just messed his head up. He's not thinking straight. I can't believe I came round here to thank him. I want to knee him in the balls on your behalf right now.'

Louise manages her first half-smile. 'I hope this isn't going to make things awkward for you. Being caught up in the middle, I mean.'

'I'm not in the middle. I'm on your side.'

'No. I don't want you to be on anyone's side. You've known him longer than I have and he's your husband's best friend. I want you to carry on being friends with both of us. Please.' She's not just saying it. She really means it. And cutting off relations with Steve would feel like cutting off a part of Adam.

'OK,' I say. 'If that's what you want. But I shall warn him that when Adam comes round he'll no doubt be giving him a piece of his mind. And I shall also tell him what a lucky bastard he is, having a wife like you.'

Louise manages another smile and hooks her hair back behind her ears before taking another sip of tea.

'So did the doctors say anything new today?'

'Not really. They don't say anything but they don't need to. They're convinced he's not coming out of it.' It is Louise's turn to squeeze my hand.

'I'm sure he's fighting really hard, Mel.'

'I know he is. I can sense it when I'm with him. And even when I'm not. Maya knows it too. There's an ache in the room when she's there because he's trying so hard to reach us. And he'll break through soon, you know. He has to.'

Fourteen

The early morning sunlight is streaming through the window. Sunlight. Through my window. Fuck. I can see. The fog has lifted, hauling up my eyelids with it. I try to move my head but I still can't. I go to speak. Nothing. But I can see. It's all a bit blurry but I can make out objects, shapes and colours. I am back in the land of the living. Even if I do still resemble the living dead. I want to scream and shout and cry all at once. I can't do any of them out loud, of course, but I do them silently just the same.

I realise I want to laugh as well. All the times I have dreamt about this, imagined the moment when I would open my eyes and see the faces of my adoring family. And I manage to do it when there is no one bloody here. I'd even be pleased to see Joan, I'd grimace through a rousing chorus of 'All Things Bright and Beautiful', anything to see a human face again. This isn't how it is in the movies. Someone should just have declared their undying love for me. Or at the very least wept at my bedside. Maybe I should close my eyes and pretend to still be asleep until a more fitting moment arises. It would probably make everyone else feel better too. All this singing, playing my favourite music and chatting they've been doing and I finally open my eyes when absolutely sod all is happening. It rather negates the whole thing for them. Come to think of it, maybe I should open my eyes for each person in turn. Give them all a self-satisfied moment of thinking they did it, they were the one who stirred something in me. The only trouble is, having waited this long for my eyes to open, I'm scared that if I close them again, if I even so much as blink, that might be it. They may never open again. Anyway, it's too late now. There are footsteps outside in the corridor. Any second the door will open. I am waiting for Cilla Black to pop out from behind my bedside cabinet and go, 'Surprise, Surprise,' as whoever it is walks through the door. Actually, an entire TV crew would be good, I could have the moment filmed for posterity. Something to play back at family Christmases when everyone's run out of things to say.

The door handle turns. There is a moment's hesitation. And then a familiar voice, though with a slight catch in it.

'Well, you've finally decided to join us, have you, Mr Adam? You sure took your time. That was one long Sunday morning lie-in you had.' I can see her. I can see Jacinta. She is standing at the foot of my bed smiling down at me. I can't see every detail clearly but it is her all right.

'I'm just sorry my ugly mug is the first one you get to see. All those pretty ladies you've had around your bed and you get to wake up to me.' She tuts and shakes her head. She is wrong though. To me her face is beautiful. Her skin is dark. Her hair is big and wavy and a slick of purple (not red as I'd imagined) lipstick surrounds that great big warm-you-up-more-than-Readybrek smile.

'Now you just stay put and I'm going to ask Dr Brooke to come and see you and phone that lovely wife of yours. She's going to be made up, I tell you. You just keep your eyes open. Don't go making a liar out of me or they'll think I've been on the rum.'

She goes. I am bereft for a moment to lose the only glimpse I have had of a face for however long it's been. But a minute later the door bursts open again.

'Good morning, Adam, delighted to meet you properly at last.' Dr Brooke grins. He is younger than I imagined and shorter too. It is not a disappointment. Nothing is a disappointment. It is all new and fresh and extremely weird. Seeing people whose voices have become so familiar to me. I wonder if I am smiling. I feel like I am smiling but I guess I'm not because nobody is reacting. I tell myself to be patient. One step at a time and all that.

Dr Brooke starts doing some tests, shining a light into each of my eyes in turn, examining reflexes (not that I have any) and checking all the monitors. A couple of young men who I'm told are student doctors come into the room. I suppose I am quite exciting to them. A medical textbook case come to life. I don't mind them being there. The more the merrier as far as I'm concerned. Dr Brooke does ask me if it's OK. He even asks me to blink if it's a problem. I try to blink, not because it is a problem but because it suddenly occurs to me that if I can open my eyes, I may well be able to blink. Nothing. I try so hard I fear there is steam coming out of my ears. It doesn't make sense to me. How did they open if I can't close them now? Are they going to be stuck open from now on? Will I be able to sleep with my eyes open? The questions keep coming but I have no way to ask them. I feel suddenly jealous of Bauby again. He may have only had one eye to see out of but at least he could blink it. It is uncharitable of me, I know. It's not as if he had it particularly good. But right now I would trade my two eyes for one which could blink. The whole world of communication is still tantalisingly out of reach. And in a way, now that I can see the world I am in, not being able to communicate is that much worse. I am being greedy, I know. One sense at a time. One day at a time. Wasn't there an awful song called that? Lena someone. Lena Martell. Fucking hell. How can I remember that but not remember how to blink my eyelid?

I hear Maya long before I see her. Little footsteps galloping down the corridor, a voice going nineteen to the dozen. And Mel's voice, soft but firm, asking her to calm down. The footsteps stop outside my room. Nothing happens for a minute. I wonder what Mel is telling her. How do you explain to a four year old that your daddy can see you but still can't give you a hug or talk to you? The door opens. There is a squeal. I am desperate to see her. It takes a moment or two before Mel realises that my eyes are in a fixed position.

'Go to the bottom of the bed, Maya. I'll pick you up, Daddy will be able to see you then.' And a second later she is there. My beautiful little girl is being held up for me to see. She is beaming down at me. She has her purple bow in her hair. She always wears it for parties and special occasions. And behind her is Mel, her eyes smiling as she cries soft, silent tears. Tears that I so want to brush away for her.

'Hello, Daddy,' says Maya. 'You've had a very long sleep, haven't you? You must have been so tired.'

'Hello, love,' says Mel softly. 'I'm sorry we weren't here. We came as soon as they phoned.' This is so typical of her, apologising as if it's her fault. 'Anyway, we're so pleased you can see again. We knew you could do it though. Knew you wouldn't give up.'

'Look, Daddy's crying,' says Maya.

'No, sweetheart. I know it looks like it but it's just where the moisture has built up in Daddy's eyes. Remember I told you that the doctor said he can't blink it away?' I want to tell her she is wrong. The doctors are wrong. That I am crying. Even on the outside.

'Do you like all the pictures I've drawn for you?' says Maya.

'I don't think Daddy can actually see them from there,' says Mel. 'Come on. Let's take them down and put them up on that wall in front of him.' Mel and Maya go in and out of shot for a few minutes. It's a bit like being a video camera on a fixed tripod. But gradually an entire gallery builds up on the far wall. Huge purple butterflies (I recognise the butterflies. She always paints them the same way), white and black blobs which I take to be rats (she has been talking non-stop about Roddy and Rita since she got them), and a host of other indistinguishable splats, squiggles and scribbles. Kid art in all its wonderful, glorious, abstract messiness. I love it. Absolutely love it. The only thing that surprises me is when I notice there are no dinosaurs. She always draws dinosaurs. The last thing in the world I want is for this to have put her off dinosaurs.

'Do you like them?' Maya asks. I lie there willing my face, my mouth, my body to say yes in some way.

'Doesn't he like them?' says Maya after a moment.

'Of course he does,' replies Mel, giving her a hug. 'He just can't smile or say thank you.'

'But I want to talk to him,' says Maya.

'Here, why don't you tickle his toes,' says Mel, pulling back the sheet. 'It can be your special way of communicating with him.'

Maya tentatively touches my big toe. For a second I think I can feel it. Then I realise that it is simply because I can see her doing it that I am imagining how it feels. I can see her fingers tickling now. I try to push the corners of my mouth up. I know from Maya's face that nothing happens.

'It's like he's still asleep but with his eyes open,' says Maya. Her voice is ringing with disappointment. Mel moves out of sight. I know it's so I can't see her crying. What she doesn't realise is that I can still picture the tears carving their way down her face.

Fifteen

MEL

'At least you can get a decent cup of tea here,' says Mum, sitting herself down next to me in the hospital café. 'Although I do wish they had a better selection of biscuits.'

My husband has just opened his eyes after twenty-one days in a coma and she's complaining about the biscuits.

'Adam's eyes are, er, looking well, anyway,' says Dad.

'Yeah,' I reply. There's nothing else I can say. He means well. It's not his fault he is hopelessly out of his depth here.

'So what happens now?' asks Dad.

'Dr Brooke's carrying out a full assessment on Adam. I don't know exactly what it involves but I'm going to see him later about it.'

'Will Daddy be coming home with us today?' asks Maya, looking up from the sea of tomato ketchup her chips are swimming in.

'No, love. Not for a long time yet, remember?'

'Can I bring Roddy and Rita in to show him, then?'

'I'm afraid not, love. They don't allow rats in hospitals.'

Maya sighs and goes back to her chips. She never used to have chips very often before she started hanging out in hospital cafés.

'Mind you,' says Mum in a hushed voice, 'there was a

story in the *Daily Mail* about them finding rat droppings at one hospital. Liverpool, I think it was, though. They're not brought up with the same sort of standards, see.' I open my mouth to say something and shut it again. There really is no point. She is a lost cause. And I don't have the stomach for a fight.

'We'll take Maya home after lunch,' says Dad.

'Thanks,' I say, lowering my voice. 'I think she's had enough for one day.'

It wasn't supposed to be like this. When I got the call from the hospital this morning I was ecstatic. Crying with joy and relief. Dancing around the kitchen with Maya. Now I am at best flatlining, at worst feeling somewhat deflated. Maya was right. Adam hasn't woken up at all. He has simply opened his eyes. Was it wrong to expect so much more? The doctors had told me enough times this wasn't going to be like in the movies. That people don't really open their eyes and start talking as if nothing has happened. But still I was hoping for something more. A flicker of recognition. A sense of Adam banging on the door letting us know he would be coming out soon. The truth is we don't even know if he can see us. If the pictures are registering at all in his head. Or whether he can hear us, for that matter. I think he can. I'm sure of it sometimes. But somehow now his eyes are open and there's no obvious recognition, no way for him to communicate, it's worse. It's like the lights are on but there's no one at home. And I keep thinking to myself, what if there is someone in but he can't make himself understood? What if he is locked in like Bauby? Adam would hate that. He would be so frustrated.

I try to pump the balloon up again. Remind myself that we are so much further forward than we were yesterday. That there is every reason for optimism. But it is hard. Because I miss my husband. And I so want him back.

'I still haven't had a reply from the BBC about that silly Evans chap,' says Mum. She is waging a one-woman crusade to get Chris Evans removed from Radio 2 and Sir Terry Wogan reinstated to his rightful place on the throne. She obviously hasn't thought to inquire as to whether Sir Terry would be amenable to that but as she has zero chance of succeeding I haven't bothered mentioning it to her.

'I read the other day that he's on his third wife, you know. What sort of people are they employing at the BBC these days?'

I look across at Dad. He shrugs. We both know better than to say anything.

'Can I go home now?' asks Maya, who has licked the last of the tomato ketchup off her plate.

'Yes,' I say, knowing Mum will have to go with her. 'Grandma and Grandad are going to take you.'

'What about you?' asks Maya.

'I'm going to see the doctor and sit with Daddy for a bit longer. I'll be home to read you a bedtime story, OK?'

Maya nods solemnly. I kiss the top of her head. I miss the time we used to spend together. I miss it a lot.

'Well,' says Dr Brooke later. 'As you know, Adam opening his eyes is a big step forward. But as I explained before, it isn't a guarantee that we're going to see any further significant progress.'

'But what about the assessment you did today?'

'I'm afraid there's still no indication that Adam is aware of his surrounding or his environment. He remains entirely unresponsive.'

'But that doesn't mean that he can't think, that he can't hear us. He can, I know he can. He knows when Maya and I are visiting. I can see it in his face.'

Dr Brooke gives a particularly patronising smile. 'Often relatives spend so much time with a patient that I'm afraid they end up seeing things which simply aren't there.'

'You still don't think he's going to get better, do you?'

Dr Brooke takes a deep breath. 'Although opening of the eyes is a good sign that functionality is returning to the arousal centre of the brain, people can remain trapped in vegetative states for months or even years after they open their eyes for the first time.'

I stare at Dr Brooke. He said vegetative state. No one's ever used that term about Adam before. He realises from my expression before I am able to formulate any words.

'Sorry. I should have explained that once an unconscious person opens their eyes but remains unresponsive they are no longer technically in a coma. He's moved into the next phase. We call it a vegetative state.'

I swallow hard. I hear the sound of air rushing out of my balloon. Dr Brooke sits there having sharpened the words that burst it.

'You mean he might never come round. Not properly. That's what you're saying.'

'I'm afraid it is a possibility. A very strong one.'

'How can you be so sure of that?'

'There's been a lot of research on this subject. For those whose eyes open between the second and fourth week, only thirty-two per cent have recovered substantially within a year. Age is a big factor. Adam falls within the middle group. Nine per cent of patients aged between twenty and forty years who are in a vegetative state at one month are living independently at one year.'

'So there is still hope then. He's got a nine per cent chance of getting back to normal.'

'Not normal. Living independently is what I said. It's a very different matter. And it is a tiny percentage of patients who achieve that. Please don't get your hopes up too high. I wouldn't want you to be disappointed.'

Disappointed, he says. Imagine how awful it would be to feel disappointed. To have had dreams shattered beyond belief, to not be able to look forward to a summer holiday together. To have to tell your daughter that Daddy may not be there for your first day at school. To lie in bed alone every night. To not have washed the pillow case that your husband used to lay his head on because you can't bear to lose the faint smell of him next to you. Jesus, imagine being that disappointed.

'No. Of course not.' I stand up, scraping my chair back noisily. I want to get out of the room as quickly as possible. If this man really thinks he can say something to prevent me being disappointed he has no bloody idea. I burst through the door, the desire to get away propelling me along the corridor. My head is down. I know that if I follow the orange line on the floor, it will take me to Adam's room. I wonder if that is why they do that in

171

Linda Green

hospitals. Paint coloured lines on the floor for directions so that when you have your head down so other people can't see you crying, you can still have some idea of where you are going. My legs are going faster, I am breaking into a trot. I am almost at Adam's door when I hurtle straight into someone. Someone carrying a cup of coffee which spills over the floor. I am about to offer an apology when I feel a hand on my shoulder. I look up. It is Steve. He puts what is left of the coffee on the ledge next to us.

'It's OK,' he says. 'I'm here.' A second later I am pounding his chest with my fists, shaking my head around, my hair flying everywhere.

'They say he's not coming back,' I sob. 'That he's in a vegetative state.'

Steve nods and takes it. Takes everything I throw at him. Not judging. Not patronising. Just being there. He waits until I am quiet. Until my arms have stopped flailing, my head shaking, my voice wailing.

'Come on,' he says. 'I need another coffee. I'll get you one too.'

I walk with Steve to the café. Neither of us says anything. I feel like a half-blown balloon someone has let go of. Having hurtled around all over the place, it is as if I am now lying on the floor, all the air having escaped, all momentum gone.

Steve gets the coffees and sits down opposite me, folding his long legs carefully under the table. He looks like a model out of the Boden catalogue, effortlessly cool and stylish. Adam used to take the piss out of him for that. Although Adam was no slouch himself.

172

'I've started thinking about him in the past tense,' I say, half to myself, half to Steve. 'It's like there are two Adams, the one who I used to have and the one who is lying in that hospital bed. They hardly even seem related.'

Steve nods. 'I know this probably sounds terrible,' he says, 'but seeing him with his eyes open just now made it even harder. I walked into his room and had to walk straight out again. That's why I went to get the coffee. I couldn't cope with seeing him like that. I wanted to shake him, scream at him to quit mucking about and wake up.' Steve looks across at me. 'Sorry, I probably shouldn't have said that. It must have sounded incredibly selfish.'

'It's OK,' I reply. 'I understand what you mean. I've been waiting for this day for so long and I'm thrilled for Adam to be able to see Maya again. It must be such a relief for him. But I can't help wanting more. The thought of him being stuck like that forever . . .'

Steve nods as my voice trails off. He moves his hand as if to take mine but stops as he appears to think better of it. 'So what did the doctor say exactly?' he asks.

'Just that Adam's moved into the next phase. He's in a vegetative state and that some people stay like that for months or years. Oh, and to try not to be disappointed. Disappointed, eh? He's my bloody husband. How can I not be disappointed?'

Steve doesn't hesitate this time. He reaches over and squeezes my shoulder. 'This must be so hard for you. You're not on your own, though. I'm here for you. We all are. But the last thing we want to see is you being dragged under by all of this.'

'What do you mean by that?'

'It's not easy to come to terms with it, is it? But maybe it would be better for all of us if we did.'

'What, give up on him, you mean?'

'It's not about giving up. It's about being realistic. Accepting how things are.'

'How can I accept how he is? I hate how he is.'

'I know. But he is how he is and it's how he might stay.'

'No he won't. He's coming back to me. He's just taking his time about it.'

'I hope you're right, Mel. But what if you're not? I'm not saying you can't have hope, I'm just saying please don't expect too much.'

'You're starting to sound like one of the doctors.'

'I'm simply trying to protect you, Mel. Adam's not here to do it so someone's got to.'

I resent the last comment. The idea that I'm some helpless damsel in distress who needs saving from herself. And that Steve can in any way replace Adam.

'Look, I'm very grateful for all the help and support you're giving me, but I'm not having anyone tell me to expect the worst. I expected the worst for years. It spoilt my happiness with Adam, I worried about it so much. And then it went and bloody happened. And the fact that I'd been expecting it – well, not "it" exactly but something – didn't soften the blow.' I am aware that this does not sound like the sort of thing you would expect to hear from someone with a 2:1 in psychology. But this is not textbook stuff. It's what's going on in my head.

'But what's the alternative, Mel?'

174

'I'm going to dare to believe that Adam will come back to me. The real Adam. The past tense one. My husband and your best mate.'

Steve shrugs and sighs. Stares at the wall behind me. I know he's hurting too. Maybe I've been too hard on him. I know he means well. I know he thinks he's doing Adam a favour by looking out for me.

'I know you're only trying to help but I guess we all have our different ways of coping,' I say.

'What's that supposed to mean?' He knows exactly what I mean. Knows that Louise would have told me by now.

'Some of us stay and fight. Some of us run away to lick our wounds in private.'

'I haven't run away.'

'Try telling that to Louise.'

'Look, this has got nothing to do with what we were talking about.'

'It's got everything to do with it because it's all about Adam.'

'What makes you think that?'

'It's shaken you up really badly. You don't know how to handle it and you can't open up to Louise so you've bolted.'

'Is that the official psychological diagnosis?'

'No but it's what Adam would say if he was here. Really here.'

'And you think that's why I've left Louise?'

'Why else would you have left her?'

Steve shakes his head. 'There's a lot of stuff you don't know about, Mel.'

'Fine. I'm all ears.'

'Stuff I'm not going to go into.'

'Because it doesn't add up.'

'No, because I'm a private kind of guy.'

'You can be private with me but you don't have to be private with your wife. Louise feels shut out. She doesn't understand what's going on. You haven't given her a chance to make things right because you haven't told her what's wrong.'

'Believe it or not, I'm protecting her. The truth hurts sometimes.'

'Not as much as silence.' Steve looks down again, fiddles with his empty coffee cup. 'She deserves to know what the problem is, Steve. She deserves a chance to work things out with you.'

'Sometimes things can't be worked out. Sometimes they're beyond that.'

'So you're not even going to try?'

'I've been trying for a long time and it hasn't worked. To be honest, I don't think it ever will.' His frankness takes me aback. I wasn't expecting that and I'm not quite sure why he's told me.

'Have you told Louise this?'

'No. Not in so many words.'

'And when exactly are you planning to tell her?'

'I told her I'd give it four months and that's what I'm going to do.'

'But you sound as if your mind's made up already.'

'Maybe it is. But it's not fair on her to tell her that. I need to give her a chance to get used to the idea of me not being around. That way, when I tell her for definite, I'm hoping it won't hit her so hard. Hoping she'll have built up some kind of life without me.'

I look up to the ceiling and shake my head, still not sure I'm hearing this right.

'So why are you telling me this?'

Steve shrugs. 'Adam's not here and you are, I guess.'

'Adam is here.'

'You know what I mean.'

'How do you know I won't tell her?'

'Because you care for her as much as I do. More, probably.'

I shake my head again. 'I can't believe you'd do this to her. She loves you so much. She's still going to be devastated, you know, whenever you tell her.'

'I don't get a kick out of this. But being with someone who you don't love isn't being fair to them either, is it?'

'You really don't love her?'

He hesitates. Looks down at the table. 'Not like I should do.'

I put my head in my hands. Thinking about Louise. About how cut up she's going to be. 'When you do tell her, please don't tell her that.'

Steve raises an eyebrow again. 'I thought you liked people to be honest.'

'Most of the time. Sometimes people need to be left with something to cling on to. Something to break their fall.'

He looks down at his coffee cup again. 'I don't want this to change anything, by the way. With us I mean.'

'Well, it does, doesn't it? You're talking about divorcing

my best friend. I'm hardly going to be thrilled about it.'

'I know. But I still want to be there for you. I owe it to Adam and I don't want to let him down.'

I let out a long sigh. I only wish he'd show the same sort of loyalty to Louise as he does to Adam.

'He's going to have such a go at you when he comes round.'

Steve opens his mouth and shuts it again. I know what he was going to say, though. That he won't be coming round. Not today. Not tomorrow. Not ever.

PART TWO

Sixteen

Tuesday, 17 August 2010

The joke's wearing a bit thin now. You know, the one about me being hit on the head by a dinosaur and ending up in a coma. I seem to remember I found it vaguely amusing at the beginning. Embarrassing but amusing all the same. Of course, that was at the point where I thought I would snap out of it at any moment. Where it was quite a novelty, having friends and family try to rouse me from my sleep. I was going to put it down as one of life's big experiences, a bit like going on one of those Outward Bound adventures at high school. Something I'd rather not have gone through and couldn't say I actually enjoyed but satisfyingly character building all the same. That was before it stopped being a life experience and became my life.

I have a calendar on my bedside cabinet now, one of those tear-off-the-day ones. Mel said she thought I'd want to know what day it was. And I guess I do. It's just that every time she tears a day off I imagine that day lying crumpled on the floor, along with all the others. Growing into a sea of lost days. Days I will never get back. She doesn't toss the pieces of paper on the floor, of course. She puts them in her handbag and takes them home. I've no idea what she does with them there. Keeps them for posterity? Recycles them? Shreds them for rat bedding? Anyway, that's how I know that we're in mid-August. Well, that and the fact that Maya keeps telling me how many days it is until she starts school. I can cope with having missed most of the summer; from what people (mainly Joan, who can always be relied upon to give me a full weather report) have told me, it hasn't been much of a summer anyway. What I can't cope with is the fact that I won't be there for Maya's first day at school. My little girl is growing up and I want to be there, want to hold her hand, see her give the boys a hard time, have her show me where she sits in class. But no, I won't be there. Because I'll be stuck here in a bloody hospital bed on a neurological ward in Manchester.

They moved me from intensive care when I started breathing for myself not long after I opened my eyes. Bad move all round that turned out to be. I had to have a tracheostomy so they can continually suction the stuff out of my throat which I can't clear myself. Which means I have another hole where I shouldn't – in my neck this time. I fear I'm beginning to look like a human colander. But the worst thing about being moved was having to leave Jacinta behind. I miss her voice, her great big smile, her giving me a bit of cheek. The nurses here are so bloody straight and polite. And my new consultant is called David McKee which means that every time he talks to me all I can think of is Elmer the patchwork elephant. I take it he's not the David McKee who wrote the books. Although I suppose that being a neurological consultant might well lend itself to imagining the adventures of a patchwork elephant. Plus, I'm not even in my own room any more. I miss that too. Company is overrated. Well, the sort of company I'm keeping, anyway. I'd never realised how noisy people are. Talking, coughing, shouting, scraping chairs, moving things around, rattling trolleys, you name it, I get it, twenty-four hours a day. If I could do anything, anything at all right now, it would be to put my finger to my lips and go, 'Ssshhh.' I miss the stillness of the moors, running along rocky trails with only the sound of the wind whooshing past my ears. And the occasional bit of verbal from Steve, of course.

It wouldn't have been so bad if they'd been able to move me nearer home. It must be so tiring for Mel and Maya to be traipsing over to Manchester all the time. (It was very inconsiderate of me, really, to have my medical emergency on the other side of the Pennines.) But apparently there isn't a neurological ward much nearer home. So here I remain, stubbornly inconvenient as well as incapacitated. Mel still hasn't missed a day, mind. She is one of those things I can rely on; night, day, the meal trolley coming round (bastards, doing that in front of a guy who still can't eat. It's probably the only thing that makes hospital food look appealing, being fed by a bloody tube into your stomach), medication time (very *One Flew Over the Cuckoo's Nest*, I know) and Mel visiting.

I imagine she'll be going back to work soon. I don't know how she's going to do it, working five days and looking after Maya and visiting me. She'll be knackered. She'll wear herself out. I can see it even now; a tiny bit of

Linda Green

brightness gone from her eyes. I'm. Wearing. Her. Out. I feel bad about that, very bad. Sometimes I even wonder if it would have been better for her if I'd died that day. Sure, it would have been hard at first but she would have had a chance to grieve and at some point to get on with her life. This isn't living for her. All the shit she's having to deal with. And me still lying here, resolutely refusing to get better or call it a day.

She's here now. I hear her footsteps approaching, I guess it's a bit like the way Mel always knew my engine if she heard the car pull up outside. She comes to the end of the bed first, puts herself into my field of vision, smiles at me in the way she's always smiled at me. Emanating light and radiance and warmth. One day, when I finally get my arse up out of this bed, I shall stand on top of the medication trolley and declare to anyone in earshot that she is a national treasure. That will make her laugh. Putting her up there on a pedestal with June Whitfield and Julie Walters. I'm not surprised at how brilliant she's been, of course. If we'd been on *Mr and Mrs* and Derek Batey had asked, 'If you were floored by a dinosaur skeleton and went into a coma, would Mel a) faint b) drop everything to care for you or c) run off with the guy next door?' I would have answered 'b' without hesitation. But it is the way she cares for me that never ceases to amaze me, the way she knows instinctively what I might like, what might be bothering me. She draws the curtains around my bed now, the way she always does. Because she knows I like my privacy. She sits next to me on the edge of the bed, stroking my arm, talking softly to me.

'It's hot outside. Maya's delighted. All summer she's been waiting for a day like this so they could get the water sprinkler out at the Ark. When I left her she was tearing around outside in her swimming costume, whooping and shrieking like a mad thing as she ran under the sprinkler. I took a photo. Here, I'll show you.' She gets out her mobile phone and holds it up about a foot away from my face. I can just about make out a purple blob with a huge smile on her face.

'Anyhow,' she says. 'Let's get you ready for the day.' She takes a large bowl from inside my bedside cabinet and disappears behind the curtain. A few minutes later she returns. I can see the steam rising from the bowl. I wonder if she realises I can't feel the warmth on my skin, only see it. Maybe she does and she simply wants to use warm water because it would seem mean, using cold just because I couldn't tell. She gets out the razor and the shaving cream, drapes the small blue towel around my neck, being careful to avoid the opening to my tracheostomy tube. She dips her hands into the water, squeezes some shaving cream on her palm, rubs it with her fingers and places her hands on my cheeks. Sometimes I think I feel her hands. Not the skin-on-skin sensation. Something far deeper than that. Love oozing through her pores into mine, radiating down through the layers to a place where it can touch me. Really touch me. In a way nothing else quite does. I watch the circular motion of her fingertips, see the soft lather on them. Occasionally I think I can smell it but actually I am remembering the smell. She uses the same shaving cream from the Body Shop that I have used for years. I imagine her going to buy it sometimes, she must do, we've got through at least a tube by now. I worked out that they are probably the only thing she still buys for me. No food, no clothes. Simply the shaving cream and razors. The only indications that I am still living. I don't suppose I'd ever really stopped to think whether people in a vegetative state need to shave. They do. The stubble keeps growing. Maya has a book at home, *Mr Follycule's Beard*, about a man whose beard grows at an alarming rate all the way out of the house and down the street. If Mel didn't do this every day for me, that's what I would probably look like by now.

She picks up the razor and draws it down my cheeks in smooth strokes. And believe me, this is the best a man can get. A man like me, anyway. She is so tender, so loving, so careful. This is far more intimate than sex. If I do ever manage to move again, I shall ask her to carry on doing it. 'Shave me,' I shall say. 'Shave me like you used to do when I was in a vegetative state.' Jeez, I sound like some weirdo. I am a weirdo, though. I'm well aware of that. I see the way other people look at me. Visitors to other patients who stare as they pass the guy in the corner who says nothing and can't move. They probably have nightmares about turning into me, being bound and gagged. Force fed into their stomach, having to pee into a tube and have someone stick a finger up their arse to get their crap out. I bet they thank their lucky stars when they leave here that they're not like me. I know I've been diagnosed as being in a vegetative state because Mel told me. The doctors think I've gone AWOL. They have no idea I'm still in here, trying to batter down the doors. I don't know what to think. Whether I've got Locked-in Syndrome or some as yet undiscovered type of brain injury. All I know is that I am still here and Mel keeps telling me I can still come out of it. People do, even after this long. But I haven't been provided with an instruction manual for how to do that. And although I keep trying different ways to get there, I don't seem to be getting any closer at all.

Mel pats my face dry with the towel. I want to reach out to her, grab her hand and pull it back to touch my face again. Beg her not to stop. To go on shaving me until my skin is raw. Sometimes I wish she wouldn't be so careful. Would nick me once or twice. I want to see blood. To know that I am truly still alive. That something flows beneath the still surface. I let out a scream; a silent scream that reverberates inside me, echoing off the walls of the tomb that is my body. At moments like this, moments when the pain and frustration of not being able to rouse myself to partake in my own life get too strong, I have learnt to leave the present and retreat to the past. Immerse myself in the events which are scored in my memory, the waymarkers of my life. In the hope that somewhere along the route I will find the key which allows me to resume that journey. To take up from where I left off.

Mel was on all fours in the birthing pool. There was something so primitive about it. My wife making noises I didn't know she was capable of. I was there in the same room as her; she wouldn't let me touch her, though. We'd been to all those bloody ante-natal classes where I'd learned how to massage her during labour and when the time came she wouldn't let me anywhere near her. She'd gone to a different place, somewhere inside her, a place I couldn't reach. The midwife smiled at me. A reassuring 'don't worry she's doing great' kind of smile. And I sat crouched at the edge of the pool in utter awe of my wife. My tiny, elfin-faced wife who often had to ask me to open jars for her, somehow pushing our baby out into the world.

'Go on, you're almost there, I can see the top of the head,' said the midwife. Mel's eyes were tight shut, her face contorted in pain. I felt helpless, pathetic. But most of all I just wanted it to be over.

'Foooooo,' she cried out. I had no idea where that came from. But a moment later I saw the head, swiftly followed by a reddish pink body which slithered out behind it. There was a second, a split second, where I felt sick in the stomach as I realised I wasn't sure it was alive. But a moment later the midwife scooped the baby up out of the water and a cry rang out. The most fantastic, tiny little cry I had ever heard in my life.

'Congratulations,' the midwife said. 'You have a little girl.'

She gave her to Mel who pulled her close against her skin and looked up at me. Her hair dripping, her cheeks red with exhaustion and her smile threatening to slip off the sides of her face. And I smiled back, tears of relief rolling down my cheeks as I leant into the pool to hug her hot, wet body, knowing that I would never, ever underestimate what she was capable of again.

'Hello, Maya,' Mel whispered. She turned Maya towards me a fraction so I could see her face.

'She's beautiful,' I said, reaching out a finger to her. And she was. But it was seeing the blood in the birthing pool which actually

started me crying. Started me shaking with sheer relief that it was over. And they were both fine.

'It's OK,' said Mel. 'Everything's all right.'

'I know,' I said. 'It is now.'

Seventeen

MEL

I am waiting for Dr McKee. I know that Adam must find it highly amusing that his consultant has the same name as Elmer the elephant's author. It's weird how being the parent of a four year old puts you in an exclusive club for in-jokes about children's book characters. I tried to explain what was funny to Steve but he didn't get it at all.

He's OK, Dr McKee. Better than Dr Brooke though not as nice as Dr Perryman. The way this is going I'll soon have a top ten of Adam's consultants in order of preference. Or maybe after a while they'll all simply blur into one, who knows. Adam's been on this ward nearly three months now. I can't say I particularly like the place. I don't think Adam does either. I expect he misses having his own room. I certainly do. I don't like the feeling of him being gawped at by everyone who goes past. He probably misses the radio too. They only have headphones here that you can plug in to hospital radio. I put it on for him every now and again but I suspect it does his head in. He never liked Alan Partridge-style BBC local radio and this is several steps down from that, firmly into Smashy and Nicey territory. It's noisy too. I've been reading up about coma stimulation programmes and I've been trying one out on Adam but all the background noise must sound rather like radio interference. There are supposed to be structured quiet times as well as stimulation and I've never heard it quiet here.

The door opens. Dr McKee is tall and decidedly large; portly would be the polite description. Unlike Elmer, he is not patchwork. 'Sorry to have kept you, Mrs Taylor. Do come in.' I do my usual thing of trying to work out whether this is going to be good or bad news by his tone of voice and the expression on his face. They are very good at this though, doctors. I suspect they are mean poker players.

'Now, I'll come straight to the point,' says Dr McKee. 'There has been no perceptible change in your husband's condition since he was transferred here. No further progress of note. Obviously there comes a time when we have to review whether we feel this is the best place for your husband to be or whether there might be somewhere else which offers more appropriate care.'

I stare at him, my brow creasing. I can see exactly where this is going. Adam's taking up a bed which they need for someone else. They want shot of him. It's as simple as that.

'What are you saying?' I'm not going to let him off the hook, I'm going to play dumb and make him spell it out. Dr McKee takes a deep breath.

'As it's now nearly four months since the accident and there's been no change in Adam's condition since he opened his eyes, it's time to consider whether his needs may be best served by being in a long-term nursing home.'

I'm not a violent woman. Really I'm not. But I have the sudden urge to kick his shins under the desk.

'You don't think he's going to get better, do you?'

'I didn't say that. You know enough about the condition by now to understand that we can never say never. But we do have to base our medical assessment on probability and I'm afraid the probability in this case is that we are talking about Adam being in a persistent vegetative state.'

I feel the pain sharply as his stiletto-heeled words stamp all over my face. Dr McKee immediately plummets to the bottom of my favourite consultant league table. I'm not even sure I'll ever be able to read *Elmer the Elephant* again.

'And do I have any say in this?'

'Obviously we do take family views into consideration and there will be a case meeting where you will have an opportunity to put forward your views, but ultimately we have to make a complex decision about a patient's medical and care needs.' This guy should be a politician. That is a very long-winded and diplomatic way of saying, 'No.'

'So how soon are you suggesting this happens?'

'There's no timetable. We understand you'll need to consider your options in terms of the various nursing homes available, but we have taken the liberty of getting some information together on those we have used previously and are able to recommend.' He hands me a pile of brochures in a clear plastic folder. It is all so cold, so final. If I saw some curtains opening and Adam's body gliding slowly through them in an open coffin I wouldn't be surprised. I have all sorts of half sentences forming in my head but none of them are making their way to my mouth. Dr McKee looks at me, he appears unsettled by my silence.

'If you're worried about the financial aspect, we usually find that compensation payouts cover the fees.'

I stare at him. Clearly he has no idea that compensation payments take years to come through. I am half expecting him to hand me a signed copy of Adam's death certificate. That is what they're doing here. They're killing him off and I haven't even been asked to sign a consent form.

'I won't be needing those, thank you,' I say, offering the brochures back.

'I understand that this is a difficult situation, Mrs Taylor. We're not going to rush you. Please at least take them so you can look through them in your own time.'

I drop the brochures on his desk. 'I won't be needing them because Adam is not going into a nursing home.'

'I'm sorry, Mrs Taylor, but there really isn't another option.'

'Yes there is. He's coming home with me.'

Dr McKee looks at me over the top of his glasses as if I have lost the plot.

'But he's going to need twenty-four-hour care.'

'I understand that. I promised our daughter that when her daddy was well enough he'd be coming home and that's exactly what's going to happen.'

'Look, why don't you take some time to think this through? Consider the implications.'

'This isn't a business decision, you know. He's my husband. I'm not packing him off to some nursing home and that's final. If you could let me know who I need to speak with to make the necessary arrangements, I'd be very grateful.' I stand up and march out of the room. I don't know who is more surprised at what I've just said, Dr McKee or me. I am aware that it's a huge decision. That it will have massive implications for everyone. But I have never been more sure of anything in my life.

I go straight to Adam. I know I should wait before telling him. It could be a while yet before it happens. There will be so much to sort out, funding to get in place and red tape to wade through. But I have made a decision and I don't want to risk him overhearing it from anyone else. Some people still talk about him as if he is not there. I want him to hear it from me. Besides, if I tell him, it's a promise and no one can get me to change my mind.

I smile at him from the end of the bed before pulling the curtain around and sitting down next to him, stroking his arm, holding his hand.

'Hey, I've got some good news. It's not going to happen for a little while yet but they're going to let you out of here. I'm going to take you home.' He stares back blankly at me. But I know that, inside, he is smiling too.

'Hi, are you all set?' asks Louise as I climb into the passenger seat beside her. We are on our way to our flamenco dancing class in Hebden Bridge. Louise has persuaded me to go back, that I need some 'me' time.

'Yes, thanks,' I say as I pull my seat belt on. 'Maya was desperate to come with me but Dad managed to distract her with one of his stories.'

'Good.' Louise glances across at me as she pulls away. 'And did you get to see the doctor today?'

I hesitate. I haven't told anyone yet. Certainly not Mum

and Dad. But the more I think about it, the more I get my head around what I have done, the more relieved I am. And I don't want to keep the news to myself any more.

'Adam's coming home,' I blurt out.

'Home?' says Louise, braking sharply at the traffic lights.

'Yeah. That's right.'

'Why? I mean, has something changed?'

'The doctor basically said he's outstayed his welcome. They wanted to put him into a long-term nursing home but I said no.'

'So who's going to look after him?'

'Me, of course.'

'But Mel, you can't. What about your new job?'

'I'm, er, going to hand my notice in.' I've been mulling it over in my head all afternoon but now I've said it out loud it sounds even scarier. 'I've got no choice,' I continue, trying to justify it to myself as much as Louise. 'I'm not having Adam shunted off into some nursing home.' The car behind us toots. The lights have changed to green.

'But you can't just give up work,' says Louise, pulling away.

'I won't give it up completely, just go part-time. I had a look on the internet this afternoon. Calderdale College are advertising for a part-time lecturer to cover maternity leave on an entry level course in childcare. Ten hours a week.' Louise looks at me as if I've just suggested trading in George Clooney for Wayne Rooney.

'Oh, Mel.'

'Well, it's a job, isn't it? It would get me out of the house for a couple of hours every day. I've found a charity that offers a sitting service which should be covered by the Independent Living Allowance Adam will get and hopefully Mum and Dad will be able to help out too.' Louise opens her mouth to say something. Something I sense will not be what I want to hear. 'Please, Louise. I know it's a big step but I need someone to back me on this.'

'But it's such a big sacrifice. What if it's too much for you? It's a hell of a commitment.'

'I understand that. But that's what marriage is. You'd do the same if—' I stop myself as soon as I realise. But it is already too late.

'It's OK,' says Louise as she pulls up outside the hall. 'I know what you mean. And believe it or not I probably would do the same for Steve – even now.'

'Look, I know it's a big deal,' I say. 'It scares the hell out of me. But what else can I do? Anyway, I can't change my mind now because I've already told Adam.'

'Oh, I see,' says Louise. 'What about Maya?'

'No, not yet. I'm going to save that one until it's all finalised. I don't think she'll be able to contain herself. It'll mean so much to her to have her daddy home. It's tearing her apart, being away from him. She needs him back at home. We both do.'

Louise gives me one of those sympathetic smiles I have become used to over the past few months. I know what she is thinking. What she has stopped herself saying. That Maya's daddy isn't coming home. Not the daddy she once had, anyway.

We walk into the community hall. The other women look up and say hello. A couple of them come up and say it's good to have me back. I can see it in their faces too, though. The sympathy. The not knowing what else to say. At least with cancer you can ask how the treatment's going or whether they're in remission. This is relentless. And even the fact that Adam is coming home isn't really something to celebrate. It's not as if he's better. He's simply not wanted in hospital any more. And although at moments this afternoon I have found myself giddy with excitement about it, I have reason to fear for the future too. The doctors have given up on him. Sending him to a nursing home was the equivalent of putting him out to grass. I know Adam would hate the thought of that. Which is why I could never let them do it. Why I'm bringing him home. But I am under no illusion that the future is anything other than uncertain.

I get changed into my flamenco clothes: swirly skirt, gypsy-style top, clompy heels. It feels wrong somehow. Dressing up and playing at having fun. I can't help feeling I shouldn't do anything showy or flamboyant, out of respect for Adam. But as the music starts and I begin stomping my feet, clicking my fingers and swishing my skirt, I manage to find some kind of escape. A chance to lose myself in another world. A world where my husband is not lying in hospital in a vegetative state. A world where I am some fiery Spanish temptress with come-to-bed eyes. It is all a big fat lie, of course. Despite my best efforts and dark features I am well aware that I don't quite cut it as a flamenco dancer. I suspect being five foot three inches has something to do with it. Whereas Louise, even with her English rose complexion, still manages to look like the most sultry señorita on the block. She smiles as I pass her but I know that she is also trying to blot the real world from her mind. She's seen Steve once since the separation, when he popped back to pick up the rest of his stuff. Hardly an effort at reconciliation. I haven't said anything, of course. Mainly because I am hoping against hope that Steve will change his mind. Will realise that life without Louise isn't half as much fun as he expected. She keeps asking me how he seems (I am embarrassed at the fact that I see a lot more of her husband than she does but Louise says she's glad that we're still friends). The truth is he seems fine. Still somewhat troubled, I think, but certainly not moping around the house. I don't tell her that, of course. I tell her he is quiet, subdued even. Not that he sometimes cracks a joke. Occasionally even manages to make me laugh, which isn't easy nowadays.

I do a couple of extra stomps after everyone else. Iris, the teacher, gives me a look.

'Sorry,' I say. 'I was miles away.'

'Do you want to come in for a coffee?' I ask Louise when we pull up outside my house later. 'Mum and Dad will be going straight away.'

'No, thanks. I've got lots to do at home. You grab an early night.'

'Thanks,' I say, giving her a hug.

'What for?'

'Getting me back there. It was good. I almost managed to enjoy myself.'

Louise smiles. 'I'm glad Adam's coming home,' she says.

'Thank you. I know it's going to be tough but we'll feel so much better having him here with us.'

'I know. And we'll – I mean I'll help as much as I can. I'm sure Steve will too.'

'Thanks. You're brilliant, you know. And don't you forget it.' I kiss her on the cheek. Give her a big hug. Because she hasn't even got an empty pillow to hug. Just a space where it used to be.

Eighteen

Home. It seems like a mirage. I worry that at the point where I finally get there, I'll discover it was nothing more than a heat haze in the distance and the disappointment will crush me. Finish me off. Mel says it's still happening. I'm going home. But I won't actually believe it until it does happen. Not because I doubt Mel's word but because it still seems so implausible. It's not as if I can simply pick up my bed and walk, is it? How will I get there? In an ambulance, I guess. It's hardly the stuff of fairy tales, is it? And he was transported home in an ambulance and they all lived happily ever after. I don't think Maya would have been satisfied with an ending like that. But now she's going to have to be. Part of me is so desperate to be back home with her, of course. To in some small way feel like her daddy again instead of the vegetable she comes to visit every other day. But at the same time I'm worried about the effect it could have on her. I mean it's not normal, is it? Having your father lying in a vegetative state in your living room. I'll take up a hell of a lot more room than her marble run and she won't be able to dismantle me and put me back in the box. Maybe they'll put me in the spare bedroom. It would probably be kindest. Out of sight from any of her friends who come round after school. Or maybe they could keep me downstairs and throw a sheet over me when people come. Pretend I'm a new sofa they don't want to get dirty. Or better still use me for something practical. Stand me up in a corner and use me as a hat stand.

I won't be sorry to leave this place. I've had enough now. Enough of hospitals to last me a lifetime. But I am under no illusions that going home is the panacea to all my ills. The frustrations will still be there and coupled with guilt now. Mel's going to be my carer. That's where she's going tomorrow. To the university to hand in her notice. She's jacking in her career to babysit me. It's the most incredibly selfless thing to do but I so wish she didn't have to do it. She was so excited about teaching an honours degree. She could have done it years ago but she put looking after Maya first. And now, just when she's got herself back to the point where she can do it, she's lumbered with me to look after. Jeez, I feel so ashamed about it. Such a burden. Like I've single-handedly put women's lib back thirty years.

Footsteps. Those same hesitant ones I remember. And a face at the end of the bed. A face I hadn't been expecting.

'Hello, Adam,' says Hannah. 'Your wife told me I could find you here. I hope you don't mind me coming.'

Mind? Why the hell should I mind? It's lovely to see her. She's had her hair cut. One of those gamine crops. Very chic. For once I'm relieved I can't say anything. If I could I'd have probably passed some comment on it which would have come out all wrong. She moves around the bed and sits down on the chair next to me.

'I'm really glad your eyes have opened,' she says, then stops abruptly. 'Sorry, that probably sounded stupid. I mean for you. I'm glad for you that you can see again.' Another pause. I feel a sudden urge to say something to make this easier for her, even though I know I can't.

'Your wife said you're going home soon. That must be a huge relief for you. To be with your family again. You used to talk about them so much. All the stories about the things your little girl got up to. Monty's back up now, by the way. There was a big meeting about it and they had him repaired and everything. I said I thought you'd want him to go back up. I hope I didn't speak out of turn.'

I'm surprised that anyone even mentioned what I may have thought about it. I wonder what the other options were, if anyone suggested having a little plaque which read, 'Here marks the spot where Adam Taylor was felled by a T-rex,' and perhaps holding a little commemorative service there for me on the anniversary of the accident every year. Maybe if I'd died, they'd have done that. Having me still alive probably made it rather more awkward for them.

'Things are the same as ever at work. Well, not the same, of course. What I mean is nothing much has changed. Apart from you not being there, that is.' I can't see her face very well where she's sitting but I hear her slap what sounds like her forehead with her hand. 'Sorry. I'm making a complete hash of this, aren't I?'

I want to tell her it's OK. She's young. People in their early twenties aren't supposed to know how to speak to their former boss when they're in a vegetative state. I wouldn't have had the guts to come here when I was her age.

'The reason I've come is I wanted to let you know that I'm, er, I'm leaving.'

I presume you can't be stopped in your tracks if you're not actually capable of making tracks. But whatever the vegetative state equivalent is, that is what I feel.

'I've got a job in the PR department at the National Museum in Wales. Not very glamorous, I know, but they're very forward thinking and Cardiff seems to be a happening kind of place. I just, well, you know, thought I needed a change of scenery.'

Slowly, the penny drops. I hate the fact that I can't say anything. Can't even join her in an awkward silence. Well, not one that she would notice, anyway. I wonder if she would still have gone if this hadn't happened to me. Or whether it actually made the decision easier for her, in a way. The fact that there could no longer even be a question mark hanging in the air. I feel wretched inside; wretched to her, wretched to Mel – for the tiny part of me that feels flattered. I want to do that little boy thing, say, 'It wasn't me, I didn't do it,' in order to protest my innocence. But sometimes you don't need to do anything. Sometimes just being is enough.

'Anyway, I'd, er, better stop wittering and let you get some rest. I've un-followed you on Twitter but don't take it personally. I still laugh at your old tweets when I read them. But I owe it to myself to make a clean break.' She leans over and kisses me on the cheek. I wish that I could feel it. Not that I could kiss her back.

'Bye, Adam,' she says. 'I'll never forget you.' I watch as she walks away without looking back. Listen to her footsteps getting further away down the corridor. What was never going to be, departing. As what was always meant to be pulls into the empty platform in my head.

'Steve thinks I'm weird,' I told Mel as we lay in bed together.

'What, because you're going to marry me?'

'No, because I didn't take up his offer of a stag weekend in Amsterdam.'

'Were there not any pole dancers at the Robin Hood tonight, then?'

I smile at her. It had been my idea to go for a quiet drink with my best man on the eve of my wedding. Although I was well aware it was a decision which had probably earned me a few brownie points from Mel.

'He kept rattling on about it being my last night of fun and freedom.'

'God, he makes it sound as if you're getting castrated and thrown in jail tomorrow, not married.'

'You mean we'll still be able to have sex afterwards?' I asked. Mel smiled and dug me in the ribs. 'And as for us spending the night before the wedding together,' I continued. 'Well, he thought that was certifiable.'

'Louise said the same. Well, a bit more diplomatically, of course. But she was almost as shocked as my mum. I had to remind her that as I live with you, I was hardly going to throw you out the night before our wedding.'

'I guess her and Steve won't be doing the same when they get hitched.'

'If,' said Mel. 'I still think Louise can do a lot better than that.'

'Hey. That's my best man you're talking about.'

'Yeah, the one who'd have you chained naked to some railings by now, if he'd had his way.'

I laughed and rolled over on top of her. 'So, any last minute nerves, Ms Summerskill?'

'Nope. Why would I have? I'll be doing what I've always wanted to do.'

'What, wearing a huge meringue?'

'Oi, I've told you. The dress is sleek and sophisticated.'

'Like the guy you're marrying, then.'

'Are you going to shut up and ravage me, or not?'

'Oh, if you insist,' I said as I started kissing her neck.

'Make the most of it. I'll be a married woman tomorrow.'

'Not in the morning you won't.'

'If you make us late for our wedding . . .'

'You'll what? Divorce me?'

She smiled and kissed me back.

As it happened, we made it in time. Just. We did at least get changed in separate rooms at the hotel. Mel wanted there to be a moment when I saw her in the dress for the first time — not have me be the one who did it up at the back for her. I still remember that moment. Turning to see her walking towards me. I'm no good at describing dresses. I couldn't tell you what material it was made out of or what sort of cut the skirt was. All I know was that she looked stunning. Cut-out-of-a-magazine-photo-shoot stunning.

'Jesus, look at her,' I whispered to Steve. He didn't look though. Just carried on fiddling with the rings in his pocket. I smiled at Mel as she drew level with me. I could still picture her at thirteen, sixteen and twenty-one. And I could imagine what she'd look like *at thirty, forty, sixty even. But I knew that picture – the one of her at twenty-three on our wedding day – would be the one I'd take to my grave.*

Nineteen

MEL

Maya stands there in her red school sweatshirt and grey skirt, looking at least three years older than she did when she was eating her breakfast in her butterfly pyjamas barely a few minutes ago.

'Fantastic. Let's get your hair tied back then. We don't want it getting in your way when you're painting.'

Maya doesn't usually have her hair tied back, it feels symbolic, taking the red scrunchy and gathering her long tresses in it. As if I am capturing a wild pony, ready to break it in. A wild pony who has no idea that it will not be able to roam free from now on. That life is about to change forever.

'Wow,' I say, stepping back and looking her up and down. 'Don't you look grown up? Come and have a look in the mirror.'

I lead her out into the hall and lift her up to see. She grins at her reflection.

'Can we take a photo to show Daddy?' she asks.

I hug her to me. 'Of course we can. That's a great idea.'

I manage to hold it together while I get the camera and even while I take the photograph. It is afterwards when I put her down and she goes to put her shoes on all by herself that I have to turn away for a second to compose myself. I can't take photographs of every moment, can't have a video diary running of everything Adam is missing. Life has to go on. But this first day of school is something I've been dreading for a long time now.

The good thing is that Maya is totally up for it. I think if she was crying and clingy and not wanting to go, I should crumble within an instant. But as I open the door and she skips out on to the path, I know I can't give any hint of how bereft I am that Adam is not here to share this.

'OK, let's go,' I say, taking her firmly by the hand as we cross the main road together.

'Will we do painting all day?' asks Maya.

'Not all day, love. There'll be time to do other things as well. Drawing and writing.'

'And playing?'

'Lots of playing.'

'Will Mrs Hinchcliffe read me stories?'

'I expect so.'

'Will she do made-up stories about dinosaurs?'

I sigh. It hangs over us all the time. She doesn't want anything to do with dinosaurs any more. Hasn't touched her toy ones for months. I keep putting them out, leaving them casually lying around but she simply puts them back in her toy box again. This from the girl who roared back at the giant T-rex at Walking With Dinosaurs Live while children much older than her cowered in their seats.

'She might not have time for made-up stories. But if she does do something about dinosaurs, that's great, isn't it? You know lots of things about dinosaurs.' Maya says nothing. We're in sight of the school now. My stomach clenches. I'm about to send my little girl off into the big wide world. And as much as I know it's a necessary part of growing up, the fear of something happening to her has intensified since Adam's accident. If Adam could talk he'd probably say there was even less reason to worry now. That lightning doesn't strike twice. But then he didn't think anything bad was going to happen to him, did he?

We climb up the steep stone steps to the school. Maya squeals as she sees Isobel and Ryan, two friends from the Ark, in the playground. She runs over to them, proudly showing off her new school shoes. A second later she lifts up her skirt to show them her red knickers which I jokingly said matched her uniform. Just at the moment Mrs Hinchcliffe comes out into the playground. I smile and shrug. Fortunately Mrs Hinchcliffe smiles back.

'It could be worse,' she says. 'At least she's not doing it on her first day at high school.'

'No, but I've still got that to worry about,' I reply.

Mrs Hinchcliffe rings the bell and the reception children line up in front of her, excitedly chattering away. A moment later they are heading off into the school, presumably the thinking being to avoid any long, drawn-out goodbyes. Maya turns and waves then skips off after Mrs Hinchcliffe. She is going to be OK. She is going to be fine. I manage a smile at a group of the other mums, whom I know by sight if not by name. And then head off quickly down the steps before any of them have a chance to ask me how my husband is.

★

There is a knock on the door later that morning. I open it to see my parents standing there. I have not invited them. My mother has that look in her eye. And she has her handbag. They have come on business. My business. I have a sudden urge to say, 'No, thank you, not today,' and slam the door in their faces. I can't do that, though. I was not made that way.

'Hi,' I say instead. The sound of hoovering is coming from the lounge. Mum looks at me quizzically. 'Denise is here.' Mum nods in a way which indicates that she does not approve of me having a cleaner. Something to do with it being wrong to pay someone to clean up my own mess. 'Come in, then,' I say, unable to bear the thought of the stand-off continuing any longer. 'I'll put the kettle on.'

They follow me into the kitchen. I know full well why they're here but I'm not going to make it easy for them by inviting comments. Mum puts her handbag purposefully on the table and looks at Dad, who promptly looks at the floor.

'The thing is,' says Mum, obviously deciding she'll have to do it herself, 'we're not sure that what you're planning to do is for the best.' I note the use of the word 'planning'. Clearly she hasn't accepted it's actually happening yet.

'Oh, and why's that?'

'It's not normal, is it? Having your husband lying in a coma in your living room.'

Dad winces even before I do.

'No, it's not. But then most people don't have a husband in a vegetative state.'

'Yes but even those who do, they don't have them living at home with them, do they?'

'How do you know?'

'Well, there'd be documentaries about it on BBC 2 if they did, wouldn't there? And articles in the *Daily Mail*.'

'I don't suppose I'm actually the only person doing this but even if I am it doesn't bother me and it certainly isn't a reason not to do it.'

'But what will people think if they visit your house?'

'I don't care what they think. Adam's my husband, Mum. And he's coming home.' I pour the teas for them. Dad hasn't even been able to look me in the eye, yet.

'The thing is, love,' he says as I hand him his mug, 'we're concerned about all the sacrifices you're making. Giving up your job and everything.'

'I don't have any choice. If I'm going to be looking after him I need to be around more. It's either this or have him packed off to some nursing home. And Adam would hate that. You know he'd hate that.'

'It's not as if he's in a position to complain, is it?' Even by Mum's standards that one plumbs the depths. I am about to ask her what she'd do if it was Dad but stop myself as I'm pretty sure what the answer would be.

'The fact that he can't speak doesn't mean he can't feel. Adam does not want to go into a nursing home so I'm bringing him home, where he belongs.'

'But what about when Maya brings her little friends home from school? It'll scare them, surely?'

'*It* is her daddy and it will be enormously beneficial to her to have him back at home. She's missed him so much.'

'But what about you? How can you move on?'

I stare at her, not wanting to believe she just said

that. The pressure valve inside me finally blows.

'Move on? What do you mean by that? Am I supposed to go out and find myself someone else, is that it? Well, it may have escaped your notice but I still have a husband, thank you. And he's coming home whether you like it or not.'

It is only as I finish that I realise Denise is standing in the kitchen with her mop and bucket.

'Do you want me to come back later?' she says.

'No, thanks. You carry on. My parents are just leaving.'

Mum picks up her handbag and Dad follows her out into the hall. I go through after them. If I'm throwing them out I may as well do it politely.

'Look, I'm very grateful for all the visiting you've done with Adam. I don't want to burden you in any way and if you'd rather not sit with him when he comes home, that's fine, just let me know and I'll ask someone else to do it.'

'Of course we'll sit with him,' says Mum. 'We'll take it in turns in the mornings, like we said.' She marches off down the path. I feel a twinge of guilt. Just a twinge, mind.

'I know you want to do what's best for Adam,' says Dad. 'I just don't want you to regret all the sacrifices you're making in years to come. Resentment isn't good for a marriage, you know. Not good at all.' He stoops to peck me on the cheek and heads off down the path to where Mum is waiting at the car. I shut the door and head back into the kitchen.

'I'm sorry about that,' I say to Denise, who has the Marigolds on and is busy cleaning the sink.

'You don't have to apologise, love. Believe me, that was a

tea party compared to the rows my family has. You never even threw anything. I'd have chucked at least a saucer.'

I smile and shake my head. 'I don't know. Maybe they're right. Maybe this is a crazy thing to do. Would you do this if it was your husband?'

'No but then I'd be well shot of my husband. All the grief he's caused me over the years. I'd pack him off to a home tomorrow if I could. One less person to clean up after.'

'You don't mean that.'

'Oh, I do.'

'So why are you still with him?'

'He's the kids' dad. Besides, the two blokes I had before him were no better, who's to say the next one would be any good? Better the devil you know, I reckon.'

I nod. I'd almost forgotten how guilty I used to feel about my relationship with Adam. How odd not to be able to join in with the general slagging off of husbands.

'He's very lucky to have you,' I say. 'I bet he couldn't do without you.'

'Course he couldn't. Men have someone looking after them from cradle to grave, don't they? The whole world would grind to a halt if we stopped looking after them, you know.'

'So you don't think I'm mad bringing Adam home?'

'Not if you want to, no. It doesn't bother me. As long as I can clean around him.'

I smile. I think Adam will like her.

I knock on the door of Margaret's office the next morning. I feel rather like Maria from *The Sound of Music* going in to

213

see Mother Superior. Hoping for some words of wisdom. For someone to make sense of it all.

'Hello, Melanie,' says Margaret, getting up from her desk as I walk in. We embrace in a rather awkward fashion and I sit down. Remembering the last time I was in here. Noting that my hands aren't shaking this time. That I feel oddly calm.

'Thank you for your letter,' she says, sitting down opposite me. 'As I explained in my email, I'm extremely sorry to lose you but I completely understand. You have to do what is right for you and your family.'

I nod, expecting her to break into 'How Do You Solve a Problem Like Melanie?' at any moment. 'I feel awful about not being able to give you much notice.'

'Well, don't. I'm only sorry we couldn't offer you anything with the sort of hours you need to fit in with your family commitments. But as I said, due to the circumstances, there's no problem with you continuing on special leave until your notice is technically up.'

'Thank you,' I say. 'I really do appreciate it.'

'We've been able to get a lecturer from Leeds Metropolitan University to take over from you so there's no problem with covering the course.'

'Oh, that's a relief. I hate having to let you all down like this.'

'You're not letting anyone down, Melanie. I'm very glad you got the job at Calderdale College but if you're ever in a position to return to us, please don't hesitate to get in touch.'

'Thank you,' I say. 'I won't.'

'And don't listen to anyone who accuses you of sacrificing your career. Your family must come first. Besides, the sixteen-year-olds you're going to be teaching are every bit as important as the graduates here. And I know you won't give them anything less than your best.'

I leave Margaret's office with a hint of a smile on my face. And the sound of the nuns' singing ringing in my ears.

I meet Nadine in a nearby café as arranged. She gets up to hug me as I walk over to her. The embrace is tentative, like when you meet an old friend you haven't seen for years and aren't quite sure whether you're close enough to hug any more. Which is crazy really. It's only been a matter of months. It's just that so much has happened, so much has changed in those months that working at the uni, having lunchtime gossips over a baguette with Nadine, seems to belong to another lifetime entirely.

'Hi,' she says, 'You're looking well.'

She's being polite. I don't think a suit and a bit of make-up can really paper over the cracks that effectively.

'Thanks,' I say. 'Sorry to interrupt the end of your summer holidays. It's just so rare I'm over this way these days.' Nadine lives in Bingley, the other side of Bradford. I didn't see her much outside of work hours before the accident but it's proved even more difficult since.

'Don't be daft. It's lovely to see you. I wish the circumstances were different but at least we've managed to meet up at last. I feel awful that I haven't made it over.'

We've texted and emailed a fair bit. Managed the odd chat on the phone. But despite various attempts at meeting up, it's never actually come off. And inevitably when you don't see someone every day, or even every month, for that matter, some of that closeness ebbs away.

'Well don't. You're busy, I know that. And I also know that you're always on the end of the phone if I need to talk.'

Nadine shrugs. I hope I've managed to offload some of the guilt she is obviously carrying about with her. She has offered plenty of times to help out in any way she can but I haven't wanted to put her out. She has three kids and a husband who haven't stopped needing her just because Adam is in a vegetative state. Life has gone on for other people. I understand that and it's how it should be.

'How did Maya get on yesterday?' Nadine asks as I sit down opposite her.

'She was fine. Trotted into the classroom happily without me, came home full of it all in the afternoon and couldn't get ready quick enough this morning.'

'Good, that must have made it a bit easier for you.'

'Yeah, it did. Long may it last. How about your three?'

'Oh, we had the usual first day back grumbles. They were fine today, though. Back to bickering amongst themselves about who had what in their lunchboxes.'

The waitress hovers above us with a crumpled notepad in her hand. I order a coffee and a toasted teacake. Nadine asks for the same.

'So how was Margaret?' she asks.

'She was lovely, actually. Probably the first person who hasn't appeared to regard me as being completely off my rocker for doing this. Or try to talk me out of it.'

Nadine fiddles with one of the sachets of sugar on the table. 'Well, for what it's worth, I don't think you're mad either. I know how devoted you two are. I wasn't surprised at all when I read your email.'

'So you don't think I'm abandoning my career?'

'No. You're taking a break. Lots of women do it for all sorts of family reasons. And I can't think of a reason better than yours, to be honest.'

The waitress returns with our order. I take a mouthful of hot, buttery teacake. Comfort food. Which is exactly what I need.

'What do you think the other lecturers will say?'

'I don't give a stuff,' says Nadine 'and nor should you. It's none of their bloody business.'

'I know. But I can still imagine some of the blokes muttering about women not being up to the rigours of teaching a degree course.'

'Well, if they do I shall tell them where to get off. Besides, anyone who sneers down their nose at further education isn't worth bothering about.'

'Thanks,' I say.

Nadine smiles back. 'Anyway, enough about work. Tell me all about the plans to bring Adam home. How's it all going?'

'Gradually coming together, I think. The social worker at the hospital's been brilliant. It's just a matter of making sure the funding and all the paperwork is in place.'

'Be sure to let me know if there's anything I can do to help, won't you?'

'Thank you but honestly, I'll be fine. I've got my parents

and Louise and her husband Steve's been really good too.'

'OK. But the offer's still there if you ever change your mind.'

I smile. I am grateful for her kindness but people's need to do something, to try to make it better, can get a bit draining at times if I'm honest. The truth is that someone cooking me a meal, looking after Maya for a couple of hours or even offering to take me out for a coffee is very nice but it's not going to change anything. It's not going to bring Adam back.

'Just keep me posted on the gossip when term starts,' I say. 'That way, if I ever do get to come back, I won't feel completely out of it.'

It's become a bit of a ritual, Steve coming round on Thursday evenings after visiting Adam. He seems to enjoy being the unofficial odd-job man. I guess it makes him feel useful. Which is why I always try to find something for him to do, even when there really isn't anything. It's also the reason I let him paint the lounge, despite the fact that I'm not keen on magnolia. It did need doing and when he turned up with a tin of paint and a roller I didn't see how I could say no.

'Hi,' I say as he steps into the hall. 'How's things?'

'OK, I guess.' He always says that. I am starting to understand how it must have driven Louise mad. His insistence on keeping everything buried deep inside.

'Coffee?'

'Yeah, that would be great. I'll sort out that dripping tap first, then.'

'Thanks. If you have a minute afterwards, the bulb's gone in the lounge, I'm afraid. I've got the ladders out but, well . . .' My voice trails off as I reach up to demonstrate. The light bulb business is one of the many downsides of being vertically challenged – and having high ceilings to boot. I suppose I should get some longer stepladders, it's just that there was no need before.

'How do you manage in supermarkets? Being a munchkin, I mean.'

'Sod off, you.' I smile. 'Anyway, that's who Ocado deliveries were invented for, those who can't reach the top shelf and are fed up with having to ask tall people.'

'I'm fed up up with being asked to reach things by short people.'

'When do you go to the supermarket?'

'I do now.'

Of course. I hadn't stopped to think.

'Why don't you do it online?'

'It's not the same, is it? You can't get away with putting chocolate in your trolley at the checkout because you're bored waiting.'

I smile. Adam used to do that as well.

I'm in the middle of dishing out the chilli I've made into individual containers when Steve comes back into the kitchen.

'That smells good.'

'You can have some if you like. I do a huge one so I can freeze it. Saves me having to cook every night.'

'No, you're OK. I grabbed a sandwich at the hospital.'

'That's not proper food. Come on,' I say, scooping some into a dish and handing it to Steve, 'you need to look after yourself.'

'Only if you have some too. I bet you haven't eaten.' He's right, I haven't. Not unless you count Maya's leftover spaghetti.

It's weird, sitting opposite Steve at the dining table. Like dancing with the wrong partner. Though to be honest, I'm glad of the company. It's not much fun, eating on your own every night.

I know I should tell Steve the news. I've managed to avoid mentioning it so far. Probably because of the way everyone else has reacted when I've told them.

'I've got something to tell you.' Steve looks across at me, having no idea what I'm about to say. 'Adam's coming home.' There is a pause while he finishes his mouthful. And another pause while he appears to be digesting the information.

'What do you mean, coming home?'

'The doctor said they can't do anything more for him. They wanted to put him into a nursing home but I said no.'

'So you're having him here?'

'Yeah. It's his home.'

'I know but who's going to look after him?'

'Me.'

'But what about when you're working?'

'I've handed my notice in. I've got a part-time job at Calderdale College. Maternity cover, ten hours a week. Mum and Dad have said they'll cover that.'

Steve appears as stunned as everyone else has been.

'Jeez. That's a massive sacrifice, Mel.'

'What was I supposed to do?'

'Put him into a home, like they said.'

'Right and that's how you'd like to be treated, is it?'

'I wouldn't have any say in it, would I?'

'Louise would do exactly the same for you.'

'I don't think so.'

'She would. She told me.'

Steve shakes his head. 'So how come I'm the last to know?'

'I just haven't got around to telling you.'

'Right. I see.' Steve puts his fork down. Holds his head in his hands.

'I don't understand why it bothers you so much.'

'I promised Adam I'd be there for you. And now I find you've gone ahead and sorted this out without me even knowing about it.'

I put my own fork down. I can't help being touched by his concern.

'Look, I didn't discuss it with anyone. I made my mind up in seconds. It simply felt the right thing to do.'

'But what about your career?'

'Adam comes before it. Maya does too. I've got to do what's right for them.' I stand up and take my half-empty bowl over to the sink. After a few seconds I hear Steve push his chair away, his footsteps approach me from behind.

'Hey, I know this is tough for you. I'm just worried about what you're taking on. And what you're giving up in the process. You were looking forward to teaching that course.'

I turn around to face him, trying hard to hold myself together. Not wanting him to see the chinks of weakness underneath my certainty.

'Thank you. But I've made up my mind and I've already told Adam. I'm not going to change my mind.'

'The thing is, Mel, I don't want to see you get hurt. And I'm worried that you think it's Adam who's coming home. Because he's not going to get better, Mel. He's not coming back.'

'You don't know that. Nobody knows that.' I'm trying to stop the tears being squeezed out by the fury. Steve puts his hands on my shoulders.

'I didn't mean to upset you, Mel. I'm simply trying to get you to face up to the truth. Adam is gone. You need to start to come to terms with that. We all do.'

'You've given up on him like everyone else. You're supposed to be his best friend.'

'I am his best friend. That's why I'm trying to help you. Trying to stop you getting hurt any more than you've already been.'

Steve's hands are still on my shoulders. For a split second I am ready to crumble; to tell him I am every bit as apprehensive about this as he is. But then I remember who I'm doing this for. For Adam and for Maya. I step aside, Steve's hands falling from my shoulders as I do so.

'I do still believe he'll come back to me. And I'm glad I do. Because if I didn't, I'd have nothing left to cling on to.'

'Yes you would. I'd be there for you.'

I give a half-smile.

'It's very kind of you but it's not what I mean. He's my

husband, Steve. I'm never going to walk away from him, no matter what happens. I love him far too much to do something like that.'

I realise as soon as I say it how wrong it sounds in the circumstances. Steve looks down at his feet, seemingly crushed.

'Look, I'm sorry. I didn't think. I didn't mean to say . . .'

'It's OK,' says Steve. 'You don't have to apologise. I know what you meant. Besides, you're right. I chose to walk away. And I know deep down that you would never do that to Adam. I guess I always have.'

He picks up his jacket. We stand awkwardly for a moment.

'I'd better be off,' he says. I nod and follow him through to the hall. He opens the front door before stopping and turning back to me.

'I'm only trying to look after you, Mel. Because whatever you might think, no one else is going to do it. Not any more.'

He pulls the door shut behind him. Instantly I feel the emptiness, swirling around between the hurt and the fear. I sink down on to the bottom step of the stairs and stare up at the ceiling. Wondering if he's right. And if I'm wrong to keep believing.

Twenty

'Dear Points of View,' begins Joan.

I know I should be grateful for the fact that my mother-in-law no longer sings 'All Things Bright and Beautiful' to me. Not since they moved me to this ward at any rate. I haven't worked out whether she is self-conscious about her voice or the nurses have told her that singing songs of worship is banned on wards, but either way, it is undoubtedly a blessing. However, I am starting to dread the reading of her letters to *Points of View* as much as I dreaded her singing.

'I would like to know how much it cost us licence payers to make that tent with the number two zip in it to promote BBC2. We are not stupid (if we were, we'd be watching ITV), we know we are watching BBC2, we have pressed the number 'two' buttons on our remote controls to get there. So why on earth does the BBC think we need constant reminding about which channel we are watching? We do not need the BBC to make special tents or cajole disabled people into playing basketball (surely it can't be good for them, all that twisting and turning? And it must ruin their wheelchairs). And as for the swimming hippos, well, that was plain cruel, training them to do that. Perhaps if the BBC concentrated more of its money on high quality programmes like *Songs of Praise* and *Cash in the Attic* instead of silly gimmicks, this country would not be in the state it is.'

Yours sincerely

Joan Summerskill (Mrs)

At least the poor bastard who receives the letter will be able to bin it after reading the first couple of lines instead of having to sit through it to the bitter end like me. Although maybe Jeremy Vine puts the ridiculous ones up on his wall like we used to do at the *Yorkshire Post*. The green-ink brigade, they were known as there. Because invariably those with enough time on their hands to write and complain about stupid things did so in green ink. I try unsuccessfully to see what colour ink Joan has used as she folds up the letter, places it back in the envelope and seals it. I'm still not sure what purpose reading these letters to me actually serves. It's not as if I can offer any editorial judgements. Or that by reading them aloud Joan can spot any which are a waste of time sending (she has not once torn a letter up after reading it). I can only presume she actually thinks I enjoy listening to them. And I suppose I do, in a so-bad-it's-actually-funny kind of way.

'There, that should tell them,' she says, putting it back into her handbag. No doubt the director general of the BBC is quaking in his boots. 'Not that they'll probably read it out. They censor them, you see. I'm certain they do.

Barry Took would never have allowed it in his day but, as you know, standards have slipped since then.'

It's going to be a long morning. Mel has gone straight to a training day at her new college. She told me about it last night. She tried to sound excited but she never could hide her disappointment from me. She's thinking about the course she should have been teaching, I know she is. Missing her friends at uni. Feeling like the new kid on the block and probably wondering why the hell she's given all that up for me.

I am torn between feeling enormously lucky to have a wife who is prepared to make those sorts of sacrifices for me and feeling like a good-for-nothing lump of lard who has forced his wife to give up her career. She keeps telling me it is her choice, that she is the one who wants to take me home and look after me. It shouldn't be like this, though. She shouldn't have to make choices like that. I try so hard not to be angry and bitter about what happened to me and most of the time I succeed. What I don't succeed at is not being angry and bitter about what has happened to Mel. She is doing more and more for me in hospital; not just the personal things she has always done like shave me and cut my nails but the practical day-to-day stuff: washing me, putting my eye drops in, moving me to prevent bedsores, even emptying the bag where my wee ends up. She says she wants to be ready for when I go home. Wants to learn to do everything so she can care for me herself. But no wife should have to clean up their husband's piss. And certainly not when they haven't even hit forty yet.

'She's a good girl, our Melanie,' says Joan, as if reading

my thoughts. 'A bit too good, probably. All that time at university, all those qualifications, and she'll end up doing what women used to do in my day. Staying at home to look after her family. I'm not sure I'd have done that. Not if I'd had opportunities and education she's had. Not if it were Tom.'

I am listening intently now. The usual backchat and quips in my head have been silenced. She continues talking, her voice hushed.

'It's not that I don't love him, you see. Just that we don't have same sort of relationship you and Melanie have. Well, it were different for you, wasn't it? You grew up together, you knew each other's foibles long before you got married. In our day it were rather like a leap of faith. You met someone at a dance. He was nice-looking, presentable, polite. Sort of chappie you could take home to meet your mother. And as long as he didn't force himself on you, or drink, or gamble, or go with anyone else behind your back, well, that were it really. Before you knew it you were engaged, then married. You didn't know them, see.'

She goes quiet for a second. I have never heard her talking like this before. I'm quite sure she wouldn't be saying any of this if I was sitting next to her having a cup of tea and a biscuit. It is one of the weird things about being in a vegetative state. People say things to you they would never dream of saying otherwise. I guess because they don't think you are really listening. Or if you are, you will never be able to repeat it.

'It's not that Tom's a bad man, you understand. Just that if we'd got to know each other properly first we might

227

have realised how different we were. How we wanted different things. I'm not sure I've ever been able to give him life he really wanted. I don't think I were enough for him. I think he had horizons far beyond Mytholmroyd. Which is unusual, really, for a Yorkshire lad.'

If I could speak I would at this point mention Captain Cook or Michael Palin, both of whom blow the stereotype of the Yorkshireman who never leaves his county out of the water. But there again if I could speak, she wouldn't be saying this to me. Besides which I am actually enjoying the genuinely new experience of listening to Joan saying something interesting.

'Anyway, enough of this nonsense,' she says, bending down to pick up a magazine. 'I thought I'd read you a couple of stories out of *People's Friend* this morning. They're quite modern ones, you know, compared to those they used to run. One of them even has a divorced lady in it. Maureen, her name is. We've got a practice nurse called Maureen at the surgery but I don't think it's based on her. She's married, for a start.'

I tune out and try to switch off. When I get out of my body, if I ever get out, one of the first things I will do is call for the ritual burning of all copies of the *People's Friend*.

'Now Gainsborough's something else,' says Tom, later that afternoon. 'If I had space, which, of course, I don't, I'd love to do something like Gainsborough Model Railway. It's one of largest 0-gauge model railways in country, you know. The whole thing is based on East Coast Mainline from King's Cross to Leeds Central. Imagine having space to do that. All their trains run to a strict timetable as well. They don't muck about there. I sometimes think they should nationalise railways and get Malcolm and his friends from Gainsborough running whole lot. I don't see why they couldn't. They'd do a damn sight better than mess we've got at moment, anyway.'

Tom sits and contemplates the model railway revolution he appears to be masterminding. I know a lot more about model railways than I did before the accident. It's as if I was channel-hopping, came across a programme called *Great Model Railways of the British Isles* on BBC2 and found that the remote has stopped working and I am now stuck with it for all eternity. Apart from the days when Joan switches me over to *Points of View*, obviously. I have come to the conclusion that Tom and Joan are not really a couple at all. Not like Mel and I are. Or were, at any rate. They seem to be more at ease when they're apart. Tom is not nearly so solemn. That sense of resignation he carries around with him when Joan is there is somehow dissipated when he's on his own. He almost has a glimmer of hope. Or maybe it's simply the way the light reflects in his glasses.

'Malcolm at Gainsborough's done all those big rail journeys, you know. Orient Express, Trans-Siberian Express, Rocky Mountaineer in Canada, even Blue Train in South Africa. I've seen his slide shows. It's not same as going, though, the sounds, the smells, the wind in your hair . . .' Tom's voice trails off. A look of resignation returns to his face.

'It's not that I didn't enjoy Settle to Carlisle train journey. It were grand. But once you get a taste for summat, well, it makes it harder in a way. To stop, I mean. I had all these plans, you know. All these hopes and dreams. But somehow they just seemed to pass me by. When young people talk about the sixties, they assume that just being there were same as having a ticket. It weren't, of course. If you weren't a student – and sons of mill workers didn't go to university – and didn't live in one of big cities like London or Liverpool, well, it kind of passed you by.

'All this talk of Isle of Wight, drugs and loose women. It weren't like that in Mytholmroyd. All I had were a bit of a fumble with Doreen from Sowerby Bridge. She were a wild one, Doreen. Wanted to go all the way first time I took her out. I don't think the Morris Minor ever really recovered from what took place on back seat. I certainly didn't. Scared me off, good and proper, she did. I met Joan Saturday after, you know. She couldn't have been more different. She were beautiful too, you know. Much better looking than Doreen. She just didn't know it. I guess that's what I liked about her, the idea of her being some beautiful, uncharted territory. Doreen had a public right of way running straight through her. She had a charming innocence, your mother-in-law. And it were good at first, we set up home and made our little lives. I worked me way up in planning department. I still thought we'd get to do all those things I wanted to do. Thought we'd just take our time, save up a bit of money. And then Martin came along, of course. And I lost Joan. Lost her completely. She became Martin's mum, instead of my wife. Not that I were jealous, you understand, or resentful. Just sad. Sad to have lost her so early in life. She put everything into Martin, you know.

All her hopes and dreams were tied up in him. I tried to tell her, tried to warn her that he'd grow up one day, want a life of his own. She didn't listen, of course. Or maybe she did listen but she just didn't want to hear. Either way, it didn't help her when he went. Inconsolable, she were. Took it out on me. I missed him too, mind. But at least I had Mel. She were always mine, you see. Always my special girl.'

I feel I should look away while Tom composes himself. Or at least signal in some way that I can hear what he's saying. I can't do either, though. All I can do is listen.

'I used to envy you, you know,' says Tom. 'Right jealous of you for taking our Mel away, I was. Taking my place in her affections. Not that I didn't like you. You were always good to her, I could see that. No, it were simply the way you were together that I used to be jealous of. Because Joan and I never had anything like you had with Mel. Never had that closeness. Soulmates, is it, they call it these days? Well, whatever you call it, we never had it. And now look at you. I feel so bad, you know. So bad for having been jealous of you. And so awful that I can't help Mel through this. I don't have words, you see. I'm no good at these sort of things. At end of day I'm no good to her. It's you she needs. Always has been, always will.'

He pauses again for a moment or two. I wonder if he can feel the hand I am reaching out to hold his. Sense the warmth from it at least.

'And I look at my life, Adam,' he continues. 'With a wife I don't really know, who I feel so distant from. And nothing stretching ahead in front of me. Nowt to look forward to apart from watching Maya grow up. And I know I shouldn't feel bad and I know I shouldn't feel sorry for myself, not with you lying there like that and Mel beside herself with worry but it's very hard, you know. Very hard not to wish I had something more. Something like you and Mel have.' He sighs and shakes his head. 'Sorry, I mean what you had. I'm a silly old bugger, aren't I? A silly old bugger who should shut up and get back to playing with toy trains.'

I had it all planned out for ages. There was never any question of 'if' only 'when'. And as soon as we hit 1999 there was no question of 'when' only 'how' and 'where'. Mel had talked about millennium eve for as long as I could remember. Right from when we were teenagers she used to speculate about where we would be, what we'd be doing. The one thing which was never in doubt was that we'd be together. But she could never quite make up her mind whether that would be at Sydney Harbour, up a mountain in the Lake District or in Times Square, New York. I'd love to say that I chose the Lake District because I knew she'd like it best but the truth was that our house had been such a money pit that year and with Mel still doing her postgrad in higher education and us only having the one wage, the Lake District kind of chose itself. I managed better than a youth hostel, mind. Llancrigg, a little country-house hotel in Grasmere, looking down over the Easdale valley. I even ran to a room with a four-poster bed. I wrapped the brochure up and gave it to her for Christmas, although she had to open half a dozen boxes before she finally got to it. She knew by then that I was taking her somewhere for the millennium, of course. I'd cracked under her relentless questioning and told her she didn't have to worry about it, I had it all sorted. And I guess she had worked out she wouldn't be needing her passport because she didn't look at all disappointed when she unwrapped it. I would have known if she was because of her being so awful at hiding things from me.

'Thank you,' she said, throwing her arms around me before jumping up and down on the bed like a big kid.

'We're staying three nights, there's a four-poster bed, a five-course meal on millennium eve and fireworks on the front lawn at midnight,' I said. 'Will that do you?'

'Perfect,' she said. 'It'll be perfect.' And she said it with such certainty that I knew it would.

I have never seen someone as excited about a bath as Mel was when we were shown to the room. It was a white enamel free-standing one on a raised plinth, surrounded by lace curtains on all four sides. She grabbed hold of my arm the second she saw it and gasped, actually gasped.

'It's a four-poster bath,' she whispered. 'I'm going to have a four-poster bath.'

Turned out she'd brought scented candles with her. Only women do things like that. I'm not sure I even knew they existed. I thought I'd done well to pack my deodorant, let alone think about candles. Anyway, that was how I found her when I came out of the shower on millennium eve. Silhouetted by candlelight behind the lace curtains, her long hair piled on top of her head, her bare shoulders glistening and one toe peeking out of the water at the other end. For a second I wished I'd packed one of the photographers from work in my suitcase and could ask them out to capture the moment. Then I realised that wasn't like packing candles at all. That was just stupid and a bit creepy, to be honest. So I stood there and watched instead. Watched the woman I *loved. The woman I was soon to propose to. And at that moment I didn't have a doubt, not one tiny doubt in my head that I was doing the right thing. I hadn't told anyone, of course. Well, not apart from Steve and he didn't really count because I knew what his reaction would be. Told me I was mad. That I was way too young to get married. That I was twenty-three, for fuck's sake, and at this rate he'd be getting me carpet slippers for Christmas.*

'You can come in and join me if you like.' I realised Mel had clocked me. I smiled back at her.

'You look far too comfortable there for me to disturb you. Anyway, you know I hate baths.'

'Well, just come and see me then.'

I pretended to hack my way through the lace curtains with an imaginary sword.

'I don't remember Prince Charming wearing a bathrobe.' She smiled.

'I don't remember Sleeping Beauty having scented candles.' I kissed her on the top of her head and knelt down beside the bath. I could have done it then, I suppose, although I'd have had to dash back to my suitcase to get the ring. But it didn't seem very gallant to propose to a naked woman in a bath. She had no place to hide, no place to run. Not that I thought for a moment that she'd do either.

'How long have I got until dinner?'

'About twenty minutes, I think.'

'OK, I'll just have five minutes longer.'

I leant over and kissed her shoulder. Blowing the bubbles away from her breast as I did so.

'Hey, don't you start. I don't want to be late.'

I scooped some more bubbles up and put them on her nose. 'Why? Is there something special happening tonight?'

We stood outside on the lawn, Mel shivering in her sleeveless dress and little jacket. The sky had been ordered especially from the God of perfect skies. Every star chiselled clearly out of the blackness. There were no streetlights, no cars. It was perfectly still. Someone had brought a radio outside to listen to Big Ben. I wrapped my arms around Mel as the countdown began. I had no idea if she thought I was going to do it at that moment but if she did she was going to be disappointed. Half the bloody population would be popping the question at midnight. I suspected that if I turned around I would see at least three guys reaching into their jacket pockets for the ring. No, she was going to have to wait. I wanted to do this right. I kissed Mel on the stroke of midnight. A cheer went up (for the new millennium, not my kiss), followed swiftly by the first firework. We did the obligatory oohs and aahs. Mel had a glass in her hand but she couldn't drink for smiling. It wasn't New York and it wasn't Sydney Harbour but it was right for us.

It was only as we turned to go back into the hotel afterwards that we realised all the lights had gone out.

'Bloody hell,' someone called out, 'must be the millennium bug.'

'It's all right,' I said. 'Keep calm. My girlfriend has some scented candles.'

It took a long time to wake Mel the next morning. Admittedly she'd only had about four hours' sleep and hadn't been expecting an early wake-up call.

'What time is it?' she said when she eventually opened her eyes.

'Five.' She groaned and turned over. 'Time to get up.'

'You've got to be kidding.'

'Nope. That's why I'm already dressed.'

Mel turned back towards me, an expression of utter incomprehension on her face.

'Why are you dressed, Adam?'

'We're going for a pre-breakfast stroll.'

'At five in the morning?'

'Yeah.'

'Is this some sort of joke?'

'No. I'm being serious for once. We're going to see the first sunrise of the millennium.'

Mel sat up. 'Really?'

'Yeah, really. I'm all packed. All you've got to do is put on your clothes.'

She smiled at me and a few seconds later scrambled out of bed.

I'd chosen the spot very carefully. Made sure it was a steady climb, nothing too strenuous, but somewhere off the beaten track. I wanted us to be alone for this. Early-morning ramblers were not welcome. We huddled down together at the top of the ridge as the morning slowly edged up the brightness control.

'Do you suppose it is the millennium bug?' We were still without power at the hotel. There was no other building or light within sight to let us know if it was just us or the whole world which had been plunged into darkness.

'You know what,' I said, 'I don't really care if it is. I could quite happily stay here forever.'

'Be a bit pricey, mind, it must have cost you a week's wages for three nights.'

'A fortnight's actually.' Mel looked mortified. 'It's OK, we can *still pay the bills. I've been saving for it since I started work.'*

'You're too good to me, Adam Taylor.'

'I've got a whole millennium to remind you of that,' I said. Mel grinned at exactly the same moment the sun came up. I pulled the glove off her left hand and reached into my pocket.

'Hey, it's freezing,' she said.

'Sorry, but it won't fit over them.' I opened my hand. The ring was lying in my palm. It looked tiny and suddenly rather unimpressive. A slim gold band. Just the one tiny diamond. I'd told the lady in the jewellers I'd wanted simple and elegant. Although at the moment I kind of wished I'd said showy and ostentatious.

Mel looked up at me. Her eyes wide awake now. Wide awake and gleaming.

'It's perfect,' she said. 'The whole thing is perfect.'

'Is that a yes, then?'

'Sorry. Yes, of course. Did you actually ask me?'

'I didn't think I needed to.'

'No,' she smiled. 'You didn't.'

'Phew, that's OK, then. Can we go down and get some breakfast now? If they've got any, that is.'

Mel smiled. I offered her back the glove. She shook her head.

'No thanks,' she said. 'I'm going to show it off to the sheep on the way down.'

Twenty-one

MEL

I thread my way through the throng of teenagers wandering aimlessly along the corridor. I keep thinking I've got the wrong place, that I'm actually back at school. Everyone at college looks so young and I am aware that even thinking that makes me very, very old. At least at university there was a fair smattering of mature students and nineteen is actually light years away from being sixteen. Still, it's sixteen year olds I'm teaching so I need to try to put my sixteen-year-old head on, remember what I thought and felt at that age in order to engage with them. And try to push to the back of my mind the knowledge that I am old enough to be their mother. Because I don't want to go there. Don't want to think about that at all.

I open the door and now it really does feel like being back at school. Rows of tables and shabby wooden chairs, posters and health and safety notices on the wall. Only the whiteboard tells me that this is not a time warp. I'm the tutor. I'm the one who's supposed to know what I'm doing.

The first group of girls arrive in the classroom. There are only girls on this course. And I suspect they will all arrive in clusters like this. I know the names from my list. Emma, Amy and Cara. Rebecca, Charlotte and Haleema. I do not know yet whether I have got them in the right clusters, but I will know soon enough. I smile and introduce myself, tell them to take a seat, grab a drink from the vending machine if they want one. This excites them. Because to them the biggest thing about college is that it is not school: being on first-name terms with lecturers, having drink machines, not wearing school uniform. They are feeling grown-up, liberated, as if they have finally arrived in the adult world.

I wait until they have all arrived and settled in their seats before I introduce myself properly, set out the course aims and objectives, tell them what they will have learnt by the end of it. I see faces that are eager, fresh and open. Others that are uncertain, not bothered and over made-up. Most of all, I see faces that are young.

'So, what I'd like to do now is give you all a chance to get to know each other and for me to get to know you. All your names are on pieces of paper in this box, I'd like you to pick one out, go and sit next to that person and both be able to tell me the answer to these three questions about your partner in ten minutes' time. Why they're on this course, what their earliest childhood memory is and which person they most admire.'

The girls look terrified and perplexed in turn. As ice-breakers go, it's one of the more interesting ones. Gets them talking. Tells you something worth knowing without them feeling they are being tested. A tall girl with long bleached hair and wearing skinny jeans is the first to go.

'Gemma,' she reads out loud. Another girl puts her hand up. They wait awkwardly for a moment before the tall girl saunters over to her.

'Introduce yourself properly,' I say, as another hand picks out a name. The noise volume rises as the girls pair off, get through the awkward introductions and start to talk to each other. Start to communicate.

'Right,' I say ten minutes later, pleased that I have to raise my voice to cut through the noise. 'Let's hear them. I'd like you all to introduce your partner and tell me those three things about them.'

The noise level drops instantly, they are back to feeling awkward again. Though not as awkward as they were before.

'Gemma and Jess, you start us off.'

'This is Gemma,' says Jess, gesturing in the style of an air stewardess. 'She's on this course because she wants to work with children or animals but being a vet takes too long. Her earliest childhood memory is drinking a can of Coke and the bubbles going up her nose and the person she most admires is Lady Gaga.'

The other girls chorus their agreement. I am not going to let them know what just went through my head. Because I am here now and I have got to make the best of it. It is Gemma's turn to do the introductions.

'This is Jess,' she says, no hand gestures and looking down at the table. 'She's on this course because hairdressing was full. Her earliest childhood memory is of a boy trying to suffocate her under a mattress at nursery and the person she most admires is Cheryl Cole.' The chorus of agreement is louder this time. I smile and praise them for their efforts. And try hard not to wonder what the postgraduates will be discussing at Bradford University.

★

Other people's children emerge from school at the end of the day looking as immaculate as when they arrived in the morning. Maya flies out of the front door with her hair flailing around her (somewhere in that building there must be a secret stash of her 'lost' scrunchies), socks down at her ankles, cardigan buttoned up the wrong way and with a general air of dishevelment about her.

'Mummy,' she screams, at once igniting the love and, in equal measure, the guilt that I don't get to do the school runs as often as I would like to.

'Hello, gorgeous,' I say, sweeping her up in my arms.

'We did a sausage roll in PE and Mrs Hinchcliffe gave me a sticker for knowing my numbers and Jake pulled my hair so he's not coming to my party.'

I nod, deciding not to come down too hard on the quest for retribution. 'Well, let's wait and see, it's a long time till your birthday and Jake might have learnt not to do that by then.'

She pulls a face, one which indicates that Jake will not be getting an invitation, not for her next party or any year after that.

I am going to tell her today. I've decided. Perhaps because I had such a disheartening morning at college that I need a lift. Is that wrong? Probably. But I won't be able to keep it from her for much longer anyway. There is a new bed to be delivered, equipment to be installed. The social worker at the hospital is hopeful it will all be ready by the end of the month.

And once Maya knows, there will be no going back.

And everyone who has been trying to talk me out of it will understand that. I'm bursting to tell her straight away but I want to wait until we get home. For it to be just the two of us and to have the chance to explain things properly to her.

She negotiates the school steps like an old pro now, after just a week. Already wanting to do it all by herself, without any help from me. We cross the road, Maya chattering to me all the way. It is the fag end of summer in the valley. Already the lush greenness seems to be fading. The odd leaf has a distinct yellow tinge. It will not be long before the familiar autumn palette is daubed across the hills. And I am so thrilled that Adam is going to be back home in the valley where he loves to see it. Yet at the same time the ache that he will only be a spectator, no longer a part of the landscape, will not go away.

Maya yanks off her school shoes and runs through to the kitchen to see Roddy and Rita. She is still usually hyper at this point. It is round about four o'clock that she visibly sags, the long school days have been a shock to her system. She won't dip this afternoon, though. Not once I tell her.

'Evie in my class says rats are dirty and they live in sewers.'

'Some of them do but not yours. Roddy and Rita are pet rats, they're different. They're cleaner than you are most of the time.' Maya giggles as I tickle her under the arms. It's now. The moment is now.

'I've got a surprise for you, love.'

'Are Roddy and Rita going to have rat babies?'

'No.' I smile, deciding to leave the 'two boy rats can't

have babies' conversation to another day. 'It's way better than that. Daddy's coming home soon.' The squeal which emanates from her mouth is enough to send Roddy and Rita scurrying into the nearest tube.

'Really?' she asks, throwing her arms around my neck. 'Is he really coming home?'

'Yes, love. He is. Not for a couple of weeks yet but he should be home by the end of the month.'

'Will he be better by then?'

'No, sweetie. He won't be better. Daddy will be exactly the same but we're going to look after him at home.'

'But how will he get here? He can't move.'

'An ambulance is going to bring him home. He'll be on a special trolley.'

'And where will you put him?'

I try to hide my irritation that she makes him sound like a new piece of furniture.

'We're going to have a special bed for him in the lounge.'

'Ohhh, I want him to go in the kitchen with Roddy and Rita.'

'There's not room there, love. He'll be fine in the lounge.'

'He'll be able to watch CBeebies with me.'

'Yes, he will.'

'But he still won't be able to read me bedtime stories, will he?'

'No, love. He can listen to them with you, though. And you'll be able to talk to him as much as you like. He loves it when you talk to him.'

Maya looks up at me suspiciously. 'How do you know?'

'Because I know how much he loves you.'

Maya smiles and hugs me. She hugs me for a long time. I can almost hear the cogs going around in her head as she works out all the implications.

'Where will you sleep?'

'I'll be downstairs on the sofa next to Daddy on Fridays and Saturdays. We're going to have people come in and sit with Daddy during the night the rest of the week, so I'll be sleeping in my bedroom as normal.'

'What people? Do I know them?'

'No, love. People from a charity. They volunteer to help look after people like Daddy.'

'But why do they need to come? I'll look after him.'

I smile at Maya. 'I know, love, but we need to get our sleep at night time, otherwise we'll be too tired.'

'Will you be tired?'

'Maybe a little bit, after the nights I've sat up with Daddy.'

'Why can't you go to sleep?'

'Someone needs to make sure he's OK. Like the nurses in hospital do at the moment.'

'Can I be his nurse one night?'

'You can be his nurse in the daytime, love. Tell him stories and make him laugh. He'll like that.'

'When he gets better, will he come back up to your bedroom? Can I snuggle in between you like I used to?'

I stroke Maya's hair. I love the fact that she still believes. And I don't want to take that belief away right now.

'Of course you can. That will be lovely. I'll look forward to that.'

She nods and pulls away, peering into the rats' cage. 'Look, Mummy. Roddy's doing another poo.'

★

I stand at the side of Adam's bed the next day. The curtains are pulled all the way around. One of the nurses is with me. Michelle, her name is. I think she is Adam's favourite. She's been really good, giving me tips about how to avoid bedsores and chafing. This is different, though. This is the big stuff. The two things I have so far felt unable to do myself. Unable to even watch. But that I now have to learn to do if I am going to look after him at home.

'Right, are you ready?' asks Michelle. I nod. As ready as I'll ever be. Michelle has the suction machine for Adam's tracheostomy next to her.

'This is the mobile one, the same model they'll give you to take home. You need to get everything ready next to you first: saline, sterile gloves, all the bits and pieces, then you give him some oxygen.' She turns to face Adam. 'OK, we're going to start now, Adam. Don't worry, your wife's only watching, I'm not letting her loose on you just yet.'

Michelle turns back to me. 'OK, the next job is to expose the tracheostomy opening.' I dig my fingernails into my palms as I watch. It's a hole in his neck, whatever they call it, and it makes my skin crawl just thinking about it. 'Then you insert the suction catheter four or five inches and apply suction as you withdraw it, for no longer than ten seconds, mind.' I nod, deciding not to ask her what happens if you do it for longer than ten seconds. 'Then you allow him to rest for thirty seconds and repeat the whole process.' I nod again as she shows me the secretions which have come out. Adam needs this done twice a day to keep his throat and lungs clear. Very soon I'm going to be the one doing it. Twice a day for – well, for however long he needs it doing. I watch as she goes through the whole thing again, trying to remember each step in my head. And trying not to gag as she mops him up and puts a fresh drain sponge around the opening. When it is over, Michelle tidies the things away and goes to wash her hands.

'I hope it doesn't hurt you,' I say to Adam. 'They tell me it doesn't but, well, I wouldn't fancy it. I'll try to be really careful, I promise.'

Michelle returns. 'Are you sure you want to carry on?' she asks. I nod and turn to Adam.

'I hope you don't mind me watching, love. I've got to learn to do it, you see. And I warn you now that Maya wants to watch me do it when you come home. Her poo obsession hasn't gone away.'

Michelle carefully turns Adam on to his side so he is facing away from us. She pulls down his pyjama bottoms and goes through the process. It's quite straightforward actually. Though it makes for decidedly uncomfortable viewing.

'And that's it,' Michelle says. 'You now know how to manually evacuate a bowel.' I nod. Although I don't suppose I'll be putting it on my CV. 'Night then, Adam,' she says. 'I'll leave you with your lovely wife. You're in very good hands.'

I smile and thank her before she walks off.

'Well,' I say, sitting down next to Adam. 'You always said you didn't want any secrets between us.' I squeeze his hand, hoping that, somehow, he's managing to see a funny side to this.

246

I don't stay for long. Maya was still hyper about Adam coming home when I left and I want to get back in case she's been playing Mum and Dad up. I am almost at the end of the corridor when I see Steve walking towards me.

'Hi,' I say. 'I didn't think this was your night.'

'It's not,' he says. 'I've been working late and I just thought I'd pop in on the way home. Is everything OK? You look a bit pale.'

'I've been learning how to suction his tracheostomy and, erm, other stuff you don't want to hear about.'

'That must have been tough.'

'Yeah. But I guess I'd better get used to it.' Neither of us says anything for a moment.

'Look, about what I said. I didn't mean to have a go. I worry about you, that's all. Worry you're taking on too much.'

'It's OK. I'll be fine. Adam will be happier at home. And Maya's thrilled about it.'

Steve nods slowly. 'You've told her then.'

'Yeah, this afternoon. She can barely contain herself.'

'Just remember that if it does prove too much you can always change your mind. No one will think badly of you for doing that.'

'Like I said, I'll be fine.' Silence again. 'You still think I'm doing the wrong thing, don't you?'

'Yeah. But I know I can't change your mind now you've told Adam and Maya. So I guess all I can do is help in any way I can.'

'Thank you.'

Steve looks straight at me. His gaze dark and intense.

'He's so lucky to have you, Mel.' I feel his eyes on my face. I find myself unexpectedly flushed. Which is ridiculous. This is Steve. My husband's best friend. My best friend's husband. He is just saying. Being nice.

'No. I'm so lucky to have him.' I smile. A small, uncertain smile. And walk off quickly along the corridor.

PART THREE

Twenty-two

Friday, 24 September 2010

The first thing I see as they get me out of the ambulance are the colours: yellow, every shade and lots of it, orange and the odd flash of red. It is my valley, these are my hills. They live. They breathe. And for the first time in ages I feel alive too. The sterile, colourless environment of hospital is labelled 'past' and inserted into a filing cabinet in my mind.

So many times I thought I would never see my home again, never see this glorious backdrop, Mel and Maya's smiling faces; here, where they belong.

'He's here. Daddy's home.' Maya's voice sends waves of emotion crashing against the rocks which barricade me inside my body. For a second I think they will do it, batter down the defences and find a way through. Nobody reacts, though. Clearly nothing is going on outwardly. Joan, Tom and Louise are standing on the front steps smiling awkwardly at me. Maya is bouncing around in front of them.

'Just give Daddy some space, sweetheart,' says Mel, who was with me in the ambulance. 'Let them get him safely inside.'

'I want him to see the banner,' says Maya. 'Let him see my banner.'

Mel asks the ambulance men to stop a minute and turn me around slightly. I see it, written in purple paint on what looks suspiciously like a pillowcase. 'Welcome Home Daddy'. I love that she did it and hate that I can't say thank you.

The ambulance men pick me up again and carry me towards the house. The picture I see jolts with each step they take. It is like watching some badly edited amateur video footage of my homecoming. Mel goes on ahead and pulls the door open wide. I didn't think about it when we bought the house, how useful it would be to have a huge front door like that should I ever be brought home from hospital in a vegetative state. They carry me over the threshold, just as I carried Mel once. Well, not on a stretcher, obviously, but you know what I mean. I can only be on the receiving end now of any lifting. I can only be done to. But I am home. I am where I want to be. And today, I am happy.

There is a lot of moving, adjusting and fussing as they put me on the bed. Joan is the one doing most of the fussing. It is only when I am finally settled in what is apparently 'my place' that I notice the colour of the walls. Magnolia. They are fucking magnolia – well, a variation on the shade, perhaps. We used to have terracotta walls in here. I liked them. I painted them myself. If I'd wanted to look at magnolia I could have stayed in hospital. I can't believe Mel did this without telling me. Maybe it wasn't Mel. Maybe it was Tom or Steve even. Mel said he's been doing odd jobs around the house. Come to think of it, where the hell is Steve? I would have thought my homecoming would have featured on his social calendar. There again, I'm not exactly sure what time it is. Maya and Louise are here so school must have finished but it's light so perhaps it's still in work hours. I guess you don't get compassionate leave for your best mate coming home from hospital. Not in IT, anyway.

The ambulance men are going now. I feel I should give them a tip though I don't know how. Or what the going rate is for safely delivering a vegetable home, for that matter. The room is decorated with balloons and another welcome home banner. I can see crisps and nibbles on the coffee table. I feel like a bit of a party pooper, lying here saying nothing. I appreciate their efforts though.

'Well, that went more smoothly than I expected,' says Joan, as if I was a grand piano which had surprisingly survived the move intact. I suppose I should give thanks that she hasn't sung 'All Things Bright and Beautiful' to me today. Although I'm aware that might start up again now I am home.

'Can we put the Twiglets down the feeding tube in Daddy's tummy?' asks Maya. Joan looks horrified but Mel simply smiles.

'I'm afraid not, love. He's not allowed party food.'

'Not even ice cream?'

'Nope.'

'I'm glad I don't have to be fed through a tube,' says Maya. Mel shakes her head. She looks like she doesn't know whether to laugh or cry.

'Oooh, I nearly forgot, I brought something for him,' says Joan, delving into a carrier bag on the floor. I can't quite see what it is she produces, only hear Mel's strained reaction.

'Right, thanks, it's, er, not really his scene but we'll give it a go.' A couple of moments later an unfamiliar song comes on the stereo.

Joan walks across to the foot of my bed. 'It's "Welcome Home" by Peters and Lee,' she says. 'I dug it out especially for the occasion. He was blind, you know, Lennie Peters. It didn't hold him back, mind. He had a lovely blonde wife. Not that he could see her, of course.'

Out of the corner of my eye I catch Mel looking down, trying not to laugh. And inside I am laughing too. Pissing myself laughing.

'Can I show him now? Can I? Please.'

'Maya, stop your mythering,' says Tom.

'It's all right,' says Mel. 'She's waited a long time for this. Come on, Maya. We'll go and get them now.'

They return a few minutes later. Maya is carrying something wriggling in her hands. Mel whispers into her ear and she steps forward to the end of my bed.

'Daddy, I'd like you to meet Roddy and Rita.' She opens her hands to reveal a small black rat and a larger white one. They are surprisingly attractive — for rats, that is.

'Can I put them on the bed?'

'Better not, love. They might start nibbling Daddy's tubes.'

'Can he stroke them, then?'

'Yeah, we can do that. Pass one of them to me.'

Maya hands her Roddy. Mel brings him over, takes my hand and moves it slowly over the rat's fur. It is smooth and sleek. At least in my head it is. Maya smiles. Mel is smiling too. Smiling like I haven't seen her smile for a long time.

Eventually, Joan, Tom and Louise go home. There is no sign of Steve. No one's mentioned him all evening. Maybe tomorrow.

Maya disappears upstairs with Mel and comes down a short time later in her butterfly pyjamas. Jeez, I never would have thought that a pair of pyjamas could have such an emotional pull. They are home. They are everything I've missed. Every silly little thing that I haven't been a part of for the past seven months.

Maya is beaming at me from the end of my bed. 'You can listen to my bedtime story, Daddy,' she says. She holds the book up for me to see. It's *Tell Me Something Happy Before I Go To Sleep*. It's her favourite book. It's my favourite too. And always will be from now on. Mel sits her up on the bed next to me and she snuggles into my side. My arms ache with trying to reach out to hold her. I can see exactly where I want them to be but I simply can't get them there. We listen in enraptured silence. Both of us. Until Willa the rabbit has fallen fast asleep.

'I want to sleep on Daddy's bed,' says Maya.

'I know, love. It's been a big day for all of us but you both need your rest now and we can't have you getting tangled up in any of Daddy's tubes in the night, can we?' Maya appears to be on the verge of tears. 'I tell you what you can do though, love. You can give Daddy a goodnight kiss.'

Maya's face brightens instantly. She leans over and gives

me a great big sloppy kiss on the cheek. I feel her. I swear I feel her lips. I send one back through the air to her. Hoping she'll catch it somehow.

'Shall I tell you something happy before you go to sleep?' asks Mel. Maya nods. 'When you wake up in the morning, Daddy will still be here.' Maya grins.

'Night, night, Daddy,' she says.

Mel takes her upstairs. She isn't gone long. When she does come back into the lounge, she looks relieved to see me, as if she feared I might have been spirited back to hospital while she was gone.

'The washing-up can wait,' she says. 'I've got company tonight.'

She walks over to the hi-fi and puts a CD on. 'Don't worry. Peters and Lee went home with my mum.' James Brown's rich, deep voice fills the air. I love that guy, even if he does make me dance like an ape, as Mel says. She sits down on the edge of the bed, holding my hand.

'I can't tell you what this means to me, to have you back here with us. I hope you're as happy as I think you are. Please don't worry about anything. It'll take a bit of getting used to but we'll be fine. And don't ever think for even a second that you're a burden or anything stupid like that. I am so, so glad I did this. So glad I've got you back.'

She folds her body down on to mine. I can feel her heart beating. Or maybe it is mine. It doesn't really matter whose it is, though. What matters is that we are here together. She lies there for a long time. Until 'It's a Man's World' has finished. It was the song we had our first dance to at our wedding (we'd toyed with 'When a Man Loves a Woman' but Mel wasn't keen because of what happened to Meg Ryan and Andy Garcia in the film). It seems a long time ago now. A different lifetime, in fact. 'I'm going to get you ready for bed now so you can get some sleep,' she says. 'I shall be on the sofa next to you. Don't worry, I shan't drop off. I won't even close my eyes. I'm going to be watching over you all night. And don't worry about me because I can tell you I'd be doing exactly the same thing even if I didn't need to. There's no way I'm going to stop looking at you tonight.'

She smiles and goes to the other end of the lounge to bring the suction machine over. And I know that James Brown is right. I would be nothing, nothing without her.

'The house has gone through today. It's sold.'

Mel sat down beside me. Put her arm around me. 'How do you feel?' she asked.

'Weird. Like my youth is officially over. My dad's dead, my mother may as well be, the family house is sold. I'm all that's left.'

'You're not on your own, though.'

'I know,' I said, rubbing her arm as she nuzzled into me. I'd never felt on my own. Not since I'd been with Mel. But I did have a strong sense that my roots had gone. The ties had been cut and I was drifting. It was up to me to decide whether I wanted to float off somewhere or put down new ones. 'I know what I want to do with the money,' I said.

'Don't tell me, trek through the Amazonian jungle, go white-water rafting in New Zealand, bungee jump from Victoria Falls.'

'No. I want to buy a house with you. Here. Well, not here exactly but in the Calder Valley.' We were living in a rented flat in

Leeds at the time. It wasn't home, though, and it never would be.

'Are you sure?' asked Mel. 'I mean, it's not just because of the whole thing of losing your dad.'

'No. I've never been more sure of anything in my life.'

A smile crept over Mel's face. She looked at me, her eyes moist and dark.

'Good,' she said. 'Because that's what I want too.'

'You know everyone's going to say we're too young. They're going to think we're crazy.'

'I don't care. It's what we both want. It'll be fantastic. Our own home. A proper home.' She was positively fizzing with excitement. I loved how she did that. It made her seem about fifteen again.

'Good. That's sorted,' I said with a smile. 'We'd better start looking then.'

We got to the house before the removal van. It wasn't a proper removal van, just a bloke and his transit someone at work had recommended. Which was fine. It was all we needed. We didn't have much stuff. I pulled up outside and turned to look at Mel. She was biting her bottom lip.

'Are you OK?'

'I can't believe it's really ours.'

'Well, it is.' I got the key out of my pocket and jangled it in front of her nose. She grabbed it from me.

'Come on,' she said. 'Let's go and play at being grown-ups.' We got out of the car and stood on the pavement, staring up at the large stone building in front of us. 'I don't remember it having this many windows,' said Mel.

'Shit. Have I bought the wrong one?'

Mel laughed and jokingly boxed my ears. 'Of course you

haven't. I love it. I want to live here forever. I want you to chase me up the stairs when we're eighty-two.'

'No chance. Not unless you get me a stairlift.' She laughed again as I held her, my arms wrapped tight around the most precious thing in the world. I gazed up at the trees on the hillside behind the house. The million shades of green. This place had lungs. It breathed. It was alive. I bent down and scooped Mel up in my arms.

'Hey, what are you doing?' she screamed.

'I want to do this properly. I'm carrying you over the threshold.'

'I thought that was when you got married.'

'Who cares? I'm doing it anyway.' I carried her up the steps, both of us laughing. I let her put the key in the door and push it open.

'Mel Summerskill, this is your new home.'

She whooped in delight. And I kissed her. Long and hard. I'd dropped anchor. The sea was calm and still again. No more drifting. I had my own family now.

Twenty-three

MEL

'Hi, Happy Birthday,' says Louise. I do my best to smile as I let her into the hall. Happy isn't really the word I'd use. It's an odd kind of birthday and to be honest I'm all over the place. The thrill of having Adam home is still there but now it is tempered with the reality of what our lives have become. It is the first time in twenty years he hasn't sent me a birthday card. Obviously I knew he wouldn't and I was actually rather relieved that my mother hadn't had the bright idea of sending one on his behalf (or if she had, she hadn't acted on it). But the inescapable fact is that there is a gap on the mantelpiece where Adam's card should be. I couldn't bring myself to put another one in the space; it would have been like letting someone sit in a loved one's favourite chair hours after they had died. Only the whole point is Adam hasn't died. He's at home with me. He just can't do cards any more.

'This is from . . .' Louise stops herself just in time. 'From me.'

'Thank you,' I say, squeezing her shoulder as I hug her. Her face is pale and drawn. She's still not finding it any easier. This notion Steve has that letting her get used to being on her own will help to soften the blow is not going to be borne out.

I open the present. It's a voucher for an aromatherapy massage session in Hebden Bridge.

'Wow, thank you. What a lovely idea.'

'Any weekend you want to use it I'll look after Adam and Maya for you. Just let me know when you're ready.'

'Thanks. I will. It'll probably be a while yet. Just going out tonight's a big deal and it's only over the road.'

'Are you sure you're up for it? We can stay here if you'd rather.'

'No. Mum's here, Adam's settled and Maya's asleep. If I don't go now I might never do.'

Louise nods and links her arm through mine.

'Come on,' she says. 'We'll do this together.'

It is drizzling outside. The sort of rain that gets you wet without you even noticing. I put my brolly up and we huddle under it together.

'So how's it going?' asks Louise as we set off down the road.

'OK, I guess. Maya loves having him home. We both do. I just haven't been able to stop worrying about him the whole time. Especially at work. I keep thinking what if something happens? What if I'm not there?'

'But something could have happened to him in hospital.'

'Yeah, but it didn't, did it? And if anything happened here, it would be my fault. I'm the one who insisted on bringing him home. I sometimes worry that was a selfish thing to do.'

Louise snorts a laugh. 'Mel, I can't think of anything less selfish. You did it because you thought it was best for him and for Maya.'

'I know. But I wanted him home too. I wanted my husband back. I wanted in some ridiculously small way to feel like part of a couple again.'

Louise says nothing. I glance across. I can see she is trying very hard not to cry. I realise that the four months is up. And that he may have told her.

'Are you OK?'

'I'm sorry,' says Louise. 'I didn't want to spoil your birthday by telling you straight away.'

'Telling me what?'

'Steve's asked for a divorce.'

'Oh, Louise. I am sorry.' We stand there under the umbrella. Me with one arm around her. Louise's body crumpled against mine, the rain pattering down around us. I feel bad for not warning her this was coming. I tried in subtle ways to suggest Steve seemed to be getting on with his own life but that is not the same. I feel bad about the fact that Steve told me in the first place. I tell myself I was simply a surrogate Adam but I am not so sure. I am not sure of anything at the moment.

'Sorry,' says Louise with a sniff. 'This was supposed to be your birthday celebration.'

'Don't be daft. Look, if you don't want to go to the pub, I'd understand.'

'No,' she says. 'It's OK. I can't stay indoors and mope around forever, can I? Besides, it's your birthday.'

'If you're sure.'

'Yeah. I am.'

It is quiet inside the Robin Hood. A few old boys standing at the bar. Some younger couples dotted around the pub. No one I know. Although that doesn't mean they don't know me. I am the woman whose husband is in a vegetative state in her living room. It's a small village. People talk. And although there are always plenty of sympathetic smiles, I still resent the fact that Adam is gossip fodder for the locals.

Louise insists on getting the drinks. I sit down at a table in the corner. There is an exhibition of landscape paintings on by a local artist. Amanda someone, I can't quite make out her surname. It's good stuff. Some of the places are familiar, would be even more familiar to Adam, no doubt. I start imagining him in the pictures; a small figure running across the hills. Running, always running. Never still.

Louise puts the drinks down on the table. They sit there solemnly. Clearly neither of us is in the mood to say cheers.

'When did he tell you?' I ask.

'Yesterday. He came round after work. Did this speech about taking stock of his life, realising he hasn't been a very good husband to me, that he didn't think it would be fair on me to carry on as before. And he didn't think he could change.'

I nod, glad that Steve had listened to me and that was all he'd said.

'I suppose I knew deep down that it was coming,' Louise continues. 'It's not as if he's made any effort to see me or try to sort things out. I just feel confused and angry that I still don't really know what this is all about. If someone asks me why I'm getting divorced, I'll have to admit I don't know. I feel so bloody stupid.'

'It's not your fault if he won't talk to you.'

'It is partly. For whatever reason I'm not someone he feels he can open up to.'

'You mustn't blame yourself, Louise.'

'Who else can I blame?'

'Steve?'

Louise shakes her head. 'I've tried that. Tried looking at photos of him and calling him a bastard. It doesn't work. I don't think he is a bastard, really. An emotionally inadequate arse maybe but that's all. Deep down I still love him. I'd have had him back like a shot if he'd asked. That's the problem; he's ended this, not me. I don't want a divorce.'

'Did you tell him that?'

'I tried. All he kept saying was that it wouldn't work. That I deserved better than him.'

'So what are you going to do?'

'What can I do? He's obviously made up his mind. It's over.'

'I'm so sorry.'

'It's not your fault.'

'I still think that if Adam hadn't had the accident, none of this would have happened.'

'Maybe. Maybe it just wouldn't have happened so soon. Things weren't exactly great between us before, were they? It probably just hurried things along. God, sorry. Listen to me going on. This was supposed to be your birthday celebration.'

'It's OK. I don't feel much like celebrating anyway. At least now we can be glum together.'

Louise smiles. 'When the Queen talked about her *annus horribilis*, she didn't have any idea, did she?'

'No. Not a bloody clue.'

'So, let's think about different ways in which very young children learn. Who can start me off?' I am trying. I am really trying to make this work even though it does feel rather like wading through treacle at times.

'The telly,' says Jess. 'They learn stuff when they watch telly. My niece Destiny can count to three in Spanish because of watching *Dora the Explorer*.'

'Yes, it's great that children can pick different languages up from TV programmes, although we're particularly talking about children under a year old here, remember.'

'Yeah, I know. Destiny's been watching telly since she was born. She used to have one bottle when *The Jeremy Kyle Show* was on, one with *Loose Women* and another with *The Weakest Link*. That's how my sister remembered when she needed feeding.' A couple of girls nod, as if mentally noting this as a useful baby-rearing tip. It's not their fault, of course. They don't know anything different. I am well aware that the parental role models they have at home aren't exactly textbook ones.

'Right, well, let's get away from television,' I say. 'Let's think about other ways young children learn.'

'You can take their crisps away,' says Becky. 'Or threaten to give them milk instead of Coke. That would make them learn not to do stuff.' I groan inwardly, it's getting harder and harder to find something positive to say about their suggestions. And sometimes I just have to pull them up on them.

'Thank you for sharing that with us but remember they shouldn't really be having Coke or crisps at that age. Now Becky was thinking about how we might teach children not to do something, what I'm really after is how children learn to do things.'

'By watching you,' says Cara. 'They learn to do things by watching and copying you.'

I smile and nod enthusiastically, relieved to get the first good answer of the morning. I like Cara. She said the person she most admired was Angelina Jolie – but for being a UNICEF ambassador rather than being gorgeous to look at and married to Brad Pitt.

'Excellent, Cara. Observation is one of the key ways in which young children learn. It's one of the reasons why it's so important we eat with young children. The social element of mealtimes is vital if they are to learn basic skills.'

'Or they could watch babies eating on telly,' says Jess. 'Like in adverts and stuff.'

I do my best to smile at her. Aware of the uphill struggle I am facing here.

It is only as I'm packing away at the end of the lesson that I realise Cara is still sitting there, her head in one of the course textbooks.

'It's good to see you so keen, Cara, but you are free to go, you know.'

She looks up, appearing rather alarmed. 'If it's all right, miss, I'd rather stay here for a bit.'

'Sure. You're welcome. I know sometimes it's hard to find the time or a quiet place at home.'

'Me mam's usually pissed when I get home. I have to sort out tea and stuff. Make sure me brothers get to bed at a decent time.'

I nod, understanding now why she seems older than the other girls.

'I take it your dad's not around?'

'Nah, he did a bunk years ago. That's when me mam started drinking.'

'Does she get help from anyone? Like a social worker.'

'Nah. She don't want anyone sticking their noses in. I make sure me brothers always have clean clothes for school and that they get there on time. That way we don't get bothered by anyone.'

'They're lucky to have a big sister like you, aren't they?' I realise as soon as I say it that I probably sound old and patronising.

Cara shrugs. 'Someone's got to do it. It's not me mam's fault. She's had a lot of crap to deal with. It's not easy when you're left on your own.'

I nod slowly. 'I've got to dash to pick my little girl up from nursery but you stay here as long as you like.'

'OK, miss.'

I turn to walk out of the door and stop. 'Any time you need to talk, Cara, I'm here, OK?'

She nods and gets back to the book.

I hear the knock on the door as I come downstairs from putting Maya to bed. Although it's a Thursday, I hadn't been expecting Steve. He didn't come last week. Texted me to say something had come up at work (although I couldn't help wondering if the real reason had more to do with Adam being home). Added to which, I didn't think he'd show his face so soon after asking Louise for the divorce.

'Hi,' he says when I open the door. 'I wasn't sure if you'd still want me to come.' He looks like an awkward teenager, wondering if he's been ostracised for dumping his girlfriend.

'Come in,' I say. 'Tempted as I am, I'm not actually going to slam the door in your face.'

'Louise told you then.'

'Yeah, last night.'

'How did she seem?'

'Ecstatic really. Reminded me of that photo of Nicole Kidman when she got divorced from Tom Cruise.'

'I thought it was only Adam who did sarcasm.'

'That one was on his behalf.'

Steve steps into the hall. He looks around awkwardly.

'Adam's in the lounge,' I say. 'I haven't told him yet. Maybe you'd better come into the kitchen.' He follows me through. The silence comes with him.

'She was OK, wasn't she?' Steve says eventually.

'She'll get through it, if that's what you mean. She's got a close family. A lot of good friends.'

'You think I'm a complete bastard, don't you?'

'Emotionally inadequate arse was the phrase Louise used, but there again she's nicer than me.'

Steve nods. Walks over to the Rayburn to warm himself.

'You wouldn't want someone to be with you if they didn't really love you, would you?'

'Probably not. And I do appreciate the fact that you didn't tell her that. I still don't understand why you don't love her, though. She's the nicest person I know.'

'Like I said, it's complicated. And if it's any consolation, I hate myself for hurting her. But I think in the long run she'll be better off without me.'

'I hope you're right.' I fill the kettle and flick it on.

'Anyway, how are you?' asks Steve. 'You look tired.'

'Thanks.'

'I'm concerned about you, Mel.'

'Well, you don't need to be. I'm very happy to have him home.'

'Are you sitting up with him at nights?'

'Only Fridays and Saturdays. We have a sitter who comes the other nights.'

'You can't keep that up forever. You'll do yourself in.'

'Maybe eventually I'll feel confident enough to sleep on the sofa. Not now though. It's too soon.'

Steve nods and thanks me for the coffee as I hand it to him. 'And how's the new job going?' he asks.

'It's fine.'

'You hate it, don't you?'

'It's just going to take some getting used to, that's all. I'm working with students at a very different level from the ones I'm used to. It has the potential to be very rewarding though. I can see that already.'

'You're turning into one of those people who get nominated for Britain's unsung hero awards.'

I smile before I can stop myself. 'You'd better vote for me, then. I might win a few hundred quid.'

'Look, if money's tight—'

'I was joking, Steve. We're fine for now. The uni are paying me until the end of my notice, which is very good of them really. And we're lucky we've only got a small mortgage.'

'Well, as long as you know that if you ever need anything, you only have to ask.'

'Thanks,' I say. 'I appreciate that.'

'So what needs doing tonight?' asks Steve.

I wrack my brain to try to think of something. Nothing obvious springs to mind.

'There is one thing,' I reply. 'It doesn't require a toolbox, though.'

'What?'

'I'd like you to tell Adam. About the divorce, I mean. He's got to know sometime and I think it would be better coming from you. Maybe you can explain it to him in a way he'll understand.'

Steve takes a sip of his coffee which can't possibly be at drinking temperature yet, even with his asbestos lips.

'I'd rather you find me a leaky tap, to be honest.'

'He has a right to know what's going on, Steve. I hate keeping things from him. I don't want to treat him like a child.'

'OK. I'll do my best. When's the sitter coming?'

'Around eleven.'

'Why don't you get an early night. I'll stay with him until then.'

'Are you sure?'

'Yeah. Looks like you could do with it.'

I nod. I'm finding it hard to equate this Steve with the one Louise talks about.

'I'll need to suction him first. Get him ready for night time. It only takes a few minutes. I'll tell him you'll be in when I'm done.'

'OK.'

I go in to Adam and close the door behind me.

'Sorry, love,' I say, stroking his head. 'It's that time again.' I gather all the bits around me. I feel like an old pro at this now. I don't even have to use the checklist any more. The community nurse says I'm a natural. Maybe it's because I'm his wife.

When I am done I perch on the edge of the bed. 'Hope that wasn't too bad. I'm going to grab an early night, love. The sitter will be here later. Steve's just arrived, he's going to sit with you until then. He's got something to tell you about him and Louise. It's not good, I'm afraid, and I don't really understand it myself but maybe it's a bloke thing. Don't worry, Louise is OK. I'm looking after her. And she'll be round at the weekend to see you.' I kiss him on the forehead. 'Night, love.'

I go back through to the kitchen where Steve is waiting. He has something in his hand.

'These are for you,' he says, stepping forward to kiss me on the cheek as he hands me a neatly wrapped present and an envelope. 'Happy Birthday for yesterday.'

I stare at him. Men don't do birthdays of women who are not their wife, girlfriend or mother. I know that for a fact. I don't know what to say. I glance awkwardly up at Steve.

'I didn't give them to you earlier because I was worried you'd throw them back in my face,' he says.

'I wouldn't have done that. Not without opening the present first, at any rate.'

Steve smiles a rather hesitant smile. I open the envelope first. The card is tasteful and appropriate. I guess he, like everyone else, decided not to risk humour this year. I peel off the Sellotape at one end of the silver wrapping paper and slide out a square, flat box. I open the lid. Inside is a silver hoop necklace with a black onyx pendant hanging from it. It's beautiful. I don't know what to say. Or whether to be delighted or embarrassed.

'Thank you. I really didn't expect anything like this.'

'I got it from Element in Hebden. I remembered Louise saying you liked their stuff. I've still got the receipt if you want to exchange it.'

'No. No, it's lovely. Really. But you shouldn't have.'

'I don't want you to think I was trying to . . . What I mean is, Adam would have got you something special. I know it's not from Adam but I did want it to be special.'

'It is. Thank you.' I close the lid and look down at the box. Telling myself he is only trying to do the right thing by Adam. Trying to look after me in a husband's best mate kind of way.

'Anyway, I'll, er, go and see Adam. You get to bed.'

'OK. Thanks. Night then.'

'Night, Mel. See you next week.'

I go upstairs slowly, holding on to the rail. When I get to my bedroom, our bedroom, I put the box in my chest of drawers. Out of sight and out of mind.

Twenty-four

Steve walks into the room. He looks about as uncomfortable as I've ever seen him. I've been trying to work out what's happened from what Mel said. I think he's been caught cheating on Louise. In which case he is an even bigger plonker than I suspected.

'Hello, mate,' he says. 'Good to see you back home.' He pulls up a chair. Runs his fingers through his hair. Fiddles with the strap on his watch.

'Mel wants me to tell you what's been going on. I didn't say anything before because, well, I didn't really want to give you my shit to deal with when you've got enough of your own.'

He pauses again, looks around the room for a second. Clearly he is finding this hard.

'The thing is, Louise and I haven't been living together for the past four months. I asked her for a trial separation. And now I've just asked her for a divorce.'

Fucking hell. What a bastard. What on earth is he playing at? He must be shagging someone else. But who? I want to ask a hundred different questions all at once. My mouth feels as if it's opening and closing like a goldfish but no sound comes out.

'I know what you're thinking and if it's any consolation I feel a complete bastard for doing this to Louise but I've been living a lie all these years and it's not fair to her to carry on like this. I don't love her, you see, Not the way I—' he hesitates for a second before carrying on. 'Not the way I should.'

Jeez, I've now turned into a mobile Relate bureau. If I lie here much longer I'll find out that there isn't a happy marriage left in the country. I blame Martin Bashir and Princess Di. They started all this touchy, feely, dissecting your marriage and pouring your heart out on TV stuff and look where it's ended up.

'Mel's tried to get me to change my mind, told me that you'd have given me a right mouthful if you were . . . you know, able to. But there's no going back, I'm afraid. I've got myself a little flat in Rishworth. I guess we might have to sell the house, Louise won't be able to afford it on her wages alone.'

Sod the domestic arrangements. I want to know why he's done this. The real reason, not the lame ones he's trotted out so far. There's someone else. I know there is. Why else would he do it?

He puts his head in his hands for a moment then looks up at the ceiling. The one good thing about not being able to say anything is that sometimes your silence encourages people to say more.

'Maybe I will regret it one day, if I end up as some sad old git living on my own. But when situations change, sometimes you owe it to yourself to take a chance. I've put other people's feelings before my own for half of my life.

I'm not going to do it any longer. I'm sorry, OK? About what happened to you, I mean. And what I'm about to do.'

What the hell is he talking about? I don't understand. He's not making any sense at all. What's this got to do with me? Apart from the fact that he's my best mate, that is. My head is hurting with thinking about it. I'm not going to get any more out of him, though. Not tonight. He's clammed up now. He's said his piece. I'll have to wait until next time. This is worse than *EastEnders*. Actually, no. Nothing's worse than *EastEnders*.

'If you can just do this room before you go,' says Mel, coming into the lounge the next morning, followed by a middle-aged woman brandishing a Dyson. They approach the end of my bed. Mel smiles down at me. 'Adam, this is Denise, our brilliant cleaner and my lifesaver. Denise, this is Adam.'

'Hello, love,' says Denise. 'Blimey, you've got yourself in a right pickle, haven't you?' The breath of fresh air hits me right between the eyes. Even Mel laughs. The very thought of someone who is not going to tiptoe around making politically correct statements and avoiding any mention of the fact that I am in a vegetative state fills my heart with joy.

'My old man's a lazy sod but even he'd be itching to get out of bed after five months.'

I am bent double inside. She is an ordinary-looking woman. I don't mean that nastily, she just is. Ordinary mousey-coloured hair, ordinary clothes, ordinary slightly bulbous, slightly red nose. But if I could, I would leap out of bed and dance around the room with this wonderfully ordinary woman.

'Don't mind me, love,' says Denise, winking at me. 'I'll whiz through here with me vac and then leave you in peace.'

'Thanks, Denise. I'd better be getting back to the gas man,' says Mel. 'See how he's getting on with the service.'

'Tell him to pull his bloody trousers up,' says Denise. 'When you've seen one crack, you've seen them all.'

Mel smiles at Denise, nods at me, as if she knows what I am thinking and leaves the room.

'If I do come back as a man, God forbid,' Denise continues when we are alone, 'the first thing I'll do is go out and get meself a bloody belt.' She turns the Dyson on and starts strutting around the room, singing above the noise. I am reminded of Freddie Mercury in the video of 'I Want to Break Free'. Noise, wonderful loud, clamorous noise. So welcome after the silence of the night. The loneliness of my thoughts. Everything Steve said going round and round in my head. And all the while watched over by a kindly looking lady from the volunteer charity who sits and smiles. Can't they bring a book? Are they not allowed to knit? I wish she would knit. I think the hypnotic clicking of needles might be just what I need to get myself to sleep. And it always gets me to thinking how lonely she must be. Oh, I know I should think that she's doing it out of the kindness of her heart and I am grateful, enormously grateful that she is helping Mel out like this. But what a terribly lonely existence she must lead if she volunteers to watch people sleep at night. Mel used to joke about it when we were teenagers. How she steered clear of older boys and purposefully landed someone a few months younger than her so she would spend less time being one of those sad old widows who continually rearrange the flowers in the front window so they can watch the world go by. It was funny at the time. It's not so funny now of course. Right now I bet she wishes she fell for someone else entirely. She has a very long time stretching in front of her in which to rearrange flowers.

The vacuuming stops.

'Right, love. I'll leave you in peace,' says Denise. 'Though I don't suppose you'll get much today with the gas man here. It's nice to meet you at last, anyway. Your Mel's told me so much about you. It's typical, isn't it? She gets one of the few good ones out there and this happens. She hasn't given up on you, mind. So just make sure you keep fighting. I want to see you out of this bed doing cartwheels across the room next time I come.'

She leaves the room. I want to ask Mel if we can pay Denise to sit with me as well as clean. I think I would like that.

'Sorry, Adam,' says Mel, coming back into the room with a balding, middle-aged man behind her. 'Mr Hodgson needs to drain all the radiators for the service. It shouldn't take long. Just shout if you need anything,' she says to him. 'I'll go and get you that tea you were after.' She disappears, no doubt off to the kitchen to hunt for the sugar. I have never yet met a gas man who doesn't take it. Mr Hodgson stares at me, reaches into his back pocket and gets out his mobile phone. For a second I think he is going to take a photo of me and post it on Facebook in some kind of freaks' gallery. He doesn't, though. He makes a call instead.

'All right, Dan. You'll never guess who I've been left in a room with. A fucking stiff. Well, not quite, I think he's breathing but he may as well be dead. There's no lights on upstairs and nobody's at home. Lying here in this woman's bloody living room, he is, and her acting like it's perfectly normal.'

I want to hit him. And knee him in the balls. What does he know? How dare he come in here and say that. I'm paying his wages, or Mel is, at least. I hate this. It was bad enough in hospital, people gawping as they walked by. But this, in my home. This is too much. I hear footsteps in the hall. Hodgson puts the phone away and immediately crouches down next to the radiator. I am willing Mel to throw the tea in his fucking face. She doesn't, of course. She even smiles as she gives it to him. She's too trusting for her own good sometimes. I bet he's going to rip her off as well. I hate myself for being so pathetic. For not being able to haul myself out of this bloody bed and kick him out of the house. As it is, all I can do is console myself with the fact that while I may be a vegetable, at least my arse isn't hanging out of the top of my trousers.

'That girl over there keeps looking at you,' said Steve. We were at a party, someone's student digs at Bradford uni. The run-up to Christmas 1995. Early hours of the morning. Mel wasn't there. She had a bad cold. Her eyes used to stream when she had a cold. She got sick of people asking her if she was all right. So she'd decided not to bother. Said she was going to get an early night.

'So?'

'Well, what are you? Man or mouse?'

'It may have escaped your notice over the past five years, Steve, but I've got a girlfriend.'

'Yeah. She's not here, though.'

'Right, so that makes it OK, does it?'

'Does if the girl in question looks like that.' I glanced over at her. She was tall with dark hair. Even darker than Mel's. She had a low-cut crop top on, tight-fitting jeans and knee-high boots. The word 'fit' could have been invented for her.

'I see what you see, Steve, but I'm still not interested.'

'Jesus, stop acting as if you're married. You're nineteen, for fuck's sake.'

'Look, if you're so interested, why don't you have a go yourself?'

'I'm not the one she's been eyeing up all night.'

'Well, she's all yours if you want a try.'

'Thanks but I'd rather not. I don't fancy being the "if I can't have him his mate'll do" second choice.'

Steve headed off to the kitchen, presumably to get another bottle. He didn't ask whether I wanted one too. Although, to be honest, we'd both already had too much. Within seconds of him going, the girl headed over to me. Fuck. I'd had it now.

'Hi,' she said. 'I'm Suzanne.'

'Hi. Adam.'

'You're doing media studies, aren't you? I've seen you around. I'm in my second year on the same course.'

'Right, yeah. I knew you looked familiar.' I tried to keep my eyes on her face. She had red lipstick on. It was slightly smudged in one corner. She had a bottle of cider in her hand but she didn't *seem pissed. Unlike me, she seemed to know exactly what she was doing.*

'Has your mate had enough?'

'Oh, yeah. I guess so.' I wasn't used to being hit on by women. The downside of going out with the same girl for five years, I guess. Not that it had ever bothered me before. But I was suddenly aware that I either needed to make a move or an excuse.

'It's a crap party, anyway. I was about to go myself,' she said. I nodded. Although up to then I'd thought it was pretty good. I had a choice now. Stay put or go with her.

'Where d'you live?' I heard myself asking.

'Sherborne Road, couple of streets before Great Horton.'

'I'll walk you home. It's on my way back to the halls.'

'Great. Thanks. I'll get my jacket.' She smiled at me before disappearing upstairs. I had no idea why I'd said that. Other than that it would have been rude not to offer to walk her home. Mel's mum had banged on about the Yorkshire Ripper as soon as Mel got offered the place at Bradford. I thought about going to find Steve to tell him I was leaving but then I thought better of it. It wouldn't be such a bad thing if he came back to find me and Suzanne gone. It would get him off my back, at least.

Suzanne returned wearing a leather jacket. I grabbed my denim jacket from the hall.

'Come on,' she said, smiling at me. 'Let's go.' I followed her out. Aware that people were looking. That they would talk. I still didn't really know why I was doing this but it was too late to back out.

'How you finding the halls?' asked Suzanne as we made our way down the road.

'OK, I guess. Though I think I'll be ready to go into digs by

the summer. It just gets a bit much sometimes. Everyone being on top of each other.'

'I hated it,' she said. 'Couldn't get out quick enough. It's been miles better this year.'

'What are your digs like?' I realised as soon as I said it that it sounded like I was angling for an invite.

'Good, well, compared to some I've seen, they are. I've got my own room on the top floor. And I'm sharing with my two best mates so we have a good laugh.'

I nodded. I had a picture in my head of the three of them eating toast tomorrow morning. Catching up on the gossip of the night before.

'Weren't they at the party?' I asked.

'No, they've both gone back to see their folks this weekend.' She didn't say she had the place to herself but she didn't really have to. We turned down the next road into Sherborne, her heels clicking along the pavement, her breath hanging suggestively in the night air. She stopped outside a gate a few houses along.

'So, you coming in then?' She didn't even try to disguise it by asking if I'd like a coffee. It was said with the confident air of a girl who was not used to being turned down.

'Look,' I started. 'It's not that I don't want to.'

'Don't tell me you're gay because I know you're not.'

'I've got a girlfriend.'

'I see.'

'We've been going out a long time.'

'Right. I won't tell a soul if that's what you're bothered about.' Her dark eyes were boring into me. The smudge of lipstick had gone, she must have reapplied it when she went upstairs. I felt her breath on my cheek, she was standing that close to me. Smelt her perfume seeping into my pores.

'I don't bite, honestly,' she said, smiling. It was hard to know how it happened. I think she leant in to me but I couldn't be sure it wasn't the other way around. A second later we were kissing. Seriously kissing, as if our lives depended on it. She tasted good. Very good. But she was not Mel.

'I'm sorry,' I said as I pulled away.

'What is it?'

'The same thing as before.'

'We haven't got to, you know. Not if you don't want to.'

'I'm really sorry. It's not you. If it's any consolation I've never even kissed another girl before. I've gone too far already. I've got to go now, before it's too late.'

I walked off down the road. Feeling good and bad and full of regrets all at the same time. And not once looking back.

Twenty-five

MEL

Maya's interpretation of the mouse from *The Gruffalo* in her class assembly is nothing if not innovative. She obviously insisted on wearing her Dora the Explorer wellies, hence she is stomping rather than tiptoeing around the school hall. She has a wide grin on her face, mouse ears which are gradually falling off, Hula-Hoops on her fingers (I have no idea why) and is hiccuping loudly. I try to keep the video camera steady, which is difficult as I am laughing so much. I asked for permission to video the parents' assembly so I could show it to Adam later. It won't be the same as being here but it's the next best thing. And Maya will love it; love being able to talk him through what's happening, sing the Gruffalo song at the top of her voice again. And it will feel, in some small way, as if he was part of it.

The hiccups stay for the entire performance but she still manages her two lines. Some of the mums smile at me as we wait outside to collect our children at the end. Genuine smiles, not the usual sympathetic ones.

'Maya was a complete star,' says Megan's mum.

'Thanks,' I say. 'She certainly left her mark.' Some of the other mums are saying what a shame it was their husbands couldn't get off work early to come. I walk away from them at that point before they realise that my husband didn't even get to ask.

'Mrs Taylor, could I have a quiet word?' It is Mrs Hinch-cliffe, gesturing at me from the main entrance.

'Yes, of course.'

'We'll go to the staffroom, it'll be quiet, which is more than I can say for Class One at the moment. I'm very relieved to have left Mrs Smythe in charge.' I nod and follow her across the hall to the staffroom. I wonder if Maya had a real paddy about the wellies. Whether I am going to be told she has to learn a little restraint.

'Please, take a seat,' says Mrs Hinchcliffe, who is looking as stylish as ever in a red and black ensemble.

I perch on the edge of one of the vinyl-covered easy chairs. Mrs Hinchcliffe sits down opposite me. She has one of those serious teacher faces on. And an exercise book and a rolled-up piece of paper in her hands.

'I don't want to worry you but I need to have a word about Maya.'

'Look, I'm sorry if she put up a fight about the wellies. She can be very headstrong.'

'This isn't about wellies, Mrs Taylor. It's about her paintings and drawings.' The tone of her voice makes me feel uncomfortable. I suspect she is not about to tell me I have a budding Rolf Harris on my hands. Mrs Taylor uncurls the rolled-up piece of paper.

'This is Maya's painting from this morning.' She holds it up. A huge dinosaur, presumably a T-rex, dominates the page. And underneath it, lying prostrate on the floor, is what appears to be a man. The whole thing has been painted in black. It doesn't actually have RIP written on it but it may as well. I look up at the ceiling, shutting my eyes and biting my lip.

'I'm sorry,' says Mrs Hinchcliffe. 'I didn't mean to upset you. I just thought you should know.' I haven't actually told anyone at school how Adam was injured but obviously they read the local papers and hear what's happening on the grapevine like everyone else in the village. She wouldn't have been concerned otherwise.

'It's OK. I'm glad you showed me. I had no idea. She's never done anything like this at home.'

'There've been several drawings of her father lying in a bed in her diary. I haven't brought them to your attention before because I knew he was in hospital and they simply appeared to be a portrayal of that. But over the last couple of weeks the drawings have changed somewhat in their nature. The colours are all very dark and the dinosaurs have started making an appearance. You might want to have a look at her diary.'

She hands me the exercise book. I flick through. Practically every page has a picture of Adam lying down on it. Mrs Hinchcliffe has helped her write 'Daddy in hospital' on one of them. But on the last few pages the bed is clearly supposed to be in our house. There is what looks like a TV and a sofa in the room. And on several of them there are also dinosaurs – too big to be her toys, even allowing for the lack of proportion in children's drawings.

'Does she talk about him much at school?' I ask.

'No more so than any other child. She told us he was

coming home, of course. She seemed very excited about it. But she hasn't talked much about him since.'

I nod. What if I've got this all wrong? What if it isn't good for her to have him at home? At least at hospital she had time out from it. At home it's relentless. Maybe it's too much for her to deal with. I should have realised. I should have talked to her more about it. Shouldn't have assumed she was OK now he was home.

'Thank you for telling me. Can I take these home so I can talk to her about it?'

'Of course. And obviously we'd like to help in any way we can. The educational psychologist is available if you wish to make an appointment. Perhaps you'd like to think it over and we can talk again soon.'

'Yes. I will. Thank you.'

Mrs Hinchcliffe smiles warmly. 'It may simply be something she needs to get out of her system. She'll probably be back to drawing butterflies in a couple of weeks.'

I nod and smile at her, although I suspect that won't be true.

'Maybe if you could arrange some play dates with her classmates, that might help,' adds Mrs Hinchcliffe. 'I've noticed she does have a tendency to play on her own much of the time.'

I nod again, feeling bad about the fact that I haven't invited any of her classmates round yet. I'm still not sure if it's a good idea for her friends to see Adam. I don't want her getting teased about him and children can be very cruel, even at that age.

'Yes. Yes, of course,' I say as we stand up.

'Don't worry. We'll keep a special eye on her,' says Mrs Hinchcliffe.

I nod, too choked to be able to speak and head back to wait with the other mums. I spot Jessica's mum. I don't even know her first name. But I do know that Maya talks about Jessica quite a lot.

'Hi, I'm Mel, Maya's mum. I was wondering if Jessica would like to come to our house and play after school one afternoon.'

She appears thrown for a second.

'Oh, right. That's very kind of you. It's a bit difficult after school at the moment, Jess is really tired, you know how it is.'

'Yes, I understand. Maya was shattered the first couple of weeks. Maybe next term when they've got used to it a bit more?'

'Yeah. We'll, er, see how it goes, shall we?'

I nod. Although I know Jess will not be coming round to play next term. Or the term after that.

I wait until I am getting Maya ready for bed that evening before speaking to her. She tends to have a small window of calm time somewhere between the last mad half-hour and sleep.

'Mrs Hinchcliffe showed me your paintings and drawings today, love. She wanted to let me see how good you are at showing your feelings. You've done a lot of pictures of Daddy, haven't you, sweetheart?'

'Daddy's easy to draw because he's always lying down. He's never doing anything.'

'How do you feel about that, love?' I ask, brushing her hair back from her face.

'Sad. My other daddy used to play with me.'

I swallow hard, trying not to react to the phrase she has just used.

'And do you like it better now Daddy's home or was it better when you visited him in hospital?'

Maya thinks for a moment. 'I didn't want this daddy to come home, I wanted my old daddy back.'

I pull her to me as the tears come. 'It's OK, love. Let it all out. It's OK.'

I hurry back downstairs once Maya has finally stopped sobbing and gone to sleep, aware that I have been up there some time. I open the lounge door and peer around it, not wanting to go right in and let Adam see me in this state. He is fine, of course. Well, not fine but the same as always. I slip out of the room and sink down on to the bottom step of the stairs, trying to compose myself. I wish I had one of those magic doodle boards Maya has, so I could erase my crumpled face and conjure up a brave one from somewhere. But I haven't and I can't. It's like someone picked up our family, wrenched us away from our nice, safe life and dropped us into a nightmare. One that none of us can escape from. One that is only going to get harder.

I hear the familiar knock at the door. I hadn't even realised what day it was. My first thought is to ignore it. Hope that he will simply go away. But I know he won't. Not without calling my mobile. Not without making sure we're OK. And although part of me resents this intrusion, another part of me is relieved to have someone to talk to.

I open the door. The hope I have that Steve will not notice is very short-lived.

'Hey. What's wrong?'

'Everything,' I say. 'Absolutely everything.' My face crumples again. Steve puts his arm around me and guides me through to the kitchen where he sits me down on a chair and crouches in front of me.

'Now tell me. Tell me what's happened.'

I sniff loudly. 'Maya's doing paintings of dinosaurs killing Adam. All her pictures are black. It's like he's the living dead. Her teacher says it started around the time Adam came home. I don't think she's coping with it at all. And I feel so awful that I, of all people, didn't notice what was happening to my own daughter.' I bend my head. Steve pulls me in towards his chest. His arms close around me and I realise how much I have missed physical contact. How good it feels to be held. I sob until I feel the dampness of his fleece on my cheek.

'Sorry,' I say, as he passes me a tissue from the box on the table.

'Don't be daft. If anyone's got the right to blub, it's you.'

I blow my nose. 'I thought bringing him home would make it better. I thought we'd somehow go back to being a happy family. I can't believe I've been so stupid.'

'You believed what you wanted to believe. I understand that, we all do.'

'You all think I'm crazy, don't you? Some deranged, pig-headed woman.'

'Determined, not pig-headed. When you set your mind

to do something, nothing in the world will stop you. You've always been like that. Ever since I've known you.' I look down. I forget sometimes. How far the two of us go back. 'And you've always put other people first. Always.'

'Don't, you make me sound like some kind of martyr.'

Steve's voice softens. 'I've got enormous respect for what you're doing for Adam, but it needn't be so tough on you and Maya.'

'What do you mean?'

'I know you don't want to put Adam into a home permanently but what about getting some respite care? He could just go into a home for a week or two every now and again, give you and Maya a well-deserved break.'

'I – I don't know. I haven't really thought about it.'

'If Maya's not coping with this, maybe you need to do it for her sake. Adam would understand. He'd be the last one to want to see you or her suffer. You know that.'

He is right. I do know that. But the idea of sending Adam away, even for a short time, when I fought so hard to get him home, seems ludicrous.

I shrug. 'It just seems wrong somehow.'

'You're not sending him to the gas chamber. We're talking about a nursing home. A place where he'll be well cared for. And you and Maya will get a chance to have some kind of life in between visiting him.'

Steve is holding my hands. I feel him willing me to do this. And I have to admit he's got a point. I could invite Maya's friends round. Let their mums know that Adam won't be here. But still something is holding me back. Something deep inside.

'He won't be loved, though. He'll simply be another patient. Deep down I don't feel anyone else can look after him the way I do.'

'Maybe not but he'll get professional, round-the-clock care. And it'll only be for a couple of weeks.'

'I don't know. It still doesn't seem right. I keep thinking of everything Adam's been through. He doesn't deserve to be parcelled off like that.'

Steve pulls his hands away and stands up abruptly. I can sense his exasperation and I do want to do the right thing. I'm just not sure what the right thing is any more.

'He'd have done it to you,' Steve says.

'Sorry?'

'If this had been the other way around, if it had been you lying there. Adam would have put you into a nursing home. Permanently.'

'No he wouldn't.'

'Of course he would. I'm not bad-mouthing him. I'm simply saying that you're one in a million. No one else I know would have done what you have, and that includes me and it includes Adam.'

'Why are you saying that?'

'Because it's true. I'm simply being honest. This is like when people die, everyone talks about how wonderful they were. No one dare say anything bad. Or even anything that makes them sound ordinary. But I don't want to see you doing yourself in by not getting respite care because you think he's some kind of saint. I love him to bits, Mel, he's my best mate. But it's not like he never did anything wrong.'

I see Steve's jaw tighten as his mouth clangs shut. But it is too late now. He said something he shouldn't have. I know it by the look in his eyes.

'What do you mean by that?'

'Nothing.'

'Yes you do. If you know something that I don't then I want to hear it.'

'There are some things it's best not to know.'

'Oh no. You don't get out of it that way. You started this. You're going to tell me what you know.'

Steve rolls his eyes and looks at the ceiling. 'Look, I shouldn't have said anything.'

'Well, you have so it's too late.' He turns to face the wall. My stomach lurches as I wonder what can be so bad that he can't face me. 'I mean it, Steve. I need to know.'

'It was a long time ago, OK?'

'What was?'

He sighs. 'His indiscretion.'

'What are you talking about?'

'In our first year at uni. There was a party. We weren't really invited. I can't even remember how we ended up there.'

I am wracking my brain, trying to remember it. Trying to work out why I wasn't there. 'Go on.'

'Well, there was a girl. She was in her second year. She'd been eyeing him up all night. I went to get a drink and when I came back they'd gone.'

'So?'

'Well, it wasn't a coincidence. Someone said they'd left together.'

'It doesn't mean anything happened.'

'I'm sorry, Mel, but I asked him the next morning. He didn't even bother to deny it.'

I shake my head. 'No. I don't believe you. He wouldn't do that to me.'

'Look, I'm not saying it meant anything. I'm just saying it happened.'

'No. He told me he'd never been with anyone else.'

'Of course he did. He wouldn't admit to it, would he? Probably thought what you didn't know couldn't hurt you.'

I shake my head. I wish I hadn't asked now. Wish I'd remained in blissful ignorance. I still don't believe that Adam would do that. But I don't know why Steve would make it up either. I look down, trying hard to blink away the tears.

'Come here,' says Steve. He walks back over to me, pulls me to my feet and wraps his arms around me. They are arms that care, that are supporting me, trying to take away the hurt. And I want that more than anything. But they are not Adam's arms. I pull away.

'I think you'd better go,' I say.

Steve looks at me, his dark eyes burning with intensity. He appears stung. 'But I was going to sit with Adam, give you the chance of an early night.'

'No thanks. I need to be with Adam. On my own.'

'Look, I'm sorry. I didn't mean for it to come out like that. But I know Adam wouldn't want to see you and Maya suffer like this.'

I stare at him, saying nothing.

'Think about what I said, won't you? And if there's

anything you need, call me. Anytime. Day or night.'

I nod. Steve picks up his jacket and sees himself out. I wait for a moment. Try to do the bright and breezy face again before I go in to see Adam. It is only when I go out into the hall that I realise the lounge door is still open.

Twenty-six

I can tell by the expression on Mel's face that she realises I might have overheard. She is weighing up whether to say anything or not. I want to scream out loud, 'He's a bastard. He's a lying fucking bastard. Don't believe a word he says.' But at the same time I want to kick myself for being so bloody stupid. Because he was right, I didn't deny it. I was nineteen. I wanted Steve off my back. I told him he could believe what he wanted. That I didn't give a toss. But despite that I thought he'd see straight through my bravado because he knew how much I loved Mel. Knew that I could never do that to her. That I'd feel bad enough just to have kissed another girl.

Mel comes over to my bedside, smiling a smile which I know is forced. She's been crying, I can tell. I could always tell. And she looks bloody knackered. I see her swallow. But still no words. She begins the night-time routine as if on automatic pilot. Gathering the things she needs around her. It took her a while to get the hang of the suctioning but she does it as well as the nurses now. I really can't tell the difference. When she has finished she picks up the sonic toothbrush and starts to clean my teeth. Maybe she believes him. Maybe she is cleansing me from the inside. In a minute she will empty the bag of wee from my leg and get the crap out of me. We have no secrets any more.

I didn't hear it all. I heard Steve ask her what was wrong and Mel say, 'Absolutely everything.' I must have drifted some place else for a while then, aware only of the distant hum of voices. Voices getting gradually louder. I came back in around about, 'What do you mean by that?' I heard all the rest. My hearing is sharp now. A bit too sharp perhaps.

Mel returns from washing her hands, removes my empty feeding sachet from the end of the tube and fixes the water one on instead. I am rehydrated at nights which is just as well as I feel so sick at the moment that I am not sure I could stomach even the excuse for food which is pumped down my tube.

Why? That's all I keep asking myself. Why would Steve do that to me? Hasn't he heard of the phrase, 'Don't kick a man when he's down'? More than just down, in my case. Paralysed and mute, for Christ's sake. A right of reply so far out of reach it isn't even visible on the distant horizon.

Mel has finished now. Finished her nursing duties, anyway. She will sit with me, though. Watch over me until the sitter comes. Margaret, I think she said it is tonight. I try to see beyond Mel's eyes as she hovers over me. Try to catch a glimpse of what is going on behind them.

'I love you,' she whispers, stroking the side of my face with her hand. 'And nothing is ever going to change that.' She doesn't want to believe it, I know that. But I am still no closer to knowing if she really does.

AND THEN IT HAPPENED

★

It was funny how many boys turned up for the gymnastics display. Normally, we couldn't get out of school fast enough and nothing would tempt us back again out of school hours. But the annual gymnastics display was different. It meant seeing lots of girls in leotards. Girls who were blossoming into adolescence. Girls who didn't yet possess anything as joy-sapping as a sports bra. We didn't tell our parents that, obviously. We feigned an interest in seeing our mates in the gym club vaulting over the box. But the truth was that was the least interesting part of the evening. The bit we had to sit through in order to see girls like Mel Summerskill doing a pike straddle off the trampette. She was cute. The cutest girl in our year. She wore her hair up in a ponytail and had two strands hanging down either side of her heart-shaped face. She reminded me of a porcelain doll who had come to life. Small but perfectly formed. Especially in a leotard.

'Awright,' said Steve who had somehow pushed his way through to find a space on the mat next to me. He should have stayed at the back really, he was the tallest one in our year. But he obviously wanted a ringside view.

'Yeah,' I said. 'Will be when it starts.'

'I'm giving them marks out of ten for artistic impression,' he replied. I grinned at him and looked up as the music started and the members of the gym club filed into the hall, toes pointing, arms swinging in time to the music.

Our eyes remained stage front as we talked, so we didn't miss a thing. The boys went first as usual. Neil Kirby in the fifth year somersaulted over the horse without even touching it. Part of me wished I could do that. Maybe I could if I tried. But I would rather have been outside running, playing rugby or football, anything other than being cooped up indoors.

The girls lined up ready for their turn. Mel Summerskill was in the queue for the trampette nearest us. She was third to go. I watched her as she ran up, arms pumping like a sprinter, legs pounding into the ground and the interesting bits in between wobbling like mad. She landed perfectly on the mat, legs together, back arched, arms outstretched, before she turned and walked right past us on the way back. That was when I glanced round and saw Steve looking at her. Not drooling like he had been at some of the others, but looking at her with such an intensity that I suspected she might burst into flames at any minute. I was going to say something but before I could, Karen James was bouncing on the trampette. She was a big girl, Karen. She made quite a dent in it. Steve started laughing and I knew the moment had gone and he'd only deny it if I said anything.

It was before school the next morning when the trouble started. Robert Hopwood, Hoppo as he was known, should have had 'trouble' tattooed on his forehead.

'Here they come, the school faggots,' he said as Steve and I walked into the playground. We'd heard it before; because Hoppo didn't have a best mate he took it out on those who did. We ignored him. We'd learnt it was the best way. But on this occasion it only seemed to make him worse.

'I saw you last night, Taylor. Looking at Neil Kirby's arse, you were.' Some of the other lads started laughing. It was all the encouragement he needed. 'You'd better watch it, Dawson, your friend might be about to ditch you for an older model.'

'Piss off,' said Steve. That was a mistake too. You couldn't let him see he'd riled you.

'Ooh, bit touchy this morning, aren't we? Wouldn't he suck your cock last night?'

'You've got it all wrong, Hoppo,' I said.

'Oh yeah? Prove it then?'

'What are you talking about?'

'Prove you're not a queer boy.'

'And how would you like me to do that?'

'Ditch Dawson here and ask one of the girls out.'

'That won't prove anything.'

'See, you can't do it, can you?' Hoppo came closer to us. He wasn't as tall as Steve but he was big and had a mean, square face. A crowd of other kids had gathered around, no doubt relieved it was not them he was picking on today.

'Stop being a prat, Hoppo.' Steve had a nasty habit of making situations like this worse.

'What's wrong?' Hoppo sneered. 'Can't face losing him, can you?'

'Drop it,' I said.

'Only if you do what I say.' The crowd had grown bigger. I hoped one of the teachers might spot it from inside and come out to break things up but there was no sign. 'She'll do,' he said pointing over to the other side of the playground where Mel was sitting on the wall with a couple of mates. Some of the other kids started laughing.

'And what if I don't?'

'We'll all know it's true then, won't we? You and Dawson are queer boys. In which case you'll get your heads kicked in after school.' Put like that it didn't seem such an attractive option. Hoppo had previous. He was only just back from suspension from the last fight. I glanced across at Steve. He appeared unable to *speak, his jaw set, his body stiff. I didn't see how I had much choice. It was the only way to get this over with quickly. I'd ask her, she'd say no and the whole thing would be over and forgotten by break time.*

'OK,' I said. 'Anything to shut you up.' I turned briefly to see Steve staring at me. Staring as if he couldn't quite believe what I'd just said. I started walking through the circle of kids, over to the far side of the playground. Mel looked up. She probably wondered what the hell was going on. Why half the school were staring at her.

'Hi,' I said. 'You were really good last night.'

Her friends giggled but had the good grace to walk a couple of paces away.

'Oh, thanks,' she said, looking down at her feet.

'I was wondering. If, erm, if you'd like to go out with me sometime. Maybe the cinema or something.'

She looked up. A huge smile lit up her face. 'Yes,' she said, without hesitation. 'I'd like that.'

I nodded, so stunned at her reply that I had no idea what to say next. 'Right. Great. See you later, then.'

I turned and strode back towards Hoppo and the other kids, finding it hard to keep a smile from forming on my face.

'Blew you out, did she?' asked Hoppo.

'No,' I said. 'She didn't actually. She said yes.'

'Tosser,' said Hoppo. He spat on the ground and slunk off. The other kids drifted off too. Leaving me and Steve standing there. I thought he might say thank you for stopping him getting his head kicked in. He didn't though. He looked for all the world as if that would have been the better option.

★

My mind comes back to the room. That's it. He's still in love with her. Steve is in love with my wife. He has been for all these years, through everything, he's never stopped loving her. That's why he split up with Louise. What is it he said? 'I've been living a lie all these years and it's not fair to carry on like this.' Fucking hell. My accident was his window of opportunity. He's trying to move in on Mel. That's what all this bollocks about coming round here to do DIY jobs is all about. He's been waiting for this, waiting for me to be out of the picture. That's why he told her about the girl at uni. He does know I didn't sleep with her. He told her because he wanted to. He's trying to make her stop loving me. He's trying to come between us. Because he wants her for himself.

Mel is still sitting next to me. She is reading a book. She has no idea. Not a clue. And somehow I've got to tell her.

Twenty-seven

MEL

I'm aware as soon as the girls enter the classroom that I look like death warmed up. There they all are with their tight skin, bright eyes and beautifully made-up faces and I'm sitting here with dark circles under my eyes and well aware that despite the hastily applied slick of lipstick and flick of mascara I look awful.

'Good night last night, was it, miss?' grins Gemma. I usually enjoy a bit of banter with them but I am not in the mood this morning. I barely slept last night, Steve's words going over and over in my head. I don't believe him. I don't believe Adam would do that to me, not even back then. But I still don't understand why Steve would make it up, either. The only answer to that is so daft, so ridiculous. I don't even want to go there. But the fact remains that now the seed of doubt has been planted it's niggling away at me.

'Afraid not, Gemma. When you have a family, you don't get many opportunities for wild nights out.'

'Me sister and her boyfriend still go out most nights. They just dump their little girl with me mum.'

'Not everyone has a family where you can do that, though. Some people's home lives are more complicated.' I catch Cara's eye as I say it. She looks down. I didn't mean for her to think I was talking about her.

'I'll babysit for you if you like, miss,' says Lauren.

I smile, desperately wishing I was in a position to be able to accept.

'Thank you. It's very kind of you to offer.'

'We'll all take it in turns,' says Haleema. 'Then you and your husband can go out more often. Can we, miss? It could be like work experience for us. And I bet your little girl's really cute.' The other girls chorus their approval of the idea. They are waiting with expectant faces. It is so sweet of them to offer. I am going to have to tell them. It's the only way not to hurt their feelings.

'That's really kind of you but I'm afraid it's not just my little girl I have to look after. I have to care for my husband as well.'

'Why, what's wrong with him?' asks Haleema.

I take a deep breath. 'He was injured in an accident at work in May. He was in a coma for a while. He's opened his eyes now but he's still in what they call a vegetative state.' The room falls silent. Clearly the girls had no idea.

'What, he can't move at all?' asks Gemma.

'No. Or talk.'

'So why isn't he in hospital?' asks Lauren.

'He was for a long while. But they can't do anything more for him. That's why I brought him home.'

'But aren't there like nursing home places he could go?'

'There are, Haleema. But I wanted to bring him home, to look after him myself.' The room is silent again.

'That must be really hard work,' says Cara.

'It is but I don't regret doing it. Not for a moment.' A couple of the girls nod. A few more smile supportively. 'Anyway,' I say, keen to change the subject, 'let's get on with some work. Different stages of child development we're looking at today.'

Cara waits until all the other girls have gone before she approaches my desk at the end of the lesson.

'It's why you gave up teaching at the university, isn't it? Because you had to look after your husband.'

'Yes. It is.'

'Whatever happens,' says Cara, 'I think it's brilliant what you've done. Putting him first and making all them sacrifices.'

'Thanks,' I say. 'Anyway, I don't suppose you get many nights off either.'

'No but it's what you do, isn't it? When you love someone, like.'

I try to speak but no words come out so I simply nod instead.

I get back home just in time to relieve the sitter who comes on Friday mornings. I grab a slice of toast and take it into the lounge with me. I always worry about eating in front of Adam. Fear it might be like someone having an ice cream in front of you when you're on a diet.

'It's OK,' I say. 'It's got peanut butter on it.' Adam hates peanut butter. I hope that somewhere inside he is managing to smile.

'Blimey, love,' says Denise when I let her in shortly afterwards. 'You've got more bags under your eyes than I have, and it's not often I can say that to anyone. Were you up sitting up with your Adam again last night?'

'No that's tonight and tomorrow night, actually.'

'You're going to do yourself in, you are,' she says as she puts her cleaning stuff down in the hall. I try to smile but I find my bottom lip quivering instead. I hurry into the kitchen, not wanting Adam to hear me blubbing again. Or wanting Denise to have to scrape me up off the floor with the rest of the rubbish. She follows me in, mop in hand.

'Some people think that just because I'm a cleaner I must be thick as shit,' she says. 'I know you don't think that and I know you realise that not a lot gets past me. So there's really no point trying to put on a brave face, is there?' I smile a watery smile as I blink the tears away.

'Go on, give me a hug, they're clean overalls,' says Denise. A few seconds later I am hugging her solid dependable frame, feeling small and weak and pathetic.

'Sorry,' I say. 'You shouldn't have to mop up my tears, that's not part of your job description.'

'You'd be surprised how often I have to do it,' she says. 'Especially some of the old dears, they get terribly lonely, you know. Some of them don't really want a cleaner, they clean the house themselves, I can tell. They're just after some company. Sad, in't it? Old folks having to pay to have someone talk to them. Too proud to admit, mind, they are.'

'I know you cheer Adam up too,' I say. 'I only wish he could talk back to you. You'd have such a laugh together.'

'You miss him, don't you?'

I nod, sitting down at the kitchen table. 'I miss him so much it's hard to even function some days. Trouble is I don't know how much longer I can carry on like this. Adam's best mate suggested I get some respite care, just for a couple of weeks. I don't know, though. It doesn't seem right somehow, shoving him off into a home so I get a break.'

'But what good are you to him if you're knackered all the time? I know I've never been able to have a proper chat with your Adam but I'm sure he's not the sort that would want you to be feeling like this.'

'So you don't think it'd be horrible of me to get some respite care?'

'Of course it bloody wouldn't. It's probably doing him in, seeing you like this. I bet he wishes you'd give yourself a break. You've got nothing to prove, you know. Anyone can see how much you love him. And you won't stop loving him, will you, just because he's in a home for a couple of weeks? And he won't stop loving you either.'

I nod. 'I should pay you for your counselling as well as your cleaning.'

'All part of the service,' she says. 'Now, is the world going to end if I don't clean your house this week?' I shake my head. 'Right, so why don't I sit with Adam and you get a couple of hours' kip.'

'Are you sure?'

'What, sit and have a cup of tea and a natter rather than cleaning the bog? What do you think?'

I smile. 'You don't need to do anything. I've just given him some more food. He'll be fine.'

'I know he will. I'll tell him about some of the stuff I see when I clean people's homes. That'll cheer him up. Now go and get your head down.'

I do as I am told. And as I climb each step of the stairs I feel the weight lightening a little to the point where, as I get to the top, I can at least see things a bit more clearly than I expected. The last thing I hear before I drop off is Adam laughing at the stories Denise is telling him. I am imagining it, of course, but I still hear it. The way I always hear what's going on inside his head.

I do it as soon as Denise has left later that afternoon. If I wait any longer I know I'll lose my nerve. I decide to try the one that was top of the pile Dr McKee passed to me. For some reason I still remember the name: Hazelwood House Nursing Home in Littleborough. When I look at the map on the Internet I realise that Adam would have driven past it every day on his way to and from work. I can't decide whether that is a good thing or not.

The phone is answered promptly by an efficient-sounding woman. I introduce myself, tell her that my husband is in a vegetative state and I am interested in respite care. Just for a week or two. I don't recognise my voice as I'm talking, still less the description I give of my husband. She asks me a few more questions. I imagine some sort of tick box list being completed at the other end. Adam seems to pass the test. She asks me when I'd like to come and have a look round. Which is how I come off the phone a few minutes later with an appointment to visit the next day.

In some ways the next phone call I make is actually harder than the first.

'Hi, it's Mel,' I say when Mum answers the phone.

'Hello. Everything all right?' She can tell just by the tone of my voice. I am sure of it.

'Yes, thanks. I was wondering if you and Dad would do me a massive favour tomorrow afternoon and look after Adam and Maya for me. I know it's short notice but I need to go somewhere.'

'Yes, I should think so. Your father'll be done with his trains by lunchtime.'

'Thanks. I really appreciate that. I'll only be a couple of hours.'

'Where are you off to?'

I make sure the kitchen door is shut but I still lower my voice. 'I'm going to visit a nursing home in Littleborough—'

'Oh, I am glad you've come to your senses. It'll be for the best, Melanie, I'm sure of it.'

'No. It's for respite care. Just for a week. I'm not putting him into a home. I thought we'd been through all that.'

'Oh, I see. I was hoping, well, never mind. Still, maybe once he's there you'll change your mind.'

I shake my head and hold the phone away from my ear. Aware that's what everyone will probably think. That I've given up on Adam. And once he's there he'll never come out again.

'Now, you be good for Grandad,' I say as I kiss Maya goodbye. 'And enjoy *Alpha and Omega*.'

'Are you sure there aren't any dinosaurs in it?' She won't even watch her *Toy Story* DVD because of Rex the toy dinosaur.

'I'm sure. It's about a couple of wolves, sweetie. OK?'

She nods. 'Have a nice shopping trip with Loo-eeze.'

Mum looks at me. I couldn't tell Maya the real reason. As hard as she's finding it, I know she won't want Adam to go either. Not even for a few days. I see Louise pull up outside the window. It's time to go.

'Hi. Thanks for this,' I say as I climb into the car. 'I don't think I could have gone on my own.'

'It's no problem. How are you feeling?'

'Pretty churned up. God knows how I'd feel if I was thinking of putting him in a home for good.'

'It's only for a week, Mel, and he's going to receive professional, round-the-clock care.'

'That's exactly what Steve said.'

'Oh. You've told him then.'

'It was his suggestion, actually. I wasn't sure about it at first. And I don't want Steve to think I've decided to do it because of what he said.'

'What did he say?'

I close my eyes and look out of the window. 'He said Adam cheated on me while we were at uni.' The words sound as if they are from a foreign language. I do not recognise them.

'Oh, Mel. What an awful thing for him to say.'

'It's not true. I know it's not true.'

'Of course it's not. Adam would never do that to you. He adored you.' She sees me twitch and corrects herself in the same sentence. 'I mean he does, he always has.'

'He said it only happened once. That Adam went home from a party with some girl. Said he didn't deny it the next day.'

'It's just not Adam, is it?' says Louise. 'It's not his style. Even back then when everyone else was putting it about, I never even saw him so much as look at anyone else. People used to joke about it, remember. How bloody besotted the pair of you were.'

'I know. That's what I keep reminding myself.'

'I don't understand why Steve said that to you. It's like he wants to dismantle everyone's lives, tear everything that's safe and familiar apart.'

'He said he didn't want me to beat myself about doing this. Wanted me to realise that Adam wasn't a saint.'

'I'm sorry, Mel. I really don't know what's got into him.'

'You don't have to apologise for him.'

'He's still my husband for now.'

'Yeah but you're not responsible for what he says. Just as long as you know that me arranging this visit has got nothing to do with what he said. It's like I said on the phone, it's Maya and the effect this is having on her that's made me consider it.'

'Of course, I understand that. Now, are you ready to go?'

I nod my head. Louise pulls away. And I try to get rid of the sense that I am committing some kind of treachery behind Adam's back.

Hazelwood House is a large 1950s-style building, bland and innocuous looking. I've driven past it myself plenty of times, without really noticing it. Louise looks at me as we step out on to the gravel car park.

'Are you ready?' she asks.

I nod and lead the way up to the front door to press the buzzer.

'Hi, it's Mel Taylor to have a look around. I spoke to Mrs Hammond yesterday about respite care for my husband.'

We are buzzed in and asked to take a seat in the reception area which has conservatory-style furniture and a plethora of artificial pot plants. I am trying very hard not to take a dislike to it so early on. An overly cheerful woman in her fifties arrives.

'Hello,' she says, 'Dorothy Hammond, proprietress. Welcome to Hazelwood House.' I get the sense that she has to stop herself saying, 'I hope your husband will be very happy here.' I realise now that this is going to be a bit like asking a double-glazing firm to come round and do one small bathroom window. I am going to get the hard sell until I agree to sign Adam over to her entirely. I suspect she has the forms hidden on her person somewhere. And a spare pen, just in case.

I introduce Louise. Dorothy asks well-meaning questions about Adam and makes suitably sympathetic clucking noises in all the right places. I am reminded of Sybil Fawlty. I know Adam would find her hilarious. I try to block that thought from my mind, scared I might break into an inappropriate laugh. Dorothy talks about the management structure, staff training and their Investors in People award. Somehow I can't help feeling I don't look as impressed as I am supposed to.

'Anyway,' she says brightly. 'Let's have a look around, shall we? It will give you much more of a feel of the place.'

I glance at Louise. She is doing her positive face for me.

I follow Dorothy down the corridor, past the prints of poppies and sunflowers on the wall and an oncoming medication trolley.

'I'll show you one of our rooms first. I understand that for many people that's one of the most important considerations. We pride ourselves on cleanliness but also, as you'll see, on creating those little homely touches that make all the difference.' She opens the door and leads us into a square room with white painted walls, a sunflower print, beige carpet and floral curtains adorning the small window which looks out on to the car park.

'As you'll see, the space is impressive, we provide above the minimum standard floor space requirement at no extra charge. And, of course, all the rooms are en-suite.'

I try to imagine Adam lying in the bed and all I can think of is that he'd hate the curtains.

'Now obviously this room is empty at the moment, we've got a new resident coming on Monday and they'll be bringing their personal belongings with them so they can really make the room their own.'

'Adam wouldn't need to do that, he'd only be coming for a week.'

'Yes, of course, dear.'

She says it in such a patronising way that I wonder if she has seen this countless times before, if everyone starts off by saying it's simply respite care until they fall under her evil spell. I realise I'm turning her into some sort of wicked witch in my head, which is probably unfair.

Dorothy takes us back along the corridor; training certificates and quality assurance awards line the walls. I do not doubt the staff's competence. What I doubt is the one thing you don't get a certificate for – love.

'And this is the residents' lounge,' says Dorothy, showing us into a large room with patio doors out to a small garden area at the far end. A collection of various sofas and arm-chairs are dotted around the edges of the room, some of them occupied by elderly ladies and several more by elderly men. One of the ladies looks up.

'Have they come to do my hair?' she asks.

'No, Elsie, love. They're just visiting,' says Dorothy, patting her on the hand. Elsie nods. The television is blaring away in the corner, Saturday afternoon horse racing. A few people have been positioned so they are looking at it. No one is actually watching.

'Do you have any younger residents at all?' I ask Dorothy.

'It tends to vary. We had a man in his forties last year but I'm afraid he's no longer with us.' I don't like to ask whether she means with us at Hazelwood House or with us in this world. 'The new lady coming on Monday is certainly younger, in her fifties I think.' I nod before following Dorothy back to her office.

'Now,' she says, 'Do you have any questions?'

'I just wonder what experience your staff have of nursing someone in a vegetative state?'

'Oh, we have considerable experience. You don't need to worry about that.'

I nod slowly. I can see Louise nodding more enthusiastically.

'We have our own little routine for Adam at home. If I gave you a list, would you be able to incorporate those things into your care?'

Dorothy smiles; if she was near enough to pat me on the hand, I think she probably would.

'What people usually find is that once their loved ones are here they soon adapt to our routines and our way of doing things. It's simply a matter of getting used to it, understanding that our professionals know exactly what they're doing.'

I nod. I don't have any more questions.

Louise and I crunch silently across the gravel car park and get into her car. I put the brochure Dorothy has given me on the back seat.

'I know exactly what you're going to say,' says Louise. 'But please don't dismiss it straight away.'

'He'd hate it,' I say. 'It would be like being prematurely aged.'

'But he'd be in his room, not with all those old bids. And it would only be for a week. A week that would do you and Maya the power of good.'

'*If* I ever did it,' I say, 'it would be for Maya. For no other reason. And if Steve, my mum or anyone else thinks they have got a chance of convincing me to leave him there, they are very much mistaken.'

Twenty-eight

'Dear *Points of View*,' begins Joan. 'Why oh why do you need to spend thousands of pounds of licence payers' money making some silly modern version of the Nativity? No doubt there will be gratuitous sex, violence and bad language in it, in a pathetic attempt to boost ratings.'

Not such a bad idea, actually. I quite fancy watching it myself now.

'Why the BBC thinks it can somehow improve on the story as told in the Bible I simply can't comprehend.' Joan clears her throat and continues. 'And to bring in someone who did the scripts for *EastEnders* to write it just about sums up the state of television today.'

She wouldn't have minded if they'd used a *Coronation Street* scriptwriter, of course. Corrie is somehow immune from criticism in the funny little world in which she lives.

'And to top it all off you put an article about it in the *Radio Times* under the label "Faith at Christmas". This is the worst case of dumbing down imaginable.' At this point she puts her letter down and holds open a copy of the *Radio Times* for me to see the offending article. I strain my eyes to try to make out the large print. Tony Jordan has written it. He did *Life on Mars* and *Hustle*, both of which I loved. I expect it will be brilliant. I wonder if Mel will put it on for me.

'I can assure you that I for one will not be sitting down in the run-up to Christmas to waste my time watching your celebrity version. I shall be supporting events at my local church.' She says this as if she is some fervent Christian. The fact is when Reverend Westwood was in charge she boycotted the place because she disapproved of the fact that he wore comedy cartoon ties. It was only the appointment of the more sombre Reverend Williams that brought her back into the fold.

'Yours sincerely, Joan Summerskill, (Mrs).' She finishes with a defiant flourish. No doubt someone at the BBC will have a good chuckle over that one. It's getting to the point where I try to second-guess her grievances now. Make up her next complaint letter in my head. I always think I am being over the top and rein them back a little. It's about time I learnt that is unlikely to be the case.

I am alone with Joan today. Mel has gone out. Tom has taken Maya to the cinema. This doesn't normally happen. Something is up. Mel was quiet this morning. Barely able to speak to me. Maybe what Steve said is getting to her, maybe it's looking after me that's getting her down. Maybe both. She looks knackered. I am a huge weight around her neck. I hate myself for that. I wish I could cut myself free and free her in the process. I am trying so hard to rouse myself. Aching and straining to find that connection, to get my fingers or my toes to do what I tell them. To force the torrent of words in my head out of my mouth. Although I fear that if I do that they will all come out at once, all the words I have wanted to say over these past five months will come whooshing out and still no one will understand me. It'll be like that scene in *Toy Story 3* when Buzz Lightyear gets switched to Spanish mode. They'll need to find my default button so we can start at the beginning again.

'I am glad our Melanie's going to get a break,' says Joan with a sigh. I hadn't noticed her sitting there wringing her hands, obviously deep in thought. 'It's so hard to see her struggling on alone. And it's not right for Maya to have to live like this, in a house which is more like a hospital ward. It's not natural, is it? Not for a child of her age. I'm sure you understand that. I'm sure you'll agree it's for the best.'

I am going to be put into a home. That's what's happening. Mel has finally snapped under the weight of caring for me. Perhaps what Steve said helped to make her mind up. Fuck, that's why he said it. That's what he's trying to do. Get me out of the picture once and for all so he can make his move. I don't blame Mel. I don't blame her at all. She has, as Steve said, been an absolute saint to bring me back here in the first place. And a part of me would feel relieved if she could have her life back. But another part, the wholly selfish part, doesn't want to go. Wants to chain myself to the railings outside, start a 'Save the Cragg Vale Vegetable' campaign. I am too young to be put out to grass. If I go to a nursing home, I will die there. I will be surrounded by old biddies and I will not be around to see Maya grow up and I will slowly wither and die. It is immensely selfish. But it is probably true.

'Daddy.' Maya's voice rings out from the hall. A second later the lounge door crashes open and she is here; jigging about, dancing all around the room and jabbering away in an incomprehensible splurge.

'The film was really good and there were these two wolves and they weren't supposed to be friends but they were and one of them went for rides in a log and then they got shot but not by baddies and they were taken to a different place and they had to find their way home and there were funny birds who helped them and the lady wolf's sister who was pretty married the wolf who made the birds fall out of the sky when he howled at the moon and that was the funniest bit.'

Phew. I'm breathless just thinking about it. They should do film reviews like that on TV. Much better than all this posturing over what the director was trying to achieve and the subtle nuances hidden within.

'Personally, I thought it were a poor man's *Happy Feet*,' says Tom quietly, coming to stand at the foot of my bed. 'You just can't beat tap-dancing penguins, in my book.' Joan rolls her eyes. I smile inside.

'Come on, Daddy, howl at the moon with me,' yells Maya, who is howling now. Howling like something possessed. I try. I try really hard. And something comes out. Not a howl but some sort of noise. I know because all three of them turn to look at me.

'You did it, you did it. Do it again, Daddy, please,' says Maya, jumping up and down next to me. I try. I try the very same way to do the very same thing but, this time, nothing.

'Ohhh,' says Maya.

'Probably just a bit of wind,' says Joan. And that is it. My triumph, albeit a minor one, dismissed as a bit of wind. I am not going to do this. Not going to break through in time to stop it. And I must stop it. Because I know what it is like to lose a parent. Know what it is like to have one of the two pillars in your life taken from you. And how precarious life is after that. Even if the other pillar remains strong.

Mum came into my room to tell me three days after my thirteenth birthday. I didn't realise at the time how significant that was or stop to wonder how long ago she'd decided to leave as soon as I was a teenager. You don't when you're thirteen. You only think about you and now. She didn't even look like my mother any more. She'd dyed her hair blond some time before Christmas. She didn't look right. She looked like someone on one of those mix and match games where you can put the wrong hair on people and see what they look like.

She had at least knocked. I'd turned my music down a bit. Joy Division, I think it was I was listening to. And then she simply hovered over the end of my bed, like the Angel Gabriel, only she'd forgotten her halo and wings.

'I need to talk to you,' she said. That was when I knew. She didn't normally come into my bedroom but on the few occasions it had happened it was to tell me off, not to talk to me. She sat down on the far corner of my Leeds United duvet. She didn't look me in the eye. She stared at the wall opposite.

'Your father and I haven't really been getting on for some time. We haven't got much in common, you see. We don't like doing the same kind of things.'

I don't know why parents do that. Try to prepare you by telling you a whole load of stuff you already know. It was like she thought I was thick or something.

'We've obviously been trying to work things out, for your sake really. But as much as we've tried, it hasn't got any better. To be honest, things have got worse.

'I'm afraid I've decided to leave, Adam. It's nothing to do with you. It's important you know that. Maybe I was too young when I married your father. The thing is, I don't feel I've lived my life yet. I want to travel, see places, meet new people.' I was trying not to listen any more. I was staring at my Leeds United poster on the wall, at Gordon Strachan and the lads. They were probably going to get promoted. I was excited about that. Or at least I had been.

'Where are you going?' I asked.

'Leeds,' she said. 'Just for a month or two. Then on to Sydney, Australia.' She said it as if it was on the bus route from Leeds. 'Maybe when you're a bit older you can come and visit. It will be a real adventure for you.'

I knew that wouldn't happen. Knew I would never see her again.

'Who are you going with?'

She sighed and shut her eyes for a moment. I obviously wasn't as stupid as she'd thought.

'Graeme from work. We're going to set up a PR company over there. Make a fresh start.'

'And what about Dad?' I asked, trying to stop my voice from going squeaky.

'He'll do a grand job of looking after you,' she said. 'A boy of your age needs to be with their father. He's a good man, Adam. Your father.'

How can she say that? If he was so fucking good why was she leaving him? Gordon Strachan had gone a bit blurry. I needed to *get out. Straight away. I jumped up from my bed and bolted for the door. I heard her calling after me as I clattered down the stairs. Past Dad, who was sitting in the kitchen with his head in his hands, and out the back door. I vaulted over the gate, along the cobbles and out into the back fields. The tears carving their way down my face, the snot running down on to my top lip. I could see for miles. Nothing but fields and trees and drystone walls. I was free to run wherever I wanted. For as far and as long as I liked. To run until the pain took the hurt inside away.*

Twenty-nine

MEL

At least this time my sleepless night coincides with one of the nights I'm not supposed to be sleeping anyway. I sit next to Adam wondering what he will think of me when I tell him. It's a bit of luck we never did the 'in sickness and in health' bit at our wedding, because I certainly don't remember there being an opt-out clause to allow you to ship your husband off for respite care if it all got a bit much. Neither of us had wanted a church wedding, which was just as well. I'd have struggled with the 'for better or worse' line. I'd have been fine saying it about Adam but how could I expect him to say it about me when he only knew my better side? And when I'd so deliberately kept my worst from him.

And so I sit here, mired knee-deep in guilt. And yet every time I reach the decision that I can't do it, I can't hand my husband over, not even for a week, I see Maya's paintings and I know I need to give her a chance to escape the blackness enveloping her. To enable her to see colours again.

It would be easier if I'd actually liked Hazelwood House. If I'd felt Dorothy was a kindred spirit instead of a profit-driven businesswoman. When I was a kid our cat Ringo had to go to a cattery every year when we went on holiday. It was a horrible place, grey, dingy, rows and rows of soulless cages. When we got him back he looked like he hadn't eaten for a week. His fur had lost its sheen, he blinked when he came out into the sunlight. But there was nothing we could do because all the other catteries were the same. Then one year a new cattery opened. Cats in Clover it was called, run by a fat, jolly woman by the name of Marjorie, who lived in a ramshackle cottage with a huge garden. One of those women who collects cat things. Who loves them. Really loves them. And when we came back Ringo was asleep in the sunshine in the garden, Marjorie stroking his big fat belly. That is what I'd like for Adam. Husbands in Clover, a special place where he will be loved, really loved. Where I will have no qualms about leaving him. It doesn't exist, though. I've checked on the internet. Hazelwood House is the only nursing home offering respite care for patients in a vegetative state within a fifty-mile radius. It is there or nothing. And I realise nothing is no longer an option.

As the room starts growing light again I know I have reached a decision. I will phone Hazelwood House later. Ask if Adam can go in for respite care. Just for a week, mind. I can tell Maya that Daddy is going on holiday. I think she will accept that. And it will give me a chance to spend some quality time with her. To be able to invite her friends round from school without fear of being refused or having them run screaming from the room. To be like other children, just for a few days.

I glance down at Adam. He knows, I am sure of it. And

whether he does or doesn't, it is only right that I should tell him. Not now, though. Maya will wake up at any minute. And I need to get Adam washed and set up for the day and Maya breakfasted and dressed and her swimming bag ready. I am taking her today. Usually, Dad takes her while Mum sits with Adam and I get a couple of hours' kip. But I want to take her today. She got a certificate last week. She can do six things I've never seen her do. That Adam's never seen her do either. He can't do anything about it. But I can.

'Morning, love,' I say to Adam. I pause for a moment, almost as if I am giving him the chance to say good morning back to me inside his head. Sometimes I think I can actually hear him saying it. That it is only other people who can't hear him.

'Mummy, Daddy.' The shout comes from upstairs, followed by footsteps clattering down them. We always used to joke it sounded like we had a centipede in jack boots, not a daughter. I wonder if Adam still smiles about that. Maya bursts in. She is wearing her butterfly pyjamas and her Dora the Explorer wellies, an endearing if somewhat unconventional combination.

'Sshhh,' I say, putting my finger to my lips. 'Daddy's only just woken up.'

'He doesn't mind,' says Maya. 'Can I get on his bed?'

'You'll have to take your wellies off first, love.'

She groans, a groan that makes her sound like a teenager before her time, kicks off her wellies and climbs up next to Adam.

'Good morning, Daddy,' says Maya. 'Did you have a nice

sleep?' She stops, frowns and turns to look at me. 'When Daddy sleeps while you watch over him, do you see his dreams?' she asks.

'It's a lovely thought, sweetheart. I wish I did see them but no, I'm afraid not.'

'Well, I think Daddy dreamed about wolves, like me. He howled at the moon like a wolf yesterday when I was doing it.'

'Did he?'

'Yes. He couldn't do it again, though, and Grandma said it was only wind.'

I look at Adam, wishing I'd been able to hear it for myself. Mum doesn't believe. And when you don't believe your mind is closed to the possibility of things happening. Things which are real, not solely in your imagination.

'Well, I'd better get Daddy his breakfast sorted. You go through to the kitchen to see Roddy and Rita and I'll be there in a few minutes.' She slithers off the bed into her wellies and marches out of the room.

'Do you remember our Sunday morning lie-ins?' I ask Adam. 'The papers, croissants, coffee. It seems a very long time ago now, doesn't it?'

When I go through to the kitchen a few minutes later I find Maya standing on a chair pouring her immune-system-boosting elderberry syrup down the sink.

'Maya, stop. What are you doing?'

'Keeping the sewer rats healthy,' she says.

I smile and shake my head. There really is nothing much you can say to that.

'I've given some to Roddy too but Rita didn't want any.'

I hurry over to his cage, fearing Roddy may have overdosed on it, but he is at least still standing.

'How much did you give him, love?'

'Just a couple of drops. He didn't seem to like it even though it's yummy.'

'That's because he's a rat, sweetie. They eat different things to us and they're much smaller than us too, aren't they? If we give them our food it can make them very poorly.'

Maya's eyes bulge and her bottom lip starts to tremble. 'He's not going to die, is he?'

'No, love,' I say, giving her a hug. 'He'll be fine. But don't give him any more, OK?'

She nods. 'Can we give Daddy some to help grow his brain back?'

I shake my head and pull her tightly to me. 'I wish we could, darling. But it doesn't help brains.'

'Is there a medicine that does?'

'No. Not even a really yucky one. But Daddy's brain will be working really hard to mend itself. It just needs time, OK?' There's a knock on the door. 'That'll be Grandad. Why don't you go and let him in while I get breakfast ready?'

Maya dashes to the door and I start begging Roddy not to die.

Through the glass screen of the viewing gallery I watch Maya swimming. It is strange to be able to see her but hear only muffled sounds and not even smell the chlorine in the pool. I wonder if this is what it's like for Adam. Always on the other side of a glass screen. Seeing everything but not really being a part of it. Not experiencing it as the people on the other side are. Maya has lifted her goggles up. She is mouthing something to me and pointing. I smile and put my thumb up. She shakes her head and mouths again. It takes me a moment or two to realise she needs the toilet. I hurry around to the other side.

'Why didn't you come straight away?' says Maya as I take her hand at the pool entrance. The irritation and frustration is etched on her face and in her voice. I multiply that in my head. By ten. A hundred. A thousand. And still I don't think I'm getting anywhere near what Adam must be feeling every waking moment of every day.

'I'm sorry, love,' I say. 'It's tricky when there's that screen between us. I'll know next time.' I hold open the toilet door and she gives my legs a hug before squeezing past. I don't mind having soggy jeans now. I don't mind at all.

It is when I am stacking the tea things into the dishwasher later in the evening that Maya comes into the kitchen holding the Hazelwood House brochure.

'What's this?' she says. 'And why are there lots of old people there?' I must have left it out last night. I meant to put it away in a drawer. I have two options now, to lie or be honest with her. And I am tired of lying. I close the dishwasher door and squat down next to Maya.

'It's a place very near here, love. A special place for people who are poorly. A lot of them are old but not all of them.'

Maya looks at me hard. 'Is Daddy going there?' she asks.

She understands so much more than I give her credit for.

'Just for a little holiday. A week, that's all. Mummy's very tired, darling. And Daddy will be very well looked after there.'

'I don't want him to go.'

'You'll be able to visit, love. Like you did when he was in hospital.'

'But I want him at home.'

'He'll be back before you know it. And it will be really nice for him to have a little holiday.' I am holding Maya's arms. She could go either way at the moment. I am willing her to go the right way. The one which will make it easier for me.

'I don't want him to go on holiday. Not without me. We always used to go on holiday together.' Her face crumples, the tears start. I have lost her now. Once she makes up her mind about something, it's very hard to change it. Adam always used to say she got it from me.

'I know, love, but Daddy can't do that any more. We'll have a little holiday here while Daddy has his. We'll go for some days out and spend lots of time together.'

'I don't want to. I hate you.' The words cut straight through me. I need to explain why I'm doing this. I open my mouth to say something about the pictures but shut it again. I know she will deny that it is a problem for her. And I don't want to give her a complex about it, stop her doing the pictures. It is important that she has an outlet. Any outlet.

'Come here,' I say, trying to pull her closer. 'Mummy loves you lots.'

'Well, I love Daddy more than you. I love Daddy to the

moon and back. I only love you to Hebden Bridge and back, so there.' She wriggles free from me, turns and runs out of the kitchen. I know that Adam would have laughed at that. I am trying to laugh. Trying very hard. But the tears keep getting in the way.

I know exactly where Maya will have run to. Or rather who she will have run to. I give her a minute or two then follow her through to the lounge where I find her standing next to the bed with her head pressed against Adam's chest and her arms draped over him as if protecting him from some evil force. Me, in this case.

'I won't let you take him,' she shouts.

'Maya, please calm down, it's not fair to upset Daddy like this.'

'Mummy's going to send you away,' says Maya, turning her back on me to talk to Adam.

'It's only for a holiday, Maya. Daddy needs a holiday, sweetheart. We all do.'

Maya starts to cry again. I sense this time that she will let me hug her. I wrap my arms around her, laying my head on her back.

'It's a family sandwich,' she says through the tears. 'I'm the bit in the middle.'

I pretend to nibble her, Maya giggles. I love the way children can do that; go from abject misery to giggling hysterically in ten seconds flat.

'Mummy and Daddy love you more than anything in the world, Maya. You have to trust me to do what's best for all of us, OK? And you wouldn't want to stop Daddy going on holiday, would you?'

The giggles stop just as quickly as they started.

'I want a proper family holiday together. I want Daddy to make sandcastles with me. I'm the only one in my class who didn't go on holiday in the summer. And I'm the only one in my class who hasn't got a brother or sister. And they've all got daddies who can play with them. It's not fair.'

I turn her around and pull her close to me so her tears can mix in with mine. Unable to tell her that of all the hurtful words she's uttered this morning, it's the one about not having a brother or sister which has penetrated deepest into me.

'It's not fair, sweetheart. It's not fair at all. But the person it's not fair to most is Daddy. And we've got to be strong for him and do what's best for our family. Because we are a family, Maya. We may be different to all the other families your friends at school have got but we're still a family and it's really important you remember that.' Maya nods her head and turns to look at Adam.

'Look, Mummy, he's crying too.' There is a tiny tear in the corner of Adam's left eye. It's happened a few times before. Mum just says his eyes are watering. I know they're not, though. Not this time.

'I told you Daddy loves you very much, didn't I?'

Maya nods. 'If I'm going to have a holiday here, does that mean I can still have ice creams?'

I smile at her. 'Of course you can. Maybe we'll even go to Blackpool for the day. It wouldn't be a holiday without ice creams, would it?'

Maya hugs me. I wonder if she loves me a bit more now. Maybe to Blackpool and back.

★

'I'm sorry,' I say to Adam, as soon as I come back down from putting Maya to bed. 'I didn't mean for you to find out like that. I didn't have a chance this morning, or maybe I was just too chicken to tell you.'

I sit down on the edge of his bed, take hold of his hand.

'It is respite care. And it's only for one week. A place called Hazelwood House in Littleborough. You'll have driven past it, though I don't suppose you'll remember it. I didn't. They recommended it at the hospital. Twenty-four-hour nursing care. Proper nurses, not me playing at being Florence Nightingale. The woman who owns it is funny. Funny weird. Dorothy her name is, just think Sybil Fawlty with a Lancashire accent. Anyway, hopefully she'll keep you entertained. Think of her as one of the redcoats.'

I stroke his hand, my thumb flicking rhythmically across his palm.

'It's because Maya's been doing pictures at school. Black pictures. Pictures of you being dead and dinosaurs standing over you. It's started since you've been home, apparently. I think she needs time to come to terms with what's happened and I need to spend more time with her. Give her all the support and comfort she needs. She loves you so much and she's trying to be brave about it but it's so hard for her. She misses you. We all do.'

I pause for a moment and dab at the tear in the corner of Adam's eye with a tissue. It's not easy, trying to strike a balance between explaining why I am doing this and not wanting him to feel bad about how his being here is impacting on us.

'I want you to know that I don't regret bringing you home, not for one second. If you turned the clock back I'd do exactly the same thing again. But I do need to do what's right for Maya. And it may be that she'll need a break like this every month or two. It may be that I do too. I know you'll understand that. Please don't hate me, please don't think I'm abandoning you and please don't think it's got anything to do with what Steve said because it hasn't, OK?'

I squeeze his hand tight so that he knows I mean it. Maya's words are still going around in my head. The ones about not having a brother or sister. She has never mentioned it before. It was almost as if she knew on some deep subconscious level that it would be too much for me. The signs were all there, though. I simply chose to ignore them. And to shoot down Adam when he picked up on them. That day at the museum when Maya was talking about Monty being lonely.

The realisation that it is time to tell Adam ebbs over me. I do not fight it. I have remained silent long enough. Adam has a right to know.

'There is one thing I do regret, though,' I say, my voice reduced to barely more than a whisper. 'Something I did a long time ago. Something that I kept from you because I was so scared of losing you.'

I pause, it is not a case of finding the right words. There are no right words. Only a cold and brutal truth.

'Maya is our second child. I got pregnant with our first just before my sixteenth birthday. After that time, well, you know what it was after. It wasn't as if we made a habit of it. I was in shock; denial, I suppose. Only my mum found the test stick in the bathroom bin. I should have realised she was that nosy but I guess I wasn't thinking straight at the time.'

I look away from Adam, up at the ceiling. Try to compose myself before going on.

'She went mental. Told me to have an abortion. Said if I did she wouldn't tell my dad or your dad and we could go on seeing each other. But that if I refused, the police would become involved and you could get sent to prison for having sex with an underage girl. I didn't see that I had a choice. I do now of course but at the time . . .'

My voice breaks off. I wipe at the tears streaming down my face with the back of my hand. The other hand. The one which is not holding tightly on to Adam, desperately trying to keep him with me as I add to his pain.

'It was sorted very quickly. A matter of days. And I was only about six weeks gone. Not that that makes it any better, I know. It was during the half-term holiday. Mum took me to a place in Manchester. I told you I was going shopping with Lisa and Julie. I hated lying to you but I didn't want you to get into trouble. And afterwards I wanted to tell you so much but by then it was done and I was so scared that if I told you it would finish us and you'd dump me. And I couldn't bear losing you, not after I'd just lost—' I screw my eyes up tight but still the tears find a way through. Forcing their way out of the darkness.

'I'm sorry, love. I'm so, so sorry.' I lay my head on to his chest as Maya had done a couple of hours ago. Wondering if Adam wants to caress it, as he would have done hers. Or whether he cannot bear my flesh to be touching his. It is a long time before I muster the courage to speak again.

'There was nothing to see or to bury or anything. They just took it away. My mum never talked about it again. Not even on the way home. I don't know how I coped, really. I was obviously traumatised by it all but I just buried it somewhere deep inside. And that's what's been eating away at me all these years. That's why I was so worried about losing Maya during the pregnancy and why I didn't want to try for another child. I know how much you wanted that and I know that Maya would have loved it too. It was selfish of me. I realise that now.'

I slowly raise my head and open my eyes and look at Adam.

'I totally understand it if you hate me. I'm not asking for or expecting forgiveness. I just felt you should know. Of all the years we've spent together, that's the only regret I have. Of agreeing to it, of not telling you at the time and then letting it fester away like this, spoiling our happiness. And when you had the accident, when I first saw you lying there in hospital, all I could think was how stupid and selfish I'd been. And how I wished I'd agreed to try for a baby. Wished I had a little bit of you growing inside of me so that if anything happened I'd have something to give to Maya. Something to help ease her pain.'

I sit in silence for a while. Waiting for the tears to subside. Wondering what is going on inside Adam's head. Maybe he wishes he was going into a home for good now. Maybe he'd be pleased to be shot of me. I don't feel cleansed at all.

I feel dirty all over again. And if I shut my eyes tight I see a seventeen year old lying asleep in the spare bedroom upstairs. A boy, I've always seen him as a boy. A boy who looks more like Adam with every passing day.

Thirty

I thought she was going to tell me she'd slept with Steve. I thought that was going to be the secret. The thing she had to confess. And the awful thing is not just that I doubted her but that for a second back there, at the part where she told me, I was actually relieved that that wasn't what it was. How sad is that? How awful does that make me?

A baby. We had a baby. Way back before Maya. I feel the pain pouring out of Mel as she lies on me. Seeping through her pores. I am hurting, really hurting. But it is nothing compared to her. All this time and I had no idea, no fucking idea at all. Can fifteen-year-old boys really be that oblivious to what is going on around them? I guess they can. All I can remember is her seeming a bit quiet, perhaps a bit off with me. And being peeved when she said she wanted to wait until after her sixteenth birthday to have sex again. The sex had been my idea. I hadn't forced her or anything but I'd started it, I was the one who got carried away, the one who asked her if we could, just this once, please forget about the waiting thing. What a bloody self-obsessed idiot I was. To think that she was going through all that on her own and all I was worried about was Leeds United getting knocked out the Champions League.

I don't blame Mel for what she did. I don't blame her at all. I blame her mum for being such a cow about it, being more bothered about what other people would think than how Mel was feeling. But as much as I hate to admit it, she was also probably right. We couldn't have had a baby. We had our whole lives in front of us. Mel couldn't have done her A levels or gone to uni or anything. And I couldn't have supported her. Not without packing my studies in and getting some crappy job in a burger joint. And where would we have lived? Would I have moved into Mel's house? It would have been crazy. But at the same time it was our baby. And to see Maya now and to think that we could also have a teenager, I mean they'd be older than we were back then. It's scary as hell but I can't help wondering what they'd have been like. Whether it was a boy or a girl. Maybe they'd have a boyfriend or girlfriend of their own by now. Jeez. This is way too much to take in.

There is so much I want to know, so many questions to ask. And yet my silence, as frustrating as it is to me, must be a nightmare for Mel. Because there's no way I can reassure her, no way to tell her it's OK. I don't hate her. I could never hate her in a million years. Not after all that she's given me. And besides, the whole reason she went through with it was to protect me. How could I hate her for that?

I try again. Try to move my arms, my hands, my fingers even. To reach out to her, to hold her, to take the hurt away. Still nothing. I won't give up though. I will go on trying. All through the night if necessary. I will find a way to break through, to show her that I might have let her down once but I am not going to do it again.

★

I come to with a start. I made a noise. A grunting sort of noise. Out loud, not in my head. I strain my eyes in the dark, trying to move them to the corners, trying to see Mel, to make sure she heard. It is not Mel, though. It is Cynthia. One of the sitters. The one with the bloody hearing aid. She is fiddling with it now. She probably thinks it was that that made the noise. Or maybe it isn't working properly. Maybe she didn't hear the noise at all. I sigh inside. I am going to have to wait until the morning to try all over again.

I feel Maya's hands on my toes. I actually feel them. Little hands. Tickly hands. Reaching under the covers to play her favourite early-morning game with me. Cynthia has gone. Mel must have been in already and gone to the kitchen to gather her things.

'This little piggy went to market, this little piggy stayed at home.'

I can feel each toe individually. Feel her fingers squeezing and pulling them in turn.

'This little piggy had roast beef, and this little piggy had none. And this little piggy went wee, wee, wee, all the way home.' Maya bends my big toe downwards. Sharply downwards. It hurts. My face contorts in pain. Maya lets go of my foot in surprise.

'Sorry, Daddy,' she says. And then she stops short. As if realising that she hasn't seen my face change expression like that for months. I did it. I broke through. I am willing her to call out. To call out right now. Right now this minute.

'Mummy!'

Mel comes flying into the room, her eyes bulging wide. She looks at me then Maya then back to me again.

'What is it?' she says. 'What's the matter?'

'Daddy pulled a face.'

'What sort of face?'

'Like this.' Maya does a pretty impressive grimace. Mel looks at me. I'm trying to do it again but I can't. Maya needs to help me. She needs to show her.

'What were you doing to him?'

'This little piggy. Like I always do.' She goes back to my feet. Starts the whole process from the beginning again. I wish I could fast forward her to the exciting bit. I pray I'll do it again when she gets there. I have no idea if I can. Maya yanks my toe even harder this time, as if desperate to prove to Mel that she was telling the truth. I grimace again. I have no idea how I managed it but I did. A smile spreads slowly over Mel's face. It spreads so high and so wide that it is in danger of toppling off it.

'You did it,' she says grinning at me. 'You really did. You're back with us, aren't you? Not that you've ever really been away. I knew that. I always knew you'd come back to us.' She rushes over to me and hugs my still body the best she can then starts covering me with little kisses. Maya joins in too, squealing with excitement, piling on to me like some crazy footballer celebrating a goal. And somewhere underneath it I am euphoric. Never has such a small, insignificant thing meant so much to one man. I can feel pain. Physical pain. Therefore I am human again. I live.

They both gaze at me as if I'm a newborn baby. Full of

awe and delight. I feel the pressure to do something; to make a sound, a movement, anything to prove it wasn't a fluke.

'Will he start talking now?' asks Maya eventually.

'Not straight away, love. No.'

'By bedtime?'

'It takes a lot longer than that, sweetheart.' Mel smiles. 'But hopefully now it's starting he'll get a little bit better every day.'

'Is Daddy still going to go on his little holiday?'

'No, love,' says Mel. She says it without hesitation. 'Well, not to the place in the brochure, anyway. If he does go away, it will be somewhere to help him get better. That's what we're going to do now. Help Daddy to get better as soon as he possibly can.'

They sit and gaze at me some more. Hugging each other. Both of their faces streaked with tears but awash with joy. And although they may not be able to see it or hear it, I am crying inside too. Crying like a baby.

The community nurse comes that afternoon. Mel phoned her before she went to work. She phoned Louise as well. I heard her, even from the kitchen. She was like a big kid who'd got the birthday present she'd set her heart on.

She is still beaming now as she shows Dawn, the nurse, into the room. Desperate to show what her new toy can do.

'I haven't had a chance to try anything else,' she says. 'Would you like me to show you what my little girl did?' Dawn nods. Mel takes hold of my toes.

'Sorry, love,' she says to me. 'You're probably sick of this by now.' I'm not though. I am every bit as excited as her. Mel does at least dispense with the nursery rhyme, she cuts straight to the toe yank. My face contorts again. Mel looks triumphantly at Dawn.

'Yes, you're right,' Dawn says, smiling. 'That's a massive leap forward.'

'So what happens now?'

'Have you checked to see if he can communicate?'

Mel shakes her head. Dawn steps closer to the bed.

'I'm going to ask you a question, Adam. Please try to blink once for yes, twice for no. Are you comfortable this morning, Adam?'

I tug at my eyelids, pulling from beneath, pushing from above. I can tell by the expression on Mel's face that they are not moving.

'Never mind,' says Dawn. 'It will come in time.'

'I want him to see someone,' says Mel. 'A specialist, not someone we've seen before. I want them to do proper tests and scans on him. Like the ones I've read about.'

'I'll do my best,' says Dawn. 'I'll go and phone the GP. Ask him to call the hospital right away. Is that OK for you?'

Mel nods, she still can't speak for smiling.

Thirty-one

MEL

It feels so different being back at hospital this time. It is in Leeds, for a start. Somewhere new, somewhere untainted with what has gone before. Somewhere full of hope. Real hope. I am not thinking about the past, only of the future. The doctors were wrong all along. And I was right. If I ever see them again, a tiny childish part of me would like to say, 'Nah, nah, nah, nah, nah,' and stick my fingers up at them. I wouldn't really, though. Partly because I am thirty-four years old and partly because this is not about point-scoring between me and the doctors. It is about Adam. And only about Adam. He has managed to claw himself back to a point where they can finally see what I knew all along. He is still with us, in every sense of the word. And not only that, he is going to come back to us.

The progress in the past two days has been painfully slow but it has been progress nonetheless. Although poor Adam must feel rather like a human pincushion with all the poking and prodding he has been subjected to. The fact is he has responded to everything. Not verbally, but physically. He has withdrawn limbs and digits in response to pain. He is gradually ticking off the boxes, doing everything the doctors ask of him.

Earlier this morning they carried out an EEG scan to map the electrical activity in his brain. And right now he is inside an MRI scanner. I am sitting at the end of it, holding his legs. They advised waiting outside because of the noise but I refused. I want Adam to know that I am here for him, he is not alone. If he is embarking on his journey back to us I am going to be there every step of the way. I have headphones on, as Adam does inside the scanner. But I can still hear the loud sporadic clanking and whirring noises coming from the machine. They are probing the dark recesses of his mind. In the room behind the screen someone is looking at the images on a computer. Looking inside Adam's brain. I have been thinking about the Chilean miners, trapped for days in the dark and how they must have felt when at last help came. When they were brought to the surface. When they saw the light again.

'It's OK,' I say to him. 'They know you're in there now. And we'll find a way to get you out.'

It is gone four o'clock by the time Dr Stephenson is ready to see me. He is young with short cropped blond hair. I like him instantly because he believes. He is the one who set up all these tests. Who wanted to find out what Adam's brain *is* capable of doing, not what it can't do.

'Sorry to keep you, Mrs Taylor,' he says, sitting down behind his desk. 'I wanted to have a chance to go through the results properly before I spoke to you.'

I nod, anxious for him to cut to the chase, to tell me what I want to hear.

'The results are encouraging,' he says. 'The neurological

and behavioural findings are that your husband does not meet the diagnostic criteria for vegetative state.'

I smile and nod my head. It is what I wanted to hear.

'What we can't say for certain is whether that has always been the case with Adam or whether he has progressed through coma and vegetative state to where he is now.'

'And where is he now?'

'I believe he's in a minimally conscious state. That's distinguished from vegetative state by the partial preservation of conscious awareness.'

'You mean he knows what's going on around him?'

'I understand that's how you perceive it. From a purely neurological point of view, we say there are islands of activation in his brain.'

I nod more slowly, I am sifting through all the research I've read over the past few months, putting all the pieces of the jigsaw together.

'I've read the studies they've done at Addenbrooke's Hospital,' I tell him. 'The ones where they've asked patients to imagine playing tennis and the corresponding parts of their brain have lit up.'

'Right, well, that's a good example. Obviously we haven't done anything as complex as that with Adam but it is possible from what we've seen that his brain could be capable of processing information in that way.'

'So how can we help him? He'll be desperate to make himself understood. To communicate.'

'That's our next step. For some patients it might be vocal, for others using a letter board or simply blinking their eyes. In the very short term I can show you some things to try with him at home and arrange for a speech therapist to visit. But what I'd really like to do is to get him on a proper brain rehabilitation programme.'

'Where would that be?'

'There's a place in Goole which deals with these sort of post-acute cases. It's run by the Brain Injury Rehabilitation Trust. If you're happy for me to refer Adam, I think it would be enormously beneficial to him.'

'There's nowhere nearer?' Goole is a good hour and a quarter's drive from our house.

'No. They run an excellent rehabilitation programme, though. I can't recommend it highly enough.'

'Then we'll do it,' I say, without hesitation. 'Whatever it takes to get Adam back.'

Dr Stephenson nods and smiles. It is a hesitant sort of smile. 'I know this is a good news day for you after what must have been an incredibly tough few months but I do have to sound a note of caution here. It's really important that you're realistic about what lies ahead. As Adam emerges from his minimally conscious state he'll go through something called PTA, post-traumatic amnesia. It will carry on for a long time, we're talking weeks. He'll be confused, disinhibited, aggressive even. It's a very difficult period for relatives but what you need to remember is that he'll not be in control and cannot be held responsible for what he says or does.'

'But he'll be fine afterwards though, won't he? When the amnesia ends. He'll be able to get back to normal.'

Dr Stephenson shakes his head, his expression now firmly set to serious mode. 'The rehabilitation process is a long, slow and often painful one. It's not a question of getting your husband back, more of adjusting to the new person who emerges.'

I let out a long sigh. The emotional roller-coaster ride continues. 'What are you saying? That he won't be like Adam?'

'Not the Adam you know, no. If he'd lost a leg in the accident he wouldn't be the same Adam, would he? And it's exactly the same with a brain injury except you haven't been able to see the damage because it's been hidden from us. But once he's out of PTA, it will be very noticeable. A severe frontal lobe injury like the one Adam suffered will have caused changes to his personality, his behaviour and his emotions. I'm very sorry but he really won't be the same person.'

I shake my head. Determined not to be fobbed off with bad news again. 'No, you're wrong. The doctors have been wrong all along. Adam has proven everyone wrong. Everyone who hasn't believed in him.'

Dr Stephenson gets up and comes round to sit on the edge of his desk. His gaze is long and steady. His voice calm.

'Look, for him to get back to where he is after such a severe brain injury is very much against the odds. But please believe me when I say this is where the miracles end. There are always a minority of patients who confound medical opinion by emerging from a prolonged unresponsive state, there is still so much we don't know about that area. But what we do know a lot about is how patients respond once they come out the other side. And as difficult as it is to come to terms with, the sooner you accept that he will not be the same person as he was before, the easier it will be for you.'

I want to scream at Dr Stephenson to stop. He is trying to burst my bubble. He still doesn't get it. Doesn't realise what Adam is capable of. I want to tell him everything that has been going on in Adam's head since the accident. But I can't do that. Because if I do, he will simply accuse me of imagining it all.

'No, Adam is different,' I say firmly. 'I will get him back. Because he's never really gone away.'

Dr Stephenson phones the following afternoon. He speaks nicely to me, even though I know I gave him a hard time. He tells me Adam has a provisional place booked at the neuro rehab unit for a week tomorrow. I feel a sharp stab of pain at the thought of Adam going away so soon. But I only have to think about how much worse I would have felt about sending him to Hazelwood House for the pain to instantly dissipate. This is not about putting Adam out to grass. This is about getting him better. Getting him back. Because he will still come back to me. I know he will.

As soon as I put the phone down I go straight to Adam to pass on the news. He knows already that it is on the cards. Dr Stephenson talked to him about it and I did too. We are in this together now. There are no secrets any more.

'You've got the place at Goole, love,' I say, squeezing his hand. 'Starting the end of next week. They're going to get you better, OK? Everything's going to be fine.'

He squeezes my hand back, the tiniest squeeze, so tiny

most people would probably not even notice. But I do.

'I felt that,' I say, sitting up with a start and grinning at him. 'I really did. Do it again, if you can.' I wait. Nothing. 'Sorry, love. I didn't feel that one but, hey, one's quite enough to be going on with.' I lay my head on his chest, feeling a childlike wonder at what is happening. It's as if he is slowly, very slowly, coming back to life.

'I know it's going to be hard, going away, but you'll be getting the best treatment available. Every time I visit, you'll be doing something new. We're moving forward. After all this time we're actually getting somewhere. You're incredible, you know. Fighting back like this. I love you very much.' I bend down and kiss him on the lips. And maybe, just maybe, he tries to kiss me back.

When I come back into the lounge that evening after getting the dishwasher going, Maya is wrapped tightly in one of the curtains.

'What are you doing, love?'

'I've made a cocoon. I'm trying to turn into a butterfly.'

I laugh out loud. As I do so, Adam makes a noise. It's not a word, more of a 'hhmmmpf' but it is the timing which is significant.

'Daddy's laughing,' says Maya, wriggling out from under the curtain and running over to his bed.

'Yes, I think he is. I think you made him laugh.'

'I'll do it again,' she says. 'I've got a joke for him. Knock, knock?'

'Who's there?' I say, doing Adam's bit for him.

'Santa.'

'Santa who?'

'Don't be silly, there's only one Santa.' I smile at the fact that she hasn't quite mastered these yet.

'Did you make that one up, love?'

'Yes. Was it funny?'

'Very funny.'

'So why isn't Daddy laughing?'

'Because he's learning to do everything again. It's a bit like you learning to write your letters and sounds. Sometimes it comes out how you want it to, sometimes it doesn't. But you're still trying really hard both times.'

Maya nods. I sense this is the right moment. I take her by the hand and lead her out into the kitchen, not wanting to upset Adam any more than necessary.

'Remember we talked about Daddy going away somewhere to help him get better. Not the place in the brochure you saw, a different place, somewhere where they can help him learn to do everything for himself again?'

'Yes. He's not going before Christmas, though, is he?'

'I'm afraid he is, love. He's going in a week. But the sooner he goes, the sooner he can get better and come back home to us.' I watch her evaluating this new piece of information, deciding how to respond.

'That's OK,' she says. 'As long as he's better for my birthday.'

'Thank you, sweetheart,' I say, giving her a hug. 'Daddy will be really proud to know how good you've been about that.'

'And when he comes home, he'll be like Daddy again, won't he?'

I stroke her head, desperate to take the pain away for her but also knowing that after listening to what Dr Stephenson said it would be wrong of me not to be cautious.

'He won't be quite the same, love. There'll be some things he'll still find tricky but, yes, he should be able to do a lot more with you.'

'Like read bedtime stories?'

'Maybe, love. We'll have to wait and see.'

We are still snuggled up with Adam reading a bedtime story when I hear the knock on the door. I frown then shake my head as I realise. I haven't heard from Steve since last Thursday. I wasn't sure he'd come back after what he said. He's early too. I wonder if he's done it on purpose, knowing I won't shut the door in his face if Maya is with me.

'Who's that?' asks Maya.

'It might be Steve, come to visit Daddy.'

'Will Loo-eeze be with him?'

'No, love. Just Steve.'

I go to the door, Maya running around my legs like an excited puppy.

'Hi,' says Steve. 'I know I'm a bit early. The roads were quiet tonight.' I'm not convinced by his excuse but open the door wide anyway.

'Come in, then,' I say.

'Are those for Daddy?' asks Maya, spotting the bunch of flowers he is holding behind his back.

'Er, your mummy, actually.'

'Why have you got her flowers?' Maya is doing a good

job of asking all of my questions. Steve glances at me and back to Maya. Clearly aware that saying, 'To apologise for telling your mummy Daddy slept with someone else' is not an option.

'Well, she's doing a great job looking after your daddy, isn't she?'

Maya nods. Steve hands the flowers to me. They are good ones from an expensive florist, not the petrol forecourt variety that he used to get Louise. The same uneasy feeling returns to the pit of my stomach.

'Thanks,' I say as Steve takes his boots off. 'You can go through to the kitchen to warm up if you like. I'm just going to finish Maya's story.'

'Daddy's getting better,' says Maya. 'He can pull faces if I hurt his toes.'

Steve looks at me, frowning, waiting for me to tell him Maya is making it up.

'It's true.'

Steve's frown deepens. 'But how? I don't understand.'

'A lot can happen in a week.' I say.

'Daddy's not going on holiday to the old people's home now, the one Mummy went to see with Loo-eeze. He's going to a place where they'll make him better.'

Steve stares at me, eyebrows raised. Maya's telling him rather too much now.

'Look, let me get Maya up to bed then I'll fill you in.'

Steve stumbles over the step up to the kitchen. He appears rather disorientated. I go back into the lounge to finish Maya's story, she says goodnight to Adam, kisses him on the cheek. I haven't told her about Adam squeezing my hand yet. I want to wait until he can do it consistently so she's not disappointed.

'Why doesn't Steve come with Loo-eeze any more?' asks Maya as she gets changed into her pyjamas. It's a fair question and at some point I'm going to have to explain about the divorce but I'm not sure that point is now. I decide to go halfway and prepare the groundwork, see how she takes it.

'Steve and Louise aren't actually living together at the moment. Steve's got himself a little flat. He wanted some time and space on his own to sort out a few things.'

'What, like his clothes and stuff?'

'Sort of, love,' I smile.

'Why can't Loo-eeze help him with those?'

'Steve wanted to do it all by himself. He needs some time on his own.'

'But he still comes round here to see Daddy, doesn't he? And to bring you flowers.'

'Yes, love,' I say, kissing her on the forehead. 'Now, you snuggle down under that duvet with Iggle-piggle. Mummy and Daddy love you lots, OK?'

'Mummy,' Maya says as I turn the light out. 'Isn't Loo-eeze a bit lonely on her own?'

'Yes, love. I think she is. I was going to ask what you thought about inviting her round to share Christmas dinner with us this year.'

'Yes. I'd like that. Will she bring presents?'

'I expect she will, love.' I smile. 'Now, straight to sleep, OK?'

I check in on Adam on my way back to the kitchen. He

is quiet and still. I guess he heard Steve's voice when he arrived. I don't have to tell him he's here. I don't want to talk to Steve in front of him, though. Not today.

'I'll be back in a bit,' I say, stroking his arm before leaving the room. And carefully closing the door behind me.

I go through to the kitchen. Steve is sitting at the table. He has already made coffee for us both. The flowers are in the sink.

'Sorry,' he says. 'I couldn't find a vase.'

I nod and sit down opposite him. I hate the awkward silence. I notice he no longer has his wedding ring on. I have no idea how long ago he took it off.

'So, you'd better fill me in on what's been happening, then,' Steve says.

'Yeah. Well, Adam's not in a vegetative state, for a start.'

'Who said so?'

'A doctor. We saw a different one. Turns out Adam's actually in a minimally conscious state.'

'What's the difference?'

'A hell of a lot, according to the doctor.'

'What doctor? Who have you seen? It's not some quack, is it?'

I am taken aback by the tone of his voice. I don't understand why he is being so negative when it's good news.

'Steve, please, just hang on a sec and let me explain.'

Steve shrugs and takes a sip of his coffee.

'Adam grimaced when Maya pulled his toe back on Sunday. He did it several times. The community nurse arranged for him to go into hospital in Leeds to see a neurologist there. He examined him, they did some tests and scans, things they've never done before, and found that he has some islands of activation in his brain.'

'What does that mean?'

'He appears to be aware of himself and his environment.'

Steve puts his coffee down so quickly some of it spills on to the table. 'Does that mean he can hear what's being said and understand it?'

'Well, yeah. But then we've always known that, haven't we?'

Steve appears unsure. 'What else can he do?'

'He's squeezed my hand back and he's made a noise when Maya said something funny.'

'But that could just be a coincidence.'

'Not any more. There's been too many of them.'

Steve nods slowly and fiddles with the handle of his mug. 'Right. So, er, what happens now?'

'He's going to a neuro-rehabilitation centre in Goole in a week's time. They say he's emerging from the minimally conscious state. The doctor's saying this, Steve. It's not just me.'

'So what was Maya saying about the home you went to with Louise?'

It's my turn to shuffle awkwardly in my seat.

'I thought about what you said, the respite care, I mean, not the other stuff. I realised it made sense, that's why I went to look round a nursing home.'

'When was this?'

'Last Saturday. The day before this all happened.'

Steve looks hurt. 'I'd have taken you. You only had to ask.'

'I thought you'd be busy. Anyway, Louise offered.'

Steve looks at me hard, as if sensing I am not being entirely straight with him. We are skirting around the issue but it is not going to go away. 'Look, I didn't ask because I didn't want you to think I'd changed my mind because of what you'd said about Adam.'

Steve nods and runs his fingers through his hair. 'For what it's worth, I wouldn't have thought that. I know you far too well.' He holds his head in his hands and sighs deeply.

'What's the matter?'

'It's a hell of a lot to take in, that's all. How long's he going to be at this rehab place?'

'I don't know exactly. They've warned me it's going to be a long process. The doctor doesn't think Adam's ever going to get back to how he used to be.'

'Maybe he's right,' says Steve. 'Maybe we all need to start getting our heads around that.'

'No,' I say, shaking my head. 'Adam will prove them wrong. Just like he has all the way through this. You know what he's like. He's never going to stop fighting.'

'It doesn't mean to say he's going to win, though.'

'Whose side are you on?'

'Yours. I'm just trying to protect you.'

We sit in silence for a moment, the tenderness in Steve's voice managing to hold at bay my frustration at his refusal to believe in Adam as much as I do.

'So what will happen?' asks Steve eventually. 'When he starts to come round properly.'

'It's not like you've seen in the films. He won't just

suddenly snap out of it. He's going to go through this post-traumatic amnesia thing that sounds really horrible.'

'Will he remember anything that's happened? While he's been unconscious, I mean.'

'I don't know. They didn't say.'

Steve nods, he brings the mug to his lips then puts it down again. 'Did they say when he'll start talking?'

'No, not really. He's going to have a speech therapist and everything. He might be able to communicate with a letter board before he can speak.'

'I see.' Steve's hand is shaking. He drinks the rest of his coffee in one go and walks over to place the mug in the sink. It slips from his hand and falls into the bowl. Luckily the water he put in for the flowers breaks the fall. 'Look,' he says, turning around. 'I wanted to say sorry about last week. That's what the flowers are for. I never meant it to come out like that. I never meant to hurt you.'

'So why did you say it?'

'Sometimes you have to tell the truth. Even if you know the other person doesn't want to hear it.'

'Why?'

He hesitates before answering. 'It doesn't matter any more, does it?' He's talking in riddles again. I can understand why he used to drive Louise mad.

'Of course it matters. I want to know.'

Steve walks over to me. 'OK, I told you because I couldn't bear to see you beating yourself up about putting Adam into a home for one week. And maybe because I'm still angry at Adam for doing that to you.'

'I don't believe he did do it, though.' I stand up, ready to take my mug over to the sink but Steve is in my path and he doesn't appear to want to get out of the way.

'I know you'll defend Adam to the hilt but I want you to know I would never have done that to you. Never have hurt you like that.'

The intensity of his gaze is beginning to unnerve me. I feel the sudden need to go on the attack.

'How can you say that when you've hurt Louise so much?'

'That was different.'

'Why?'

'Because she wasn't the person I'd always loved. The person I longed to be with.'

'Well, who was then?'

There is a pause. Steve doesn't take his eyes off me. He steps closer, takes my face in his hands and kisses me. Hard on the lips. For a second I am rendered incapable of speech or movement. It is like he has pressed the pause button on the remote. I feel the warmth of his breath, the roughness of his stubble against my face and the sense of pure desperation in his touch. Finally I manage to wrest the remote from him and press play. I pull free and stagger back a step or two.

'What the hell are you doing?'

Steve's face is flushed, his eyes bulging.

'I thought you realised. I thought . . .'

I shake my head. 'Get out,' I say, my voice barely above a whisper. My whole body quivering as I point towards the door. 'And don't ever, ever come back.'

Steve picks up his jacket from the back of the kitchen chair and heads straight for the door in long, quick strides.

My heart is going so fast I can't feel the individual beats any more. Only a constant hammering. I count the seconds until I hear the front door close behind him. I sink down on to the floor, holding my head in my hands, unable to believe I have been so naive. So bloody, bloody stupid.

Steve was lying when he said there was no one else. There is. It's me.

PART FOUR

Thirty-two

ADAM

Friday, 3 December 2010

'I haven't got time for exercises. I need to go on the computer. I've got a story to file. I've got a deadline.'

'There's plenty of time, Adam, this won't take long at all.'

Tracey is a physiotherapist. It says so on the door. She doesn't understand that when you're a journalist you can't miss your deadline. You can't just lie there lifting your legs up and down.

'That's great, Adam. You've got a great range of movement now.'

'Why couldn't I learn to walk again by myself? Why do I need you?'

'Because the part of your brain which deals with walking was damaged in the accident. And my job's to help people like you.'

They all talk about 'the accident'. I've been told about it enough times to know what happened. They say a dinosaur skull fell on my head at the museum where I worked. I remember working at the museum. I remember a dinosaur skeleton but I don't remember the bit where the skull fell on my head. At first I thought they had made it up but they have told me it so often now I don't think they did.

'OK. Let's have you sitting up now.' Tracey beams at me as I sit up on the bed. I don't know why she makes such a big deal about the fact that I can sit up. You'd think I was a baby or something. I am not. My name is Adam Taylor. I am thirty-three years old. I live in Cragg Vale in West Yorkshire but I am not there at the moment. I am staying here in Goole because of my accident. It is like being back at school. I am having to learn how to do everything again. They don't realise that I am fine. That there is nothing wrong with me.

'There's a press conference starting soon I've got to go to.'

'I won't keep you much longer now, Adam,' says Tracey. 'You're doing really well. I just want to get you up on your feet.'

She helps me into my wheelchair and pushes me over to the two bars at the side of the room, positions me between them and helps me stand up. I grasp a bar with each hand. My legs feel disconnected to my body. It is hard to get them to move.

'That's great, Adam. Keep going.'

'When can I start running again?' I ask.

I love running. I do remember running. Outside, on the hills. Over the tops. Wind and cold and rain and mud. All of them on my body. My legs just kept moving.

'All in good time,' says Tracey. 'We're taking things one step at a time, remember? People wouldn't believe that when you arrived here a couple of months ago you could barely move, let alone walk.'

'How did I learn?'

'You practised. Every day here with me. Like you practised to learn to speak again and to eat.'

'Where did the food go when I couldn't eat?'

'Through a tube into your stomach. Do you remember we looked at your scar last week, where the tube used to be?'

I think I remember but I'm not sure. I have a scar on my head as well. It is under my hair but I know it is there. I lift my hand up to try to touch it. As I do so, I stumble and have to grab hold of the bar with both hands. I thump the air with my fist. I hate it when that happens.

'OK, Adam. I think we'll leave it there for today,' says Tracey, getting my wheelchair and turning me around to sit me down in it. 'You've done really well. I'll see you same time tomorrow.'

I hear that a lot. 'Same time tomorrow'. There is a timetable like we had at school. It is lunchtime now. I wheel myself back down the corridor to the dining room. I sit in the same place as usual. The man sitting opposite me is being helped by one of the women wearing a uniform. He is young, younger than me.

'That's it. You sit down here with me and Gary,' the woman says.

'How old are you?' I ask him. He looks across at the woman.

'Twenty-one, aren't you?' says the woman. 'Mind you, that's what they all say.' She laughs as if that is funny. Gary knocks his water over, it goes down his trousers. It looks as if he has wet himself. I start laughing. Gary starts laughing too.

'I've peed my pants,' says Gary. Some of the others laugh

too. The woman in uniform mops it up and gets him some more water. She doesn't seem to find it so funny.

I finish my jacket potato. Another woman brings me some sponge pudding. Everybody gets sponge pudding. I don't know if we always have sponge pudding. I can't remember what we had yesterday. I can't remember what we had for breakfast.

'I don't want this. I want custard.' Gary throws the sponge pudding on the floor.

'We don't do that with our food, do we, Gary?' says the woman.

'I want custard,' says Gary.

'He wants custard,' I repeat. The woman does not seem to understand. She cleans him up and gets him some more sponge pudding. He eats it this time.

'I thought you wanted custard?' I say. The woman looks at me. She still isn't laughing.

Mel arrives after lunch. It is when she always comes.

'Hello, love,' she says, bending to kiss me on the lips. Mel is safe, Mel is good, Mel is always. 'Tracey tells me you did really well walking this morning.'

'When did you see Tracey?'

'Just now. On my way in.'

'I thought you came straight from work.'

'I did. I just passed her in the corridor. We only spoke for a minute.'

'How long does it take from the university to get here?'

'I don't work at the university now, do I, Adam? I work at Calderdale College in Halifax.'

'Why didn't you tell me that?'

'I did. But you don't always remember things you've been told and it's not your fault.'

'Why don't you work at the university?'

'It didn't fit in with looking after you and Maya. I wanted to be nearer home and work less hours.'

'Is Maya here?'

'No, love. She's at school. She'll come tomorrow. She always comes at the weekend.'

'I want to see Maya.'

'I know, love. And she's desperate to see you too. She'll come tomorrow.'

'Why can't she come today?'

'She's at school.' Mel gets up and walks over to the window of my room and rearranges the flowers in my vase. She does it for a long time. When she turns around to look at me again she has a funny expression on her face. It is kind of smiley and kind of sad.

'She was in the gold book at school again this morning.'

'Who?'

'Maya. Dad went to the assembly so she had someone there to wave to.'

'From the train? Did your dad wave from the train?'

'No. There weren't any trains. He was in Maya's school assembly.'

'The trains are never late at Gainsborough.' There is a pause.

'Did Dad tell you that?' Mel sounds as if she really wants to know.

I shrug. I have no idea how I know that.

Mel smiles and nods. She used to smile a lot. When I think about her, when I remember seeing her face, it was always smiling.

'I've got another joke for you,' I say. I've been doing ones I remember from when I was a kid. I used to know a lot of jokes. 'Knock, knock.'

'Who's there?'

'B-4.'

'B-4 who?'

'B-4 I freeze to death, please open this door.'

Mel smiles again. It is not a very good smile.

'You know, like before I do this,' I say.

'Yeah. It's OK, I get it.'

'Had you heard it before, then?'

'Before. That's a good joke.'

'What is?'

Mel says it doesn't matter and goes back to rearranging the flowers.

I have always been with Mel. I do remember that. She says she loves me. I know she is really good to me. But I don't know what she wore last time she came or what she told me last Friday. I hate that. I hate not being able to piece everything together. My fist comes down heavily on the bedside table.

'Hey, it's OK,' says Mel, rushing back over to crouch down next to me. 'It won't be long now. They say you'll soon be able to remember lots more. The worst is over.'

Mel puts some music on. All my favourite tracks are still on my iPod so I haven't lost any of them. I still know all the words to everything James Brown ever sang. 'It's a Man's World' comes on.

'I played this the first night you came home from hospital,' says Mel. 'I lay with my head on your chest and we listened to it together.'

Mel is looking at me. I don't remember that. I can remember something else, though.

'We had it at our wedding,' I say. 'And the band is going to play it at our anniversary party. It's a surprise for you. When is it going to be our party?'

Mel smiles and squeezes my hand. 'We had to postpone it, love. Maybe we can have it another year.'

'Next year. We could have it next year. Don't let your mum come, though. In case she starts singing. She's such a crap singer.'

'How do you know that?'

I think for a moment. Sometimes I just know things, I don't know where from.

'I remember from our wedding. And Maya's christening.' Mel squeezes my hand again. 'Anyway,' I say, 'where is Maya?'

Thirty-three

MEL

'How are you doing?' asks Dr Daines. She is tall and elegant and remarkably approachable for a consultant in neuro rehabilitation.

'I'm OK,' I say.

'No, really. How are you doing?'

I give a half-smile in acknowledgement of her determination not to be fobbed off with my stock answer.

'It's hard. I thought nothing could be worse than the first week. But when it goes on and on and on, it gets to feel like groundhog day. I know it sounds terrible but I actually dread visiting him sometimes. I certainly dread bringing Maya to see him in case Adam says something inappropriate.'

'It doesn't sound terrible at all. Loads of people feel like that. From what I've seen and heard, you're doing remarkably well. So many people show their frustration and that gets the patient even more agitated.'

'It's when he keeps asking the same thing over and over again.'

'I know but you're doing exactly as I asked you to. Remaining calm, not telling him you've told him that already. Not arguing with him when he says he's got a press conference to go to.'

I manage the other half of the smile. I always knew Adam missed journalism. In a bizarre way that's the one good thing about this. That, temporarily at least, he thinks he has got his old job back.

But the rest of it is tough, incredibly tough. Adam has been like this for weeks now. Actually, no, that's not true. He's been far worse than this. I can't say they didn't warn me but when you actually see your husband shouting and swearing at other people, or are aware that he's masturbating under the bedclothes while you're talking to him, it's hard to remember that he can't help it, it's because he's got a brain injury and not because he's an objectionable individual.

And even though Dr Daines and all the other staff reassured me that it was perfectly normal and lots of patients go through this phase during post-traumatic amnesia, it still upset me that my husband was doing it.

I say my husband, but in truth the man I have been visiting these past few weeks bears only a physical resemblance to Adam. My real husband is somewhere underneath his skin, still waiting to be revealed to me. It has been hard, incredibly hard to keep the faith while all this has been going on. And there have been moments, dark, lonely moments during long, sleepless nights, when I have thought maybe the doctors are right. Maybe the old Adam will never come back to me. But in daylight hours it does not pay to think like that. I need to believe. I need to be seen to believe and to be strong for Adam so that he can find the strength to come back to me.

'How much longer do you think?' I ask. 'Before he's out of PTA completely.'

'Only a week or so. His answers to my questions are becoming more and more consistent. It may not seem like it to you but he is retaining much more information.'

'And what will happen then? Will he start to remember things?'

'He'll be able to lay down new memories but I'm afraid he won't be able to remember anything from his time in PTA or from when he was in a minimally conscious state, or the coma, obviously.'

She says it so matter-of-factly. Clearly she has no idea what that means to me. How I have to cling to the belief that Adam has been with me all the way through this. That he has been aware of everything.

'He says things sometimes and can't remember where he heard it before or knows it from. He did it today, about my mum's terrible singing and something my dad said about trains. Things that he knows from when he was minimally conscious.'

Dr Daines smiles, a sympathetic, supportive kind of smile but a smile of a non-believer.

'I can only imagine how hard it must be to accept that there are no memories there but it doesn't in any way negate what you and your family and friends did for Adam and what it meant to him at the time.'

'But surely some people remember?'

She shakes her head. 'Not really. Very occasionally a person may come out with something that they think they remember from that time; a nugget of information, an unexplained understanding of a situation. But even then it can't be proved. And as I said, that's extremely rare. You need to prepare yourself for the fact that Adam won't remember anything at all.'

I nod, knowing I have to ask but suspecting I already know the answer.

'I told him something while he was in a minimally conscious state. Something important which happened in the past that he didn't know about. I take it you don't think he'll have any recollection of it?'

'No.' She shakes her head firmly. 'Not at all.'

'Would it be wise to tell him again? When he's out of the PTA, I mean?'

'Was it something that could upset him?'

'Yes.'

'And is there any reason now that he needs to know?'

'No. I guess not.'

'Best leave well alone then. He'll need stability, security and familiarity. It could do a lot more harm than good to tell him something upsetting.'

I nod. I know she's probably right. But I also know that I'll always be wondering whether he does remember and is just not telling me.

'And how quickly will he make progress? Once he comes out of PTA, I mean. How long before we start seeing the real Adam?'

Dr Daines looks serious for a moment. She hesitates before answering.

'I know we've talked about this before but the answer's still the same. Adam has made remarkable progress in so many areas but it's so important that you recognise that the Adam you remember from before the accident is

371

not the one you'll eventually be taking home.'

I nod. I like Dr Daines and I have learnt it is not worth arguing with the doctors about this. I will simply wait for Adam to prove them all wrong.

'I have got some good news, though,' continues Dr Daines. 'I've spoken to the neuro-rehab unit at Leeds, the one for patients who are ready for more advanced rehabilitation, and they've got a place for Adam.'

I smile. It's the next step forward. Leeds is good. It's nearer home. It'll be easier for Maya to visit him, easier for all of us. And most importantly it means that Adam's making progress. Real progress.

'When can they have him?'

'As soon as he's out of PTA. It should be just before Christmas. Is that going to be OK for you?'

I still don't like the thought of Adam being away from home for Christmas but I've had a long time to get used to the idea. Plus I know he'll be getting the best treatment possible.

'Yeah. That's great.'

'Good. As I explained, they have a twelve-week assessment programme. It's going to be a long haul but it's the next step along the road for him.'

I nod. I feel we are getting closer to Adam all the time. It's like he's a fossil. The longer we dig, the further we get, the more of the real Adam will be revealed.

I stand on Louise's doorstep feeling ridiculously nervous and uncomfortable. I haven't been round since Steve kissed me. In fact I've barely seen her at all. I've stopped going to flamenco dancing, blaming it on being too tired with all the travelling to and from Goole. But though that's true, it's not the real reason. The real reason is that I cannot bear to look my best friend in the eye. Because although she doesn't know it, I am the reason her marriage has broken down.

I have lain awake going through it all in my head on more nights than I care to remember. But still I come to the same conclusion. It is my fault. Somehow I must have given him the impression that I was interested, that he was more than just a shoulder to cry on to me. I can't even begin to explain my naivety. I think back to all the times I thought he was talking in riddles and, of course, he wasn't, it was simply me being incredibly dense. The necklace he gave me for my birthday, for Christ's sake. And yes it did make me uncomfortable at the time and that can only be because I realised it was inappropriate but somehow I managed to convince myself it was just Steve trying to do right by Adam. I didn't realise he was trying to replace him.

I'm aware that if I stand here much longer, one of the Neighbourhood Watch types in Louise's road will probably call the police. I ring the bell. The bunch of flowers I am holding suddenly seems a rather pathetic offering for wrecking a marriage. Although Louise will not realise that, because she still doesn't know what I've done. However many times I've decided to tell her as I've lain in bed at night, the courage has always deserted me by the following morning. The lame excuse I come up with is that no good can come from telling her, it will only cause her more pain. It is the same excuse I used not to tell Adam about the abortion for all those years. Although, as with that, protecting myself from losing someone I love is clearly a bigger factor than I would care to admit.

'Hi,' says Louise, opening the door. 'It's so good to see you.' She gives me a hug. I am paralysed by guilt. So much so that Louise has to look at the flowers in my hand and back to my face a couple of times before I am finally galvanised into action.

'Here, these are for you.'

'Thank you. They're gorgeous. You didn't need to do that.'

I grimace inside. All I can think of is the flowers Steve gave me. The ones I binned the next day, telling Maya it was because they had greenfly.

'It's been so long, hasn't it?' I say.

'Far too long. Anyway, come in out of the cold.'

I step into the hall. Louise is looking fantastic: scoop neck top, little shrug, figure-hugging trousers. Her face never needs much make-up; a slick of pink lipstick and a wave of mascara is all she normally bothers with. I think for a second that she has got blusher on but actually she hasn't. It's just that she has a little bit of colour in her cheeks.

'You're looking great,' I say, as we walk through to the kitchen. It is still strange, the idea that this is no longer her marital home. Just Louise's place.

'Thanks,' she says, turning to face me with a huge grin on her face. 'Things seem to be looking up.'

'Have you met somebody?' I ask.

Louise laughs. 'And who might that be? Nursery school

teachers don't exactly get to socialise with many single men.'

I realise straight away. And the very thought of it turns me cold.

'You've heard from Steve, haven't you?'

She blushes and looks down at her feet. Which is ridiculous considering he's still her husband.

'I sent him a Christmas card,' she says. 'You know how I always like to get in early. He'd given me the address to forward any post to. I don't know why I did it, to be honest. Maybe it was desperation or some sad attempt to call a Christmas truce. Anyway, he emailed me today. Apologised for the fact that as he didn't have me to write cards he wouldn't be sending any this year.'

Steve's rather black sense of humour washes over me. I am too busy trying to work out what he's playing at.

'So what else did he say?'

'He suggested meeting up for a pre-Christmas drink.'

I nod, sitting down at the table. Louise is twiddling her wedding ring. Unlike Steve she never took it off.

'I don't know if anything will come of it,' she says. 'But what I do know is that everything's gone quiet on the divorce front. My solicitor hasn't heard from his since the beginning of October.'

I nod again, unsure what to say.

'You don't seem very pleased,' says Louise.

'I just don't want you to get hurt again. To build up your expectations when you don't know exactly what he wants.'

'I guess I'll find out soon enough.'

'Would you have him back?'

'What do you think? I haven't exactly been having a whale of a time in my new life, have I?'

'You've been to lots of different places. And you really enjoyed that singles holiday you went on. You've made lots of new friends.'

'Oh, I've been busy. But that's not the same as being happy, is it? Busy is good at covering up how you're feeling. Pretending to yourself that everything's fine. Busy doesn't work at bedtime though. Or first thing in the morning when you wake up.'

'So what are you going to do?'

'Just wait and see what he says, I guess. The ball's in his court. Always has been. Just depends whether he's going to pick it up and start playing with it.'

I nod, unable to bring myself to say anything positive.

'I know what you're thinking, Mel. And I'd probably think the same if it was the other way around. But I can't simply write off our marriage, not if there's even the tiniest chance that it could be resurrected.'

I nod and smile at her. As much as I feel I should do, I can't tell her. I can't own up. Not when she still has so much hope. I shall have to find another way to make it up to her.

I feel bad about going out two evenings in a row but Dad was fine about babysitting Maya again. He loves it. They both do. It's like he's got his little girl back. I told him I wanted to go and see Louise again. That I was worried about her. And part of that is true, at least.

I got Steve's address from Louise. Said I wanted to send

him a Christmas card. She doesn't know I haven't seen him since the beginning of October. Or phoned him. I did send him one text. To let him know Adam had gone to Goole and only close family would be visiting. He texted back to say thanks for letting him know. And that was the last I heard.

I am not entirely sure I am doing the right thing going to see him unannounced like this. But I have questions I need answers to. And I could not bear to see Louise hurt again.

The flats are a modern, low-rise, two-storey affair, squeezed in between a convenience store and a row of new-build houses. I ring the buzzer. It hasn't occurred to me until this moment that he might not let me in. Although I'm pretty certain curiosity will get the better of him.

'Hi, it's Mel,' I say when he answers. There is a pause before the door buzzes open.

'I'm on the first floor,' he says. When I get to the top of the stairs he is standing there, the front door open behind him, his face trying hard to work out which expression is required.

'Hi,' he says. 'It's good to see you.'

'I need to talk to you.'

'It's not bad news?'

I feel a pang of guilt for having worried him. 'No. Adam's fine.'

'Good. You'd better come in then.'

I follow him through to a square hallway. The doors to the lounge and kitchen are open, the other two are closed.

'Can I get you a coffee?'

'No thanks.'

'Let me take your coat then.' I slip it off and pass it to him. He puts it on a hook next to his. Even that makes me feel uncomfortable. I follow him through to the lounge and sit down awkwardly on the edge of a beige armchair.

'So how's Adam doing?' he asks, hovering above me uncertainly.

'Really well. He's almost out of the post-traumatic amnesia now. He'll be moving to a different rehab centre in a week or so. A place called Shaw House in Leeds. It'll be good to have him nearer home.'

'Great. Can he talk yet?'

'Yeah. He talks a lot.'

'What about?'

It suddenly dawns on me why he's so bothered about the talking.

'You told him, didn't you?'

'Told him what?'

'That there was someone else. That it was me.'

Steve stares at me. His eyes dark and intense, searching my face for clues as to how to respond.

'Not in so many words. I kind of hinted at it.'

'Why?'

Steve shrugs. 'He's my best mate, isn't he? I thought it only fair that he know.'

I shake my head. 'Some mate you've been to him.'

Steve looks up at the ceiling, his lips pursed. 'I know what I did was wrong, Mel. And I'm sorry it upset you but I can't help how I feel. How I've always felt. And although I may not have been much of a mate to Adam over the past few months, over the past twenty-odd years I've been a damn good friend. I let him walk off with the girl I loved and sacrificed my happiness out of loyalty to him. That's a pretty high price to pay.'

I don't know where to look, what to say. Nor, it seems, does Steve. I had no idea it went back that far. That a kiss when I was eleven years old could still be lingering on his lips. I feel awful, all the times we went out as teenagers, me and Adam, Steve tagging along. It must have been a nightmare for him, like having your teeth pulled in public without anaesthetic and yet not being able to scream.

'I'm sorry,' I say. 'I had no idea. I feel so stupid.' I sense the colour rising in my cheeks.

'It's OK,' says Steve. 'You weren't to know. I've always played things pretty close to my chest.'

'You never even told Adam?'

'No. We didn't talk about stuff like that. Boys don't. I think he guessed, though.'

'Why do you say that?'

'He seemed embarrassed after he asked you out. Like he knew he'd shafted me.'

'So why didn't you tell him then?'

'I only thought it would last a couple of weeks. I certainly didn't expect it to last a lifetime.'

My mind is racing ahead now. Joining up the dots of our lives. Forming a picture.

'Is that why you went out with Louise? Because she was my best friend.'

Steve sits down opposite me, holds his head in his hands.

'It was a factor, yes.'

379

'Jesus. And do you think that was fair to her?'

'Of course I don't. That's why I've been going through hell all these years, beating myself up about it. Trying to love her in the way I knew I should. In the way I love . . .'

He shrugs as his voice trails off. But the sentence is already finished in my head. All I can think of is whether I'm somehow responsible for this. Whether I've been leading him on, flirting with him without realising. And then I remember Hannah. The young woman who used to work with Adam. Remember the way she looked at him that time I went into the museum with Maya. I'm quite sure Adam didn't do anything to make her feel like that. Sometimes you don't have to. Sometimes just being is enough.

'Please, Steve. Don't.' I shut my eyes for a second. 'Look, I'm sorry if I ever gave you the impression I was interested.'

'You didn't. But I guess I just couldn't accept it. I kept my feelings to myself all these years but it ate away at me. That's why things were so difficult with Louise. And then when Adam had the accident . . .'

'You saw an opportunity to make your move,' I say.

'No. It wasn't like that.'

'Well, it was very convenient, wasn't it? You volunteering to be my odd-job man.'

'I wanted to help. I felt useless. I couldn't bear to see you hurting.'

'But you did more than just help, didn't you? You over-stepped the mark.' I reach into my bag, take out the box containing the silver necklace and put it on the coffee table in between us. 'You can have this back. It wasn't from Adam at all. It was from you.'

His eyes are fixed on the box. He fiddles with the strap on his watch. 'It was hard not to get carried away. For a while back there I could actually see us having a future together.'

'That's why you made it up. About Adam and that girl at uni.'

'I didn't make up anything, it was like I said. He didn't deny it.'

'Oh, and Adam always plays a straight bat with you, does he? You never wind each other up. Resort to a bit of sarcasm.'

Steve shrugs.

'You believed him because it suited you to. Gave you some kind of moral superiority in your head if you could kid yourself he'd cheated on me. But to come out and tell me that, when deep down you knew it wasn't true.'

'You were hurting, Mel. I couldn't bear to see you suffer, see you throw your life away and make a martyr of yourself.'

'I was looking after my husband.'

'You were punishing yourself because for some reason you thought it was your fault. Well, it wasn't, OK? Shit happens. And the last thing Adam would have wanted is for you to do yourself in on his account.'

'Don't start all this "I was doing it for Adam" crap. You wanted him to go into a home. You wanted him off the scene so you could move in on me once you were divorced.'

'OK, I admit it. Maybe I did. But can you blame me?

And can you say I've been anything other than loyal to Adam, all these years? He stole my girl. Stole her from right under my nose. And I never put up a fight. Never complained. Never said it wasn't fucking fair.'

The pain etched in his face and in his voice takes me aback. It's real. This thing he has for me. It must be to have lasted all these years. I feel for him. I really do. And I can't help somehow feeling responsible.

'Look, if it helps you to hear it, I am not your girl, Steve. I never have been and I never will be. Please try to accept that, for your own sake as much as anything.'

We sit for a while. Neither of us saying anything. Neither of us able to look the other in the eye.

'Are you going to tell Louise?' Steve asks eventually.

I shrug and walk over to the window. I think she has a right to know. But I also think it will break her heart. It's not good for anybody to be told they've always been second best. She deserves so much better than that.

'Are you prepared to make a go of it with her?' I ask.

'Yes. I am. That's why I got in touch with her. Why I stopped the divorce proceedings. I think it will be easier, now it's finally out there. Now you know.'

'And now you know nothing will ever happen. Nor would it have. Even if Adam hadn't woken up.' I turn around to see him nodding his head slowly. His tall frame suddenly seeming smaller somehow. 'You need to go away with her, though,' I add. 'It won't work here. Not with me around.'

'But won't you miss Louise?'

'Yeah. I'll miss her like hell. But I want her to be happy.

And she thinks she can only be happy with you.'

Steve nods. 'But what about you and Adam?'

'We've got each other,' I say. 'We'll be fine.'

'But you haven't got him, have you? Not really. Louise said he's completely different. That you were finding it really tough to cope with that.'

'She's right. And I am. But three months ago he couldn't speak a word or move a muscle. Who's to say what he'll be like in three months' time?'

'And if he doesn't get back to how he was?'

'He's still my husband, Steve. And I still love him. Nothing's ever going to change that.'

I pick up my bag. Steve jumps up and goes through to the hall to get my coat.

'Just make sure you're good to Louise,' I say. 'Be the husband she deserves to have. One who lets her in. One who never, ever hurts her again.'

He nods. 'I'll do my best.'

He holds the door open for me. He doesn't go to kiss me this time. 'Bye, Mel.'

'Bye.' I smile at him. A small smile but enough for him to know that despite everything, I still care for him. Still care very much indeed. I step out on to the landing then turn back to him.

'You could start by giving her some flowers for Christmas,' I say. 'Good ones, mind. Nothing from a petrol station.'

Thirty-four

ADAM

We pull up outside a modern, low, red-brick building on the outskirts of Leeds.

'Here we are, then,' says Mel. 'I'll come round to give you a hand.' We are in my car. Though Mel is driving. They won't let me drive even though I know I can. I only need the wheelchair for longer distances now. Most of the time I walk with the help of sticks or a frame.

Mel opens the door, helps me swivel around and swing my legs out then holds me under my arm as I push up on to my feet.

I shuffle into the reception area, which is festooned with Christmas decorations, including a garishly decorated tree. A lady called Sheila comes out and introduces herself as the service manager.

'Hello, Adam. Welcome to Shaw House. We hope you'll be very happy here.'

She is looking at me and smiling. Mel is looking at me too but I don't know what I am supposed to say.

'Thank you,' Mel says to Sheila after a pause. 'We're really grateful to be here.'

We follow her along the corridor. There are pictures on the walls. Not the same pictures as at Goole, though.

The room she shows us to is bright and clean. There is more space than in my room at Goole. I have a window and a little television on a desk and my own shower and toilet. I sit down on the bed.

'It's very bouncy,' I say. 'Here, Mel, come and try it.' Mel sits down next to me and puts her arm around my shoulder.

'You can go now,' I say to Sheila. 'We'll be all right, we are married you know.'

Sheila smiles. 'I'll leave you to settle in, then,' she says, nodding at Mel.

'I know you didn't mean it to be, love, but that sounded a bit rude,' says Mel. 'She was only making sure everything was all right for you.'

'Oh. OK.' I get up and put the television on and use the remote to flick between channels. 'Great, look. They've got CBeebies. There's Mr Tumble.' I laugh as he ducks and misses a custard pie then slips on a banana skin. 'He's great, Mr Tumble, isn't he?'

Mel nods. 'Maya'll be happy.'

'When's she coming?'

'Straight after school. Mum and Dad are bringing her. I should warn you she's rather excited about this little celebration.'

It is Maya's birthday in four days' time. She will be five. Or maybe it's five days' time and she'll be four. It's ten days before Christmas, anyway. I remember that much. We were going to call her Holly at one point. I had the idea of calling her Maya while eating a bar of Green and Black's Maya Gold chocolate. Although Mel doesn't like me telling people that. I don't know why. It's not as if we called her Malteser.

'Why isn't she having a proper party?'

'She is. Tomorrow at Upsy Daisy's in Mytholmroyd. Lots of her school friends are coming. Remember I said I'm going to video it all for you so you can watch it?'

'So why are we having a party here for her today?'

'It's not a party, just a celebration. I wanted her to open her presents from us with you. It'll be too far for her to come on her actual birthday. She's still shattered after school.'

'I haven't got her a present.'

'It's OK. I've got one between us.'

'Is it a dinosaur thing?'

'No, love. She's gone off dinosaurs a bit. I've got her a beautiful butterfly dressing-up costume and a huge rat puppet that she'll love. One that looks just like Roddy.'

'Roddy who?' I can only think of Roddy Frame out of *Aztec Camera*. And I don't think he looks like a rat at all.

'Sorry. Her pet rat, Roddy. You met him when you were at home.'

I try to picture Roddy in my head but the only rat I can remember is Roland Rat.

'I'll bring in a photo of him next time,' says Mel. She has been bringing in a lot of photos to show me. People we know, places we've been. Steve and Louise and holidays in Cornwall. She seems very pleased when I remember them. And I do remember them. It is only the recent ones that draw a blank. The ones since the accident.

'Why doesn't she like dinosaurs any more?'

Mel hesitates. 'Oh, you know what children are like at this age. They go through phases, don't they? Anyway. I need your help with another present. I need to think of something to get Mum and Dad for Christmas. I'd like to get them something special as a way of saying thank you for everything they've done for us since your accident.'

I think for a moment. Only one thing comes to mind. But it is one thing which seems so obvious to me that there is no point in thinking of anything else anyway.

'A train ticket,' I say.

'Sorry?'

'For one of the great railway journeys of the world.'

'Why did you say that?'

'Your dad's always wanted to go on one.'

'Has he? He never told me.'

I shrug.

'But what about Mum?'

'Do the Orient Express one. They have nice waiters on there. Very polite, nothing is too much trouble. She'll like it.'

There is a knock at the door. Mel opens it. Sheila is asking if we're ready to do the tour of Shaw House. We head off down the corridor. There is a man in a suit walking towards us, whistling 'Here Comes the Sun'. Which is a bit weird when it's pissing it down outside but maybe that's why he's doing it.

'Hey, you must be Adam,' he says, stretching out his hand. I let go of my stick for a moment so I can shake it. 'I've been hearing very positive reports on you from our friends at Goole,' he continues. 'Sounds like you've been working bloody hard.'

'I won't need to stay here long,' I tell him. 'I'm fine. I'll be ready to go home soon.'

'Well, we're going to do everything possible to help you but you will need to be patient. We don't believe in rushing things. We like to make sure that people are fully equipped for what lies ahead. And that includes our clients' families,' he says, turning to Mel. 'Anything you want to ask, my door is open.'

'Thanks,' says Mel. He pats me twice on the shoulder, nods at Mel and hurries off, still whistling.

'He's a busy man,' says Sheila. 'But he always makes time for people. Right, next stop, the physio room.'

The physiotherapist is a man. His name is Danny.

'I had a woman called Tracey at Goole,' I tell him. 'She wasn't fat like you.'

'Ah,' he says. 'But I bet she didn't have a sparkling personality like mine.'

Danny smiles. I look at Mel. She is not smiling.

'Come along, then,' says Sheila. 'Plenty of other people still to meet.'

Mel comes into the dining room with me to eat at lunch-time. Some of the other blokes are looking at her. Mel is quiet. Quieter than usual. She is keeping her head down. We are given tomato soup and a roll.

'This is nice,' she says, dunking her roll in.

'Yeah.'

'What do you think of it here then?'

'It's good. I won't be here long before I go home, though.'

'Remember what Dr Andrews said. It might take a bit longer than you think.'

'No it won't. There's nothing wrong with me. Not compared to these people. Look, he can't even feed himself.' I point to a young man on the next table with ginger hair.

'Try to keep your voice down, love,' says Mel. 'And it's a bit rude to point.'

I shrug. We eat the rest of our lunch in silence then get up to leave. A man at another table, not the ginger one, does a wolf whistle. I swing around and lunge towards him. As I do so my foot goes from under me and I start to wobble. Mel catches me just in time. A couple of people who work here rush over and help her to sit me down. Mel starts to cry.

'It's OK,' I say. 'I didn't hurt myself.'

We are back sitting on the bed in my own room later when Maya arrives. She charges in with her arms outstretched.

'Daddy,' she cries, giving me a huge hug. I love the feel of her hair in my face and her little fingers clinging to my back. For a moment I can't speak. I am scared I've forgotten how to again. And then something clears in my throat and the words find a way through.

'Hello, sweetheart.'

I love Maya. I really do. She squeezes the sad out of me. Fills me with joy.

It is only when I open my eyes and look up that I remember Joan and Tom are here too.

'Hello, Adam,' says Tom, coming over to shake my hand. 'Looks like you've landed on your feet here. Very swish, in't it? Like being in a hotel.'

'It's certainly better than that hotel we stayed in at

Cleethorpes last year,' says Joan. 'They didn't even have proper soap in the bathroom. Just that silly liquid rubbish.' She leans down to kiss me on the cheek. 'Anyway, nice to see you.'

'To see you nice,' I say, grinning. Mel is looking at me as if she doesn't understand.

'You know, Bruce Forsyth,' I say.

Mel nods. Joan and Tom sit down on the two chairs in the room. Maya bounces up and down next to me on the bed.

'Can we do the presents now?' she squeals. I look at Mel.

'We certainly can,' she says. 'And we've got a welcome to your new home gift we want to give to Daddy first, haven't you?'

Mel reaches down to a big bag she must have tucked behind the bed when I wasn't looking and takes a flat, rectangular present from it and hands it to Maya.

'This is from me and Mummy,' she says, passing it to me. 'We had it done especially. We had to go to a studio and the man kept trying to make me laugh and he gave me a sweetie at the end for being good. Shall I help you open it?' She starts tearing the paper without waiting for a reply. A moment later I am looking at a framed photograph of Mel and Maya. Maya has got her arms draped around Mel's neck and they are both laughing. Mel is wearing the blue dress I bought her for our anniversary last year. And Maya has got her purple and silver party dress on as well. The one she is wearing today.

'You've got your party dresses on,' I say. 'You both look really pretty.'

'Thanks,' says Mel, beaming.

'Do you like it?' asks Maya.

'Yes. Yes I do.'

'It's got a stand,' says Mel, taking it from me for a second. 'We thought you might like to put it up on your bedside cabinet here. Make you feel more at home.'

She stands it up and turns around to look at me and I nod. Maya whispers into my ear, 'Daddy, you've forgotten to say thank you.'

'Oh. Right. Thank you.'

'I've made you a card, as well,' says Maya, running over to Mel and producing a folded piece of purple card. 'I painted a picture of Roddy and Rita for you.' I look down at a white blob and a black blob on the front of the card.

'They don't look anything like rats,' I say.

'Adam,' says Mel. The sharpness of her tone throws me. I look up and see Maya staring at me, looking as if she is about to burst into tears. 'Daddy was only joking, sweetheart. It's a lovely painting.'

I look at Mel. She looks cross. I am about to tell her that I wasn't joking at all when she puts her finger to her lips.

'Right then, missy. I suppose you'll be wanting your present now?'

Maya squeals and starts bouncing on the bed some more. Mel passes me a present.

'There you are, love,' she says. 'You can give it to her.' I hand Maya the parcel. She immediately rips open the paper to reveal the purple and pink butterfly costume inside. She squeals so loudly Mel has to tell her to be quiet as well. A few moments later she is dancing around the room flapping her wings, singing a song about a butterfly.

'I think we can take it that's a hit.' Tom smiles.

'Thank you, Daddy,' says Maya. 'It's my best present ever.'

'Well, you're very lucky because you've got another one yet,' says Mel, handing her another parcel. Maya rips the paper and her eyes almost fall off her face.

'It's a Roddy puppet,' she squeals, bouncing up and down. 'Look, Daddy, it's just like Roddy. Now I can bring him to see you when I come and visit.'

'That's if the health and safety rules allow it,' snorts Joan.

'What does Grandma mean?' asks Maya.

'Nothing. She's just joking,' replies Mel.

'People aren't making very funny jokes today,' says Maya.

'I'll tell you a funny joke,' I say. 'Knock knock.'

'Who's there,' asks Maya.

'Boo.'

'Boo who?'

'Don't cry, it's only a joke.'

Maya bursts out laughing. Everyone else just kind of smiles.

Thirty-five

MEL

I pull up outside Shaw House. I am not going to see Adam first today. I have an appointment with Dr Andrews. I am hoping he will give me the answers I want to hear. I knock on the door.

'Come right in,' calls Dr Andrews. He has a slight Scottish accent, Edinburgh, I think, but probably from a long time ago.

'Hello, Dr Andrews. Thanks for seeing me so quickly.'

'No problem and please, call me James.'

'OK. As long as you call me Mel.' He smiles and gestures to me to take a seat. It's a comfy one, looking suspiciously like something I saw in IKEA once. The walls of his office are covered in framed certificates and framed album covers. The Beatles mainly but a few Rod Stewart ones and one from Simple Minds. The shelves behind him are lined with psychology books and lots of volumes with the word 'brain' in the title. There's also a considerable section of Ian Rankin novels.

'I take it you're an Inspector Rebus fan.' I smile.

'Sadly so. I am one of those neuropsychologists who foolishly think I can work out whodunit before him. Misguided, I'm afraid. Still, never stops me trying and, besides, it's always good to be reminded of home. Anyway, enough about me. You've come to find out where your husband's gone, haven't you?'

For a moment I think I must have come to the wrong place. That it actually said 'Professor Marvel' on his door and he is peering into a crystal ball, not his coffee cup.

'How did you know?'

'It's actually one of the most common conversations I have with relatives. That and "when will they be ready to come home?"'

'Sorry, we must be very annoying.'

'Not at all. It's completely understandable. You want your loved one back. In every sense of the word.'

'I thought once he came out of the PTA, that the old Adam would gradually return. He's still in there, you see. I know he is.'

Dr Andrews nods slowly, gets up from behind his desk and walks over to the window, which looks out on a small patio beyond.

'Adam tells me you lecture in child development. And that you're a fellow psychology graduate as well.' I nod. 'I bet you've done a lot of research,' he says. 'Bet you've Googled the Internet dry.'

I smile. He's actually a cross between Inspector Rebus and Professor Marvel.

'I needed to know everything. All the possibilities.'

'So you've read Dr Owen's research at Addenbrooke's Hospital, the playing tennis stuff?'

I nod.

'And Professor Laureys' at Liège University, the Houben

case?'

I nod again.

'Interesting stuff, isn't it? Makes you think about all sorts of possibilities.'

'Adam's doctors said he was in a persistent vegetative state. Then they said he was in a minimally conscious state. How do I know even that was true?'

Dr Andrews pauses again. 'I've dealt with a lot of family members who have been convinced their loved one was aware of everything.'

'But the research says that the brain can process things when people are in a minimally conscious state.'

'Somebody can still be processing things but have no conscious awareness. A whole lot of brain processes go on unconsciously, even when we're awake.'

I sigh. I thought he was a believer but he isn't. He's just like all the rest.

'You think I'm crazy, don't you?'

'Mel, we are all capable of deluding ourselves, particularly when we're going through an incredibly traumatic time. We pick out the information that suits our belief, we discount everything that doesn't.'

'So you don't think I'm going to get Adam back?'

'You have a husband out there who is making great progress, who is obviously an intelligent and strong-willed man. Will he still be telling knock-knock jokes when you see him? Yes. Will he make inappropriate and embarrassing remarks? Yes again. Will he stop to ask you how you're coping? Probably not. We can work on those things but if that's what you mean when you say you want the old

Adam back, I'm afraid there are no miracles in store.'

'You think I should be grateful for what I've got, don't you?'

'No. I think it would help you to let the old Adam go and focus on what this Adam can achieve.'

I nod. Although I have no idea if I could do that even if I wanted to.

'That was great, Lauren,' I say, handing her essay back the next morning. 'You managed to remember a lot of points from our last lesson. And Cara, fantastic. Really thoughtful, I loved the way you applied some of the new approaches you've been learning about to practical situations.'

Cara beams at me. Her confidence has grown so much since she started the course. She is beginning to believe in herself. Believe in her ability to rise above everything and be the person I know she can be. I am going to miss her when I leave. I am going to miss them all. Which is funny, as if you'd told me that three months ago I would probably have laughed in your face.

'Right, that's it then, girls. All that remains is for me to wish you a very happy Christmas. You've got one more term of me then your new tutor Carole will be back from her maternity leave. It's been a pleasure to teach you this term and I look forward to seeing you all again in January.'

I look around the classroom. A minute ago the girls seemed demob happy, now they are oddly quiet. Cara stands up, picks up a large paper bag at the side of her desk and walks up to me.

'Happy Christmas, miss. This is for you from all of us. We

didn't know what to get you but I hope it's OK.'

I am choked already, I wasn't expecting this. Not from a bunch of seventeen year olds. Not when I've only been teaching them for a few months.

'Thank you,' I say, taking the bag from her. 'You really shouldn't have, you know.'

'Don't say that, you haven't opened it yet,' says Haleema. 'You might not even like it.'

'I'm sure I will,' I say, taking the bulky present from the bag. 'Do you want me to open it now?'

'Well, yeah, otherwise it'll be like watching *The X-Factor* but missing the results show when everyone cries,' says Gemma.

I smile and peel off the sticky tape, opening the paper up on my desk. Inside is a pair of wooden lovebirds, delicately carved and brightly painted. It is a moment or two before I am able to speak.

'Thank you,' I say, looking around the sea of expectant faces. 'I love them.'

'We thought they were like you and your husband,' says Haleema. 'You know, a couple of lovebirds.'

I'm aware I have started to cry. They don't seem bothered, though. Most of them are crying too.

'See, it is like *X-Factor* now,' says Gemma.

'I'm hardly Cheryl Cole, am I?' I laugh.

'No, miss. I was thinking more like Susan Boyle.' Gemma is smiling as she says it. And wiping away the tears.

Cara hangs back at the end, while all the others give me their Christmas hugs. She waits until they have left before coming up to my desk.

'Did you choose the present, Cara?' I ask. She nods. 'Thank you. I really do love it.'

'I'm gonna really miss you when you go,' she says. 'Won't they let you stay? Find another job for you here?'

'I don't know. There's nothing at the moment. It's not the best time to be looking for an opening. People are tending to stay put in the current climate.'

'Will you go back to the university then?'

'Depends if they've got anything which will suit the hours I can do.'

Cara looks concerned.

'Don't worry,' I say. 'I'll be OK. Something will turn up. What about you? What are you planning to do at the end of the course?'

'I want to go on to the NVQ level two in childcare. If you think I can do it.'

'Of course you can. I was really hoping you'd say that. I was also going to ask if you've got anything sorted out for your work experience in the summer yet.'

'No. It's been a bit difficult at home lately. I'll try to find the time to sit down and write some letters after Easter.'

'How about I put in a good word for you at the Ark? It's only in Cragg Vale. You could get there on the bus. My little girl used to go there. I know the women who run it.'

'Would you, really?'

'I'd be delighted.' Cara can't seem to speak for grinning. 'Right then,' I say. 'Are you going to give me a Christmas hug or not?'

Cara practically throws herself at me and sobs into my shirt.

'How about some time you come round and babysit for me?' I say. 'I think you and my little girl would really hit it off.'

'I'd like that,' says Cara.

'Great. We'll sort that out in the New Year, then. Are you staying in the classroom for a bit?'

She nods. I give her shoulder a squeeze, put the lovebirds back in the bag and pick up my briefcase.

'I know Christmas must be a tough time for you, but I hope you manage to have a happy one,' I say.

'Thanks,' says Cara. 'You too.'

I pop into Mum and Dad's on my way home from college. I'm going to have to give them their Christmas present early. I've booked the Orient Express tickets for February and the passport office said to try to get their applications in before Christmas. Neither of them have ever had a passport – it's not as if you need one for Cleethorpes.

'Hi,' I say, when Mum opens the door. 'Santa's making a special early delivery.' I hand her the train tickets which I've wrapped up along with the itinerary, brochure and passport application forms.

'What's this?' says Mum, looking at the present.

'You'd better open it and see.'

I slip off my boots and follow her into the lounge where Dad is sitting in the armchair reading a copy of *Inside Track*.

'Hello, love,' he says, looking up. 'Everything all right?'

'Our Melanie's brought us a Christmas present,' says Mum.

'You need to open it now,' I say. 'You'll see why in a minute.'

Mum shrugs and hands it to Dad. 'There you go,' she says. 'You'd better do it.'

Dad nods and obligingly waits until Mum has fetched some scissors for the Sellotape. Tearing wrapping paper is not approved of in this house and Dad is nothing if not well trained. He snips the tape and slides out the contents. His face is blank for a second, then a frown as he reads followed by an unadulterated grin.

'It's tickets for Orient Express,' he says, looking up at me, then to Mum and back to me. 'Seven nights, Paris and Venice. Departing on February fourteenth.'

'That's Valentine's Day,' says Mum. 'We don't normally do owt for Valentine's Day.'

'Well, you are next year. I wanted to say thank you for everything you've done for us this year. I couldn't have managed without you, I really couldn't.'

'I can't believe it. Thank you,' says Dad, his face still lit up. 'I'm lost for words.'

'Good. Adam said you'd like it.'

'Adam?'

'Yeah. It was his idea.'

Dad nods and frowns again. Mum still has a bemused expression on her face.

'He thought you'd like it too,' I say, turning to her. 'The waiters are very attentive, you know. Nothing is too much trouble. And I don't think there'll be any riff-raff on there.' I am smiling as I say it. Dad is still smiling too.

'Thank you,' Mum says. 'You needn't have gone to this expense but it's very kind of you. I'm sure it will be lovely.'

That is about as good as it gets from her. I stay for a bit

longer, just long enough to go through the passport application form with Dad and for Mum to give me an update on Mrs Cooper's gallbladder problem. When I go to leave, Dad puts down the Great Rail Journeys brochure he has been avidly reading and follows me outside.

'Where's your car?' he asks.

'There,' I say, pointing to Adam's car which is parked further up the road.

'Why are you not in the Polo?'

'Oh, I sold it,' I said. 'We don't really need the two now.'

Dad looks at me. His face serious for a moment.

'You really shouldn't have gone to this expense on our account, love.'

'Why not?' I say, giving him a peck on the cheek. 'It's not every woman who's lucky enough to have a dad like you.'

I've not long come down from putting Maya to bed later that evening when there is a tap on the door. Instinctively I think of Steve until I remember that it's a Friday – and that he doesn't come round any more. I open the door to see Dad standing there.

'Hello again,' I say. 'Did I leave something?'

Dad shakes his head. He looks serious. So serious it scares me.

'Can I come in?' he says. 'I need to talk to you.'

'Of course.'

He steps inside and follows me through to the kitchen without another word. I offer a chair but he shakes his head. Whatever it is, he needs to say it standing up.

'You sold your car to buy us Orient Express tickets, didn't you?'

I open my mouth to deny it but think better of it. Dad strikes me as being in the mood for some straight talking.

'It's like I said, we really don't need two now anyway.'

Dad shakes his head and looks up at the ceiling.

'You really shouldn't have, you know. We've helped out like any parents would in the same situation and the last thing we want is you making more sacrifices for us.'

He reaches into his jacket pocket, takes out the tickets and puts them on the kitchen table.

'Hey, I don't want them back. Has Mum put you up to this?'

'Your mother knows nothing about it,' he says. 'I told her I were going to shop for a pint of milk.'

'Well, I want you to take them back.'

'I don't deserve them, Mel. I feel like I've got them under false pretences.'

'What do you mean?'

There is a long pause during which Dad wrings his hands so much I half expect to see water dripping out of them.

'It wasn't your mother,' he says finally.

'What wasn't?'

He hesitates. 'It weren't her who insisted on you having the abortion.' The word sounds cold and hard coming from his lips. It is not a word I'd ever associate with someone so warm and comfy looking.

'How do you know about that?'

He sighs and looks down at his feet. 'I'm one who said you should have it.'

I stare at him, unable to comprehend what he is saying.

'Your mother told me. Well, that's not true either. I walked into bedroom and found her crying. The test stick were still in her hand.'

'But she said you didn't know. That if I agreed to it she wouldn't tell you.'

'That were all her idea. She seemed to think it would be better coming from her. Because she wasn't as close to you, like. She said that if you were going to hate anyone it were better that you hated her. That you wouldn't be able to deal with losing me as well as losing . . .'

His voice trails off. I sit down heavily on a chair. My head is trying desperately to equate the story as it has just been told with the one I have always believed to be true.

'You wanted me to have the abortion?'

He nods and hangs his head like a dog who has been told off by its master.

'I couldn't bear it, you see. You were my little girl.'

'I was nearly sixteen.'

'Not to me you weren't. You were still apple of my eye. The one ray of sunshine in my dreary, humdrum life. It were bad enough for me that you were going out with Adam, that he'd replaced me in your affections. For him to get you pregnant . . .' He shakes his head and looks down at the floor.

'You were going to try to split us up, weren't you?'

'I told your mother that only way I'd let you carry on seeing him were if you got rid of it.'

'It was my baby, Dad. Not an it.'

'I know. And second Maya were born I realised what I'd lost.'

'What you'd lost? What about me?'

'I know. And I feel awful about it. It's eaten away at me all these years. But I also know that if you'd had that baby, things might not have turned out as they did. The pressure might have been too much, you and Adam could have split up. You might never have had Maya.'

I look down at my hands clasped together on the table. The emotions have all bubbled up now from below the surface and are swirling around madly inside me, jostling for position. Maybe he's right. Maybe we wouldn't have survived it. Maybe things would have worked out completely differently.

'It was still wrong of you, though. Not to give me the choice.'

'We play God as parents, don't we? We make calls all the time based on what we think is best for our children. And when I saw you go on to get your degree, then your Masters, teach at university, have such a strong marriage and be a brilliant mum to Maya, there couldn't have been anyone prouder than me. And I guess if I'm honest I thought that justified what I'd done.'

I sit for a while. Thinking. Trying to take it all in.

'So why tell me now?'

'I'm very grateful for present but I don't feel I've any right to have a special place in your heart. Your mother made a lot of sacrifices, her relationship with you being one of them. She's still never got over Martin going to

Belgium. I wanted her to have a chance to try to rebuild some kind of relationship with you.'

I nod slowly, realising as a mother what an incredibly selfless thing she did in taking the blame. And knowing that without her, things could indeed have turned out very differently.

'Thank you,' I say. 'For telling me, I mean. I hope that whatever decisions I make as a parent, I'll be able to justify them to Maya one day.'

Dad nods. Comes over and kisses the top of my head. Just like he used to do when I was a child.

'Has your life really been that dull and boring?' I ask him.

He shrugs. 'I had dreams, love. Like we all do. I told Adam about them once, when he were in hospital.'

'About the train journeys you'd always wanted to go on?'

'Yeah. I think I did.'

'Did you ever tell him before that?'

'I'm not sure, love. Maybe I did. Anyway, I'd better be getting back. Your mother'll be wondering where I've got to.'

He gets up and heads for the door.

'Aren't you forgetting something?'

'What?' he says, turning back to me. I pick up the envelope with the tickets in and press it into his hand. 'No, love. I told you, it's not right.'

'You've told me now,' I say. 'It's up to me to decide if I still want to give them to you. And as far as I can see, there's no reason not to. You did what you thought was best as a parent, I can't blame you for that, can I?'

'Are you sure, love?'

'I want you to have them, Dad. I want you both to have them. And I want you to have the best time ever.'

'Thank you,' says Dad, his voice trembling as he puts the tickets back in his pocket. 'That'll be right good, that will.'

Thirty-six

ADAM

I walk into Dr Andrews' office and sit down. I don't even need a stick now. I can do it by myself.

'Hey, look at you,' he says. 'That's fantastic progress you're making, Adam.'

I grin at him. I like Dr Andrews. He talks to me like I'm a grown-up. He doesn't think I'm stupid.

'I'm going to start running again soon,' I say.

'Let's just concentrate on the walking for now, shall we?'

'I like being out in the elements.'

'You'll be able to go for plenty of walks soon. Nothing to lift the spirits like exercising outside. How are you feeling generally, Adam? About your progress, I mean.'

'I want to start running again. I want to go back to work.'

'It's understandable that you're frustrated. You see that you've made fantastic progress as well, though, don't you?'

'I guess so.'

Dr Andrews nods, slowly. 'How about I give you a new goal? Something achievable you can work towards?'

'OK.'

'What have you enjoyed doing since you came here? What do you most look forward to?'

'Maya visiting.'

Dr Andrews gets up and comes round to sit on the desk in front of me. 'How would you feel about looking after her, Adam? About being her carer.'

'What, when I get home?'

'Yeah, I think you could. We'd have to do some work on your decision-making processes, make sure you were going to be OK with the safety side of things. But we've had other people from here who have been able to take over the main child carer role. Maybe that's something you could work towards?'

'But I'll be going back to work.'

'How about you just do it to start off with? See how you get on.'

I frown. I'm not sure.

'I don't know. Mel's very good with Maya. She's more patient than me.'

'But being a childcare expert she'd be ideally placed to help you learn.'

'Yeah. I guess she would.'

'And maybe if you helped out with Maya she could increase her hours lecturing? Go back to the university even?'

'Maybe. She's very good at her job, you know.'

'Great. Sounds like that's something you could work towards then.'

'Can I tell her? She's coming in later.'

'Of course you can. Ask her, though, don't tell her. Remember what we said about finding out how other people feel about the things you want to do? And ask her to come and see me if she's got any concerns.'

I nod and gaze up at the album covers on the wall behind Dr Andrews.

'How did you get Rod Stewart's autograph?' I ask.

'Ah,' he replies. 'Now that's a long story.'

Mel arrives after lunch. She comes in my car. She has sold her one. I don't know why she didn't sell mine. It's not like we need it for the wheelchair any more.

'Hello, love,' she says, bending to kiss me as she comes into my room. 'I've got some post for you this morning.' She hands me a white envelope.

'Who's it from?'

'I don't know, love. Why don't you open it and see?'

I do as I'm told and pull out a Christmas card with a multi-coloured reindeer on. I open it and read, 'To Adam and family, so good to hear you're up and about. Wishing you a Happy Christmas and continued recovery in the New Year. Hannah X'

'It's from Hannah at the museum,' I say, handing the card to Mel.

'That's nice of her,' she says. 'She's in Cardiff now, you know.'

'Is she?'

'Yeah, she got a new job while you were in hospital. She visited you a couple of times before she left, and I think she keeps in touch with your progress through the museum.'

'She was nice, Hannah,' I say.

'Yeah, she thought a lot of you. Anyway, have you had a good morning?'

I shrug. 'Dr Andrews says I might be able to help you look after Maya when I get home. If you don't mind.'

Mel's face lights up. 'Mind? Of course I don't mind. I'd be delighted.'

'Good. He thinks I can do it.'

'Well, I can't think of anyone I'd rather have looking after Maya. And if you did make a few little mistakes at first, it wouldn't matter, would it? I made mistakes too. Besides, she's old enough to show you the ropes herself now.'

'It won't be for a while. Not till I can go home.'

'Sure. Well, that will give us plenty of time to get things sorted, won't it?'

'Will you get your job back at the university?'

'I don't know. Things are tough out there right now, Adam. All these cuts starting to bite, thanks to your friend Mr Cameron.'

'He's not my friend. I never liked him.'

'No, I know. Sorry. I was trying to be . . . it doesn't matter.'

'What's Brown doing about it?'

'He's not the Labour leader any more. It's Miliband.'

'I never liked him either.'

'No, not that one. His brother, Ed.'

I frown and shake my head. 'Jeez. I missed a lot, didn't I?'

Mel smiles and nods. 'You'll get there,' she says. 'In your own time.'

'But I want to get there now.'

She moves over to sit down next to me on the bed. Puts her hand on my knee.

'All you need to remember is that Maya and I love you and we'll wait as long as it takes.'

'I'm very lucky to have you, aren't I?'

'Don't ask me,' she whispers. 'Tell me.' She puts her arms around me and holds me for a long time. When she finally looks up she smiles and kisses me on the lips.

'I kissed another girl once,' I say. 'While we were at uni.'

'Oh.' The smile disappears from Mel's face. She looks worried.

'Nothing happened. Apart from the kiss, I mean. I blew her out because she wasn't you.'

'I see,' she says, letting out a long sigh.

'Are you mad at me?'

'No. Not at all. I'm very glad you told me the truth. We all make mistakes, Adam. I let someone get too close to me after your accident.'

'Who?'

'Steve.'

'Steve my best mate?'

'Yeah.'

'I didn't realise how he felt, you see. I forgot that we all go back such a long way.'

'He fancied you at school.'

'I know, he told me. I never realised. I should have because he kissed me at our primary school Christmas disco. I feel a bit stupid about that.'

Adam shrugs. 'Can I tell Maya?'

'About what?'

'About me looking after her.'

411

'Yes,' she says, smiling. 'You can tell her on Christmas Day when she comes to visit.'

Steve arrives after tea that evening. He'd phoned them to check it was OK to come. They said I had a friend to see me. I couldn't work out who they meant until he walked in.

'Hello, mate,' he says. 'Long time no see and all that.'

'You came while I was in hospital and when I was at home.'

'How do you know?'

'Mel told me.'

'Oh. I see.'

'Where's Louise?'

'She's gone dancing with Mel. You know, the flamenco thing.'

'Do they still do that?'

'Yeah. They stopped for a while but they've started again.'

Steve walks further into the room. He is tall and dark just like I remember. Apart from a couple of grey hairs.

'You're going grey.'

'Yeah, I know,' he says. 'Must be the worry.'

'The worry of what?'

He pauses for a second. 'Having my best mate get done over by a dinosaur, I guess.' He is smiling. I don't know why.

'I can't remember it at all.'

'Right. Probably just as well.'

He points at the chair. 'Is it OK if I sit down?'

'Yeah, sure.'

'Seems a decent place.'

'Yeah. I guess so.'

Steve looks at the photo of Mel and Maya on my bedside cabinet.

'Mel came earlier,' I say. 'She told me you kissed her.'

'Did she?'

'When you were kids at primary school.'

'Oh. I see. Did she say anything else?'

'Only that she felt a bit stupid about not realising you used to fancy her.'

He nods. Looks down at the floor. 'I came to tell you I'm leaving.'

'But you've only just got here.'

'No, I mean I'm leaving the area. Moving away.'

'Where to?'

'Cornwall. Padstow.'

'Where we went on holiday that time? The four of us?'

'Yeah. I always said how much I liked it there.'

'You liked the restaurant. The Rick Stein one.'

'Yeah. I did, didn't I?'

'Is Louise going with you?'

'I don't know. I've asked her and she's thinking about it.'

'Doesn't she want to go?'

'It's kind of complicated.'

'When are you going?'

'In January. As soon as I've worked out my notice.'

'Have you got a job down there?'

'Not yet.'

'It's tough out there at the moment because of your friend Cameron,' Mel said.'

Steve smiles. 'If I can't find anything I'm going to set up my own business. Freelance computer consultant. There's a lot of self-employed people down there, should be quite a market for it.'

'I suppose you'll go running on the beach.'

'Yeah. I guess I will. Do they think you'll be able to get back running again?'

'I don't know. No one will talk to me about it. They keep saying I have to take it one day at a time.'

There is a long pause before Steve speaks again.

'I haven't been as good a friend to you as I should have been.'

'About the Panini sticker album, you mean? Mel showed me that you'd brought it back.'

Steve holds his head in his hands. 'Not just about that. Other things as well. Anyway, I want you to know I'm sorry. It's all in the past now. I'm going to make a fresh start.'

'OK,' I say. Though I'm not really sure what he's talking about. All I do know is that I'm not bothered that he's moving away. We sit for a bit longer in silence.

'Right. Well, I'd better be going then,' he says, getting to his feet. 'Got lots of things still to sort out. Have a good Christmas. You being back with us is the best present Mel could ever have.' He is hovering in the doorway, he seems a bit upset about something. I don't know why he doesn't just go.

'Right. See you, then.'

'Yeah. I'll be in touch. Maybe you can come down for a holiday sometime when you're out of here.'

I nod. I don't think I ever will, though.

Thirty-seven

MEL

'Are you sure he's going to be able to cope with it, though? It's a lot of responsibility, looking after a child.' I didn't want to express any doubts to Adam, not when he seemed so keen on the idea and when it had at least taken his mind off all the things he couldn't do, softened the blow of not being able to return to work. But I couldn't go home without seeing Dr Andrews first.

He leans back in his chair, removes the end of his pen from his mouth.

'I know, but if, as you say, you're going to be at home for at least the spring and summer, it gives you a great chance to assess how he's doing before deciding if you can go back to work. Just build it up gradually so he's got a chance to find his feet and for his confidence to grow. And you need to be hands-off with him as well. As long as you're there to offer advice and support when he needs it, let him learn by his own mistakes. As long as they don't put Maya at risk, of course.'

I nod. I love the idea. Maya will be delighted. She seems so much more settled since Adam went into rehabilitation. She's taken his absence from home really well. And I think it has given her a chance to breathe, to feel like a normal little girl again. She's painting butterflies again at school. Butterflies and rats.

'And you still think he might be home around May time?'

'As you know, we can never guarantee these things. But I'm hoping that at the end of the twelve-week assessment period he'll be ready to move into our bungalow to learn to live independently again. And what we'll do, if it's OK by you, is get Maya in there with him for an afternoon so we can video them together, look for any potential safety issues and be able to talk them through with Adam afterwards.'

'Yeah, that sounds good. I think it would do Adam's confidence the power of good as well as putting my mind at ease.'

'There will be several visits home before he comes home for good. We're going to take everything very gradually to make sure we get it right.'

I smile at Dr Andrews. 'That's good to know,' I say. 'I'm really grateful for all your support.'

'Not at all. And remember when Adam does go home, that support carries on.'

'Thank you.'

'And how about you? How are you doing?'

I shrug. 'Good days and bad days, I guess. A bit like Adam. It's a weird mixture of hope laced with disappointment.'

'It's the toughest thing imaginable for families. Have you thought about getting some help?'

'What sort of help?'

'You've been through an incredibly traumatic time.

There's a woman I know in Huddersfield. A hypnotherapist.'

'Oh, I don't know.'

'No, a proper clinical hypnotherapist. I wouldn't recommend her if she wasn't the best in her field. She does EMDR. It stands for Eye Movement Desensitisation Reprogramming. Basically, it helps your brain to process the trauma and allow you to move on.' He reaches into his desk and pulls out a purple and white business card which he hands to me. 'Give her a try. You never know, it might help you get over that final hurdle.'

'Thank you,' I say, taking it and slipping it into my pocket.

Louise texts me to ask if it's OK to come round after Maya's gone to bed. That's when I know something's wrong. You don't make an appointment to catch up with your best friend. Only if you need to have a serious talk.

Even her smile as I let her in is tissue-paper thin. And the warmth in her hug feels like a storage heater at the end of a long day.

'Go straight through to the lounge,' I say, sensing we might be glad of the comfy seat later on. 'I'll get the coffees.'

'It's weird,' says Louise, a few minutes later when I return. 'I can still kind of feel Adam's presence in this room.'

'I know what you mean. I still come in sometimes expecting to find him here.'

'Have they any more idea about when he'll come home?'

'Around May time, hopefully. The doctor still hasn't told Adam he won't be able to go back to his old job. Thinks it will be too much for him to deal with right now. But he did suggest he could look after Maya so I can go back to working longer hours from September.'

'Oh, Mel, that's great. Are you going to try to go back to the university?'

'I don't know yet. I'm not sure there'll be any jobs, for a start.'

'I'm sure Margaret will find something for you. And Maya will be thrilled to have her daddy looking after her.'

'I know. He's going to tell her on Christmas Day. I think it will blow all her other presents out of the water.'

Louise smiles. 'I still can't believe how far he's come since October.'

I nod. Every time I get frustrated at what he can't do or say, I have to remind myself how three months ago I'd have given anything just to hear him say a single word.

'You still miss him, don't you? The old Adam, I mean.'

'Yeah, I do. Although it feels terribly ungrateful to say so.'

'Don't be daft. It's only natural to want him back. It doesn't mean you don't appreciate what you've got.'

'Thanks,' I say. 'You're the only person I know who would say that.'

We sit in silence for a while and sip our coffees. I sense Louise is gearing herself up to say something. Something which accounts for the lack of festive good cheer she has tonight. Louise is usually a Christmas-holic; counting down the days, humming the songs. And yet she hasn't even remarked on the Christmas tree in the corner.

'I met up with Steve yesterday,' she says finally.

I nod. Instantly understanding that things are not going to be as straightforward as I'd hoped.

'Oh, how did it go?'

'Not as I expected, really.'

'Why?'

'Well,' says Louise, 'for the first time ever he really opened up to me. About all sorts of things.'

There is something about the pause before the last sentence and the change of tone in Louise's voice which makes me wonder. When I catch her eye I know for certain. I look straight back down again.

'It's OK,' says Louise. 'It didn't come as a total shock, to be honest. He's known you longer than me or anyone else apart from his family. I always knew you had a special place in his affections. I guess I just didn't realise how special. Or maybe I did and I simply didn't want to believe it.'

'I am so sorry,' I say. 'I can't begin to tell you how awful I feel about it. I would have told you as soon as I found out but you were so down at the time I didn't want to hurt you any more than you'd already been hurt.'

'It wasn't your fault, Mel. It wasn't like you did anything to encourage him. Quite the opposite, in fact. You've been utterly in love with Adam for as long as I've known you. Anyone could see that. Well, anyone apart from Steve, it seems.'

'He does love you,' I say. 'I think it's just taken him a long time to realise how much. What he felt for me wasn't love. Not really. He thought Adam stole me away from him but I was never his to steal.'

Louise nods, although it is a nod utterly without

conviction. 'He wants us to get back together. He asked me to move away with him. Said he thought it was best for everyone.'

'Right. Where to?'

'Cornwall.'

I nod. It sounds like the end of the earth but as I never stipulated where to move to, I guess I can't complain.

'When are you going?'

'I'm not.'

'Sorry?'

'He's moving down there in January,' she says. 'But I'm not going with him.'

If I felt bad before, I feel wretched now. I've single-handedly wrecked my best friend's marriage.

'But you love him. You've been miserable without him, you said so yourself.'

'I know but I owe it to myself not to go. I've been second best for too long. I don't want to live like that for the rest of my life. Always feeling I'm not quite what he wants. Trying to be a poor imitation of you.'

I put my arms around her, pull her towards me as two sets of tears start to fall.

'You're not a poor imitation of anyone, Louise. You're you and you're brilliant.'

'I can't go back to him, though. As much as I may want to. I've wasted too much of my life with him already. I need to start again.'

I shake my head. Wipe the tears away from her face. 'I can't believe I've caused you so much pain. So much for being your best friend. You have every right to hate me.'

'No I haven't. None of this is of your making. It's Steve who let me down. He let us all down.'

'I know he's hurt you but I also know he never meant to. And I know he feels awful about the way he's treated you. He really wanted to make a go of it, you know.'

'You've spoken to him about us?'

I nod. 'I went to his flat a few weeks ago. I'm sorry, I should have told you. I was trying to protect you from the truth because I knew how much it would hurt you.'

'Sometimes lies can hurt just as much.'

'Believe me, I know that.'

Louise sits quietly for a moment as if trying to take it all in.

'I suppose it was you who suggested the flowers?'

'Yeah. I didn't suggest he tell you about me, though. That was his idea.'

Louise gets a tissue from her bag and dabs at the corners of her eyes. 'I haven't told him yet. I'm going to pop round to see him tomorrow before he goes to his parents. Although I feel a bit of a cow doing it on Christmas Eve.'

'He can't complain, can he? This is all of his making.' Even as I say it, I realise I don't really believe it. And I can see from the expression on Louise's face that she doesn't either.

'As much as I want to, I can't bring myself to hate him,' she says. 'I feel sorry for him, to be honest. It was big of him to tell me when he didn't have to. And losing the three people he loves most in the world is a pretty heavy price to pay.'

She's right. I'm trying not to think about Steve, though.

What matters now is how I can help Louise.

'I understand that but if this is your decision and you're sure about it, you've got to think about yourself from now on. You deserve so much better.'

'Maybe I'll meet a hot male flamenco dancer in the New Year.' She is smiling as she says it. We both know it's not going to happen.

'Look, I understand if you don't want to but the offer of Christmas lunch is still there.'

'Thanks,' she says. 'I'd like that.'

I lean over to give her a hug. Grateful for the opportunity to continue our friendship, although I suspect it will never be quite the same again.

'I should warn you that Santa's bringing Maya a Rita rat puppet to go with the Roddy one.'

'It's OK,' smiles Louise. 'As long as the real ones stay in their cage I'll be all right.' She looks at me, eyes still laden with tears. 'I hope you get what you want for Christmas too.'

'Thank you,' I say. 'Let's hope we both have a happier New Year.'

Epilogue

Friday, 6 May 2011

I wake up early on the morning of our eleventh wedding anniversary. My midnight-blue dress is hanging from the wardrobe. I am going to wear it for the party later. Like I always said I would. And tonight Adam will share this bed with me. Adam is coming home today. For good.

I get up and pull on old jeans and a fleece which has seen better days. I peer into Maya's bedroom on my way past. She is still sleeping, the Roddy and Rita puppets tucked under her arm. Her purple and silver dress is hanging from a chair, washed and ironed and ready to go.

I pad softly downstairs, make myself a cup of tea and go through into the lounge. The walls are freshly painted in terracotta. Adam said he didn't like the magnolia, the first time he came home for the weekend. My laptop is still set up on the coffee table, the email from Margaret offering me a full-time position teaching on the Early Years MA from September still top of my inbox. The DVD I watched last night is still in there, too. The one they did of Adam at Shaw House; of him playing with Maya, showing her how to crack an egg without spilling it, using the oven gloves when they got the cake out and blowing on it to cool it down before giving her a slice – and not the size of slice she wanted. He has proved beyond doubt that he is ready for this. And I, finally, am ready for it too.

There is a soft tap on the door. 'Thanks for coming, Mum,' I say, letting her in.

'It's OK. It's rather nice to be up early on such a lovely day. Your father's going to set off to get Adam shortly. Is there owt you need me to do to help with lunch?'

'Not really. Most of it's in the fridge ready to go. And Louise will be bringing a few extra bits round when she comes.'

'Is Maya OK?'

'Yeah. She's fine. Just a tad excited. I've left loads of colouring stuff out for her. She wants to make a card for Adam. One with a dinosaur on.'

Mum smiles and nods. 'And what about you?' she says. 'How are you feeling?'

I look at her, unable to believe this is my mother speaking but pleasantly surprised all the same.

'Nervous, excited, sad, happy, exhausted, relieved. All of those really.'

'You don't need to pretend, Melanie. I know this has been right tough for you.'

'Please don't feel sorry for me, though,' I say. 'Because if you'd told me a year ago when Adam was lying in a coma that this is where we'd be today, I'd have been delighted, really I would.'

'But you still don't have your husband back.'

'I know but unlike Louise I still have a husband and

most importantly Maya has a father. A father who is going to take such good care of her.'

Mum smiles and nods. 'I'm very proud of you, Melanie. You're a better wife and mother than I've ever been.'

I look at her, seeming suddenly small and fragile, and I know it's time to tell her. 'That's not true. You did something incredibly selfless for me and Dad. Something which has cost you dearly. You put your own happiness last, didn't you? Put yourself in the firing line to protect your daughter and husband. And never breathed a word about it.'

She stares at me, her lower lip trembling. 'He told you?'

'Yeah. After I gave you both the Orient Express tickets. He felt he didn't deserve them and I told him then what I'm going to tell you now. That you did what you thought was best for your child at the time. And I of all people am not going to hold that against you.'

She manages a watery smile. 'It were a lovely trip on the train, Melanie. Your father's not stopped talking about it since. And the waiters really were ever so attentive.'

I smile and kiss her on the cheek.

'Oh, I nearly forgot,' says Mum, reaching into her handbag and handing me an envelope.

'What's this?' I ask.

'A cutting from *Halifax Courier*. They used the press release Adam wrote about model railway museum open day. Your father's ever so chuffed.'

'Thank you,' I say, putting it on the shelf above the radiator. 'Adam will be too.'

Mum potters off into the kitchen. I go to pull a

waterproof on just in case then stop myself. There's no need. The forecast is dry.

I know exactly where to go. I've been there several times before on walks. I've always marvelled at how somewhere so desolate can be quite so beautiful. It takes a while to climb up there, the hill is steep in places, the ground muddy underfoot.

I stop for a moment when I reach the top. Partly to get my breath back, partly to check out the view. To reassure myself that this is the place it has to be. I look down on the valley below. Our valley. From Adam's hill. You can even make out our house from here, bathed in early morning sunlight. Clearly I have done my homework well. There are no doubts left. None at all.

The stones are easy to come by, certainly to start with. You don't have a landscape littered with drystone walls without there being one or two loose ones. One or two which have fallen by the wayside. I work quickly and deftly, searching out the stones and putting them in two piles of appropriate size. When I have gathered all I need I set to work on the tiny one. Taking care to set every stone in line, even though my vision is increasingly blurry.

Once the last stone is in place, I hesitate before starting the larger one. Scared for a second that it is somehow disloyal, somehow ungrateful. I've been through all that, though, with Karen, the woman who did the EMDR therapy with me. I've recognised that I haven't had the chance to grieve. For the baby or for Adam. And that without doing so, it is nigh on impossible to move forward.

I place the first stone down on the ground. Followed by

another and another in quick succession. As I do so I also dismantle the life-support machine in my head. The one which kept him alive all that time. In order that I too could survive. Could be strong enough to get Maya and me through this. As I place the last stone down, a gasp of air slips out with it. He is quiet now. He is at peace.

I step back and look at them. The large stone cross and the much smaller one next to it. Already blending into the landscape. Becoming part of the backdrop of my life. I take the flowers from my rucksack, place the yellow rose at the foot of the small cross and stand holding the red rose at the end of the large one.

'I hope you understand why I have to do this,' I say. 'It's not about giving up, it's about letting go. I hung on to you, you see. After the accident I kept you alive in my head, imagined what you'd be thinking, feeling. Heard your voice giving a running commentary on everything around you. Helped you sort through your memories to find good ones to hold on to. Karen said a lot of people suffering from post-traumatic stress disorder do things like that. Delude themselves about what has happened in order to survive. Only I need to do more than survive now. I need to be strong for Maya and for the new Adam. And I can't do that unless I let you go . . .'

I pause as my voice falters, as the tears run down my cheeks and fall gently on to the rose.

'I'm not giving up on you, a part of me will always go on hoping you'll come back to me, but I can't let myself become a bitter twisted person. I have to live in the here and now. Not in the past or in the future. So this isn't goodbye, Adam, I guess it's more of an au revoir.'

I lay the rose down on the cross and see Adam's face grinning at me, hear his voice in my head, mimicking Jim from *The Royle Family*. 'Au revoir, my arse.'

I stand for a long time; smiling, remembering, letting the wind dry my eyes. And then I walk back down the hill. To Maya. To Adam. To our new life together. A life that doesn't scare me any more. Because I, like those stones, have withstood everything which has been thrown at me. I am weathered and worn but I am still standing. I am still strong. And my love cannot be broken.

I was eleven years old the first time I saw him but I still knew straight away. It was something about the darkness of his eyes and the way his face scrunched up when he smiled. I didn't tell him, of course. That wasn't how it worked, I understood that even then. I had to wait for him to realise. Two years it took. Though it felt more like an eternity to me. Still, it was worth the wait. I knew it then and I know it now. Twenty-one years later.

About the book

WARNING: Spoiler Alert!

As a trainee reporter on the *Enfield Gazette* back in 1989, I interviewed Tim and Valerie Barton whose fifteen-year-old daughter Joanne had gone into a coma after being knocked down on a pedestrian crossing by a motorist jumping a red light. Speaking to such loving parents and meeting Joanne, who unfortunately died not long after her sixteenth birthday, brought home to me how the lives of a whole family can be devastated in an instant.

Barely a few months later, forty-year-old John Dennis suffered a heart attack during the ambulance dispute of December 1989. The army crew who attended him took the wrong turning on the way to hospital in Coventry and did not provide adequate treatment during the journey. John's brain was starved of oxygen and by the time he arrived at hospital he was in a coma.

I met John in 1997 when I interviewed his wife Jean for the *Coventry Evening Telegraph*. By that time John had been in a persistent vegetative state for seven years, the past six of them having been spent at home being cared for by Jean, who had refused the offer of a long-term nursing home place for John in favour of looking after him herself.

Witnessing the tenderness, love and utter devotion with which Jean cared for John was incredibly moving. And yet she was adamant that any woman would have done the same in her situation. Sadly, John never recovered and died in 2006, almost seventeen years after slipping into the coma.

Jean and John's story had a lasting impact on me. The idea of trying to capture the range of human emotions involved took hold in my head and by the time I had to come up with an idea for my fourth novel, I felt I was ready to tackle it.

I embarked on a lengthy period of research into coma, persistent vegetative state and minimally conscious state. For someone who flunked her O level biology, I ended up knowing a surprising amount about the human brain!

The task was then to apply my research to the characters and situation in the novel. *And Then It Happened* is entirely a work of fiction. But, whilst allowing myself a bit of artistic licence, I wanted to ensure that the characters' experiences were as accurate as possible.

Adam's recovery from such a serious traumatic brain injury and lengthy unresponsive state is undoubtedly against the odds but not unheard of. It is estimated that forty per cent of comatose patients are wrongly diagnosed as being in a vegetative state when they are, in fact, in a minimally conscious state. It is not known whether people in a minimally conscious state can process emotion but certainly there are cases when they appear to respond emotionally, for example, to being shown photos of loved ones. There are also stories of patients appearing to respond to the voices of loved ones.

However, if patients do finally emerge from a coma to a point where they can communicate, they very rarely have any memory of their time in an unresponsive state. In rare cases there might be an unexplained understanding or knowledge of something but very few, if any, specific memories.

If you look back at the chapters told from Adam's point of view after the accident you will find that they are not headed with 'ADAM', as the chapters before the accident and after he emerges from the post-traumatic amnesia are. Mel makes it clear in the novel that she imagined how Adam would have been feeling and what he would have been thinking during these times, in order to keep him 'alive' in her head. This is one of the examples where I used my artistic licence. The inference is that these chapters have been imagined by Mel but if anyone wishes to believe that these are indeed Adam's real point of view chapters, I have left that option open.

The one thing that remains certain is that traumatic brain injury has a devastating effect on people's lives. Each year in the UK, almost 12,000 people will suffer a head injury so severe that they will remain unconscious for six hours or more. After five years, only fifteen per cent of these people will have returned to work.

Two charities that help brain-injured people and their families have also been an enormous help to me. I will be making a donation from the royalties of this book to each of them. If you have been moved by Adam and Mel's experiences and would also like to make a donation, I know they would be enormously grateful. Thank you in advance.

Headway, the brain injury association, is a charity set up to give help and support to people affected by brain injury. The Headway Helpline provides information, advises on sources of support, finds local rehabilitation services and offers a listening ear to those experiencing problems. The free telephone number is 0808 800 2244 and their website is www.headway.org.uk.

The Brain Injury Rehabilitation Trust (BIRT) helps people regain the skills lost as a result of brain injury – whether caused by road accident, assault, stroke or illness. The charity, which is a division of The Disabilities Trust, offers a range of services designed to meet the needs of people at different stages of rehabilitation. For more information and to donate go to www.birt.co.uk or call 01924 266 344.

Writing Adam and Mel's story moved me immensely and I know their story will stay with me always. Thank you for reading it and I hope their story will stay with you too. Please do get in touch via my website www.linda-green. com or by Facebook (Fans of Author Linda Green) or Twitter (@LindaGreenisms).

Acknowledgements

Warmest thanks to the following people: my editor Sherise Hobbs, for letting me write this book in the first place, and my original publishers Headline; also, everyone at Quercus for their support with the reissue; my agent Anthony Goff for his shrewd advice and much appreciated support throughout; everyone at David Higham Associates; Jean Dennis, whose love for and devotion to her husband inspired me in the first place and for providing so much useful background information; Andrew James, Consultant in Neuropsychology and Rehabilitation at Daniel Yorath House in Leeds, for sparing a huge amount of his valuable time, picking apart the original plot for this book, then very patiently working with me while I built it back up again in a (hopefully!) more credible way; Sandra Hughes at Daniel Yorath House and Sally Rogers of the Brain Injury Rehabilitation Trust; Richard Morris of Headway for advice and information provided; Luke Griggs and all at Headway; Natalie Rodgers at Central Manchester Foundation Trust and the Emergency Department consultants at Manchester Royal Infirmary; Dr Adrian Owen, formerly of the Impaired Consciousness Study Group at Addenbrooke's Hospital, and his team for their ground-breaking research, John Cornwell for writing such a terrific article about it in *The Sunday Times Magazine*; the late Jean-Dominique Bauby for his inspirational memoir *The Diving Bell and the Butterfly*, painstakingly dictated with the blink of an eyelid (if you haven't yet read it, please do so); Lance Little for the great website (www.linda-green.com); my friends and family for their on-going support; my fantastic readers, whose positive feedback helps keep me going while writing the next book; my wonderful son Rohan for providing some of Maya's best lines, having brilliant ideas for the plot and for promising to adapt this book for the stage or screen one day (I shall hold you to that!); and, as ever, my husband Ian for childcare and household chores far beyond the call of duty, listening to me babble on about this book incessantly, believing in it and me and making a truly stupendous whale for Rohan's *Finding Nemo* party while I was busy writing. Thank you.